Praise for Rachael English's novels:

'A sensory and nostalgic delight. At its heart, it's a moving story about the vulnerability of youth, the importance of friendship and the abuse of power'
Irish Times

'A true storyteller who keeps you turning the pages'
Cathy Kelly

'A cracking page-turner in the best tradition of Maeve Binchy'
Patricia Scanlan

'I read [it] greedily, unable to put it down . . . beautiful, compelling and sincere in the way of the very best stories and the best books'
Sunday Independent

'Richly imagined and searingly empathetic . . . compelling reading'
Business Post

'[English] weaves a tale with the natural ease of a born storyteller . . . heart-breaking and uplifting all at once and I highly recommend it'
RTÉ Culture

Rachael English is a bestselling novelist and RTÉ Radio 1 presenter. During more than twenty years as a journalist, she has worked on most of RTÉ Radio's leading current affairs programmes, covering a huge range of national and international stories. *The Last Song* is her seventh novel.

Twitter: @EnglishRachael
Facebook: rachaelenglishwriter

Also by Rachael English

Going Back
Each & Every One
The American Girl
The Night of the Party
The Paper Bracelet
The Letter Home

The Last Song

RACHAEL
ENGLISH

HACHETTE
BOOKS
IRELAND

First published as *Whatever Happened to Birdy Troy?* in Ireland in 2024 by
HACHETTE BOOKS IRELAND
First published in paperback in 2025

1

Cataloguing in Publication Data is available from the British Library

ISBN 978 1 3997 2683 2

Typeset in 11.5/14.75pt Arno Pro by Jouve (UK), Milton Keynes

Printed and bound in Great Britain by Clays Ltd, Elcograf S.p.A.

Hachette Books Ireland policy is to use papers that are natural, renewable and recyclable products and made from wood grown in sustainable forests. The logging and manufacturing processes are expected to conform to the environmental regulations of the country of origin.

Hachette Books Ireland
8 Castlecourt Centre
Castleknock
Dublin 15, Ireland

A division of Hachette UK Ltd
Carmelite House, 50 Victoria Embankment, London EC4Y 0DZ

www.hachettebooksireland.ie

For all the people in Shannon
who have been so supportive.
Thank you.

PART ONE

Chapter 1

Now, Dublin

Stacey edged towards the top of the queue, reminding herself that when she got there, she would need some small-talk. Nothing too adventurous. A bland observation about the weather would do. She didn't want rudeness added to her list of failings.

The Pear Tree Café was humming, conversations overlapping as customers bought their morning fix. Two women sat at a nearby table, dressed in neck-to-calf black Lycra, heads bent together in a conspiracy of laughter. A man in a striped shirt held a one-sided phone conversation. 'If you ask me,' he said, 'things can't get any worse.' The coffee machine hissed and whirred.

The line shuffled forward until Stacey was beside the silver-fronted machine. She twisted to avoid her reflection. A glance in the mirror before leaving the apartment had been a mistake. What she'd seen – swollen eyes, sunken cheeks, skin like cold porridge – had reminded her of a mugshot on one of those American police websites where people went to revel in the chaotic lives of others. Her dark brown hair was calling out for a wash, and her pale grey T-shirt needed ironing.

The day had begun with the arrival of a stiff cream envelope. Good news rarely came in expensive envelopes, and this was doubly true when the back was embossed with the words 'Silver Eagle Property'. The rent must be going up. Again.

Making the payments had been hard enough when two of them had lived in the apartment. On her own, it was almost impossible. Another increase and . . . No, she wouldn't think about it. When the caffeine was chugging through her system, and she was feeling sufficiently brave, she would open the letter and face the bad news.

One more shuffle, and she was at the front of the queue.

'We haven't seen much of you lately,' said Detta, the Pear Tree's owner, as she took Stacey's order for a skinny cappuccino. 'Will you be having the coffee here?'

'Eh . . . yes. Yes, please.'

'You've been busy, I'd say.'

'Well . . . busy enough. You know the way.'

'Anyone interesting on your radar?'

'Not especially. No one who stands out, anyway.'

Detta gave up and turned to make the coffee. Stacey had told herself that this was the day she would return to doing real work. But if swapping chit-chat with a regular acquaintance was such a struggle, she couldn't imagine how she would cope with strangers.

Hello there, I'd like you to tell me about your life. Please excuse the fact that I'm an incoherent mess.

With the cappuccino in front of her, she tapped her debit card to pay. Up popped a red circle containing a large white X.

'Not to worry.' Detta pressed a button. 'That machine's forever acting up. Give your card another tap there, like a good woman.'

She did, and again the X appeared.

'Third time lucky,' said Detta. 'Do you want to put your card into the machine?'

Transaction declined, read the screen.

'I'm sorry,' said Stacey. Her immediate impulse was to tell a face-saving lie. To blame a computer malfunction or to question the reliability of the card reader. In truth, there was every danger her bank account was bare. For the past few days, she'd been afraid to look. 'Let me see if I have the cash.'

She dug into the pocket of her jeans while adopting what she hoped was an endearingly goofy expression. An expression that said, 'disorganised but basically sound'. All she could produce was a tattered bus ticket, a green button and a fifty-cent coin. Oh, and her customer loyalty card.

A shiver of second-hand embarrassment passed along the queue. The woman directly behind her muttered about not having all day to fritter away. A baby began to cry.

'I'm sorry,' Stacey said again, heat spreading up from her throat. 'I shouldn't have come out without cash.'

'Here, give me that,' said Detta, taking the loyalty card and giving it three extra stamps. 'It's full now, so you're entitled to a free cup.'

The woman behind her gave a performative sigh.

The temptation to turn around and say something sharp was strong. Stacey resisted. She dropped the fifty-cent piece into the tips mug. 'I owe you,' she said to Detta. 'Thanks.'

She walked to a small stripped-pine table on the far side of the café, the eyes of other customers sweeping over her. She knew this was a minor incident. Detta probably dealt with something similar every day. Yet Stacey was close to tears. The old political saying was right. It was the little things that tripped you up.

For several minutes, she drank her coffee, only looking up when someone new entered the café. Each time the door opened, warm air wafted in. There was a heaviness to the day, a sluggishness, that was unusual for Dublin in early June.

She considered checking her bank balance, then decided it could wait. She looked at the letter from Silver Eagle but stopped short of opening it. The company name was unfamiliar. Ronan had always taken care of the forms and contracts. Unlike Stacey, he was good with bureaucracy.

She opened her email. Her personal account contained nothing she felt like reading. Companies clamoured to sell her clothes and holidays she couldn't afford. In her work inbox, there were thirteen new messages. Most looked like complaints.

For eighteen months, Stacey had been presenting and producing a podcast called 'Whatever Happened To . . . ?' It had started as her hobby, her passion, but had quickly taken over her life. At the end of the second lockdown, when it had become possible to do interviews in person again, she'd quit her job in PR. Back then, she'd believed that following your heart was a viable route through life. Now she saw how naïve she'd been.

The idea behind the series was simple. She spoke to people who had once been famous. Or, if not fully famous, moderately well-known. She'd talked to footballers who'd been hailed as the next Pelé/Maradona/Messi before dropping to the wastelands of the lower leagues. She'd heard from politicians who'd been tipped for greatness only to end up on the wrong side of a long-forgotten scandal. She'd tracked down singers and writers, actors and athletes.

And then there were the television presenters. Legions of television presenters. She'd learnt that children's TV was particularly savage and that light entertainment was exceptionally dark.

Not all of her subjects were conventional celebrities. Some of the most popular episodes featured the accidentally well-known: a teenager who'd foiled an armed robbery, a man who'd led a long and rancorous strike, a woman whose childhood illness had been chronicled by the media but who now regretted this.

Stacey hadn't been surprised by the interest of the listening public. *Schadenfreude* was a powerful emotion. In other cases, listeners were genuinely curious about the fate of her guests. Had they walked away from fame – or had they been pushed?

What did surprise her was how many people were willing to talk. A few did so because they wanted to relive their glory days, others because they hoped that renewed exposure would deliver fresh opportunities. Most had scores to settle.

There were episodes where the listening was bleak. She had broadcast tales of backstabbing record executives, indifferent publishers and rapacious managers. She'd heard about crushed dreams, unanswered phone calls and festering resentments. Sometimes, she found people, then decided against telling their story. The once-beloved DJ who had spent much of the year in a psychiatric hospital? The feted young author who'd blown her large advance, realised she had no more to say and passed her days watching trash TV? The public didn't need to know about their troubles.

The most challenging stories were the ones in which a potential subject wouldn't accept that the circus had moved on. *What do you mean,* after *I was famous?*

Stacey had worried that the ideas would run dry. In a small country, the list of the previously famous was finite. And yet the emails continued to flow. *You know who I was wondering about?* they'd say. Or *I'm not sure if you remember, but in the late nineties, there was a fellow who . . .*

Given this engagement, it was strange to find herself sitting in the Pear Tree without the price of a coffee. The last two weeks had been rough. Not only had a relationship she'd believed in fallen asunder, 'Whatever Happened To . . . ?' had tumbled out of the podcast Top Ten.

The public had no time for the bitter journalist who'd featured in the most recent pod. There'd been even less enthusiasm for the petulant influencer who'd appeared the week before. In her heyday, Ella Fox had been the queen of the #sponcon circuit. She'd been a #brandambassador for everything from lip fillers to concrete blocks. Had the fee been high enough and the photos cute enough, she would probably have endorsed weapons of mass destruction. Then, a phone conversation in which she'd made cruel comments about her fellow influencers had been leaked to a gossip website. Overnight, Ella had been banished to #paidpromotion Siberia. Or, as she put it herself, she had 'pivoted to a more fulfilling role'. She now worked in the civil service.

What an entitled bore, one email had read. *Where have all the interesting people gone?* Stacey had lost two lucrative advertisers, and a prospective sponsor had backed out.

'You've got to adapt,' the man who ran the studio where she occasionally worked had said. 'Do you know anything about mental health or reality TV? They never go out of fashion. Or how about talking to successful people? You must have interviewed every loser in the country.'

She opened the emails. As she'd feared, the majority were complaints about the fact that an episode hadn't appeared the previous week. Stacey picked at the skin around her left thumbnail, peeling it away until she drew blood. She didn't know how to reply. Saying she hadn't been in the right frame of mind would sound frivolous, and the listeners weren't keen on frivolity.

The final email was different. It was from a man called Senan O'Reilly who asked what had happened to an all-woman rock group called The Diamonds. They'd been from Steelstown in County Clare, he said. Stacey knew Steelstown. It was only twenty kilometres from Limerick where she'd grown up. Despite this, she couldn't recall having spent much time there. Steelstown wasn't the sort of place that prompted visiting Dubliners to post 'And breathe' on their Instagram. Nor did it tally with the media's preferred version of the west of Ireland. There were no turf fires, cliff walks or wellness retreats.

A quick search brought up a website about Irish bands of the 1980s. It told her that The Diamonds had formed in 1979 and broken up in 1982. Rock critics had labelled them 'U2 for girls'. Because they'd been on the cusp of international success, the split had been unexpected and had never been properly explained.

The paragraph was accompanied by a black-and-white photo of four women, their hair unruly, their eye makeup heavy. So fuzzy was the image that it might have been taken in the 1880s. The only other thing Stacey could say for sure was that The Diamonds had been very young, possibly no more than teenagers.

She looked at their names. Vocals: Loretta Saunders. Guitar and Backing Vocals: Birdy Troy. Bass Guitar: Gail McGeehan. Drums: Yvonne Hayes. None meant anything to her.

She did the sums. 1982. Forty years ago. Ten years before she was born. She rarely tunnelled back that far. Experience had taught her that the 1980s was the last decade in which it had been possible to disappear.

She swallowed the dregs of her coffee and turned her attention to the letter from Silver Eagle. Like the envelope, the paper was thick, expensive. She began to read.

Oh.

Dear Ms Nash,

I'm writing to you about the property you currently rent at 12, Whitethorn House, Briarstown, County Dublin.

As you may be aware, Silver Eagle has purchased the apartments in this development. It is our intention to renovate and refurbish these residences.

Our records show that your lease expires on 5 September next. You are hereby notified that it will be terminated at that point. You will have the whole of the 24 hours of the termination date to give up possession of the dwelling. It would, however, be preferable if you could vacate the premises prior to this date.

This notice is fully in accordance with the law. Please be aware that failure to comply with its terms will result in legal proceedings.

Yours,

George Sheffield

Stacey considered the letter. It was, she assumed, designed to intimidate. To make people feel smaller than they already were. She was caught in one of those moments when, even though she understood what was happening, she didn't want to acknowledge it. A cold feeling, like being dunked in seawater, passed over her. It hadn't occurred to her that she could be evicted.

She placed her elbows on the table and rested her head in her hands. The man in the striped shirt had been wrong. Things could always get worse.

Chapter 2

Forty-one years earlier
June 1981, Steelstown, County Clare

Birdy was busy with her pricing gun, attaching labels to tins of grapefruit segments and mandarin oranges, when the Tannoy crackled to life.

'Miss Troy to the office, please. Miss Troy to the office.'

She decided to finish what she was doing. No doubt her supervisor, a wasp of a woman called Vera Cheevers, wanted to complain about her timekeeping. That morning, Birdy had clocked in at four minutes past the hour, something Vera viewed as a mortal sin.

After less than a minute, the supervisor's voice returned. This time, it had an extra layer of frost. 'Phone call for Miss Birdy Troy. Miss Troy to the office *now*, please.'

'Ah, hell,' said Birdy, to no one in particular. She shoved the gun into the pocket of her sludge-brown polyester uniform and made her way past Canned Vegetables and Baking Supplies before rounding the corner into Cleaning Products.

At eleven thirty on Friday morning, Save-A-Lot teemed with women doing their weekly shop. Many had babies or toddlers in tow. The fluorescent lights gave them all a jaundiced, hollow-eyed look. They snapped at their kids and fretted about the prices.

In Jams and Spreads, someone had dropped a pot of marmalade, and its contents were oozing across the floor, like nuclear waste. Birdy would have to clean it up when she got back, by which time the sticky mess would have been trampled into the next aisle.

In the year since she'd left school, she'd been working full-time at Save-A-Lot. For two years before that, she'd had a Saturday job. She knew every shelf and fridge, every line and price. No matter what a customer wanted – crispy pancakes or candied peel, fish fingers or furniture polish – she was their woman.

As she clattered up the metal stairs to the office, she tried to imagine why someone had phoned her. Even harder to imagine was why Vera Cheevers had passed on the message. Vera didn't approve of personal lives.

The office was laden with files and folders and smelt of dust and corned-beef sandwiches. Vera was standing in the far corner, her blonde bouffant – part Bond girl, part Margaret Thatcher – starched into place. She gestured towards the shiny black phone, her expression as rigid as her hair. 'Your mother wants you.'

Birdy's heart speeded up. On the one hand, her mam wouldn't ring unless something was wrong. On the other, and this was a tantalising thought, the call might be enough to free her from work. She picked up the receiver. 'Mam? Is everything all right?'

'It's me,' came the muffled reply, 'only you're to pretend I'm your mother and I'm phoning to say your aunt has died. Have you got that?'

'I'm sorry?'

'I'm in the callbox around the corner. Yvonne's here too. We're after getting a great gig. In Limerick.'

Birdy took a moment to realise that the voice at the end of the line belonged to her friend and bandmate Gail McGeehan. With Yvonne Hayes and Loretta Saunders, they were The Diamonds, the best rock band in Steelstown. (And, yes, it was possible they were the only rock band in Steelstown.) Birdy played guitar.

'Oh, that's fa—' She quickly corrected herself. 'That's desperate, Mam. When?'

'There's the snag. It's this evening. We're playing support to A Nest of Vipers in the Old Mill.'

'You're not serious?'

'The original support band broke up yesterday. That's why the notice is so short.'

'I see.' Birdy turned around. Vera was watching. She would have to ham it up a bit. She pressed the phone more tightly to her ear. 'That's awful news. Yourself and Angela were very close. What are the arrangements, do you know?'

'I'm beside myself with grief, pet,' said Gail, voice splintered with laughter. 'You've got to tell Mrs Cheevers you're needed at home because of the tragic news. Then you're to meet us at my house.'

Birdy risked another glance in the supervisor's direction. 'It mightn't be that easy. We're really busy this morning.'

'Now, Birdy Troy, are you going to let down your poor old mother in her hour of need?'

Birdy pictured her friend's brown eyes crinkling with laughter. A giggle climbed up her own throat. Just in time, she managed to suppress it. A squeak escaped. She hoped Vera would mistake it for a mewl of sorrow. She paused and rearranged her face. 'Of course not.'

'Good girl. As quickly as you can, get out of there and head over to my place. Loretta's meeting us in ten minutes. Are you with me?'

'Yes, only—'

'We'll be waiting.'

After Gail had hung up, Birdy stopped to think. Her brain fizzed with the news. When you were in an all-girl rock band, support slots weren't always welcome. Gig-goers, impatient for the main act, had been known to send a hail of cans in The Diamonds' direction. A couple of months back, a great gob of spit had landed on Birdy's face and slithered down, like frog spawn.

This was different. A Nest of Vipers were massive. Well, okay, not massive. But they were popular and would attract a good crowd. The Diamonds couldn't afford to say no.

'So,' said Vera, 'a dead aunt, I believe. Was she sick for long?'

'No. It was sudden. Mam says she needs me at home.'

The supervisor gave a look that suggested anything short of Birdy's own death wouldn't be sufficient to secure her early release. 'I'm sorry for your troubles. I don't see why you have to leave straight away, though. You'll probably want time off for the funeral, am I right?'

For five minutes, they argued. All the while, Birdy's thoughts were with everything she needed to do before the gig. Eventually, Vera agreed to let her go, but only on condition she worked extra hours the following week. Birdy wasn't listening. Next week could take care of itself.

She'd left the office and was back on the stairs when Vera called after her.

'Birdy?'

Damn. 'Eh . . . Yeah?' she said, heart gathering pace again.

'Don't forget to clock out.'

*

It was as she stepped into the midday glare that Birdy remembered Declan. Her sixteen-year-old brother had a summer job in Save-A-Lot. For fifty pence an hour, he roamed the streets and estates rounding up stray trolleys. She would have to alert him to their family tragedy.

When she spotted him, he was at the edge of the car park, wrangling with a trolley.

'Dodgy wheel?'

'Isn't there always?' He squinted through his fringe. 'Aren't you supposed to be at work?'

'I'm in mourning,' she said, before explaining the true reason for her early departure.

'What'll I say if anyone enquires after Aunt . . . ?'

'Angela. God rest her soul, her name was Angela.'

'We don't have an Aunt Angela.'

'Vera doesn't know that. If anyone says anything, you're to play along. Tell them Mam needed consoling.'

'That's a lot to ask.' Declan pulled a face. 'What if I make a mistake?'

Birdy dipped into the pocket of her denim skirt and took out a wrinkled pound note. 'Here you go. This should help.'

'You can do better than that.'

'Ah, Dec, I haven't any more to give.'

'You'll get paid tonight, won't you?'

'We're not exactly headlining Madison Square Garden. It's a support gig in a glorified pub.' She returned to her pocket and removed a fifty-pence piece. 'That's as much as I've got.'

'All right,' he said, taking the cash. 'It'll be money well spent. If Cheevers says anything, I'll lay it on thick. She'll be praying for the late Angela's soul by the time I'm finished.'

'Fair play to you. Loretta will be grateful.'

There was no point in mentioning Gail or Yvonne. In common with half of the boys in town, Declan's fantasies were of The Diamonds' lead singer. With her thick golden hair, high cheekbones and thigh-skimming skirts, Loretta looked as if she'd stepped out of a magazine. Not a knitting-patterns-and-soup-recipes magazine, but something cool, something American or French. She wore anklets and diamanté earrings, and ringed her round eyes with navy kohl.

Declan pushed the money into the front pocket of his jeans. 'If the lovely Loretta would like to show her gratitude, she knows where to find me.'

The thought of Loretta hanging out in the Save-A-Lot car park made Birdy smile.

'Dream on,' she said.

If Birdy had to describe Steelstown in one word, it would be 'loud'. Most of the noise came from children. At times, it seemed as if every spare inch had been taken over by skipping games and makeshift football pitches. They whooped and chattered and sang, like exotic birds.

Older kids hung in small groups, the boys exchanging insults, the girls reciting the latest chart hits. Right then, they were crazy for Shakin' Stevens and Adam Ant. 'Seriously, girls,' Birdy would say, as she passed by, 'you've got to get some better tunes.'

Although Birdy was fond of Steelstown's sharp edges, she doubted anyone would make their fortune selling postcards there. The town centre's narrow streets quickly gave way to a sprawl of housing estates. Gail lived in the largest estate, All Saints Park. To reach All Saints, Birdy walked along a ribbon of pockmarked tarmac. The lane was bordered on one side by a thicket of spruce trees, where children built dens and fourteen-year-olds played kissing games. Depending on who you believed, visiting the lane after dark meant meeting either a ghost or a flasher.

That summer, black flags hung from the lampposts, marking the deaths of the hunger strikers in the North. In the last week, the flags had been joined by election posters. Birdy felt as if the dour faces, almost all of them men's, were watching her. Her father said he wouldn't be voting because the politicians were vermin who'd sold the country down the river. Her mother said this was no example to be setting, and that anyone with enough courage to put their name forward deserved respect. For the first time, Birdy would be able to vote. She didn't think she'd bother.

She walked with a gathering sense of freedom, her shoulders relaxing, her brown suede bag slapping against her hip.

When she got to the McGeehans' house, the others were already there. It was easier for them. Loretta was on her summer holidays from university. Gail, The Diamonds' bass player, had been let go from her factory job two months before, and Yvonne, their drummer, rarely had a problem taking breaks from the office. She claimed this was because she sometimes slept with one of her managers. Birdy thought she was joking but wasn't completely sure.

They were in the kitchen, drinking mugs of coffee and smoking. Everybody smoked in Gail's house and, apart from the occasional eye-roll, her mother didn't mind. Birdy was convinced none of the family had a sense of smell. Gail's sister, Donna, had once smoked a joint, or 'a bamboozler' as she called it, in the front room while their parents watched *Dallas*. Neither had noticed.

'Here she is, the bereaved niece,' said Gail, scraping her fingers through her cloud of dark hair. 'Have you made the funeral arrangements yet?'

Birdy removed her combat jacket and joined them at the table. 'You're a terrible woman. We'll all go to Hell, you know that?'

'Listen, it was either a dead relation or a bomb scare, and I didn't want to shut down the entire town when all we needed was you.'

'Is that a confession?'

Gail tapped the side of her nose and smiled.

During their Leaving Cert year, classes in St John's Community School had repeatedly been disrupted by hoax bomb warnings. While suspicion had fallen on Gail, no one had been able to prove her involvement.

Birdy and Gail had first bonded during school music lessons when they'd sung 'O Sacred Head Surrounded' and 'The Battle Hymn of the Republic' with gusto. In a class where everybody else had mumbled or mouthed the words, that had felt subversive. At the time, Birdy had been playing acoustic guitar with the parish youth group. Gail had been teaching herself to play an elder brother's bass.

For them, music wasn't a hobby, it was life. They were the girls who obsessed about new sounds; the girls who spent twenty minutes twisting their old transistors one way then the other to hear John Peel; the girls who bought as many records as they could afford and went to the library to read the *NME* and *Melody Maker*. In the way that some of their classmates liked reading about boarding schools they would never attend or glamorous lives they would never lead, Birdy and Gail dreamt of venues they'd never play and musicians they'd never meet.

Through a friend of a friend, they'd found Yvonne, who'd been introduced to the drums by her father. He'd been a drummer in a showband and was keen for one of the family to follow his lead. If The Diamonds weren't to his taste, he hid it well.

Finding a vocalist had been more challenging. The threesome were competent and able to hold a tune, but they didn't have *it*. If they were going to form a band, they needed *it*.

They placed an audition notice in the window of Save-A-Lot. When Loretta turned up, Birdy was surprised. The would-be vocalist went to the convent, and there was a strong, often caustic, rivalry between her school and theirs. According to Loretta, her classmates believed that St John's pupils were given special lessons in how to claim the dole. They also maintained that a third year had given birth at the back of the woodwork room. 'Nah, you've got it wrong there,' Gail replied, in her most matter-of-fact voice. 'It was the chemistry lab.'

Immediately, the first three Diamonds knew that Loretta was the one. It wasn't just that she looked like a frontwoman, she could sing. Really sing. Her voice had depth and range. It could be tough, it could shimmer, it could soar.

Birdy stirred her coffee and took a sip. 'So,' she said, 'what's our plan for tonight?'

'Our plan,' replied Gail, 'is to storm out the gate and keep on storming.'

Yvonne pulled on her cigarette and blew a curl of smoke. 'We might put together a set list too. I always enjoy the night more when we're not a total shambles.'

Yvonne had taken the booking. At twenty, she was two years older than the others and tended to handle the practicalities. Although capable of hammering the drums like a maniac, her personality was steady. Methodical. She had bobbed auburn hair, milk-pale skin and four piercings in her left ear. She was also blessed with a long fuse. When they fell out, she was the peacemaker.

'How long will we get on stage?' asked Loretta.

'Half an hour.'

'Not much time, so.'

'Well, the way I look at it, it's short enough not to annoy the lads who're only there for A Nest of Vipers. And long enough . . .' Yvonne took another drag of her cigarette '. . . to impress Kieran Mitchell.'

'You're kidding,' said Birdy. 'As in *the* Kieran Mitchell?'

'The very man. According to the guy who runs the place, he's going to be there tonight.'

Kieran Mitchell was a Dublin-based manager. He had a small roster of bands, all of them successful. His main group, Future Heroes, were just back from an American tour. Their last single had received a rave review in the *NME*. The Diamonds had sent Mitchell a demo tape but hadn't received a reply.

'Dead on,' said Gail. 'Why didn't you tell us before?'

'I'm telling you now, aren't I? Anyway, it's A Nest of Vipers he's interested in. He doesn't know we'll be playing.'

'The Vipers are no better than us,' said Birdy.

Gail slapped the table. 'Too right they're not.'

The prospect of performing in front of Kieran Mitchell focused their thoughts. In the two years they'd been together, they had honed their act in bars and parish halls, at parties and in community centres. They'd played in places where the night ended with the national anthem – and where it ended with a brawl. Along the way, they'd accumulated a solid collection of songs: 'Away From Me', 'The Fire Inside', 'Ordinary Girl', and Birdy's favourite, 'Too Much Not Enough'. If they had an anthem, that was it.

Mostly, the band wrote together, combining scraps of ideas then rehearsing the music and lyrics until they were satisfied. As much as Birdy loved performing, writing songs was her favourite part of being a Diamond. She'd had no idea how exhilarating it would be to create something. To call it hers. She couldn't hear anyone else writing about her life, about their lives, and that was what she wanted to do. (The nagging feeling that this sounded too pretentious stopped her saying it out loud. In Steelstown, people didn't have much time for airy-fairy notions.)

Loretta looked at her watch. 'I'd better go home and tell my mother about the gig.'

'That should be fun,' said Yvonne. Patrice Saunders wasn't a fan of the band. 'I'll walk with you.'

'Now, ladies,' said Gail, 'you can't leave until you've done your duty.'

'Go on,' said Yvonne, stubbing out her cigarette. 'What have you got for us?'

This was their ritual. On the day of a gig, they danced, throwing themselves around the room as if they were hearing music for the first time. It was their way of psyching themselves up. Of saying, 'Here's what it's all about.'

Gail pushed back her chair and went to the kitchen counter. There, she pressed rewind on the cassette player. It finished with a light *thunk*, the cue for the rest to get to their feet.

As they did, Gail pressed play, and Talking Heads' 'Once In A Lifetime' bubbled from the speakers. There wasn't much space in the McGeehans' kitchen, but The Diamonds made the most of what they had. They strutted and twirled, shuffled and clapped.

They were carefree. They were fans. They were rock stars.

'Have you forgotten that home taping is killing music?' said Yvonne, with a wheeze of laughter.

'You won't be joking when you're losing millions in record sales,' replied Gail.

Next came 'It's Going To Happen'. They sang along, raising their voices still further when The Undertones were followed by

Martha and the Muffins and 'Echo Beach'. Loretta used a sweeping brush as a mic stand and Yvonne bashed a wooden spoon against the lid of a biscuit tin. Birdy and Gail swayed their hips and stomped their feet in a glorious free-for-all.

It was at this point that Mrs O'Malley next door decided she'd had enough. Three heavy thumps echoed through the adjoining wall.

'Fuckity-fuck,' said Gail. 'I'd better turn it down or she'll be moaning to Mam again. "You've got to teach that girl how to behave,"' she said, adopting her neighbour's adenoidal voice.

Birdy's chest ached from laughing. She leaned forward and cupped her hands over her knees.

When she straightened up again, she looked at the others. Did they feel, as she did, that this summer would decide their future? That they would either strike out beyond Steelstown or fall apart? Not for the first time, she had a sense of being tugged in opposite directions. As much as she craved success, she would hate to lose this silliness. This closeness.

She wanted everything to be different and nothing to change.

Chapter 3

From the side of the stage, Loretta assessed the crowd. The evening was mild, and already the venue felt clammy. The Old Mill was gloomy, poorly ventilated, borderline seedy. The paint was chipped, the floor tacky with the residue of a thousand spilt drinks. It was their kind of place.

The audience was mostly male. Thin as wire, they wore bomber jackets and jeans, and drank pints of Carling. The smattering of women were in their Friday-night best, hair teased, heels high. Loretta spotted two or three Steelstown faces. They were loyal, the Steelstown girls. Although reluctant to acknowledge it, she was also watching out for someone who might be Kieran Mitchell. Someone older and more sophisticated. Someone who didn't look as if his mother had bought his clothes from the local drapery and cut his hair with pinking shears.

Back in the storeroom where The Diamonds were getting ready, Birdy was staring into the speckled mirror and applying wings of black eyeliner. The solitary light-bulb, a hundred watts at most, meant it wasn't easy.

Arms out, palms up, she spun around to face the others. 'Am I okay?'

'You look great,' said Yvonne.

'I'd nearly hop on you myself,' added Gail.

Birdy looked sheepishly pleased but stayed quiet.

Loretta realised that she was expected to add to the compliments. 'Fab,' she said. 'The eye makeup suits you.'

Birdy gave her broadest snaggle-toothed smile. 'Cheers, Loretta.'

If she was honest, there were still days when Loretta felt slightly apart from her bandmates. When she worried that she'd say the wrong thing or express the wrong view. It wasn't just that she'd gone to a different school or was attending university. Sometimes the subtle distinctions were the most significant. She'd never had to share a bedroom or use another person's bathwater. In her family home, there was no lock on the telephone, and they ate dinner, not tea. While it was easy to say none of this mattered, the fact that she could list the differences showed that it did.

She was also less physical. The other Diamonds hugged and kissed and backcombed each other's hair. They could be volatile too, singing together one moment, snapping at each other the next. Loretta was never relaxed enough to join in.

Even her name was wrong. She'd never liked 'Loretta'. It was too fussy, too old-fashioned. It belonged to an elderly woman in a tweed skirt, not a girl who wore black mini-dresses and sang in a rock band.

At the start, her parents had encouraged her interest in music. Her mother had been keen for her to play the piano – or the harp. The harp was a suitable instrument for well-brought-up girls. Neither Patrice nor Des Saunders had foreseen their elder daughter's desire to learn the guitar or join a band.

That was the problem with them. Yes, they were ambitious for her. But their ambition was unimaginative.

At fifteen, Loretta had bought *Easter*. She'd played 'Because The Night' over and over and over again until she feared the needle would wear a hole in the vinyl. As the song's tentative opening built to its irresistible chorus, she'd marched across the front room.

'This,' she'd said to her parents. 'This is who I want to be.'

Her mother had scrutinised Patti Smith's picture on the album cover before declaring that there were more attractive women cleaning offices in the industrial estate. She'd always placed a premium on conventional good looks. Anything quirky wasn't to be trusted.

Yvonne's brother, Gary, who owned a Transit van, had driven The Diamonds and their gear to Limerick. He frequently came to see them, as did other members of the Hayes family. The McGeehans turned up from time to time. Despite being underage, Birdy's brother was a regular, and her mother had been known to call in for a song or two. Loretta hoped her father and younger sister might yet come to a gig. She'd given up on her mother.

When she'd told her parents about this evening's booking, her mam had put on a pained expression. 'I thought that after a year of university, you'd have got that carry-on out of your system,' she'd said.

That carry-on. The words had lodged like a boulder in Loretta's brain.

Rather than arguing, she'd turned away. After a minute of silence, her mother had accused her of being sullen. 'You've got so much to look forward to,' she'd said, her voice crisp as a November leaf. 'So many opportunities. I can't understand why you're wasting your time with those girls.'

That carry-on. Those girls.

Loretta's mother hadn't wanted her to spend the summer back in Steelstown. She couldn't understand why her daughter hadn't gone to Montauk or Cape Cod like others in her year at college. London would have been acceptable too. She might have met a better class of person there. Instead, here she was, still palling around with Birdy, Yvonne and Gail. Patrice had especially strong feelings about Gail, whom she'd once described as 'the sort of girl who'd let anyone paw at her'.

Commerce hadn't been Loretta's choice. She'd been keen to study English or psychology. Her career guidance teacher had put her straight. 'Why do an arts degree when you'll have the results for something better?' she'd argued. 'These days, girls are going for all sorts of courses.' Loretta's parents had agreed.

That was how she'd found herself in UCD, where the grey buildings blended into the grey sky, and everyone she met had been to one of a small number of fee-paying schools. She'd expected college to be filled with fascinating, friendly people. She'd hoped it would be more colourful, more sophisticated, than Steelstown. Yet somehow it felt less interesting, more regimented.

When she explained that she was from Clare, the other students assumed her father was a farmer. They weren't able to grasp that the county had more than fields and stones. In their minds, she'd grown up surrounded by donkeys and drunks and old men who played the concertina and drank tea out of saucers. They didn't understand that Steelstown people lived in rows of houses and worked in factories and offices.

Mostly, Loretta tried to fit in, but one night during her second term, she'd decided to dress up. She'd changed into a small black skirt, fishnet tights and black ankle boots. She crimped her hair and applied deep plum lipstick with a smear of gloss on top. At home, her look would have been considered cool. Gail would have *swit-swoo*ed, and Birdy would have admired her makeup.

The reception from her classmates was different. As she returned from the bathroom, she overheard one of the interchangeable south Dublin girls with interchangeable south Dublin names use the word 'tacky'. Another, speaking in an exaggerated west of Ireland accent, said, 'I'm in a band, you know.' A third snorted with laughter. Five months on, Loretta still felt the chill of social rejection.

Two weeks later, she'd played a gig with The Diamonds. It had gone well, and afterwards, they'd shared a flagon of cider. At one point, Birdy tapped her on the shoulder. 'What you don't understand,' she said, with glassy-eyed sincerity, 'is that this band is my salvation.' Taken aback, Loretta fumbled her reply. She wished she'd said, 'Mine too.'

In some ways, she envied The Diamonds' guitarist. The thing about being Birdy Troy with the gangly legs, sinewy arms and stuttering laugh was that no one expected anything from her. She reminded Loretta of a sea creature on land. In everyday life, she could be awkward. On stage, her movement was fluid, her purpose clear.

Loretta considered them now, those girls. There was Yvonne in khaki shorts and a navy halterneck, staring at her hands and nodding in time to an imaginary beat. There was Gail in a leopard-print skirt and grey top, her nerves revealed by the way she took quick pulls on her cigarette. And there was Birdy, black T-shirt, black jeans and silver ankle boots, pacing between the crates of empty bottles and throwing out scattered thoughts.

A head poked around the door. A girl of no more than fourteen or fifteen gave a twitchy smile. 'The manager says there's enough folks in now. Ye can start.'

'Thanks, love,' said Yvonne. 'Right. Come on, you lot.'

It was time.

*

They opened with 'Shadow And Smoke', which was a mistake. It was too new, too plodding. Even the sprinkling of audience members who'd heard the song before didn't show any great enthusiasm.

They segued into 'Ordinary Girl'. Another mistake. It sounded too low-key. Oh, and Loretta couldn't quite get her voice around the higher notes. *Of all the nights* . . . A section of the crowd started talking. A shriek of laughter cut through the room. The Diamonds were two songs in, a quarter of their set, and they were flailing.

Loretta glanced to her right and saw Birdy mouthing 'Too Much Not Enough'. She wavered. It was their big number. Their climax. They couldn't throw it away here. Or, maybe, they had no choice. They needed to rescue the set.

As 'Ordinary Girl' shuddered to an end, she called, 'This is "Too Much Not Enough".'

If Gail and Yvonne were surprised, they didn't let it show. As soon as the first throb of music passed through her, Loretta knew Birdy had been right. She felt the beat in her blood and bones. She heard her own voice, and it sounded strong:

You say I'm too soft, you say I'm too rough,
I'm too much, you say, I'm not enough . . .

The crowd howled their approval. How did so many of them know the words? The boys bounced up and down, the girls waved their arms. The room vibrated.

This was The Diamonds' sound as she liked to think of it. Tight. Uncluttered. Fierce. Without pausing, they lurched into their cover of 'My Sharona'. A roar rolled across the room. Birdy's solo sounded better than the original record, and her backing vocals were just right. Gail was precise, solid. Yvonne was fire.

When she got the chance, Loretta searched the room for someone who might be Kieran Mitchell. He had to be there. He had to see them, hear them, at their sparkling best. But the place was a frenzy of flushed faces, and it was hard to know where one body ended and another began.

The band played on. Never before had 'The Fire Inside' sounded so melodic. Never had 'Away From Me' sounded more strident. Next came 'Harder', another new song. But where the opening number had sunk, this one flew.

They had time for one more.

'"Too Much Not Enough"', came a shout from the floor.

'We've already played it,' said Loretta, wiping the sweat from her face.

'Do it again.'

So they did, only this time it was even faster, louder, wilder:

I've never known easy, I've always known tough,
What you once said was too much, is now not enough . . .

The Diamonds had the audience by the throat. They played one last song, 'Friday Afternoons'. It wasn't their most powerful number. That didn't matter. They were too caught up in the communal sense of joy and freedom to care. They were playing as though their lives depended on it, which in a way they did.

Afterwards, when they'd packed the gear into Gary's Transit, they went to collect their money. They were buzzing from their performance, giggling and trading compliments and larking about. They'd played enough gigs to know that the sensation would pass, but in that moment they were invincible.

The venue's manager was a fleshy man with thin sideburns and thick glasses. A Nest of Vipers would be on in a few minutes, he said.

He took off his glasses and polished them with the end of his maroon shirt. 'For four young girls, you make an awful lot of noise.'

'Cheers,' said Birdy.

'I was worried at the start. I thought to myself, *This crowd aren't much use.* You managed to turn it around, though.'

'We like to give ourselves a challenge,' replied Gail, sending a pointed look towards Yvonne.

'You told me that Kieran Mitchell might be knocking about,' said the drummer. 'Is he here?'

'He was around, right enough. I haven't seen him in a while, mind. He'd somewhere else to go.'

'We sent him a tape. We wanted to see if he'd got it.'

'Not that he mentioned. I'd say the same man gets tapes by the lorry load.'

'We'd like a quick word, that's all. Have you any idea where he went?'

'No,' said the manager. 'And there's no sense in annoying him. If he's not interested, he's not interested. There's a fierce lot of rejection in this business. You'll have to get used to that.'

'Thanks for the advice,' said Gail.

Figuring that Mitchell had to return, they waited through A Nest of Vipers, drinking vodka and accepting praise from people who'd been there for their own set. Yvonne, who'd snipped a picture of the band manager from *Hot Press,* insisted she would recognise him.

A Nest of Vipers were worth seeing but, honestly, not as compelling or energetic as The Diamonds. What they didn't lack was confidence. When the crowd appeared indifferent to one of their songs, the lead singer drawled, 'If you've got something better to do, why don't you fuck off and do it?'

When they'd finished, The Diamonds went backstage to say hello.

'What's the story with Kieran Mitchell?' asked Loretta, trying – and failing – to sound casual.

'He's arranged to meet us tomorrow,' said the singer, a wall of a guy called Justin Turley. 'He's a busy man.'

'So everyone keeps telling us,' said Birdy.

Turley then asked Loretta if she was spoken for. His choice of old-fashioned language sounded calculated, as though he saw making a move on her as a bit of a joke, something to be done with a raised eyebrow and a smirk.

'Yes,' she lied.

'Arrogant tosser,' muttered Gail, almost loud enough for him to hear.

Yvonne took her by the arm. 'Let's go,' she said. 'I'm starving.'

They found Gary, who said he was staying for another drink. The four went to a nearby chipper and climbed into a booth. The red vinyl seat covering stuck to Loretta's thighs. The stench of fried onions and dirty chip-fat hit the back of her throat. All of a sudden, the day felt achingly long. She wouldn't have minded another vodka, but she didn't want to be here, surrounded by messy drunks.

'I reckon Kieran Mitchell saw the first song or two and left,' said Birdy, who looked exhausted, her hair tangled, her makeup smeared under her eyes.

'There are other managers,' said Yvonne, waving a chip in the air. 'There'll be other opportunities.'

'I hear you,' said Loretta. 'It's just . . . I feel like tonight was as good as we might ever be. And it wasn't enough.'

Birdy placed her can of Coke on the table with a decisive thud.

'You can't believe that. And, even if you do, you shouldn't say it. It's bad luck.'

'I'm only saying what I think.'

'Ah, here,' said Yvonne. 'Can we stop sniping at each other? Especially when there are better targets . . . like our friend from A Nest of Vipers. Talk about loving himself.'

'Hey, lay-dees,' said Gail, mimicking Justin Turley's drawl. 'Won't you spread your legs for me?'

'Puke,' said Birdy. 'I'd go with Pat Joe Hoey before I'd let Turley near me.'

In Steelstown, Pat Joe was known as the human equivalent of knotweed. Wherever he went, havoc and heartbreak followed.

As they tore into the Vipers, Loretta noticed a man entering the chipper. His eyes scanned the room. Then he began walking in their direction.

Go away, she thought. This wasn't the night for being hassled or leered at or having to bat away half-brained questions about why they'd no men to keep them company.

Yvonne, too, appeared to notice. 'Oh,' she said, giving Loretta a nudge.

The man took another step in their direction. He was tall with collar-length brown hair and wore a suit jacket and dark jeans. It was unlikely his mother had bought his clothes or cut his hair.

'So, girls,' he said, 'this is where you've been hiding.'

Chapter 4

Now, Dublin

News of the letters spread, fast as fire.

'Everyone?' said Stacey to Rhiannon, as she sat down at her neighbour's kitchen table.

'Every last one of us. Or that's how it looks at the minute. A few people say they haven't seen a letter, but that's only because they'd left for work before the post arrived.'

'And can this Silver Eagle crowd . . . whoever they are . . . can they evict everyone? I mean, are there not laws against that sort of thing?'

Rhiannon shook her head. 'You know Piotr down the hall?'

'Uh-huh.'

'He looked it all up. There are a million loopholes, and Silver Eagle could be using any one of them. Apparently, they're based in London and they buy up apartment blocks all the time. Then they wait for the leases to expire.'

'Why?' asked Stacey, knowing the answer but wanting to hear Rhiannon say it out loud.

'Why does anybody do anything? To make money. They'll tidy up the building, then rent out the apartments to folks who can pay twice as much as us. And you can be certain they've got teams of expensive lawyers making sure we don't get in the way.' Rhiannon's voice twanged with anger, and when she'd finished, she slapped her cheek. 'Sorry, Stace. I'm just so worried, y'know. Where are we going to find another place like this?'

'I don't know.'

The implications were forcing their way through the sawdust in Stacey's brain. Not only would she have to find a new apartment, she'd have to get a new job, a proper job, to pay the rent.

Once, she would have balked at the idea of living somewhere like Briarstown on Dublin's southern fringes. She'd seen herself as a city girl in a redbrick terrace; someone with a relentless social life and a cottage filled with colourful souvenirs from adventurous holidays in warm countries. But to enjoy an artisan lifestyle, you needed a management wage. Well, either that or wealthy parents, and Stacey failed on both counts.

Whitethorn House didn't need tidying. If anything, the six floors of pale brick and smoked glass were overly sterile. The building had a complicated entrance system, a no-washing-on-the-balconies policy and a vigilant residents' association. Despite her initial misgivings, Stacey had grown fond of it. Whitethorn had become her home.

Rhiannon Dempsey, her partner Carmel and their six-year-old daughter, Mia, lived in the apartment next door. Carmel was a hairstylist, but Rhiannon's job as a bookkeeper meant she worked part of the week from home. Thankfully, this was one of those days. From the tree of hand-painted mugs to Mia's drawings on the fridge to the smell of washing powder and lavender, the apartment was as welcoming as Stacey's was cheerless.

Rhiannon lifted her coffee mug. 'Have you seen the WhatsApp? It's gone wild.'

In Stacey's view, the world contained two types of people: those who saw neighbourhood WhatsApp groups as an opportunity and those who viewed them as a menace. As a rule, she tried to avoid the Whitethorn group. Its competitive neighbourliness set her on edge.

She took out her phone and had a look. The usual chirpy tone had been replaced by disbelief – and anger. Liam in number twenty-seven said Silver Eagle couldn't throw them all onto the side of the road. Jasmine in fifty-nine disagreed. It was well known that vulture funds could do whatever they liked, she said, her message dotted with emojis 🤑🤮😈. Pat and Bróna in thirty-three argued that the government actually wanted to evict them so that young people with well-paid jobs in high-tech companies could move in. Aengus in eleven thought this was far-fetched, and Marek in fifteen claimed it was an insult to someone like him who worked in tech. Pat and Bróna responded by sending an attachment to an impenetrable article about housing supply and late-stage capitalism.

Stacey muted her phone.

'Will you tell Ronan?' asked Rhiannon, passing a teaspoon from one hand to the other.

'I'm not sure.'

'Which means you won't.'

Stacey picked at her thumb, which was bleeding again. She was only slightly less tongue-tied than she'd been with Detta in the Pear Tree. 'It's not really any of his business.'

'Fair enough, only . . .'

'Only what?'

The two women sat in silence, their eyes not quite meeting.

'I'm not saying you should get back with him or anything,' said Rhiannon. 'But look at you. You've licked your wounds down to the bone and you're still miserable.'

'That's not fair.'

'Come on, Stace. You don't even look like yourself. You've gone all bland.'

This was hard to deny. Usually Stacey enjoyed making mismatched clothes look as though they belonged together. She would wear a Breton top with a lime green floral skirt and a pair of cream Converse. She paired neons with pastels, and stars with polka dots. Even on her quieter days she would add something a bit adventurous, like large resin earrings or a vintage school scarf. At college, a girl had told her that wearing clashing clothes was her one true talent. Today, she was in ill-fitting jeans, a wrinkled grey T-shirt and flat black sandals. The sandals showed that her feet had not wintered well. There were deep ridges on her yellow toenails, and the skin on her heels was so thick the best way to tackle them would be with a potato-peeler. Stacey's style had abandoned her.

'Answer me this,' said Rhiannon. 'Have you eaten this morning?'

'No, but I'm okay.'

Stacey didn't know how to explain that a broken relationship and an eviction notice weren't her only problems. Until she received an overdue advertising payment, going to the shop was pointless. She didn't want anyone to know that she'd run out of money. Thirty-year-olds should not be left with little more than a jar of coins.

Objectively speaking, she knew that thirtieth birthdays no longer had the same significance. Being single and childless wasn't an automatic source of shame. But thirty remained a staging post, a point by which you should be well along the path to full adulthood. Instead, Stacey was meandering through the weeds, taking wrong turns and stumbling over obstacles.

The most popular word in her vocabulary was 'congratulations'. She congratulated friends on their engagements, pregnancies and promotions. She congratulated new parents and new home owners. Her life was a succession of weddings, christenings and hen weekends. But while others were bounding up life's ladder, she appeared to have landed on a long and slippery snake.

She'd spent the past fortnight in a trough of self-pity, her mind roving over everything she'd got wrong. She should have known it wouldn't work out with Ronan. Her relationships never lasted. Nor could she settle on a career and stick with it.

On her worst days, she'd slobbed around in frayed pyjamas, capable of nothing more strenuous than eating toast and scrolling through Instagram. There was something about summer Instagram, with its ceaseless waves of parties and festivals, Photoshopped thighs and Amalfi coast holidays, that she found particularly draining. Yet, the more inadequate an account made her feel, the more intense her attachment to it. She wondered if there was a word for her behaviour. If not, there should be.

'You're not with me, are you?' said Rhiannon.

'Don't mind me. I was having another mope.' Stacey attempted a smile. 'Like I say, I'll be all right.'

Rhiannon got to her feet. 'I'm going to make you a sandwich. Honestly, though, Stace, I hate to see you like this.'

Although she'd initially dismissed the idea of finding out more about The Diamonds, and although there were a hundred other things she should have been doing, Stacey couldn't shake the band from her thoughts. There couldn't have been many all-woman rock groups in early 1980s Ireland. Even if they hadn't been any good, they must have had novelty appeal. When she returned to her apartment, she decided to take another look.

Most of the online references were part of broader pieces about the Irish music scene of those years. The articles had a pro-forma feel: the country had been a monochrome place and young people had yearned for colour. If you couldn't start a revolution with a guitar, you could at least hope it would aid your escape. Journalists and DJs spoke about how Dublin had pulsed with music. Every garage had become a rehearsal space, every pub a venue.

The Diamonds, she learnt, had recorded one single, 'Too Much Not Enough'. After that? Nothing. They'd had a sharp ascent. And a sharper fall.

Hoping that the single had a video, she tried YouTube. To her delight, an excerpt from a June 1982 edition of *Top of the Pops* jumped to the top of the screen. A baby-faced presenter was surrounded by exuberant teenagers with frizzy perms and garlands of plastic beads. 'And now,' he announced, 'this week's highest new entry. Big things are expected from these girls. Straight from Ireland, it's The Diamonds.'

What followed was mesmerising. The four grainy figures from the photo came to life. Stacey's suspicion that they'd been very young was confirmed. What she hadn't expected was how good they'd been. 'Too Much Not Enough' began quickly and gathered pace. A thunderstorm of drums gave way to a ridiculously catchy chorus.

When the clip finished, she watched again. Was this what 1982 had looked like? High cheekbones, matte red lipstick, high-waisted black jeans? While the lead singer was conventionally lovely – smoky eyes, wide mouth, tousled blonde hair – it was the guitarist,

Birdy, who attracted Stacey's attention. There was agility in her movement, grace in the way her fingers glided along the neck of the guitar. At one point, she looked up at the camera. Her gaze had a surprising intensity. How could someone so compelling have melted back into ordinary life?

As Stacey watched for the third time, the weight of the day eased. She felt the sweet release of coming across a story that interested her. Fleetingly, she wondered if The Diamonds, who must now be in their late fifties or early sixties, ever looked at themselves online. Did it hurt to see yourself as you once were? Did you think about an alternate history in which the hits had kept on coming?

It was easy to get swallowed by a YouTube sinkhole, and the temptation to view the other acts from that night's *TOTP* was strong. She allowed herself a brief diversion, watching ABC and Echo and the Bunnymen. Then she returned to The Diamonds and clicked open the comments.

What amused her was the number of people who wanted a time machine to transport them back to 1982. It wasn't just the music they craved. They spoke of the 1980s as a lost paradise of fun and freedom, sunshine and opportunity. No decade in history had been so laden with promise. Growing up had been a privilege. Stacey thought of the articles she'd been reading about recession and unemployment. Not for the first time, she was fascinated by the siren call of nostalgia.

The remarks about The Diamonds were mostly positive: Saw them live back in the day. Amazing!! That song is the elixir of youth. Simple perfection. Why didn't these girls make it big?

A few were sleazy: I'd have done all four in a heartbeat. The singer looks well up for it. What a honey!!

The most significant posts were at the bottom of the page. JBT wrote: Loved The Diamonds. Should have been more than one-hit wonders. Wonder why they never did anything else.

Gus McNamara replied: Great story to be told. Shame it never was.

AllSaint62 said: Oh? Tell us more.

There were no further messages.

Next, Stacey turned to social media. Reasoning that middle-aged women were most likely to be on Facebook, she went there first. (A voice in her head, the one that sounded like her mother, complained about the ageism behind her assumption.) She toggled from profile to profile before discounting them. The women she found were too old, too young, too far away.

It occurred to her that if any of the band had married, they'd probably changed their name. She could be looking for Loretta Aaronson or Loretta Zywicki or anything in between. Also, there was every chance the guitarist had reverted to her real name. What had Birdy stood for? Breda? Bernie? Bridget? Or had the nickname been prompted by something else?

Instagram contained several references to #TheDiamonds, mainly from eighties obsessives who admired the women's style. There were a couple of screengrabs from *Top of the Pops* and a portrait of them posing in front of a white wall. The accounts also paid homage to The Go-Go's, Bananarama, Madonna and The Bangles.

On Twitter, she came across a Gail McGeehan-Davis. A rush of anticipation quickly turned to disappointment. While this Gail appeared to be in her fifties, she was also an academic in the United States, specialising in political theory. Stacey ruled her out.

After two hours of blind alleys and dead ends, she gave up. Forty years on, even the seediest corners of the internet were indifferent to The Diamonds' fate. She'd found a tantalising glimpse of them, but not much more.

So, Birdy, Loretta, Gail, Yvonne, she said, as if they were standing in front of her, *why did you split up and where did you go?*

Stacey ran through the possibilities. Had they been torn apart by 'creative differences'? Had the split been caused by too much partying or too little money? By drugs or disillusionment? Or had The Diamonds got a different story to tell? There were a thousand other bands she could track down. Bands who'd had their ten minutes behind fame's velvet rope before being reclaimed by obscurity. Was there anything special about these four women?

Something told her there was.

Chapter 5

June 1981, Steelstown

'No,' said Birdy's father, as he rose from his chair. 'I've not interfered before now. In fact, I've been very reasonable.' He nodded, as if to emphasise his good behaviour. 'This time the answer's no. You're not moving to Dublin. And if you stop to think about what this man is saying, you won't want to go either.'

'I thought about nothing else all night,' said Birdy. 'I want to go, and so do the others.'

Half past eight on Saturday morning, and she was in the kitchen with her parents. Declan was already at work. No sooner had she started talking about Kieran Mitchell than her mother's face had taken on a pinched look and she'd squeezed the bridge of her nose. It was a look that Birdy knew well. It said, 'I'm not sure I need to hear this.'

Her father was less subtle. Oliver Troy didn't trust Dubliners, considering them little better than the English. And he definitely didn't trust Dubliners who managed rock bands and wanted his daughter to leave her perfectly acceptable job and move to the other side of the country. His claim that he didn't usually interfere was correct, but only because he hadn't expected The Diamonds to get anywhere. Birdy's dad didn't have much faith in good news.

Her thoughts swung back to the night before and Kieran Mitchell's sudden arrival. Gary Hayes, who'd remained in the Old Mill, had told him where to find them. They'd talked in the chipper and, later, at his hotel where he'd bought them drinks in the residents' bar. They could go all the way, he'd said. But they'd have to leave Steelstown, and they'd have to write and rehearse and perform like never before. There'd be no time for work or men or their families. The band would be their lives. If they followed this advice, he'd said, the rewards could be huge.

He'd done the bulk of the talking, waving his arms in expansive gestures while throwing out lines about sessions and tours and record companies. They'd sat, rapt, almost incapable of believing that this was happening. Birdy had tried to arrange herself so that she appeared poised and sophisticated, the person she wanted to be rather than the scrappy small-town girl she actually was. She'd sensed that the others, even Loretta, were doing the same. They'd waited for the caveat that would bring everything tumbling down. It hadn't come.

When, finally, they'd got home, she'd slid into the house as quietly as possible. Then, she'd lain on top of the bedclothes, her head overwhelmed by thoughts of the future. In the past, when she hadn't been able to sleep, it had been because she was anxious or annoyed. This time pure elation had kept her awake.

'Suppose this man isn't lying to you,' her father said now. 'I still don't like what he's suggesting.'

'He's not lying. And I promise you, this is a big deal. He's really well-known.'

'Not to us he's not, pet,' said her mother. 'Perhaps we could talk to him.'

Her dad, hovering at the far end of the Formica table, scratched his neck. 'We'll be talking to no one, Mary, because she's not going to Dublin.'

For as long as Birdy could remember, her father had worked in the butcher's shop around the corner from Save-A-Lot. Gail claimed the job suited him because he had a head like a boiled ham. Birdy pretended to be offended but secretly she found the remark funny. That he'd spent more than twenty years parcelling the same cuts of meat for the same customers said a lot. He viewed any surprise, no matter how promising, with suspicion.

'I'll bet Loretta Saunders isn't giving up university,' he said.

'She is.'

'I'll believe that when I see it. Des Saunders will have talked sense into her – you can put the house on it. And I doubt Yvonne Hayes is walking out on her job either. Hasn't she a grand cushy number above in Flexatron?'

Birdy didn't know if she was supposed to answer. Before she had the chance to speak, he moved on.

'As for Gail McGeehan . . .' He widened his eyes. 'Granted she'll probably be on the first bus to Dublin, but she's got nothing to lose. She's unlikely to find much of a job. She'll be like her sisters, pregnant and married before she's twenty-one.'

'That's not fair,' said Birdy. 'You hardly know Gail.'

'I know her well enough. I'm not saying she's a bad person. But girls like her? They're a magnet for every class of loser and waster. Education is wasted on them.'

Birdy's mother sighed. 'There's no call for that sort of talk,' she said, her voice barely audible. 'She's got a big heart, has Gail.'

'And it'll be taken advantage of.'

It was at moments like this that Birdy hated the smallness of everything. The shoddiness. Life doesn't have to be this way, she wanted to say. It doesn't have to be about Save-A-Lot and Normoyle's Butchers and dusting and ironing and the occasional trip to the seaside. It doesn't have to be narrow and respectable and 'Keep your head down' and 'Don't make a show of yourself.' It doesn't have to be about putting on a performance and then forgetting the insulting things you said. Because, even as her father spoke, they all knew he was going through a well-practised ritual. When it came to reactions, his repertoire was limited.

She often ran ideas like these around her brain but rarely voiced them. Another look at her mother, and she abandoned any notion of doing so now. The pinched look remained.

'The more I think about this, the less I like it,' said her father, who'd decided to sit down again. 'I've read about what's happening in Dublin at the minute. All those youngsters taking drugs. Innocent boys and girls walking around like zombies.'

Birdy shifted in her chair. 'If I don't do drugs here, why would I take them in Dublin?'

Thwack. The sound came from outside.

'Because they're not available here.'

Thwack. There it was again.

'Thanks for the vote of confidence.'

Thwack.

'For the love of God,' said her father, 'have those fellows nothing better to be doing on a Saturday morning?'

Thwack.

The Troys lived at the end of a terrace of five houses in the middle of Connolly Park, and boys used the gable end to practise their football and hurling skills. Birdy's dad got to his feet once more. 'I'll go and sort them out.'

Thwack.

When he'd left, a streak of morning sunshine peeped through the window, illuminating her mam's face. Mother and daughter had similar features: round grey eyes, a snub of a nose and a pointed chin. But while Mary Troy's hair was sleek and well-behaved, Birdy was cursed with a thousand uncooperative waves and kinks. She always thought of her mother as a more orderly version of herself.

Although her mother was a bit of a neat freak ('Pick up your anorak, Declan. Put those records away, Birdy. Am I the only one who notices dust?'), the kitchen had a higgledy-piggledy quality. Implements and utensils lined the wall beside the sink: here a ladle, there a sieve. The shelves were stacked with condiments while the dresser bulged with crockery.

When Birdy went to Dublin – because she was going to Dublin – she would miss this room.

While she didn't dislike her father, she did dislike his inability to understand what mattered to her. Declan understood. As did her mother. Otherwise, why would she have taken out a credit-union loan to help Birdy buy an electric guitar?

As if she could read these thoughts, and maybe she could, her mother reached over and squeezed her hand. 'He'll calm down.'

'Thanks, Mam.'

Another squeeze. 'Your heart's set on going, isn't it?'

''Tis.'

Her mother stared into her teacup, as though the leaves offered the solution to the world's problems. 'I'll miss you.'

After the footballer had been shooed away, and her father had returned, his attitude changed. The truth was working its way in. She was eighteen, and he couldn't stop her leaving. What he could do was continue complaining.

He nodded towards the sliced pan. 'Put some bread under the grill, Bird, would you? I'll have to get off to work in a minute, and so will you.'

Deciding not to say anything about Save-A-Lot, she did as he asked.

'And what about Mike?' he said. 'What'll he make of this Dublin business?'

They sat on a low wall near the community hall. There were two walls, just three or four feet apart, with a path in between. As kids, they'd played show jumping here, hurdling the obstacles in quick succession, pretending they were horses rather than riders. It had been easier to imagine being an animal than having the money to own one.

The afternoon was warm, the sky a hard blue. About twenty metres away, a wire trolley lay on its side. Birdy would have to tell Declan. Next to it, three boys were playing marbles, their competitive yelps cutting through the quiet.

Mike ran a hand over his hair. He hadn't looked at her since she'd begun speaking.

'I guess this has been coming for a while,' he said.

'It has.'

Birdy had been going out with Mike Slattery for more than a year. At the start, he'd got a kick from her playing guitar in a rock band. It had made her interesting. Glamorous, even. More recently, his enthusiasm had waned. He'd complained that The Diamonds took up too much of her time, that Gail was trouble, Yvonne bossy,

Loretta a snob. The week before, he'd told her she was becoming one of those people who confused their taste in music with their personality. Mike liked sugary pop music and middle-of-the-road ballads.

'Are you sure?' he said. 'I mean, not just about the band thing. You know how I feel about that. But you'll all be living together as well. Is that a good idea?'

'Why wouldn't it be?'

'Because, apart from Loretta, none of you has ever lived away from home. There's every danger you'll drive each other mad.'

She twisted her hands together. 'I'd say we'll cope.'

'There's another thing. You don't know Dublin. How many times have you been there?'

'Loads.'

The truthful answer was five. She'd been to a pantomime with the Girl Guides and to the National Museum with her class from school. She'd also been to three gigs. The last, U2 in the TV Club, had been the best. She'd thumbed a lift with Gail, and they'd met Loretta in St Stephen's Green. They'd stayed up most of the night, dissecting U2's performance and arguing about their strongest song. At five in the morning, they'd finally settled on 'I Will Follow'.

Birdy could reel off a list of Dublin's most popular music venues: the Baggot, the SFX, McGonagles, the National Stadium. The names were stardust on her tongue. When it came to more practical matters, her knowledge was limited. She would struggle to tell one side of the Liffey from the other.

At last, Mike turned so that his gaze met hers. 'I used to think we wanted the same things.'

'We did. We wanted to go out and enjoy being together.'

'Yeah, only you can't do that for ever. There has to be . . . oh, I don't know . . . a plan or a purpose to it all.'

'We're only kids, Mike. It's too soon to be settling down.'

Lately, Birdy had been thinking about how little time there was to be young, only a handful of years between being a girl in white knee socks and being a grown woman with adult responsibilities. She wanted to make the most of those years.

In the months they'd been together, she'd had sex with Mike, proper sex not just messing about, twelve times. If she hadn't found the experience especially thrilling, it hadn't been awful either. They'd been getting better at it, she thought.

Strange as it might sound, the main benefit of sleeping with him had been the status it gave her among other girls. Although you didn't have to talk about what you'd done, anything you said was welcomed and analysed. In turn, they trusted you with their stories. You became a full member of the sisterhood.

Birdy had often heard people say that sex before marriage was taboo. In reality, you could do whatever you liked. Getting caught was the problem. In Steelstown, a speedy wedding in an empire-line dress was the favoured solution to an unplanned pregnancy. The few women who became single mothers were treated as oddities. They weren't disowned but neither were they particularly popular. 'You wouldn't want to be encouraging them,' her father had said.

Others, like Mags Mounsey who'd been in Birdy's home-economics class, were sent to a special home and forced to give their baby away. A year after Mags had vanished, she'd returned to Steelstown. Her hair was short now, and even on the hottest day of the year, she wore a brown duffel coat. From time to time, Birdy saw her in the supermarket. When they spoke, it was as if Mags had been reassembled with some of her parts missing.

Mike leant back and tilted his face to the sky. He was getting ready to leave. He wasn't going to get emotional or ask her to reconsider. She was part disappointed, part relieved. No matter his feelings today, he would move on pretty quickly, she reckoned.

When he looked at her again, she smiled. 'I hope everything goes well for you. You know that, don't you?'

'I hope you don't get hurt,' he replied.

That evening, she met Gail and Yvonne in the lounge of the Hunter's Inn. The Hunter's was an old man's pub, glued together by years of nicotine and grease. It was also quieter than their usual haunts, and they needed somewhere to talk. They'd arranged the get-together in the early hours when they'd been high from their meeting with Kieran Mitchell.

Forty minutes passed, and there was no sign of Loretta.

Birdy took a mouthful of beer. 'Do you think she's okay?'

'Telling her mother won't have been easy,' said Gail. 'I can't see Patrice Saunders shrugging and saying, "No bother, love. You follow your heart." I'd say she went ape.'

'Should we give Loretta a call?'

'We might only make the situation worse,' said Yvonne. 'Her ladyship doesn't have any great love for us.'

'That's one way of putting it,' said Gail, lighting a cigarette. 'Let's face it, Mrs S thinks we're out-and-out savages.' She exhaled a plume of smoke. 'Mind you, there's no deal without Loretta. You heard how Kieran spoke about her.'

Yvonne laughed. 'Twenty-four hours ago we hadn't met the man, and now he's "Kieran".'

'I'm hardly going to call him "Mr Mitchell", am I? I'd sound like a right eejit.'

Birdy emptied her glass. In the background a man was singing about carrying a coffin down a narrow road. There was no jukebox in the Hunter's, just a tape of deep-voiced men singing wistfully about the farm they'd lost and the Ireland they'd left. In many ways, she thought, Gail and Yvonne were their usual selves. But there were subtle differences. There was a suppressed energy about them, an excitement that was impossible to hide. Like her, they were probably finding it hard not to punch the air with joy.

She told them what Mike had said about getting hurt. 'Wasn't that odd?'

'I wouldn't read too much into it,' said Yvonne.

'He was put out because you were the one breaking it off,' added Gail. 'You know the way it is. Men like to think they're in control.'

'I suppose,' she said. 'Can we afford another drink?'

'We surely can. Aren't we on our way to the big-time? Give it a year, and we'll be drinking champagne in New York City.'

'Oh, yes,' said Yvonne, 'and we'll give Justin Turley a job opening our fan mail.'

'Ah, no,' said Birdy, 'we've got to save that gig for Vera Cheevers.'

They stayed until last orders. Loretta never came.

When Birdy went to bed that night, she surprised herself by crying. Not because she was sad – how could she be? – but because she sensed that one part of her life was over.

Chapter 6

Now, Dublin

Ultan Dowdall had a politician's ability to make it look as though every part of his body was listening. Perhaps that was why he had survived for so long. He'd been writing about the Irish music scene since the late 1970s, and this wasn't the first time Stacey had tapped him for information.

She also planned on recording a short interview about The Diamonds. Ultan had a great broadcasting voice. Despite decades in Dublin, his warm drawl remained true to his County Louth roots. With any luck, if she played the interview at the end of the next podcast, someone who knew what had happened would contact her.

The overdue advertising payment had come through and, with her account back in the black, Stacey could afford to meet Ultan in a city-centre café. Once upon a time, he had smoked, snorted and swallowed most of the toxic substances available to man. Ten years earlier, he'd become sober, a status he'd embraced like another addiction. He was drinking green tea and eating gluten-free ginger cake.

With his shaved head and angular face, Ultan cut an ascetic figure. Stacey reckoned his black leather jacket dated from the last millennium. In five years or so, it would probably be back in fashion.

She was bone tired, the consequence of four nights with little sleep. No sooner had she dropped off than she woke again, her head a whirl of worries. During the day, her mood fluctuated between fragile optimism and full-scale panic. A public meeting was taking place that evening, and some of Whitethorn's residents maintained that if they made enough noise, they would delay the evictions. Others went further, insisting the decision could be reversed. The WhatsApp group was alight with messages about people power and resistance. Stacey wished she could share her neighbours' confidence.

Her fascination with The Diamonds had reignited her enthusiasm for 'Whatever Happened To . . . ?' She'd edited the next episode, about a cancelled comedian, until it was almost ready for uploading. While she didn't kid herself that her work was making a lasting contribution to humankind, she liked to think she provided a worthwhile listen. She also cherished the fact that the podcast belonged to her. It was about her ideas, her research, her creativity. It gave her a glimpse into other worlds. Accepting that it was no longer viable was hard.

She would begin her search for a new job the following week. That should give her enough time to find out something solid about The Diamonds.

'The early eighties, huh?' said Ultan, unfurling his long legs. 'You're going back to my youth with this one.'

Stacey smiled. 'Long, long before my time.'

'I was only a kid myself.'

'But you do remember The Diamonds?'

'Oh, God, yeah. I reckon they turned up in Dublin in the summer of '81. They weren't alone, mind. Every night of the week, you could head out and see a new band.'

'I've read about how tough times were,' said Stacey, 'but why did everyone want to be a musician?'

'The short answer is . . . why not? What do kids want to be now? Gamers? Influencers?'

Ultan's tone suggested that he viewed these contemporary ambitions as broadly comparable to crack-dealing and contract-killing.

Stacey fought to keep the amusement from her voice. 'I think plenty of teenagers still dream of being rock stars.'

'Maybe so. But back then, music was everything. *Everything.* You've also got to factor in the hype about U2. The London A&R men had started pitching up in Dublin. For a while, it felt like every second guy in the Baggot Inn had an English accent and an expense account. They were looking for a star, so why wouldn't a youngster give music a shot?'

'From the little I know about The Diamonds, they seemed better placed than most to make it. Is that how you remember them?'

'It is. You had all these young guys throwing shapes. But posing on Grafton Street is one thing, delivering the goods is another. The Diamonds were different. They were a proper band. Good tunes too.'

'Have you any idea what happened?'

'I wish I did. Somehow they dropped off the radar. After you called, I looked up their chart placings. "Too Much Not Enough" made it to number one here and number ten in Britain. For a debut single, that was impressive. Looking back, I should have questioned their disappearance. But, hey,' Ultan raised his palms to the ceiling, 'there was so much going on, so many contenders, it was easy to lose track.'

'Fair enough,' said Stacey. 'But was being in the British charts and getting on *Top of the Pops*, was that not a big deal?'

'Mmm, it was. It's hard to explain how much singles mattered.' Ultan's tone became more reverential, as though he was a historian talking about a particularly important era. 'You went out and bought a seven-inch because it was the only way you could listen to a new release over and over again. And record companies were obsessed with the charts. They were all about pluggers and mid-weeks and what-have-you. It was as corrupt as hell, but great fun.'

'Happy days?'

'Happy days. Only if a band didn't make progress, something newer and shinier came along, and everyone moved on. It always was a fickle business.'

'I was wondering, though,' said Stacey. 'The country can't have had many all-women rock bands. Did that not make them stand out?'

'Absolutely. Some of the show bands had female vocalists. And you got the occasional folk singer. But four girls in a rock band? It just didn't happen.'

'So, given how unusual they were, surely someone has to remember what went wrong?'

'You'd think so but . . .'

'. . . it was a long time ago.'

'That's the problem.'

This was what Stacey had feared. The Diamonds belonged to a different era. A different century. Over the course of forty years, hundreds of groups had flourished and withered. They'd gone from being the next big thing to churning out Garth Brooks covers at country weddings. Why should one band stand out?

'Did you ever interview them?' she asked.

'No. I did come across them, though. They were up for a laugh.

Big-time. I remember meeting the bass player, Gail McGeehan, at a couple of parties. She was quite something.'

'Oh?' said Stacey, rubbing her palms together. 'Tell me more.'

He chuckled. 'Nothing happened, which is not to say I didn't try. Anyway, as far as interviews were concerned, Kieran Mitchell tended to keep his bands on a tight leash. He liked to be in control.'

'For truth? Kieran Mitchell was their manager?'

'Uh-huh,' said Ultan, picking at his cake crumbs. 'I remember that because in those days he was always giving hacks the hard sell. There wasn't much subtlety to his approach. Nowadays, I see him on TV, looking as smooth as glass, and I think, *I knew you before the money planed away your rough edges.*'

Kieran Mitchell was a legendary manager who'd guided several acts to international stardom. His biggest group, One Scarlet Morning, had been releasing albums for more than thirty years. Even if the high glare of their fame had dimmed, they remained hugely popular. There were others too, like The Latecomers with their bouncy summer anthems and toothsome good looks, and Iona Daunt, whose moody tunes had provided the soundtrack to a million Instagram stories.

From what Stacey could recall, Mitchell lived in New York. When he gave interviews, they were about his contemporary art collection or his appreciation of modernist literature. Even though logic told her he must have begun as a hustler, it was difficult to picture him hawking his bands around the clubs and radio studios of Dublin. Hearing that he'd managed The Diamonds was like hearing that Beyoncé had played the local community hall.

She thought of the listener who'd asked where all the interesting people had gone. By the sound of things, this story was filled with interesting people.

'Do you have a number for Kieran Mitchell?' she asked.

Ultan grinned, the lines fanning out across his face. When he spoke, there was a rumble of humour in his voice. 'The days when Mitchell had space in his diary for the likes of me are long gone. He has a Dublin office, but I don't think he spends much time there. Your best bet is the New York HQ. I have an email address for one of his assistants. I can give you that.'

'Thanks.'

Stacey drank some coffee and told him about the cryptic online comments suggesting the group had a tale to tell. 'Of course,' she said, 'if a band like The Diamonds split up now, there'd be loads of speculation on forums and Reddit and the like.'

'And it'd probably be way wide of the mark.'

'Maybe so, but it would give me somewhere to start. What do you think happened?'

'I suppose if I was to think about it . . . and I won't say this when we do the recording . . . I assumed they'd burnt up on re-entry.'

'I don't follow you,' said Stacey.

'Like a rocket, you know? You've got to understand they were only kids. And they were from a small town, so I'm guessing they had quite sheltered backgrounds. Then, almost overnight, they were shooting into the stratosphere. When it didn't work out, coming back down again must have been tough.' Ultan played with the silver rings on his left hand. 'There were a lot of casualties in those days, and a lot of chancers who'd be happy to take advantage of girls like The Diamonds.'

'That sounds grim.'

'That's the way it was, I'm afraid. Where did you get that line about there being a hidden story?'

Stacey took out her phone and found the YouTube video. 'The comments are underneath.'

Ultan put on his reading glasses and watched. 'Does it sound weird if I say I find that difficult to look at? Like, Jesus, all that promise. Where did it go, huh?'

'That's what I'm keen to find out.'

He bent closer to the screen. 'That's a funny one. The comment about the split, I mean.'

'How so?'

'The video was uploaded eight years ago, and almost all the comments are a few years old, yeah?'

Stacey nodded.

'But the most important posts – the last three – have only been there for a week or so.'

Ultan returned the phone, and she looked again. 'I can't believe I didn't spot that. It might be a coincidence only . . .'

'You don't believe in coincidences?'

'You're dead right I don't.'

'Me neither,' he said.

Chapter 7

August 1981, Dublin

Birdy sat on the stained beige sofa, watching Loretta gather up stray underwear. The bras and knickers, which had been drying on the backs of their sitting-room chairs, were bright and mismatched: here a shot of turquoise, there a splash of acid pink. As Loretta worked, her face was free of expression.

Birdy was tinkering with the lyrics for a new song. The right words kept skittering away, but she was confident they would come together in the end. Yvonne was hunched in the far corner, writing a letter.

'Hey,' said Gail, announcing her arrival. 'What's going on? I put my stuff there to dry.'

'It's dry enough,' replied Loretta. 'Kieran will be here any minute. You don't want him sitting here surrounded by your underwear.'

'He's a married man. I'd say he's seen knickers before.'

'It's hardly the same.'

'That's true,' said Birdy, keen to ease the tension. 'I doubt his wife buys her smalls from market stalls. I'd say she's more of a department-store lady.'

Gail ignored her. 'Give them to me. I'll take them upstairs. I wouldn't want to be offending anyone.'

'You're not offending me,' said Loretta, handing over the underwear. 'I'm tidying the room. That's all.'

'I get it. You're civilising the rest of us. Your mother would be proud.'

One of the reasons Birdy valued Gail's friendship was that she said the things others were reluctant to say. In doing so, she made you question your own opinions. Sometimes, though, she went too far.

Yvonne sat up. 'Seriously, Gail. That's out of order.'

Generally, they avoided mentioning Patrice Saunders. Loretta's mother wouldn't forgive her for dropping out of college, and they hadn't spoken in two months. That her daughter's band had been signed by a respected manager and were on their way to securing a record deal didn't matter. Being a musician wasn't Patrice's idea of achievement.

Loretta's face had gone slack, and she appeared to be on the edge of tears.

'I'm sorry,' said Gail. 'I can be an awful witch. Forgive me, huh?'

''S okay. It's a drag that we've nowhere better to dry our clothes. I should have asked before moving them.'

'Nah. I was being a cow. Next time, I'll bring them to the launderette.'

'Righty-ho,' said Yvonne, 'we can all agree that you're a witchy cow. Now pop the underwear upstairs, would you? Loretta's right. Kieran's due in a few minutes.'

Their new home was a terraced house in the web of redbrick streets near Croke Park. The landlord had decorated it in musty shades of brown and purple, as though on a mission to make the rooms as ugly as possible. The cooker was temperamental, and the fridge buzzed and clanked. To wash your hair, you knelt on the cracked lino and used one of those rubber attachments that provided only a dribble of water. That being said, the rent was low, they were within walking distance of the city centre, and their neighbours didn't care how much noise they made.

It was a good job the house was cheap. Their earnings were thin, and they were permanently broke. They survived on toast, sausages and instant mashed potato. Nights out were sacrosanct, and they could usually scrape together the cash for a drink or two.

Dubliners amused Birdy. Ask about their city, and they'd call it a kip. They'd claim the streets were rancid with dirt and overrun by feral kids and drug addicts. All the buildings were dilapidated, they'd say, all the politicians corrupt. But if anyone from outside the city agreed with even a syllable, they were told to eff off back to the bog.

It was difficult to argue with their complaints. Once-majestic buildings were crusted with soot. The Liffey was disappointingly oily, and there was a dirty caramel froth on the Royal Canal. Piles of rubbish grew sour in the summer heat. While a year at college had helped Loretta to adjust, the others often felt grubby. Yvonne said this was because in Steelstown they'd been scoured clean by the wind and rain sweeping in from the Atlantic. They'd spent their lives feeling newly washed.

To begin with, Birdy had found it hard to adapt. She'd made basic mistakes, like asking for a return fare on the bus. Having taken her father's warnings about thieves to heart, she'd carried her money in her sock. While this worked with a pound note, having a sock full of change was awkward. When Gail had noticed her limping, Birdy had been forced to confess her secret. Her friend's laughter had probably been heard in Steelstown.

Despite its flaws, Dublin was growing on her. She got a kick from its bustle, its attitude. She liked its amber double-decker buses with the conductors shouting, 'Fay-ers, puh-lease.' She was fascinated by the young people, some only twelve or thirteen, who congregated on Grafton Street to pose and bicker. There were tribes galore: punks and mods, metalheads and rude boys, New Romantics and hippies.

Most of all, she loved the music swirling around her. Walk down any street, and there was a record shop. On O'Connell Bridge, a man sold bootleg tapes, while along the quays, the grey dereliction was relieved by vivid posters for gigs and records. The radio dial was crammed with pirate stations where Dubliners adopted Californian names and accents. *This is Randy St James with the weather for the bay area. Stand by for the red-hot sound of REO Speedwagon.*

Although guitars were Birdy's mainstay, she had no time for musical barriers and snobbery. If a song made her feel something, she didn't care whether it was played on guitars, synthesisers or trumpets. That summer, the radio glowed with pop music. From the eerie chords of 'Ghost Town' to the 'miaow miaow miaow' at the beginning of 'Love Action' to the driving beat of 'Tainted Love', everything sounded fresh.

The Diamonds were gigging, gigging, gigging. When they weren't on stage, they were writing or rehearsing. Some nights, they played to a great crush of people. On others, the crowd was sparse, and they asked themselves if leaving Steelstown had been a mistake. On their best nights, everything was simple and good and strong. Exhilaration would surge through them, and they'd believe their ambitions were within reach.

There were times when Birdy missed home and she found herself pining for the gossipy chat in the Save-A-Lot canteen. Her mother wrote lengthy letters filled with the minutiae of Steelstown life. The under-fourteens had won a football tournament, and the town had erupted in celebration. Cars had lapped the housing estates with their lights flashing and horns honking. *Heaven help us if the town ever wins anything important*, she wrote.

The Troys' next-door neighbours, the McNamaras, had fallen out over the royal wedding. Mrs McNamara had been keen to watch Lady Diana marry Prince Charles, but Mr McNamara maintained it would be an insult to the hunger strikers in the North. If men were prepared to die for Ireland, he said, the least she could do was turn off the telly. According to Birdy's mother, their argument was the talk of Connolly Park.

Occasionally, Birdy missed Mike. Then she reminded herself that there were thousands upon thousands of men in Dublin and, as Gail liked to point out, they were better-looking than the men in Steelstown. Opportunities would come.

Kieran arrived, as he always did, with a rush of activity. He was busy and couldn't stop so he wouldn't have a coffee, only now that he thought about it, a coffee was exactly what he needed, so that would be two sugars and a dash of milk, please.

'I have some news for you,' he said, flinging himself into their best armchair.

'Oh?' said Yvonne.

'I'll get there in a minute . . . and I promise you'll like it. There's something else I've got to mention first, though.'

'Go on.'

'I've been asking a few trusted friends for their assessments of your show. And the consensus is that while your sound gets better by the week, your look needs . . . well, it needs some work.'

'Our look?' said Gail, flicking back her hair. 'What's wrong with us?'

Birdy wondered who the 'few trusted friends' were. Or if they existed. She'd noticed that Kieran tended to place criticism in the mouths of others. It had been a 'veteran venue manager' who'd complained that their set sagged in the middle and a 'savvy journalist' who'd argued that Gail and Yvonne should work harder at being in sync.

'I don't want to be negative,' he said, sinking further into the chair. 'But sometimes you look like you're in four different bands. And that was fine until now, I guess. Perhaps, though, you ought to . . . I don't know . . . coordinate a bit more.'

This was another one of their manager's tricks. When it suited him, he became hesitant, bumbling almost. He adapted his voice to sound more working class. Not full scale 'Ah, Jaysus, howarya,' but slightly less Trinity College. Birdy suspected that he also adjusted his personality to suit his audience.

'Coordinate?' said Gail. 'We're not the Nolan Sisters. We're a rock band. Nobody makes the Ramones coordinate.'

'Except,' said Loretta, 'they do. They all wear leather jackets and have the same haircut.'

'I'd wear a leather jacket if I could afford one. Anyway, we're all too different. You and Bird are lanky. Me and Yvonne are small. We'd look daft in the same clothes. And we're never going to have the same hair.' She pointed from one to another. 'Blonde, red, mouse and black.'

'Would you get away with your "mouse"?' said Birdy. 'My hair is brown.'

Gail leaned over and tousled it. 'Okay, mousy-brown then.'

Birdy stuck out her tongue but she was only play-acting. She didn't want to add to the ill-feeling caused by the knickers incident.

Yvonne pulled the cuffs of her sweatshirt over her knuckles. 'I'm not quite with you, Kieran. What is it you're asking us to do?'

'Maybe you could check with each other before you go on stage? Like, if one of you is wearing a white dress,' he glanced towards Loretta, 'another one,' a swift look at Birdy, 'shouldn't be in a combat jacket and big boots. Do you get my drift? And sometimes you could . . . how shall I put this? . . . make a bit more of yourselves.'

'I haven't worn a white dress since I made my first communion,' said Gail, 'and I spilt a glass of blackcurrant down the front. Mam was ripping because my cousin was due to wear it the following week. Sandra, that's my cousin, had to go up to the altar in a navy top and skirt. There was *war*. Mam took my communion money and paid the electricity bill with it.'

Kieran sent Gail a look of studied indifference. He knew she was trying to blow his plans off course. 'Listen,' he said, 'I have a vision for you – for your success. And how you look matters. I know that's not a cool opinion any more, what with women's lib and whatnot. And I know that, in the ideal world, nobody would care what you wore. But I can't change the world. All I can do is try to get you a deal.'

'And you really think a record company is more likely to sign us if we dress well?' said Yvonne.

'I can't see it doing any harm. You don't need me to tell you it's incredibly competitive out there. You're nice-looking girls. You could use that to your advantage.' He raised one shoulder. 'Obviously . . . It's up to you, though.'

Birdy studied him but said nothing. Her first instinct was to chafe against his proposal. It sounded too like a uniform and, between school and Save-A-Lot, she'd had enough of uniforms. Surely, the point of being in a rock band was that you could wear whatever you liked or be whoever you chose. The more she thought about what he was saying, the clearer it became: he wanted them all to dress like Loretta. He wanted shorter skirts, tighter T-shirts, more straightforward glamour.

Finally, as it always did, reality crept in. She was part of the teeny-tiny band of people who got to do something they loved. There was no Vera Cheevers hovering at her shoulder with news of a spillage in Juices and Minerals or a shortage of plastic bags in Fruit and Veg. No tedium or irritation. No resentment of colleagues or customers. Instead, she woke up feeling as light as a dandelion seed. Birdy wouldn't consciously do anything to jeopardise this new life. If Kieran suggested she take to the stage in a shroud, she probably would.

She slid her eyes towards Gail and then Yvonne. 'I suppose there's no harm in looking our best.'

Gail hesitated before responding. 'I suppose. Only no white dresses or pink lipstick. And definitely nothing frilly. Anything frilly and I'm out.'

Kieran smiled his most charming smile, the one he used when he'd won an argument. 'Now, would I do that to you?'

Loretta appeared relieved. 'We can work together. None of us is interested in looking too girly. That's not who we are.'

'So what's this news you promised us?' asked Yvonne.

'Aha!' he said, followed by a pause.

'Don't get all tricksy on us, Kieran,' said Gail. 'Spit it out.'

He laughed. 'I'm assuming you're familiar with the sessions on *The Dave Fanning Show*.' Another pause. 'How are you fixed for recording on the twelfth of next month?'

The four exchanged looks.

'Are you serious?' said Loretta.

'Class,' said Yvonne.

'What do you think we should wear?' asked Gail.

Birdy felt her mouth curve into a smile. A session on the *Fanning Show* didn't just mean getting to record songs in a proper studio and having those songs played on the radio. People who mattered would hear their music. The session could lead to more gigs and better opportunities. It might even lead to a record deal.

Another door had opened.

Chapter 8

Away they went, into the sticky August evening. Gripped by the freewheeling giddiness that came with good news, the three planned on walking into town. They'd spent the previous hour swapping lipsticks and applying each other's eye-shadow, the air solid with hairspray.

'We're only going for the one,' said Yvonne.

Gail winked. 'Two at the most.'

'And we might drop into The Magnet,' added Birdy. 'There's a new band playing. Five lads from Tallaght. I've heard they're pretty special.'

'It makes sense to keep an eye on the competition,' said Gail.

Loretta knew she should join them, but after the argument with Gail and the tension with Kieran, she wanted some time alone. She wanted peace.

The radio session was a breakthrough. They were one step closer to achieving their ambitions. That didn't mean the questions stopped chasing around her brain. *Are we good enough? Am I good enough?*

She slumped onto the sofa and lit a Consulate. According to Gail, only pregnant women should be allowed to smoke menthol cigarettes. She liked Gail. It was impossible not to. But sometimes . . . how should Loretta put this? . . . sometimes it felt as if she sucked up everyone's energy. From the moment her feet hit the floor in the morning, her personal amp was set to eleven. Every situation was an opportunity for a quip or a story, every disagreement an excuse for battle.

What Loretta hadn't anticipated was Gail's interest in the workings of the world. Alone among the four, she was a regular newspaper reader, treating tabloids and broadsheets with equal respect. During the riots in England, she'd gone to a pub to watch the news. 'You have to hand it to the English,' she'd said, voice tinged with envy. 'They know how to riot.'

While Loretta often felt as if she was playing a role, Gail was fully herself. From the legalisation of abortion to the best-looking member of Duran Duran, she had well-argued positions on matters Loretta hadn't considered. Something similar was true of Yvonne. With Birdy, it was hard to know. There were days when she never stopped speaking and days when she was quiet and watchful. She seemed happiest when talking about music.

Outside, a group of little girls were playing a rhyming game. Their chanting reminded Loretta of home. The words were different – *Johnson, Mooney and O'Brien bought a horse for one and nine* – but the rhythms were the same. The Dublin she was experiencing now – boisterous, dishevelled, defiant – was far more interesting than the city she'd known at college.

When she'd left Steelstown, Loretta had been surprised to discover that her father had slipped a note and a hundred pounds into her case. The message, wishing her good luck, had meant more than the money. She kept it in her underwear drawer. The cash was gone, blown on nights out, new shoes, lighter blonde streaks and a quarter share in a second-hand record player.

Although she appreciated why her dad had hidden his kindness, she wished he'd been bolder. How great would it have been if for once he'd stood up to her mother? Instead, he'd meekly accepted the flurry of words she'd launched in Loretta's direction. The warnings: 'You're throwing your life away for a fantasy world.' The snide dismissal of the band: 'They're dragging you down to their level.' The self-pity: 'What did I do wrong?' Later, when her mother's initial flare of anger had subsided, her attempts at understanding had been even more cutting. 'Is college too challenging for you?' she'd asked. 'You could switch to a less demanding course, I'm sure.'

Loretta's father had given a wishy-washy defence of his wife. 'She's invested so much in you,' he'd said. 'Women of your mother's generation were rarely allowed to go to university. Educating girls was considered a waste of money. So it's hard for her to see you turning your back on the opportunity.'

'What about Susannah?' Loretta had asked, referring to her fifteen-year-old sister. 'Why can't Mam invest in her?' Even as her mouth had formed the words, she'd known they were pointless. Susannah had neither the ability nor the ambition to do well at school. She floated along, untethered by practical considerations, like exams or job prospects.

In the way that the tongue seeks out a sore tooth, Loretta's thoughts frequently returned to her mother. This didn't mean she regretted her choice. She'd spent too long walking the path of least resistance.

As she lit another cigarette, the phone rang, its rasping tone cutting through her thoughts. They had an old coin phone, and anything other than a quick local call required a sizeable pile of five-pence pieces. She went out to the hall. Then, reasoning that the call was likely to be for one of the others, she let it ring off. In a finger click, it began again. This time, she answered, but when she said hello, the line went dead. From the *clink clink* of coins, it sounded like the caller was in a phone box.

She returned to the sitting room and put on a record: disc two of *The River*, the side with 'Point Blank' and 'Stolen Car'. Their stories of bruised lives suited her mood.

Fifteen minutes later, when Springsteen was singing about once bright rooms being filled with the coming night, there was a knock at the front door. When she didn't answer, the knocking became more aggressive.

So much for a peaceful evening.

Kieran was carrying two plastic bags of groceries, one of which contained two bottles of white wine. As always, he moved swiftly. By the time Loretta had told him that the others were out, he was in the kitchen searching for a corkscrew.

'That's cool,' he said, his tone suggesting he already knew. Had he made the phone calls? It was an uncomfortable thought, and she pushed it away. 'It was you I'd hoped to talk to.'

He removed a punnet of nectarines from one of the bags, cut two into slices and put them on a plate. Then he opened a bottle of wine and poured two substantial measures. The house didn't have any wine glasses, so they had to drink from tumblers.

'Philistines,' he said, with a small laugh.

'Wine wouldn't be the drink of choice around here,' replied Loretta, before sinking her teeth into a crescent of nectarine. 'Gail says it's for people who're only pretending to like alcohol.'

'She says a lot, that girl.'

In the sitting room, Loretta flipped over the disc then joined Kieran on the sofa. He told her that he'd gone to London a couple of months ago to see *The River* tour. Springsteen's stagecraft was stunning, he said, as good as everyone claimed. Loretta said she couldn't imagine travelling to London just to see a band. Immediately, she regretted this. It made her sound childish, unadventurous.

Kieran raised his glass. 'That day will come.'

She waited for him to explain why he wanted to talk to her. Should she be nervous? What if he was unhappy with her vocals and didn't want to humiliate her in front of the band?

She took another mouthful of wine. It was better than anything she'd tasted before. Cold. Crisp. She had the feeling it was expensive.

Loretta was aware of her power over men. Or, to be more accurate, over certain types of men. Mostly they were either young boys with limited imagination or older guys who assumed that because she was in a band, and because she sang lines like, *Don't try to teach me, don't try to tame me, you'll never tie me down, you'll never ever shame me*, she must be an easy conquest. The older men, with their corned-beef skin and scouring-pad hair, were as predictable as they were unattractive.

Kieran didn't fit into either category. He was twenty-seven, nine years older than her. Old, but not scarily so. Not wrinkled and flabby and tired. Also, his conversation contained occasional references to his wife, Imogen. Such a pretty name. Loretta doubted there was a single Imogen in Steelstown. The couple had met at Trinity where they'd studied English. The band hadn't been introduced to Imogen, but Loretta pictured her as petite, with elegant features and small straight teeth. She probably watched French films and read hardback books.

'Right,' he said eventually. 'I was thinking about our earlier discussion, and I wanted to reassure you that anything I said about the band's image, et cetera, didn't apply to you.'

'Oh, I didn't think it did,' she said, her reply coming too quickly. 'I mean, I worried it might. But I kind of took it as being about all of us . . . as a unit, you know.'

'Well, it didn't refer to you. You have a certain style. I saw that from the start. It's probably because you're more mature than the other three. You've spent a year at university, living away from home . . . *with all that entails*.'

With all that entails. Loretta knew what he meant. He was wrong. Alone among the four, she'd never had sex. In theory, she was eager for the experience. Once or twice, she'd come close before shying away. She simply hadn't felt the way other girls had told her she should: so filled with desire, so intoxicated, that if she didn't follow through, she'd regret it. One former boyfriend had called her a prick-tease. Another had suggested she had a psychological hang-up. She hadn't revealed this to anyone. When Gail, because it was usually Gail, asked about her sex life, she danced around the truth.

Living together meant they'd become immersed in each other's business. Gail and Yvonne had sufficient sexual experience to have formed tastes and preferences. They spoke about what they liked and what they found off-putting. While Birdy revealed less, she did have a vault of stories about the adventures of others. The tales swung between entertaining and unsettling and made Loretta wonder if that was how she ought to be living.

She picked up another section of nectarine and tried to sound casual. 'I suppose my experience has been different from the other girls'.'

Kieran must have noticed something in her voice because he

said, 'Sorry, I didn't mean to embarrass you.' Then he slapped his knees. 'I'm going to top up our glasses.'

When he came back from the kitchen, they riffed about what The Diamonds should do next. Kieran said he was talking to record companies. If one of the other Diamonds was here, they would press for more information. She was content to ramble around the subject. She'd had little to eat all day, and the wine had brought her to that place where the world was pleasingly hazy. The conversation was good, and she didn't want to risk derailing it.

'Do you have any regrets about leaving college?' he said.

'No. The band comes first. As Birdy says, "Whatever it takes."'

'She's intense, isn't she?'

Loretta took a second to absorb the question. 'Birdy?'

'Yeah, Yvonne's fairly straightforward, and Gail's all mouth. But Birdy? I find it hard to know where she's at. It's like she's always sizing people up, trying to get their measure.'

Loretta wasn't sure that she bought into his assessments. And despite their earlier argument, she felt she should come to Gail's defence. Still, she liked that Kieran was confiding in her.

'I reckon,' she said, 'that Birdy wants the band to be successful and she wants to keep on being a full-time musician. Simple as that.'

'What about you? What do you want?'

'The same, of course.'

'You have options, though. Options not available to the others.'

'Now you're sounding like my mother.'

'What do you mean? Actually, hold that thought. We need more wine.'

He returned, holding the second bottle. How could they have finished the first already?

'You were going to tell me about your mother,' he said, as he poured their drinks. 'I have the impression she mightn't be the founding member of The Diamonds' fan club . . .'

He allowed his voice to fade away, encouraging her to fill the silence. Because he'd moved closer, she had to twist her body to look him in the eye. He smiled. It was an appealing smile. She'd thought as much since the night they'd first met. The rest of him was good-looking but not exceptionally so. His greenish-brown eyes drooped at the corners and his nose was a shade too broad. Gail had described him as having the appearance of a bit-part actor. He could be an unnamed soldier in a Vietnam film, she'd said, or a random New Yorker in something by Woody Allen.

Loretta took a sip of her drink, then told him about the difficult relationship with her mother. She'd intended to talk solely about their latest disagreement but, under gentle questioning, she returned to her early teens. She spoke about misunderstandings, mismatched ambitions and the unshakeable feeling that she would never meet her mam's expectations.

Once she'd started, Kieran said little. He made encouraging noises and gave the occasional supportive nod.

'You won't like to hear this,' he said eventually, 'but I'm sure your mother worries about you. It must be tough to send someone so beautiful out into the world. Especially when you know how much danger that world contains.'

Under normal circumstances, Loretta would have cringed. Then she would have laughed. These weren't normal circumstances. She felt her face turn pink. Or maybe it was pink already from the wine and the evening's humidity.

He brushed her hand. 'It's important that you realise how talented you are. I've never come across someone with the same potential. I saw it in Limerick and I see it every night you walk out on stage.'

What he was saying had the air of a rehearsed speech. It was designed to appeal to her vanity. That didn't prevent her from enjoying his flattery. Who wouldn't want to be flattered by Kieran?

He rested a hand on her knee. She was wearing a short canvas skirt, and his fingers were cool against her skin. He leant in and started kissing her. They were good kisses. Adult. Practised. Entirely different from the efforts of the suckers and slobberers she usually encountered.

As their kissing continued, she felt a swoosh of pleasure unlike anything she'd experienced before. She hoped she was getting it right. Was her tongue in the correct place? What should she do with her hands? How should she control her breathing? Then she told herself not to let her insecurities get in the way. *You're okay. You're enough.*

Was this seduction? she wondered. If so, she would go with it. She would see where it carried her.

Chapter 9

Now, Dublin

When Stacey got home, she sent an email to Kieran Mitchell's assistant. Even if he hadn't stayed in touch with The Diamonds, there was a chance he would know where they'd gone.

Then she ran his name through Google. Articles cascaded down the screen. Because of his lengthy career, there was a considerable amount to wade through. He was pictured with various bands, television hosts and high-profile politicians. There were shots of him receiving honorary degrees and lifetime achievement awards. One profile claimed music ran through his 'Irish veins'. Another lauded his longevity and described him as a 'cultural arbiter'. In the main, the coverage was ridiculously sycophantic. Stacey wouldn't have been surprised to read that he was well-known for giving refuge to stray dogs and helping old women cross the road.

The one exception was a piece in an American online publication that questioned the ongoing influence of an 'old white guy' like Mitchell. The writer also argued that, rather than being a trailblazer, his main skill was bandwagon jumping. Iona Daunt was dismissed as a 'cut-price Taylor Swift' while The Latecomers 'made Ed Sheeran sound like death metal'.

Nowhere could Stacey find a reference to The Diamonds. Neither were they listed on his Wikipedia page, even though two other bands he'd managed in the early 1980s, Future Heroes and Aces Wild, did get a mention.

Was it possible that Ultan had been mistaken?

The meeting was held in Briarstown community centre. Local gossip had it that George Sheffield or another representative of Silver Eagle Property would be there. Carmel offered to stay at home with Mia so that Rhiannon could attend.

The hall was packed. There was a scramble for extra chairs, and even then, people had to stand at the back.

The councillor who had organised the residents' meeting, Shay McKenna, looked as though he could do with a spray of starch and an iron. From his forehead to his black T-shirt and jeans, everything about him was crumpled and weary. By contrast, the man from Silver Eagle was wearing what Stacey guessed was an extremely expensive jacket. He had the type of floppy haircut favoured by his kind. His name was Logan Walsh, and he was a stand-in for the infamous Mr Sheffield. A local stand-in. Not local-local, but definitely Irish. Oh, and he was young, possibly younger than Stacey.

'The state of him,' whispered Rhiannon, in her soft Wexford accent. 'He looks about fourteen. I wouldn't trust him to go for a litre of milk.'

Sitting beside her neighbour made Stacey feel untidy. Including her nails, Rhiannon was wearing four shades of taupe. On anyone else this would look sickeningly dull, but she made it work.

Shay McKenna plucked a wad of paper from the pocket of his jeans, unfolded it and called the meeting to order. He was aware, he said, of anger and fear in the community. Of women who cried themselves to sleep and men who couldn't sleep at all. For five minutes, he recited moth-eaten lines about the decent hard-working people of Whitethorn House. As he droned on, his worn face took on a beatific glow.

With every second that passed, the heat rose. Eventually, a man at the back intervened. 'With respect, Shay,' he said, 'we know all that. We want to hear from the vulture man.'

Stacey looked around the room. It was filled with couples. She was surrounded by people who had someone with whom they could pool their money – and share their troubles. No one else was going through this alone. That wasn't all. Most of Whitethorn's tenants had jobs. Proper jobs with regular hours and staff canteens. Her neighbours weren't one mediocre podcast away from penury. These were people with gym memberships, health insurance, wine racks.

Even when she'd had a proper job, Stacey had been poor with money. In her early twenties, she'd spent two years in Australia. On her return, she'd hoped to become a journalist. Thin freelance pickings followed by a year reading overnight radio news bulletins had changed her mind. Perpetual exhaustion wasn't for her. Next, she'd blundered into a job in corporate PR. She'd toned down her dress sense, bought a nice pair of navy pumps and tried to fit in.

Hand on heart, she'd been useless. Too slapdash, too giddy, too cynical. Referring to a client's plans for International Women's Day as 'corporate cringe' had been a mistake. As had telling another client about his reputation for exploiting workers. Even on her best days, she'd never felt as though she was doing anything positive. Her working life had been about damage limitation. The knowledge that she would have to return to that life rested heavily on her.

At the top of the room, Shay McKenna appeared to have grasped that the more he spoke, the more votes he was likely to lose. He handed the microphone to Logan Walsh, who tapped it twice before beginning his speech.

The facts were simple, he claimed. Silver Eagle Property, a reputable international company, had acquired Whitethorn House. After appropriate renovations, it would either sell the apartments or rent them at a realistic market rate. He continued, stringing words together in a way that made it almost impossible to interrupt.

Bróna of WhatsApp group fame was first to succeed. 'If you've nothing good to tell us,' she said, 'I don't know why you came. We shouldn't have to leave our homes.'

'I'm aware that securing alternative accommodation presents something of a challenge,' he said, his tone suggesting he was flicking away a gnat. 'However, there are agencies to assist you.'

Bróna's partner, Pat, stood up. 'Like that man at the back said, you and your cabal are nothing but a flock of vultures. You should be run out of the country.'

The comment received a burst of applause and a shout of, 'Go on ya boy ya, Pat.'

Councillor McKenna gestured for the microphone, cleared his throat and turned to Walsh. 'Tenants were hoping for something more by way of reassurance. Have you anything to offer them?'

'First of all, I'd like to say that in this context the use of the term "vulture fund" is not appropriate. Also, I've heard the word "eviction" being thrown around. It's not the 1840s. No one is being evicted. Silver Eagle is simply exercising its right not to renew tenants' leases.'

Indignation passed across the room, but no one spoke.

'Now,' he added, 'to address the substantive issue. I think you may have been under a misapprehension about the purpose of this meeting. As I thought I'd made plain, I'm not here to haggle or negotiate. Our purpose is to deliver a profit for the company's investors. While you may consider this unpalatable, it's the way of the world.'

Clearly taken aback, the councillor ran out of words. 'Ahm, what would you advise tenants to do?'

'Have they considered buying a property? I'm not saying it's easy, but it's not impossible either.'

Stacey snorted. Buying an apartment was about as feasible as rowing across the Atlantic or qualifying as a surgeon. While technically possible, it was not something she was likely to achieve.

Rhiannon crossed her legs. 'The condescension is oozing out of him. I don't know if I can listen to much more.'

Perhaps it was the heat, which had risen to tropical levels, but lethargy had settled over the community centre. It was as if everybody was wilting from the temperature and the bad news. Their hopes were fizzling out.

They had underestimated Logan Walsh. For all that he looked like an office boy, he had the cold confidence of a man twice his age. As much as Stacey disliked him, there was something impressive about his indifference to the crowd's hostility.

The unfortunate truth was that the only person on the tenants' side, Councillor McKenna, was no better than useless. There was no chance of a delay, much less a change of heart.

*

The following morning, when Stacey checked her phone, she saw a reply from Kieran Mitchell's assistant. She hadn't expected such a speedy response and opened it immediately. *Please,* she thought, *please contain something I can use.*

Dear Ms Nash,
Thank you for your inquiry about The Diamonds.

You are correct, the group was managed by Mr Mitchell at the beginning of his career. As you are no doubt aware, he has, over several decades, guided the careers of many musicians. Most have been successful. Unfortunately, this was not the case with The Diamonds.

His association with the band was brief, and after the passage of forty years, he is not in possession of any relevant information. He has no knowledge of the current whereabouts of the group's members. Because of this, Mr Mitchell must decline your invitation to take part in the podcast.

Yours,
Maren Calvert-Pruitt
Mitchell Artist Management

While Stacey hadn't believed that Kieran Mitchell would grant her an interview, she was disappointed he had nothing to offer. No tips or suggestions. No anecdotes. No warmth. She felt deflated.

When she read the email again, her feelings swung towards irritation. The tone wasn't just chilly, it was dismissive. Okay, The Diamonds had been eclipsed by his subsequent successes. They'd never played a sell-out stadium tour, written a James Bond theme or had a Vegas residency. But when Mitchell was starting out, they'd given him a Top Ten song in Britain. Why downplay what they'd done? Why sound so clinical? She found herself annoyed on the band's behalf.

The morning's second surprise was that Whitethorn House had made the papers. Stacey couldn't read the stories because they were behind paywalls, but she could see enough to gather that a couple of reporters had been at the previous night's meeting.

She pulled on a clean T-shirt and skirt and decided to go for a coffee. There was usually an abandoned newspaper in the Pear Tree.

She had just begun the five-minute walk when her phone jangled to life. She let it click through to voicemail. Almost immediately, it rang again. When she saw the name on the screen, she hesitated. After another fitful night's sleep, she didn't have the energy to talk to him. She also knew that if she didn't answer, he would keep on calling. He must have seen the Whitethorn story in the papers.

'Hi, Ronan,' she said. 'It's not a great time. I—'

He jumped in. 'Why didn't you tell me what was going on, Stace? I thought we said we'd stay in touch.'

Because when I agreed to that, I didn't mean it. 'There didn't seem much point. I'm not sure there's anything you can do.'

'Maybe not. But I'd like to have known. Are you looking for somewhere new?'

'Not yet. I will, though. I will.'

'Sorry. I didn't mean to sound like I was hassling you. It's . . . Well, you don't need me to tell you it's rough out there right now.'

'Yeah, I know. I . . .' Her voice ran dry. 'Like I said, this isn't a good time.'

Before Ronan could reply, she hung up.

Chapter 10

December 1981, Dublin

'Hey,' said Vivienne, as she swerved around a group of partygoers and made her way towards Birdy. 'That was a fantastic show tonight. Seriously, you were *hot*.'

'Thanks a million,' said Birdy, tucking her hair behind her ears. 'Even when you think it's all gone well, you can't be totally sure.'

Vivienne Lane was a photographer who'd taken pictures of The Diamonds. The shoot had been fun, and afterwards she'd insisted they go for a drink. They'd spent the afternoon in the Bailey, acting like they'd already made it.

Three weeks later, here they were, at her Christmas party. The house was enormous: two storeys of redbrick over a grey-fronted basement. The interior was ... Birdy searched for the right word ... opulent, that was it. There was marble in the main bathroom, a crystal chandelier in the hall and a Jack B. Yeats in the front room. (With a B in Leaving Cert art, Birdy considered herself skilled at identifying the works of Ireland's greatest painters. She'd never expected to be in a house where someone actually owned one. That it hung on the same walls as confirmation photos and a sentimental portrait of a family dog, made the experience even more bizarre.) Vivienne explained that the house belonged to her parents who were spending the holidays in Switzerland.

Christmas lights were strung along the staircase and around every door and alcove. They glittered and glowed like constellations of multicoloured stars. Birdy could hear her father tut-tutting about the electricity bill and her mother asking if the displays were safe.

She was sitting in the corner of the kitchen, possibly the quietest place in the house. The room was dense with smoke. Yvonne was in the hall, debating the future of music with three guys in black suits and immaculate eye makeup. Gail butterflied about. Loretta had disappeared.

Earlier, in McGonagles, The Diamonds had played to their largest crowd so far. Just stepping onto the stage had given Birdy a jolt. How could she be performing in such an amazing place?

The band had been in command, defiant one moment, joyful the next. Loretta had been especially powerful. She'd stood at the edge of the stage, one hip cocked, hair swinging. And the audience? Oh, the audience! They'd been magical. In raucous voices, they'd called for favourite songs and demanded a second encore. Luckily, at Kieran's suggestion, the band had rehearsed a cover of Darlene Love's 'Christmas (Baby Please Come Home)'. The room had responded, singing and dancing until it had felt as if even the foundations were shaking. Their sound had billowed out into South Anne Street and soared through the roof. For an hour, Dublin had been theirs.

After the radio session, everything had shifted. The Diamonds had been approached by venues all over Ireland. They'd travelled to Belfast, Cork, Galway and Tralee. They'd returned to Limerick, this time as headliners. Their Dublin audience was growing too. In the beginning, their following had been confined to young lads with mushroom clouds of blond hair and floor-sweeping coats. Now they attracted all sorts, from glammed-up girls to long-haired boys in denim jackets and biker boots. A review in *Hot Press*, titled 'Shine Like a Diamond', had called them the hottest unsigned band in Dublin. According to rumours, A&R men were flying in from London to take a look. Birdy suspected the stories were planted by Kieran. Rather than annoying her, his audacity made her laugh.

And yet, for all the positive vibes, they hadn't been signed. They continued to jostle for attention alongside the other hopefuls. While one part of Birdy marvelled at how far they'd come, another part was restless. The Diamonds had written a batch of new songs, including one called 'Brighter Than The Sun', which she reckoned was better than 'Too Much Not Enough'. Fingers crossed, this would make a difference.

Birdy was discovering that Dublin winters could be harsh. Their sheets felt wet, and the bathroom was furred with black mould. Even when the weather was fine, the evening began at lunchtime, the light slipping away more quickly than it did on the west coast. On the worst days, their street was smothered in thick smog, and soot fell like snowflakes. At other times, she would see the lights blinking across the city, and her heart would soar.

Vivienne, who was carrying two bottles of beer, handed one to Birdy and pulled up a chair. Blessed with unshakeable self-confidence, she had a look that demanded attention. Tonight, she was wearing a midnight-blue taffeta miniskirt, a small black T-shirt and white stiletto heels. Her shoulder-length hair had a plum sheen. In Steelstown, girls dyed their hair with cochineal food-colouring to try to get the same effect.

They spoke about music, about who was on the up and who

was falling apart. It was standard stuff, strong on frivolity, weak on anything of significance. Birdy liked listening to the photographer's accent. She pronounced the *o* sound in that strange south Dublin way, so that lost became 'lawst' and off turned into 'awf'.

After a few minutes, Vivienne moved her chair closer. 'Listen,' she said, 'you can tell me to butt out if you like, but I hope your friend is being careful.'

'Which one?'

'Loretta, of course.'

'I'm not with you.'

'Shit,' said Vivienne. 'I assumed you knew.'

'Knew what?'

Vivienne said nothing. In the front room, someone had put on a record. Roxy Music throbbed through the walls. On the other side of the kitchen, a spindle-thin woman boasted about her planned move to New York.

Finally, Vivienne replied. 'I assumed . . . given that you share a house . . . I assumed . . .'

'I'm sorry, I'm—'

'I thought you'd know about her and Kieran. Their relationship, I mean.'

Birdy's hand tightened around her beer. Otherwise, she would have let it fall. 'Relationship' was not a word she tended to use. In Steelstown, people said 'going with' or 'doing a line'.

'Um, that's news to me. Are you sure?'

'Yep. I saw them outside a pub in Dalkey the other day.'

'That doesn't mean they're a couple.'

'Believe me, Birdy, they were together.'

'Maybe it was a once-off. Maybe they were drunk or fooling about.'

Vivienne gave a dismissive shake of the head. 'They were fairly sloshed, all right. And they were fooling about. But I promise you this wasn't a one-time thing. Other folks know about them. That's why I figured you had to be in the picture.'

Birdy stopped to reflect on what she'd heard. For a second or two, she thought that perhaps it was okay. No big deal. Something adult and cool. But that wasn't true.

'I'm . . . Actually, I don't know what I am,' she said. 'Is he still with his wife?'

'Oh, God, yeah. I think I told you I've known him for quite a while?'

'You said you met at college.'

'That's right. He was two years ahead of me. He started going out with Imogen at Trinity. They were in the same year. He was definitely one of the in-guys. She was . . . well, I always found her sort of drab. Sorry, that sounds too rough. Like, she's pretty and everything. But only in the way that those girls usually are.'

'Those girls?' said Birdy, peeling the label from her beer.

'You know, the ones who went to one of those snooty schools where Leaving Cert girls are taught how to play tennis and hold dinner parties.'

Birdy couldn't imagine such a school. 'I've never met her.'

'She was attached to him at college, like . . . What's that thing that burrows into you and swells?'

'A tick?'

'Yeah, a tick. The thing is,' said Vivienne, offering Birdy a Marlboro Light, 'even then Kieran rode all around him. He was an absolute hound, if you know what I mean.'

'Shhh,' said Birdy. Not that there was much danger of being overheard. Everyone was at that stage of drunkenness where they didn't realise they were shouting. Despite rarely smoking, she took a cigarette. The beer label was shredded, and she needed something to do with her hands. 'Do you know how long they've been seeing each other?'

'At least two or three months, I'd say.'

'And Imogen? Has she any idea what's going on?'

Vivienne took a drag of her cigarette. 'Who knows? She's not much of a socialiser, and his job gives him an excuse to be out every night of the week. Perhaps she doesn't mind.'

'That's crackers. How could she not mind?'

'It wouldn't be for me. But that's how some women live their lives. He won't leave her, anyway.'

'Why not?'

'For one thing, her old man is Garret Faulkner.'

'You've lost me again,' said Birdy.

'He owns half the hotels in Dublin. The Mount Vernon, the Fairley, the Temple Lane – they're all his. And it doesn't stop there. He's got houses and apartments all over the country. A complete Monopoly board of property. Our place probably looks fancy,' Vivienne waved her cigarette towards the ceiling, 'but my folks are in the ha'penny place compared to the Faulkners.'

'I had the impression that Kieran's people had money too.'

'They're comfortable, that's true, but they're not in the same league as Imogen's family.'

The Christmas lights danced in and out of focus. Tears were pooling at the backs of Birdy's eyes. Why she was in danger of crying, she couldn't say. Shock, maybe. Or a sense that this wouldn't end well. She steadied herself. 'Would Imogen leave him, do you think?'

'No. Daddy wouldn't approve. Not only is he massively rich, he's a serious Catholic of the old school. There's practically a smell of incense off the guy. Take my word, there are no second chances in the Faulkner family. Kieran is married for life.'

*

The next morning, Birdy woke with a screeching hangover. For a while, she lay in the fuzzy borderland between sleep and full consciousness. She reached out for the pint glass of water she'd remembered to place beside the bed, took three quick gulps and flipped the pillow to the cool side. Bob Marley's voice bounced in from the next room. Gail was going through a reggae phase.

The events of the previous night returned, and she replayed what Vivienne had told her.

What troubled her was the level of deception involved. Loretta was her bandmate, her housemate, her friend. It had never occurred to Birdy that she might have a secret life. That she did, and that it involved their manager, felt like betrayal.

The previous afternoon, they'd performed their gig-day ritual, and, honestly, it had been special. Gail had made a tape with some of the year's highlights. She'd placed 'Harder' from their radio session into the mix. For the first time, they'd sung along with one of their own recordings. The tape ended with the Christmas number one, 'Don't You Want Me'. Loretta had taken the male verse, Birdy the female response, and they'd sashayed around the sitting room, tossing their hair and punching the air. By the end, their singing had disintegrated into squawks of laughter.

Now all Birdy could think of was what she'd missed. When they'd been larking about, when they'd stood together on stage, singing into the same mic, should she have been more observant? She hadn't spotted any particular spark between Loretta and Kieran. Yeah, it was clear she was his favourite. Yeah, they'd flirted a little. Nothing exceptional, though. Nothing to suggest they were lovers.

Jesus, she thought. *Kieran.* He had a wife. He had responsibilities. He had a life in a well-groomed suburb where ruddy-faced men drove BMWs and drank gin and tonic. Where women played golf in Rupert Bear trousers and went for weekly blow-dries. He was twenty-seven, much older and more mature than Loretta.

Birdy had read about the sleazy side of rock 'n' roll. Those stories, all suntanned debauchery and azure swimming pools, felt distant. They focused on wizened men in leather trousers frolicking with LA blondes at the Whiskey A Go Go. They didn't take place in a rickety redbrick on the back-streets of Dublin with sleet slapping against the window and the electricity meter running low on credit.

She saw how the affair was possible. Frequently, Loretta went out alone. According to her version of events, she spent those evenings with friends from UCD. When she failed to come home, she claimed to have crashed on the floor of a flat in Ranelagh or Harold's Cross. But she only named her friends in the most general way – 'one of the Orlas, Mary Mac, Gráinne from Foxrock' – and she never revealed anything about them.

Birdy sat up, the sudden movement sending her stomach into revolt. She took a sip of water. The plan had been for all four to get the bus home tomorrow. It would be the first time in six months that Loretta had returned to Steelstown. Birdy couldn't face her. Neither could she handle Gail and Yvonne.

Quickly and quietly, she packed her clothes and the presents she'd got for Declan and her parents. Then she left a note and set out for the bus station. She bought a bottle of Lucozade and a Mars bar and boarded the bus to Steelstown. Almost all the seats were taken, and she had to sit beside a man who smelt of vomit and wet clothes. She closed her eyes and pretended to sleep.

All the way home, as a steady rain fell and the bus lurched from pothole to pothole, Birdy mulled over what to do.

Chapter 11

Now, Dublin

Stacey had hoped that her interview with Ultan Dowdall would encourage listeners to come forward with tips about The Diamonds. In the event, all she received was another email from Senan O'Reilly, the man who'd first contacted her about the band. There were people who might be able to solve the mystery, he said. People who'd been part of the Dublin scene in those days.

She was perplexed. If the guy was so obsessed, why was he bothering with her? Why wasn't he doing the work himself? She wrote a polite email, asking if he had any specific information to share. He didn't reply.

Never before had she spent this much time attempting to track down a potential subject. Usually the pieces fell into place. If they didn't, and an interviewee remained out of reach, she abandoned the search. That was what she should do now.

And yet . . .

The story had sparked something in her. She would see a woman in the supermarket and convince herself she'd found a Diamond. *Yvonne!* she'd want to call. *Gail!* Then the truth would hit her: the woman who'd attracted her attention was too young.

Just as Stacey was increasingly poor at gauging the ages of children and teenagers, she also had trouble with the over-forties. Even if any of the band lived in Dublin, she was unlikely to recognise them. They were of a similar age to Detta in the Pear Tree – or to her own mother. She found herself examining women in their fifties and sixties. She scrutinised their eyes, their hair, their frame. *Could you be Birdy? Could you be Loretta?*

Through his hive of connections, Ultan had unearthed a bootleg cassette of a gig from Christmas '81. With help from a friend, he transferred it to his laptop, then sent the file to Stacey. The concert had taken place in a venue called McGonagles. *Look it up,* he wrote. *It was a kip but a legendary one. There'd be no U2 without it. I think there's a clothes shop or a hairdresser's there now. Progress, huh?*

The bootleg's sound was tinny with a persistent background hum. No matter. Stacey was spellbound. On this evidence, The Diamonds had written an album's worth of songs. Two tracks, 'Brighter Than The Sun' and 'Harder', stood out. Time and distorted sound couldn't diminish their impact. Their intensity made her shiver. They should have been hits.

Ultan had also come up with a name. A photographer called Vivienne Lane had been friendly with the band and might be able to help.

Stacey did a search for her. Vivienne Lane Power, as she'd become, had been a social fixture in Dublin during the eighties. A photographer/model/muse, she'd been born into a wealthy family and married into another. The online images showed a wide-eyed woman with a narrow nose and an artful tangle of hair. She wore chandelier earrings and stacks of bangles. Stacey rang the number Ultan had given her. The ringtone suggested that Vivienne was abroad. Of course she was. It was high summer. She was probably drinking rosé on the terrace of a French villa or sunbathing on a yacht in the Adriatic. *Damn.*

By the time Stacey had done all of this, dusk was setting in, the room becoming tinged with silver. Another day had passed without any serious effort to find a new home or a new job. Almost three weeks on from Silver Eagle's letter, and all she'd managed were a few soul-sapping hours on various rental websites. By contrast, Rhiannon and Carmel were compiling lists, sending emails and making calls.

Stacey knew that too much of her energy was devoted to the podcast. When it came to the pod, and to The Diamonds in particular, there was no detail too small, no fact too obscure. If only this enthusiasm could filter through to the rest of her life.

Tomorrow, she told herself. Tomorrow she would put aside the podcast and focus on what mattered.

And yet . . .

The questions continued. The story didn't make sense. No record company would abandon a group whose debut single had reached the Top Ten. Few musicians, having experienced that first flare of popularity, would walk away.

The cancelled comedian, Albie Laffroy, had bought Stacey some time. His robust, unrepentant interview had been picked up by the papers and debated on Twitter. Depending on whom you believed, he was a refreshing change from the woke orthodoxy or a toxic misogynist who should never be platformed again. On Stacey, too, opinion was divided. She was a conniving misandrist who'd stitched up her interviewee or she was hapless and completely out of her depth. It would be great to claim that she had shut out the negativity, but she doubted there was a person alive who could handle the more vitriolic side of Twitter.

Either way, the interest had pushed 'Whatever Happened To . . . ?' back up the charts and brought a new advertiser on board. She had a hunch that the next episode, featuring a celebrity chef who'd burnt through investors like cheap saucepans, would also attract attention.

It was as she was going to bed that Ronan's message came: Have to meet a man in Briarstown tomorrow. Free for a coffee afterwards?

She considered turning off her phone and ignoring him. By now, he should understand that she wasn't able to do friendship. Perhaps she'd feel differently when she'd cleared up the debris of her past life and moved on. Perhaps.

It wasn't that Stacey didn't want to see Ronan. She did. And that was the problem.

OK, she replied. Give me a shout in the a.m. & I'll see if I'm free.

They went for a walk in Briarstown Park. Usually a kaleidoscope of colour, it was jaded, its flowers shrivelled, its grass parched.

Dublin was enjoying a different country's weather, each day as warm as the one before. In the morning, the sky was a blur of rose gold. In the evening, it was streaked with neon. Stacey wondered if she should worry. Was the heat further evidence of climate change? That was how she felt: even the outwardly positive was actually a sign of damage and decay.

A jokey claim by Rhiannon that she'd begun to resemble a 1970s religion teacher had convinced her to make an effort with her appearance. She was wearing a star-splashed midi-dress and cerise Birkenstocks. She'd painted her toenails a vibrant shade of blue and tied up her hair with a black silk scarf. A coat of red lipstick completed the look. She hoped it struck a balance between 'Don't think I've gone to much trouble' and 'I'm doing fine here on my own.'

Ronan looked like Ronan: dark brown hair in need of a cut, grey-blue eyes behind nerdish glasses. In his teens and early twenties, he'd had a minor degree of fame as a cross-country runner, representing Ireland several times before a series of injuries forced his retirement. In the podcast's early days, they'd joked about this. If she was stuck, she would feature him, she'd said. He'd claimed she couldn't afford his fee.

'Who were you meeting out this way?' she asked.

'I was dropping the car in for a service.'

'There aren't any mechanics near your new place?'

'All right, you've got me,' he said, sounding like a man who was happy to be found out. 'I wanted to see you. Is that such a bad thing?'

Yes. Yes, it is. 'Well, as you can see, I'm still standing. Still cogging along.'

Ronan did most of the talking. He told a couple of anecdotes about his job in the Department of Justice and a couple of others about mutual friends. He was going home to Galway at the weekend because his mother wasn't well. He didn't know if it was anything serious.

Not that long ago, Stacey would have offered to accompany him. Their lives had been intertwined. His plans had been her plans.

She'd met Ronan Egan more than two years earlier, just as the first reports of a mystery virus were emerging from China. They'd been guests at a wedding. Stacey was a friend of the groom, Ronan a neighbour of the bride. He'd been on his own. She'd been with a date of convenience. Both would rather have been somewhere – anywhere – else.

In her experience, weddings either brought on a crushing desire to conform or they stirred up every rebellious instinct you'd ever possessed. In Ronan, she'd recognised a fellow rebel. They'd agreed that not only did too many couples turn their wedding into an occupation, some were also intent on seeing it as a commercial opportunity.

'I guarantee you,' Ronan had said, with a sweeping motion towards the overblown floral displays, grandiose table-settings and multi-tiered wedding cake, 'this will be up on the 'gram, and the suppliers will be tagged.'

'Yuck,' Stacey had replied. 'Even the thought of all that fuss tires me out.'

'You're not alone. There's a lot to be said for eloping.'

Three days later, they'd gone for a drink. And that had been that.

Ordinarily, she would have followed convention and taken her time returning his calls and messages. From the beginning, this had been different. They'd had the right blend of physical attraction and general compatibility. Both were only children, both had spent time in Australia, both had known they couldn't settle there. Their conversations had veered from acerbic to sentimental and back again.

Within weeks, their hand forced by the first Covid lockdown, they'd started renting in Whitethorn. To begin with, she'd been apprehensive. They were working from home, which meant being together every hour of every day. There was no time for the standard rituals. No first weekend away. No getting to meet each other's friends.

The outside world was fractious, febrile. On social media,

everyone was turning on everyone else. The restrictions were too harsh or too lenient. The virus was a calamity or a conspiracy. They were all living through what felt like an enormous social experiment.

There were days when being cooped up with a relative stranger was challenging. Basic things could grate on Stacey. How could a thirty-year-old man sleep so much? Why did they invariably end up watching his choices on Netflix? And did he have to give her a running commentary on his day, like a hyperactive four-year-old? But she was mad about Ronan. Stone mad, as he would say. Gradually, they settled into a rhythm.

As the months passed, and one lockdown merged into another, she basked in an unspoken sense of relief. Here, at last, was someone with whom it was possible to relax – and also have great spontaneous sex. Someone who ticked almost every box on her virtual checklist. At their best, they shared the exhilarating sense of conspiracy that a relationship can bring, the feeling that you are the only two to see the world as it truly is.

Stacey's past relationships had started brightly and burnt out. When she'd heard women complain about men not being ready for commitment, she'd tuned out. In truth, she had usually been the fickle partner. She would get so far before finding excuses to leave. *Is he the right one? Am I the right one? Should I be feeling more?* She would analyse and pathologise until the inevitable split.

If anyone had asked, she'd have said that one of the qualities she valued in her relationship with Ronan was its candour. Not that she believed in total honesty. Only a very strange person would reveal their full self: their fantasies, their internet habits, their less-appealing judgements. Everyone was entitled to hold something back. Still, she exposed more to Ronan than she had to any of his predecessors.

And all the while he was keeping a secret.

One night, when they were drinking tequila, he confessed that in the early days of their relationship, he'd slept with a woman from work. It hadn't meant anything, he said. It was just something that had happened after a hassle-filled day and too much alcohol, and he was telling her because it was on his conscience.

'I could have stayed quiet,' he'd said, 'except that wouldn't have been right.'

'What do you want? A medal?' she'd replied.

Ronan had looked wounded by her response. He'd been contrite, but not overwhelmingly so.

Stacey's thoughts had skipped back to those first days when even a WhatsApp from Ronan had given her a thrill. She could no more have had sex with someone else than she could have eaten her own hand. It was then she discovered that the relationship she had viewed as well-balanced was actually lopsided. She also discovered that while she admired stoicism in others, she didn't have any aptitude for it.

She instructed herself not to overreact. She was supposed to be cool. Wasn't that one of the hallmarks of her generation? She was expected to coin a few droll putdowns before returning to the dating apps. Instead, she crumbled like burnt paper.

Two days later, Ronan moved out. A room had come free in a friend's rented house, and he could crash there for a while. Everything he said made it plain that he saw the break as temporary, a small bump on a long road. Stacey felt differently. For her, this was fundamental. Her perception of their time together had changed. One thought kept returning: if you value honesty, and if that isn't there, what else have you got?

At the edge of Briarstown Park, they sat down. Except for an occasional feather of cloud, the sky was purest blue. The sun's rays stung her skin. Two teenage girls perched on a nearby bench, squinting at their phones and laughing. Their carefree giggles reminded Stacey of her younger self. Now, even on her strongest days, she felt as if she had a concrete block on each shoulder.

'There was another reason I wanted to have a chat,' said Ronan. 'It's about the eviction thing. Have you made any headway in finding somewhere new?'

No, she longed to say. *I'm too busy wallowing in what might have happened forty-odd years ago to bother with the present day. Engaging with the present makes me sad.* She gave a more pedestrian, less truthful, answer. She was making enquiries. She'd get somewhere before she was due to leave Whitethorn.

'I'm confident,' she lied.

The newspaper articles about Whitethorn had landed with a thud of indifference. Yes, there'd been a bit of muttering in the area, but no one with influence had taken up their cause. There had been no support from well-known politicians, no slot on the TV news. She could hear reporters saying, 'Haven't we covered this type of thing a million times before?'

Ronan rubbed his hands together, a gesture Stacey recognised. He was nervous.

'If you're stuck,' he said, 'Aaron, one of the lads in the house, is leaving. So there'll be a spare room and, ahm . . . I thought I'd let you know. You can have it if you like. No strings attached or anything, I promise. And for fear you're wondering, there's another woman in the house, Marina. So you wouldn't be living with a bunch of lads.'

For a second, she thought about saying yes. Saying yes would strike one item from her list of worries. But even if Ronan's motives were genuine, she couldn't allow herself to share a house with him. In solving one problem, she would create twenty others. The unpalatable truth was that, despite everything, she wanted to reach out to him. She craved the comfort of him. Worse, there remained a crackle of attraction. She imagined kissing him.

She composed herself, removed her sunglasses, turned and looked him in the eye. 'I appreciate the offer, but it wouldn't be a smart move. We both know that.'

'I thought I'd ask anyway . . . in case you were stuck because . . .' Ronan wasn't usually this inarticulate, and his voice fell away.

'Honestly, I'm really grateful only . . . well, you know yourself.'

'I do.'

'I reckon I should go,' said Stacey.

'No. I'd better get back to work. You stay here if you like. It's your 'hood, after all.'

'I'll let you know when I've found somewhere new.'

'Thanks.'

Stacey closed her eyes and counted to two hundred. When she opened them again, Ronan was gone.

Chapter 12

January 1982, Steelstown

After Christmas, it snowed. Not their usual two squally showers and three hours of slush, but a proper fall with staying power. It was the sort of snow they'd seen on TV but had never experienced in real life. Children left their homes, squealing with delight. They zigzagged down Steelstown's two half-hearted hills on abandoned election posters and torn fertiliser bags.

The next day, the flakes thickened until the entire town was swaddled in white. Across Ireland, schools stayed closed, and factories sent workers home. Shops shut their doors, and roads became impassable.

Every town was its own world.

Gail and Loretta had returned to Dublin before the weather changed. Birdy and Yvonne were stranded in Steelstown. On the third day, they went for one of those aimless walks that reminded Birdy of her early teens. *Will we fly to New York and live in a skyscraper? Will we go to Hawaii and take up surfing? Or will we do another circuit of Pearse Park?* With nothing to do and nowhere to go, they trudged through the snow, their breath smoking in the freezing air. Birdy was wearing two overcoats while Yvonne wore her pyjamas under her clothes. Their hats were pulled low, their scarves wrapped tightly around their necks. Their faces were mottled from the cold.

'If Kieran saw the state of us, he'd be raging,' said Yvonne. 'We're like refugees from a horror film.'

'At least we match,' replied Birdy, ducking her head to avoid the wind.

They crunched on, swapping their news. As Birdy had predicted, Mike had been quick to find a new girlfriend. He was going steady with Joan Finnerty. At school, Gail had labelled her 'Moan Finicky' because of her permanent dissatisfaction. She spent her life complaining about Steelstown but would never leave. Mike could do better.

Their chat careened from one topic to another. All the while, Birdy's thoughts were elsewhere. Throughout Christmas, she'd obsessed about Vivienne's revelation. With every day that passed, her feelings grew more complex and her attitude towards Loretta softened. If anything, she felt protective of her.

'Does Mike going out with someone new bother you?' asked Yvonne, while they rounded a mud-smeared drift.

'Honestly? No, only I'm baffled that he took up with Moan. She must be the most tedious woman in Steelstown. I'd say she started planning her wedding the day after her confirmation.'

'You're worked up about something, though.'

'Ah, it's nothing.' Birdy faltered. 'Well, that's not true.' She had toyed with keeping the story to herself. But, if she was going to confide in anyone, it had to be Yvonne. Her bandmate's judgement was sound. Also, in a place where the water seemed to be contaminated with deference, Yvonne had managed to acquire a steely authority. 'It's Loretta,' she said. 'And Kieran.'

Once she began, the words tumbled out, like pennies from a slot machine. Save for the occasional question, Yvonne said little. Birdy worried that she'd misjudged her friend. Suppose she didn't believe her? Suppose she didn't believe the affair mattered? After all, before leaving Steelstown, they'd joked about Yvonne sleeping with one of her bosses.

At last, as they teetered past a mammoth snowman, Yvonne spoke. 'No wonder Loretta was in such an almighty rush back to Dublin. I just can't get my head around this. Is she mad?'

'In a way, I feel the same. Except the longer I've had to think the more pissed off I am with Kieran. Not to excuse Loretta or anything, but he's the one who's married.'

Again, it took Yvonne a while to respond. 'It's funny, isn't it?' she said. 'I'd always reckoned Loretta must have loads of self-confidence. On stage, she's a total superstar. It was only when we started living together that it hit me. She's two different people. When she's not putting on a performance, she's actually quite insecure.'

Birdy kicked a clump of snow into the air and watched its powdery fall. 'She must know she's good-looking, only she doesn't get any buzz from it. If I had her face, I'd be shifting men every night of the week. I'd also find it impossible not to talk. You'd all be bored senseless with tales of my adventures.'

Truth to tell, Birdy wasn't surprised by Loretta's ability to be two people at once. She was the same. Standing under a spotlight was easier than negotiating real life. No matter how ill at ease or inadequate she felt in the outside world, on stage she could act like she owed nothing to anyone. Unfortunately, that confidence dissolved as soon as the final chord rang out.

She was also starting to understand that it was possible to be too beautiful. She thought of the most popular girls in her year at school, like Noeleen Kelleher and Majella Henshaw. Noeleen was so flat-chested she hadn't worn a bra until third year, and Majella's hair had been ruined by a series of disastrous home perms. Both, however, had been pretty enough, and approachable enough, to attract the best-looking boys. No one would accuse Loretta of being approachable. She was best appreciated from a distance.

The snow was falling again. Yvonne hunched her shoulders against the cold. 'From what Vivienne said to you, Kieran does this all the time. If . . . when . . . he moves on, what then?'

'That's one of the things that bothers me. A messy split would mean trouble for the band. God, that sounds selfish but . . .'

'You want things to work out for us? I know.'

At the wall where Birdy had broken up with Mike, they came across a group of lads. She recognised them as part of a gang from school: would-be hard chaws with sparse moustaches, acne-splashed skin and a thorough knowledge of cheap highs. They even chewed gum in an aggressive way. Their musical taste began and ended with AC/DC. In defiance of the weather, they were wearing short leather jackets. No hats, scarves or gloves. They could be glazed with ice and still they wouldn't admit to feeling the cold.

'Have ye made it to the cover of *Smash Hits* yet, girls?' shouted one.

'They're too ugly for that,' yelled another. 'Where's your fit friend?'

Yvonne raised a finger in their direction, and they laughed.

'We'll send you a signed copy when we do,' said Birdy. 'It might be sooner than you think.'

Once, she would have been keen to impress lads like these. Despite not wanting to hang around with them, she would have hankered after their approval. *Consider me cool. Consider me worthy of attention. Admire me from afar.* With some pleasure, she realised that she no longer cared what they thought.

'What about Gail?' said Yvonne, as they turned towards home.

'We'll have to fill her in.'

'Yeah. If we don't, and she finds out, she'll go ballistic on us.'

Birdy peered up at the quilted sky. A scattering of snowflakes settled on her face. 'Which brings us to the other question: what are we going to say to Loretta?'

That night, the lights went out. In a low growl of a voice, the newsreader on Birdy's transistor said the snow had toppled electricity lines around the country. It was unclear when power would be restored.

Her mother bustled about, fetching the candles she stored in the dresser drawer and placing sheets of newspaper in front of the fridge for fear it would defrost. Her father maintained the supply would return sooner if the engineers made more of an effort.

'No one wants to work any more,' he said.

The four sat in front of the fire, its glow providing most of the room's light. When her mam put on a new log, sparks flew into the air like tiny fireworks.

Birdy and Declan tuned and retuned the transistor. Without saying a word, they both knew what they were doing. Finally, they came across The Atrix and 'Treasure On The Wasteland'. This was it, a song guaranteed to annoy their father.

As reliable as rain, he harrumphed, 'If that's what young people are listening to these days, I'm glad I'm on the way out.'

'Dad,' replied Declan, in his best deadpan voice, 'you're forty-three.'

Birdy giggled. Her mother joined in. Soon, even her father recognised the absurdity of his comment and allowed himself a chuckle. They were still laughing when they heard a rattling knock on the front door.

Birdy eased herself off the floor and picked up a candle. 'I'll get it.'

'What class of fool goes out on a night like this?' said her dad.

It was Yvonne, now wearing her brother's parka and a balaclava.

Perhaps Birdy had spent too long in her father's company, but she expected bad news. 'Come in,' she said. 'What is it?'

'I'll tell you in a sec. I'm absolutely frozen. The cold out there would skin you.'

Yvonne followed her down the hall, shedding clothes as she went. In the kitchen, the candlelight flickered across her face. For a few seconds, she was perfectly still. Then, she slapped the table, causing the flame to shudder.

'Have you any champagne?'

'Let me ask Mam. I think she keeps it with the lobster. They're probably out in the garage with her sports car.'

'You're a comedian, Birdy Troy, and no mistake.'

'Are you going to let me know what's up?'

'Okey-dokes. Here's another question. How are you fixed for moving to London?'

'Why would I do that?'

'Because . . .' Yvonne paused, as if waiting for the roll of her own drums '. . . it's where we'll be recording our album.'

'You're kidding me.'

'I'm not, you know. Kieran called this evening, saying he had news. I got quite a shock, I can tell you. Anyway, we've got a deal. An actual record deal with an actual record company. In London!'

'How can anyone be offering us a contract? Have they no snow in England?'

'There are telephones, Bird. And telexes and what-have-you.'

Cocooned in Steelstown, it was easy to forget that, outside, life continued. Even though a record deal was what they'd been working towards, Birdy couldn't quite believe what she was hearing.

Yvonne sketched out what Kieran had told her. The company, Supreme Records, was a subsidiary of one of the big multinationals. They'd heard The Diamonds' session tape, and their main A&R man had been to see the band more than once. The money wasn't brilliant, but Supreme was promising a top producer and a major promotional push. That was fine with Birdy. This wasn't about possessions or even about fame. She had the rest of her life to worry about money. This was about the freedom to keep doing what made her happy.

While Yvonne spoke, the candle melted down to its nub. In the gloom, Birdy could barely make out her face.

'When do we have to go?' she asked.

'From what Kieran said, fairly soon. As soon as the snow melts, I'd say.'

'That'll go down well with Dad. I can hear him: "London, is it? You'll be off to Australia next, I suppose."'

Yvonne clapped. 'Lahndan, baby,' she said, sounding like she'd escaped from the set of *Minder*.

Although Birdy had never been to London, she felt she knew it. She'd seen the city so many times on television that the images flashed in front of her, like a slideshow. In her mind, it was a magical place. It was The Stranglers and The Clash, Siouxsie Sioux and The

Jam. It was the Marquee Club and the Roundhouse, King's Road and Kensington Market. It was Princess Diana and the Brixton riots and everything in between.

She savoured the moment. If The Diamonds had a number-one album, if they had ten number-one albums, if they played every stadium in every part of the world, the sensation couldn't beat this.

And still it gnawed at her. 'What about Kieran and Loretta? Where does this leave us?'

'I reckon it solves the problem,' said Yvonne. 'If we're in London, he can't just call around to the house any more. He can't meet up with her any time he likes.'

'Fair enough, only I don't trust him. He's got the money to fly over and back as often as he wants.'

'Think about it: at the minute, it's easy to see why Loretta would have a crush on him. He's always around. London's different. We'll meet loads of new people. Loads of men. She's bound to move on.'

'I'm sure you're right,' said Birdy, who wasn't sure at all.

Chapter 13

Now, Dublin

'I first did some portraits of them in late '81. Then, after they'd moved to London, I got a fantastic commission to take shots of them there. For a magazine, you know.'

Vivienne Lane Power leant forward as she spoke. They were sitting in the shaded part of her garden, not far from an explosion of flowers. The house, in Leeson Park, was as impressive as Stacey had expected. What was more, it was comfortable, lived-in. A family home rather than an antiseptic show house. The garden was a delight. At the bottom of a perfect lawn, there was a wooden swing set. 'For the grandchildren,' Vivienne had explained, in her slightly husky voice.

Stacey tried to imagine what it would be like to have so much space.

Vivienne was a surprise in that, unlike many women of her background, she had allowed herself to age. Her long, smooth hair was grey, her tanned face lightly lined. It was an expressive face. She wore a white T-shirt, a ruby-coloured wraparound skirt and flat silver sandals. She was also surprisingly jittery.

Stacey had been relieved to hear from her. She was in Portugal, she'd said, but would be back at the weekend and could arrange a meeting then. She'd stressed that while she was willing to talk, it would be for background purposes only. 'I don't want to be quoted,' she'd added, as though she was speaking to an influential journalist about state secrets. That had deepened Stacey's interest.

'My memories of them are so clear, it's as if I saw them last week,' Vivienne said now. 'Ridiculous, of course. But memory's funny, isn't it? I can forget where I was yesterday and then recite the lyrics of an entire album from forty years ago.'

Stacey smiled. 'They obviously left an impression.'

'Birdy was my favourite. She had a real spirit about her. Gail was more of an attention-grabber. Yvonne was sound. I know the drummer's supposed to be the mad one, but she was solid. And Loretta . . . Well, we can get to her in a minute. Birdy had this watchful thing going on, like a small child. Like she was taking it all in and would report back at a future date.' Vivienne opened a crisp brown folder, which was sitting on the wrought-iron table in front of her. 'Here you go. These are the London shots. I wanted to capture their energy.'

'I didn't know they'd moved to England,' said Stacey, accepting the black-and-white prints, which had yellowed with age.

'Uh-huh. They went in early '82. They only spent a few months in Dublin.'

In Vivienne's pictures, the four Diamonds goofed about on a city street. Their hair was backcombed, their clothes black, but there was none of the faux-coolness that was in vogue at the time.

They were exuberant, playful, happy. They were luminous. For a brief flash, Stacey felt as if she was on the street with them.

'The photos are great. The four of them look so alive.'

'Thanks.' Vivienne reached into the folder again and pulled out the article in which The Diamonds were interviewed. It came from a long-defunct Irish music magazine. 'Don't mind the writing style. In those days every hack thought he was Hunter S. Thompson.'

Stacey read hungrily. The piece revealed that the band had been living in a flat in Shepherd's Bush and recording in a nearby studio. 'London's like Steelstown only the tea is rubbish, and no one knows who we are,' Gail told the interviewer. 'Oh, and we have to keep reassuring people that we're not nuns and we're not in the IRA.'

The article swung between pompous and insightful. It wasn't just the writing style that jarred. The author was determined to compare the band to men. They were 'like a female Undertones' and, if they worked hard, might yet be as successful as 'their male counterparts, U2'. He asked if they needed much help with their song-writing and how important their image was. Elsewhere, he sneered at their backgrounds. It was easy, he wrote, to see all four Diamonds 'dancing around their handbags' in their 'gritty' home town. Birdy was described as a 'shop girl'. Yvonne's look was 'small-town Ireland meets Soho-chic'. Gail was 'fresh from the dole queue'. Loretta was 'the hottest girl in your class at school, the one who's snapped up the bank manager's son.'

Reading between the lines, the band had taken this on board and had fun with him. They joked about being true daughters of Steelstown. According to Gail, they had drawers filled with Irish dancing medals, ate fish on Fridays and saved Green Shield stamps. Birdy added a cryptic comment: 'Then again, who knows what secrets we have? Perhaps one of us is leading a double life.'

'I'm amazed they didn't give that journalist a slap,' said Stacey, as she took photos of the article. 'Talk about patronising. Is he still knocking around?'

'Fiachra Purcell? No, the poor man died twenty years ago.' Vivienne mimed a hand raising a pint. 'Young as they were, I think they'd already learnt to let an awful lot go over their heads.' She fidgeted with her bangles. 'You've also got to remember that back then every woman put up with behaviour that wouldn't be acceptable now. Not just condescension and general pettiness but physical stuff too. A guy feeling you up at a gig? It was no big hassle. Something you shrugged off. These days, quite rightly, it'd be called sexual assault.' Another fidget. 'If you don't mind me asking, what year were you born?'

'1992. I was thirty in February.'

'Lucky you. Don't get me wrong. I'm not saying everything's easy for your generation. In some ways, it's tougher. I mean, it was possible for The Diamonds to turn up in Dublin with barely a penny to their names. They were able to chase their dreams in a way that wouldn't be feasible today. I get that.'

Tell me about it, thought Stacey. She decided against raising her own troubles. If she allowed the discussion to veer off-topic, she might miss something.

'To be fair,' continued Vivienne, 'it wasn't only the music business that was dark. Ireland could be dark, and any woman who complained was belittled or dismissed.' She waved one hand, causing her bracelets to tinkle like wind chimes. 'I can't imagine how much sleazy bullshit The Diamonds had to put up with. Well, I can . . . but I'll come to that.'

Stacey's back stiffened. Did Vivienne know something specific about what had happened to the band? Why else mention sleaze? Before she could frame a question, Vivienne had moved on.

'You've also got to remember that when those days are written and spoken about, it's usually by men. Most of the bands were men, most of the journalists, all the managers, all the record execs, all the DJs.'

'What puzzles me,' said Stacey, 'is why so many people, including women, remember the 1980s with such fondness. When I go on YouTube, it's all "My heart aches for those years" and "Condolences to anyone who missed the eighties." What's that about?'

'You ask a good question. I wish I had a good answer. The simple explanation is . . . we were young.'

'Surely there's more to it than that.'

'Yes, but I find it impossible to explain. When the subject comes up, I tend to say the "correct" thing – "Nostalgia is corrosive, it's for the simple-minded," and all the rest of it. And then I hear an old song or see an old photo and I turn to mush. Or a musician from that era dies, and it's like I've lost a friend.'

'But you don't really think those were better times?'

'No, but we had lots to fight for. And the fight was exhilarating . . . because we felt like it was possible to win, you know?'

Stacey watched a powder-pink rose petal fall to the ground. She suspected that the dark allure of the 1980s could be Vivienne's *Mastermind* subject. As interesting as this was, she needed to steer the conversation back to The Diamonds.

'What I did take from the interview,' she said, 'is that the band definitely recorded an album.'

'Absolutely.'

'What happened to it?'

'I wish I knew.'

'So you didn't hear any further talk about it?'

'No.'

'And Birdy . . . I assume she wasn't christened that. You don't by any chance know her proper name?'

Vivienne gave a warm smile. 'As it happens, I do. Her real name was Jacqueline or Jackie. Jacqueline Bernadette Troy. She was born in 1962, at the height of Jackie Kennedy mania. There were two or three other girls with the same name in her class at school. At home, they called her Birdy. Because she was always singing, you know? By the age of eight or nine, everyone knew her as Birdy. She said it made life easier for her teachers. The reason I'm smiling, and the reason I remember the detail, is because it took endless coaxing to get her true name from her. She definitely preferred her nickname.'

'Can I ask you about Loretta? You said you'd come back to her.'

'Yes, I did. I've debated whether to tell you this, only I've always sensed that it might be relevant to what happened afterwards. So here goes. The story, or my part of it at least, starts at a party in my parents' house.'

For the next five minutes, Vivienne spoke about the events of late 1981. In particular, she spoke about a covert affair between Loretta and Kieran Mitchell. Or perhaps it hadn't been so covert. If she had known, and if she'd told Birdy, how many others had been in the loop? When she'd finished, she ran a hand through her hair. Again, her bracelets tinkled.

'After you'd spoken to Birdy,' said Stacey, 'did she mention the affair again?'

'Not to me, no. Within a few weeks, they'd gone to London. Mind you, I did wonder about that line in the interview.'

'Where she talked about one of them leading a double life?'

'Yes.'

'And did you see her again after the London photo shoot?'

'No. They all said they'd give me a shout when they got back to Dublin. But I figure that when the day came they'd already broken up.'

'Did you not have questions about what had become of them?'

Vivienne bristled, as though she'd been accused of negligence. 'I asked Kieran. As I recall, he was vague. He said it hadn't worked out. And he called Birdy a troublemaker. With hindsight, that should have set off a warning siren. It didn't tally with the girl I knew. Birdy loved that band. Loved everything about it. She can't have let go easily. But the music business is the landfill of dreams. You can be incredibly talented and still not make it.'

'I understand.'

'And then, a year or so later, I left Dublin. I'd fallen for an American guy. I spent two years in San Francisco with him. Those were wild, wild days. By the time that all came undone, and I returned to Dublin, a lot had changed. Kieran was managing One Scarlet Morning, and they were beginning to make a name for themselves. I met Thomas, my husband, and became more . . . let's say settled. I lost my appetite for following bands around.'

The more she heard, the more Stacey was fascinated by Vivienne. Fascinated and envious. Once again, she wanted to veer off course. She wanted to ask about California. And she wanted to ask how Vivienne had known that Thomas was the one. What had separated him from Mr San Francisco or any of the others?

She forced herself to focus. 'Did you come across Kieran Mitchell again?'

'Oh, I did.' Vivienne's voice hardened. 'For years, he was impossible to avoid. I bumped into him at theatre first nights, exhibition openings, events like that. As far as I know, he comes back to Ireland fairly regularly. The last time I met him was three or four years ago. Before the pandemic, at a cultural thingy in New York. He was friendly – but in a superficial way. Even Kieran has only so much charm, and he wouldn't want to waste any of it on a middle-aged woman. He's put a lot of effort into his public image, and he hates being reminded of the old days.'

'You don't like him much, do you?'

Immediately, Stacey feared her question had been too blunt.

That didn't stop Vivienne answering. 'I don't and I'm not alone. From everything I've heard, he can be pretty ruthless. The trouble is, he's also indestructible. I honestly think that, in the end, it'll be Kieran Mitchell and the cockroaches, fighting it out for global supremacy.'

'That's quite an image.'

The sun had moved so that light was splintering around Vivienne. 'If you find them,' she said, 'if you find Birdy, promise you'll let me know. And tell them I said hello. Will you do that for me?'

'Of course.'

'I've never forgotten them. That's the reason I've held on to the article and the photographs. And that's the reason I've spoken to you. Every so often, a song comes on the radio, and I hear a glimmer of The Diamonds. Of what they might have been. Not just another band trying to make it in U2's slipstream, but genuine talents in their own right.'

'I'm very grateful,' said Stacey. She had an inkling that Vivienne had more to say, but wasn't sure how she should ask. 'Is that . . . everything?'

Vivienne stayed silent.

'Or is there something else?'

The silence stretched.

'Yes,' she said, at last. 'There's something I didn't know when I spoke to Birdy, something I only discovered after the trip to London. The thing is, it mightn't be of any consequence. But it also . . . It meant that some of what I'd predicted was wrong. No one's life panned out in the way I'd expected. But I suppose some of that's a matter of public record.'

'Go on.'

Once more, Stacey waited for Vivienne to explain. Eventually, she did.

Although she still didn't know why The Diamonds had split or what they'd done afterwards, Stacey's mind was alive with what she'd learnt. As soon as she got to the car, she went to her phone and searched for women called Jackie or Jacqueline Troy. Yet again, she was disappointed.

If a woman's social media suggested she was the right age, she looked wrong. If she looked right, she was ruled out by location or taste. It was unlikely that Jacqueline Troy of Winnebago County, Wisconsin, a cross-stitch embroidery enthusiast and active member of the Lutheran Church, was the woman Stacey was seeking. Neither did Jackie Troy Webster, a former show-jumper from Lincolnshire, sound like a strong match. Jacqui Troy of Inverness who recommended that Stacey visit her page on OnlyFans could be ruled out, as could Jackie Glenna Troy, an amusement-park worker from Lubbock, Texas. The one outside possibility lived on a farm in New Zealand. Jacqueline Troy Brown was fifty-nine years old and had wished her friends a happy St Patrick's Day.

Prior to today, Stacey hadn't taken any interest in Kieran Mitchell's personal life. It hadn't seemed relevant. She returned to his Wikipedia page. What she saw reflected what Vivienne had told her.

It was then that she noticed the change. Since she'd last

visited, someone had inserted a line about The Diamonds. They were described as one of the first bands Mitchell had managed. The reference was straightforward, unadorned. But it was there. There was something satisfying about the fact that The Diamonds were no longer erased from their manager's history. A link brought Stacey to the *Top of the Pops* video on YouTube.

She told herself not to read too much into this. There was a chance the edit had been made by someone who'd heard Ultan's interview on her podcast.

She looked again at the comments under the video. There was a new message, posted two days ago. Steelstown4eva wrote, Always wondered why they couldn't work together any more. Time the truth was told. Gus McNamara, who had originally suggested there was a story, replied, Someone should be nervous. And JBT, who had started the conversation, added, Really?

Stacey held her breath. JBT: now she understood the initials. Even if the person using that name wasn't the real Birdy, there must be a connection. She wanted to reply. She wanted to say, *Who are you?* But that wouldn't be wise. She would think about it on the way home.

Chapter 14

April 1982, London

If Loretta was making a TV drama featuring a couple having clandestine sex, this would have been the ideal set. The worn navy carpet, the skew-whiff curtains, the smell of stale cigarette smoke: all spoke of a hotel room that might once have been considered classy but was long past its best. The dressing-table was dotted with burns and there was a troubling red stain on one wall. If Gail was here, she would be hypothesising about finding a body under the floorboards.

While the room wouldn't have been Loretta's choice, she was happy to be alone with Kieran. Just the two of them, without distractions. Without Yvonne asking questions or Gail telling stories or Birdy being a bore about their album.

Except there were distractions. In normal circumstances, they'd be having a drink. They'd be flirting. Teasing. Kissing. Instead they were at opposite sides of the room.

When she'd met Kieran at Reception, he'd said he needed to talk. This had set her on edge. Immediately he'd started complaining about the magazine article. Relief had washed through her. *Is that all?* she'd wanted to say. In the months they'd been seeing each other, she'd learnt that he could work himself into a froth of irritation about the unlikeliest issues. Then, before she'd had the chance to adjust, he would become calm again, his anger spent, his mind moving on.

She'd also learnt that he could be surprisingly possessive. He winced when she spoke about parties or nights in the pub. He wouldn't be able to bear it if she slept with another man, he said. Was it wrong that she didn't mind? If the alternative was indifference, she would prefer him like this.

'I'm a bit worried about Birdy,' he said now. 'What's all this bullshit about someone leading a "double life"? Has she said anything to you?'

'No. Why would she?'

'Because maybe you've let something slip? She's sharp. It wouldn't take a lot to get her mind working.'

'I promise you I haven't. She was only messing. We all were. The journalist was a complete pain.' Loretta told herself not to sound too whiny. Kieran had made it clear that he disliked whining. 'I don't think there's any reason to worry.'

Usually, she was the worrier. Worry was never far away, nipping at her heels, whispering in her ear. What if one of the other Diamonds guessed the truth? What would she say?

In the beginning, she'd been convinced they would notice. She'd barely been able to eat or sleep. The sight of Kieran, the sound of him, had brought a lightness to her chest and a lump to the base of her throat. Every note she'd sung had been for him. *Are you watching me?* she'd think. *Are you listening?*

Her desire had been so overwhelming that she'd had no interest in anything or anybody else. The rest of the world had annoyed her. Despite this, the others had remained oblivious to how her life had changed. To the fact that she was breathing different air.

She'd had sex with Kieran a week after their first kiss. He'd brought her to a hotel in Wicklow. The suite had been decorated with antique furniture and muted paintings of faraway hills. The carpet was so thick her bare feet had disappeared into its fibres. She'd been incredibly nervous, her anxiety heightened by their grand surroundings. Thankfully, Kieran had assumed she was jumpy because she feared someone would spot them. He hadn't known it was her first time. She preferred it that way.

Did she feel guilty? Of course. She didn't like hiding from the others. Both Birdy and Yvonne had new boyfriends while Gail was making the most of every opportunity.

They went to parties in Camden Town and Ladbroke Grove where they met musicians and students, wannabes and never-woulds. They drank strong lager, smoked weed and told each other how special they were. Forget the hippies. Forget punk. Forget the past. This was their time.

Loretta also felt bad about Imogen. She'd have felt worse if Kieran's marriage was otherwise sound. It wasn't. His wife, his immensely privileged wife, was a drinker who took no interest in his life. Because her family was wealthy, she was insulated from the real world. Although he said relatively little about their marriage, it was plain that he regretted it.

Over the months, Loretta had come up with stories to conceal the relationship. She'd invented friends and relatives and parties. To this day, she maintained a bank of tales and excuses. This evening she'd claimed she was meeting her cousin Carole who was down from Birmingham. Two weeks previously, she'd said she wanted to take a stroll around the West End. 'On your own? On a miserable evening?' Birdy had asked. Loretta had ummed and aahed about being restless, and Birdy had let it drop.

'It's my fault,' said Kieran. 'I should have vetted that Purcell guy more carefully. I'd heard he was talented, but he comes across as just another hack with ideas about himself. Him and his "shop girl" jibes. Mind you, in my experience, people quite like shop girls. They're easy to relate to.' He pressed his palm against his forehead. 'Did any of you ask Birdy what she meant?'

'I couldn't do that. Then she'd suspect I did have something to hide.'

'Okay. And sorry. I didn't mean to get at you. I've always trusted you to be discreet.'

This was not how Loretta would have liked to celebrate her nineteenth birthday. Her actual birthday had been two days ago. The band had spent it in the studio and then gone to the pub. The other three had bought sugary drinks – a brandy and Babycham, a Malibu and pineapple, a Black Russian – and told tacky jokes about making the most of her last months as a teenager. The following morning, she'd felt as if her mouth was lined with chalk and her skull coated with lead. 'Never again,' she'd croaked, as she tried to keep down a plate of dry toast and a fistful of Anadin.

Loretta had dressed up to meet Kieran. She was wearing a red dress from Topshop in Oxford Circus and a pair of black patent heels. It was, she thought, more grown-up than her usual look. If he'd noticed, he hadn't said. Neither had he mentioned a present. The room was cold, a draught wafting through the curtains, and she wished she'd worn tights.

In many ways, Loretta was ambivalent about London. That the city was everything the others claimed – exciting, vibrant, filled with possibility – was beside the point. Her Dublin life had been more satisfying. Simpler too. She'd been able to see Kieran all the time. Was it bad that she thought of those months as a golden period?

Compared to the energy rush of performing live, recording was a grind. She was forced to sing the same lines over and over again until they were stripped of meaning. Birdy and Yvonne obsessed about tiny details. They wrote and rewrote. Their producer, Ian Montgomery, kept demanding more. Another take. A fresh approach. A bit higher. No, a bit lower.

If she complained, one of the others would round on her. Ian was class, they'd say. They were lucky he was willing to work with them.

The Diamonds were still gigging. They'd played in Huddersfield and Doncaster, Nottingham and Cardiff. Usually, the audience was made up of drunk students and the sort of men who shouted, 'Get your tits out,' and 'Go home to your husbands.'

The best nights were the ones with Irish people in the crowd. Most were recent arrivals. They'd hated Ireland, they said. They'd hated being on the dole, relying on scraps of black-market work. And they'd hated older people telling them to stop complaining. They were tired of hearing how times had been even tougher in the fifties and sixties. A new life in England was what they craved. And yet they clung like hot tar to anything from home. They drank in Irish bars and supported Irish bands. Their stories were laden with references no English person would understand: red lemonade, the Child of Prague, *Wanderly Wagon*. On the Tube, they spoke in Irish. Were they homesick? Or did they want Londoners to consider them exotic?

Encouraged by their record company, music journalists had been coming to see The Diamonds. They'd received two great reviews, one describing them as 'hot as lava', the other as 'the sound of a new Ireland'. A third had been cutting. The writer maintained they dressed more like groupies than musicians. Their lyrics were described as 'typical teenage girl angst'. Loretta was a 'charity-shop Debbie Harry'. Kieran had crackled with anger.

His mood that evening was harder to pin down. His rant about the magazine segued into a speech about the pressure he was under.

'I don't see myself as being a manager in the traditional sense,' he said. 'And in a way I'm not. It's not like I'm going to ask you to clock in. But I do have responsibilities. People depend on me. When I'm not making plans, I'm fighting fires. And I'm doing my best, you know.'

A hum in Loretta's head told her that something wasn't right. There was more to this weird humour than a so-so magazine article. 'Of course you are,' she said. 'Doing your best, I mean.'

He was on his feet, walking to her side of the room. He sat on the edge of the bed, facing her. It sighed in protest. She wished she knew him well enough to interpret his actions.

'There's something I've got to tell you,' he said, 'and I need you to hear me out.'

Chapter 15

Birdy picked up her post, a letter from Declan, and stepped into the kitchen. The room had one slim window, and the light from the bare bulb gave it a cosy feel. Yvonne was stirring a vegetable stew, the aroma filling the small space. The Jam were on the cassette player. 'Town Called Malice' had become a regular part of their gig-day ritual. It was, in Birdy's opinion, physically impossible to hear it without wanting to dance.

She remembered how, at the start, she'd found Dublin difficult to navigate. Now, she thought of her time there as training: training for this city of different faces and languages; this city where the smells and sounds and colours bore no relation to those she'd known before; this city where people lived in gated mansions and tower blocks, gleaming streets and cardboard boxes.

She'd grown up in a small, easily defined place. Steelstown began at a set of traffic lights and ended where the land was swallowed by the Shannon estuary. London felt as though it went on for ever. As though there was an infinite number of alleyways and courtyards, cafés and corner shops. You could devote your life to exploring it and still not complete the task.

The Diamonds were living near the perpetual motion of the Westway. No sensible person would have called their flat luxurious, but it was no worse than their house in Dublin and far better than the squats where many bands lived.

She turned down the music and sat at the table beside Gail. 'So,' she said, 'does anyone else doubt that this cousin Carole exists? Or am I just a cynic?'

Yvonne, chopping parsley and tossing it into the pot, made a clicking noise. 'I don't think I'd ever heard a mention of Carole until this afternoon.'

'Me neither. And have you noticed how she always disappears the night before Kieran's due to arrive?'

'You reckon Loretta meets up with him, does the deed, comes home and then the next morning they both act like he's straight off the flight?'

'Yep, that's about the size of it.'

Gail, who was going through a reading phase ('Why did none of you tell me about books?'), looked up from *The Women's Room*. 'He's always been the slipperiest eel in the tank. And now she's no better. The way she's sneaking around bugs me. But without confronting her, I'm not sure what we can do.'

'Fair enough,' said Birdy. 'Only it's getting harder to pretend we don't know.'

After the snow, Birdy and Yvonne had told Gail. They'd argued back and forth about what to do before deciding that distance would probably cause the affair to fizzle out. Best to say nothing, they'd agreed.

They'd been wrong.

Birdy's feelings towards Loretta had hardened again. It wasn't just the flimsy stories that bothered her. It was the fact that she'd become increasingly distracted. This was especially true in the studio.

Over the past few weeks, Birdy had been forced to accept that they all viewed recording in different ways. For her, it was mind-blowing. A blast of technicolour in a hazy grey world. The challenge – to make a record that sounded both crafted and spontaneous – filled her head. And, yeah, Ian could be tough with his 'Try it this way. No, try it that way.' There were days when his perfectionism was tedious. But he was an expert. Like her, he breathed music. He dreamt music.

With part of their advance, Birdy had bought a new guitar. The sound from the second-hand black Stratocaster was immense, and she practised and practised until the others begged her to stop. When she heard her music being played back on quality speakers, the work felt worthwhile. Just seeing the little sound-bars rise and fall gave her a thrill.

In her view, creativity didn't last for ever. You only got so many ideas. Every time she flicked on the radio, she heard proof of this. Old bands churned out the same riffs, the same beats, the same themes. But what had sounded exciting at twenty was lame at forty. This was The Diamonds' shot at producing a great piece of work. At producing something pure. They would be fools to waste it.

Their first single, 'Too Much Not Enough', was due to be released in late May. 'Brighter Than The Sun' would follow in August. Their album would come out two weeks later.

The recording studio was where Birdy had met Andy Chisholm. He was twenty-two and had left university the year before. He worked as a gofer: making coffee, taking phone calls and going out for takeaway. Birdy hadn't intended to get together with him. The plan had been for her and Gail to be free women, slutting their way around London (Gail's phrase), breaking hearts and having adventures. But she'd found herself drawn to Andy's combination of awkwardness and charm.

Was he the best-looking guy she'd met? No. But if he wasn't ride-of-the-century material (another Gailism), he wasn't a horror show either. He had pale blue eyes, sandy hair, an extensive knowledge of indie bands and a knack of asking interesting questions. With Andy, Birdy was learning that sex could be more than a one-time act. It could be how you spent an entire day. After their first night together, she'd found herself thinking, *Ah, so that's what the fuss is about.* Along with Gail and Yvonne, she joked about English sex being completely different from Irish sex. No guilt, they said. No sin. She had a feeling every Irish person in London said the same thing.

Despite a lack of free time, Birdy was a frequent visitor to Andy's place in Ladbroke Grove. There, they spent hours enjoying each other, listening to music and talking about their lives. Sometimes, they turned off the music and just listened to the sounds of the street below. Occasionally, she wondered what he was doing with her. He would, she thought, be better suited to the type of wispy English girl who wore floral dresses and had skin like Princess Diana.

According to Ian, Andy's university, Bristol, was only one step away from Oxford and Cambridge. He'd also had something called a 'gap year', during which he'd travelled around Africa. He was puzzled by Birdy's admission that she'd never been on an aeroplane. 'How did you get to England?' he'd asked. When she'd explained that, because of their gear, they'd got the ferry to Holyhead, he'd promised that one day soon the two of them would fly somewhere.

In anticipation, she had applied for a passport. The small, green-covered booklet had now arrived.

To begin with, she'd been reluctant to talk about her parents or Declan or Steelstown. Her pre-Dublin life sounded too poor. Not interesting poor, like the world of an English kitchen-sink film or a New York rap record, but plodding, nondescript poor. Andy's response to her stories showed she'd been wrong. He was genuinely interested in her tales of Save-A-Lot, St John's Community School and the band's early gigs.

Although Birdy tried not to dwell on Kieran and Loretta, they infected her thoughts. The Diamonds needed Loretta. They couldn't exist without her. What they didn't need was her dishonesty.

Gail returned to her book, and Birdy opened the letter from Declan. She didn't receive many letters from her brother and was intrigued to see that this one contained a newspaper cutting. The letter itself was short and written on a page torn from an A4 pad.

While Yvonne tossed fistfuls of brown rice into boiling water, Birdy began to read:

How's it going, Bird?

One of the lads at school gave me this. It's from last week's Sunday Independent. *It's a good job Mam and Dad don't read the* Independent, *or they'd be worried about the company you're keeping. Dad would be on the next bus to London to drag you home!*

By the way, they're really into the band thing now. Mam has the picture of you from that magazine Blu-tacked to one of the cupboards in the kitchen. And I heard Dad telling Senan O'Reilly that you were working with the best producer in England. Senan said you'd always been a grand girl, and Dad agreed.

You probably know all the stuff in the paper. In case you don't, here you go . . . Your manager sounds like he has a busy life.

Any news on the record? No crack here. Trying to keep the head down before the Leaving. You know the score.

Talk to you soon,
Declan

PS Vera Cheevers was asking after you, so if the band doesn't work out, there's always Save-A-Lot.

'It'll be ready in five,' said Yvonne, shaking salt into the stew. 'Could one of you get out the bowls?'

'Give me a sec,' said Birdy, already scanning the article, which was from the paper's gossip page.

Rock 'n' Roll Baby

Congratulations to up-and-coming music mogul Kieran Mitchell. The manager and man-about-town is about to become a father. The snag? The mother isn't his wife, heiress Imogen Faulkner. Regular readers will know that the beautiful Imogen is the eldest daughter of property tycoon, Garret Faulkner.

Word reaches us that the lucky lady is Cork glamour girl Dairena Lennox. While Mitchell wasn't keen to confirm the happy news, we have it on good authority that the baby is due in the coming weeks.

The Glenageary man has a lot on his plate. His much-hyped charges, The Diamonds, are currently recording their debut album in London town, while another of his bands, Future Heroes, are writing material for their second LP.

Stay tuned for developments.

At first, Birdy didn't know whether to believe what she was reading. A few seconds' thought told her it rang true. Unfamiliar as she was with newspapers and the law, she was confident they couldn't make up something like this.

Assuming the article was accurate, Loretta would have to be told. And she'd have to call a halt to her affair with Kieran. Maybe, in a funny way, this would turn out to be good news for the band. Maybe it was vindication. If so, vindication didn't taste quite as sweet as Birdy had imagined.

'Here,' she said, placing the newspaper cutting in front of Gail. 'You'd better take a look at this.'

Chapter 16

When Kieran began to talk, Loretta had difficulty focusing. *Whoosh*: his words rushed past her ears. What he was saying couldn't be true. But it was. In less than a month, he would become a father. A baby boy or girl, another human being, would enter his life. She did the sums. Dairena Lennox must have become pregnant at around the time Loretta and Kieran had started seeing each other. Unease rose inside her, salty liquid gathering behind her teeth.

Every so often, Kieran paused, as though waiting for her to comment. The news was such a shock that she wasn't able to form a coherent sentence. He reached out to her. She recoiled.

'Don't,' she said, surprised by the force of her own voice. 'Leave me alone.'

'Okay, okay,' he replied, as he retreated to the edge of the bed.

Loretta attempted to unscramble her feelings. She'd always known that Kieran was married, and if she hadn't been fully comfortable with this, it hadn't driven her away. In truth, she'd viewed his marriage as a temporary arrangement. Something to be discarded when the moment was right, like a boring job or an unflattering hair colour. She'd also believed that, until she came along, he had been faithful to Imogen. All that time, she'd been deceived.

'Talk to me,' he said. 'Tell me what you're thinking.'

That was when she started to cry. There was nothing gentle or romantic about her tears. They were hot and furious and accompanied by shivers and shakes. Even when her sobbing subsided, the silly hiccups and tremors continued.

'Please talk to me,' repeated Kieran.

She ignored him, choosing instead to look in the dressing-table mirror. It showed silver tracks carving through her makeup. Her nose was pink, her eyes puffy. In one way, she hated herself for crying. Tears were ugly. Childish. In another, she was glad she hadn't been able to suppress her emotion. She needed Kieran to see how much he'd hurt her.

Loretta's mother crashed into her thoughts. There she was: frosted mauve lipstick bleeding into the lines around her mouth, hair blow-dried into neat sausages, buttons shining on her royal blue blazer. What would she say if she found out about Kieran? If she could witness this scene? The dictionary would be drained of insults.

In an effort to stop shaking, Loretta breathed in hard. Then again. And again. That was better. She looked at Kieran. His eyes were rooted to the floor. She rose, went to the bathroom and pulled out a wad of toilet paper. She tried to blow her nose and dab at her swollen face, but the paper was crisp, like the tracing paper they'd used in primary school.

When she returned to the bedroom, she was more composed.

She was also numb from the cold. Goosebumps ran up and down her thighs. Kieran remained at the edge of the bed.

She warned herself not to sound angry. Neither did she want to come across as simpering or overly conciliatory. Insecurity was not an attractive trait. God knew, she'd heard him say that often enough. If ever there was a time to act like the cool girl she wanted to be, this was it.

'You know what you didn't tell me?' she said. 'You didn't say how long you've known about the baby.'

Kieran sat up, as though taken aback by her voice. He took a few moments to reply, and when he did, the answer was vaguer than she would have liked. 'Since earlier in the year.'

'So why didn't you talk to me before? If the story about your baby hadn't been in a newspaper, would you even have mentioned what was going on?'

'Please, Loretta, I admit I'm in the wrong here, but that's not fair. I didn't tell you because I knew it would upset you. And because you'd think there was still something between me and Dairena. And there's not. You have to believe me on that. It ended as soon as I got together with you.'

'I see.' What Loretta saw was that she was no longer unique. No longer special. She was an item on a conveyor-belt. 'Have there been other women?'

Kieran's head tilted upwards. 'That's another reason I was reluctant to tell you. You were bound to think the worst. But I swear there aren't any others. And even the fling with Dairena . . . That's all it was. A fling. If it wasn't for the baby, we wouldn't be in contact at all.' He sighed. 'Life isn't always easy. Marriage isn't always easy.'

'That's what my mother says, but she's been married for twenty years. You only got married three years ago.'

His chin dipped again. 'I'd always viewed our marriage as an arrangement with a certain amount of leeway. A certain amount of openness. I'd been under the impression that Imogen felt the same. Like I've told you before, she leads her own life.'

Loretta was sceptical. Did such arrangements exist in Dublin? For her, open marriages belonged on the pages of a Harold Robbins novel. There was, however, no sense in arguing. His marriage wasn't the issue. The issue was that another woman was having his baby.

Her initial anger had faded. What she was left with was sadness. Deep, deep sadness. She had convinced herself that she was beginning to know him. That she was with the real Kieran Mitchell, the one the others didn't get to see. Not the professional glad-hander but someone warm and passionate and thoughtful. Someone whose talent and intelligence would bring success to The Diamonds. She'd also told herself that the day would come when she would receive his undivided attention. Instead, she was part of a fragile arrangement, an arrangement that was on the verge of falling apart.

Did she love Kieran? Initially she'd been scared to say the word, even to herself. *I love being with him*, she'd think. Or *I love how he makes me feel*. Step by step, she'd been forced to acknowledge that it didn't end there. Yes, she did love him. But for all the compliments he'd given her, he'd never used the word. Until he did, she'd decided to remain quiet.

'What are you going to do?' she asked.

'Imogen has said she needs some time alone, so I've moved out. I'm renting an apartment in Ballsbridge.'

That explained the cheap hotel room. His marital home had been a gift from Imogen's father. Garret Faulkner had also subsidised their spending. For once, Kieran was having to pay his own way.

Loretta had fantasised about Kieran leaving Imogen, but none of those fantasies had contained a twist like this. Curiosity continued to tug at her. 'Will you get to see the baby?'

'I hope so, if Dairena's all right with that. And I'll pay my fair share . . . obviously.'

'Tell me about her.'

'Dairena? There's not much to tell. She's twenty-four so she's a bit older than you. She's an architect. I met her at a gig in Cork when Future Heroes were playing down that way.'

An architect. Loretta found something unsettling about the fact that this other other woman had qualifications and a career. 'Is she good-looking?'

'Ah, Loretta. Seriously. Why should that matter? As it happens, she's nice-looking. Not nearly as beautiful as you, though. Not in the same universe.' He patted the bed. 'Come over and sit beside me. Please.'

She regretted her last question. It betrayed her jealousy. Jesus, how could she be jealous of a woman who was about to become a mother with no man by her side? What sort of person was she? She hesitated, then did as Kieran asked. She was careful not to sit too close.

'Listen,' he said, 'in just over a month "Too Much Not Enough" will be released, and your lives will change. I'm not exaggerating. I've never been so certain of anything. This is dreams-come-true territory, and for the next while, that's all that should matter to you. You've got to make the most of every second of every day. And you can't allow yourself to be distracted.'

He inched along the bed towards her, then placed his hand under her chin and lifted up her face. 'You're the best thing about my life. You understand that, don't you? You're always in my thoughts, and I hate to see you upset like this.'

A familiar pulse of pleasure passed through her. She tried to fight it by moving her face away. 'It's all getting very tough.'

'I appreciate that, and I admit it's my fault. You have no idea how sorry I am for screwing things up. But if you can hang in there, everything will become more straightforward, I promise.' He stood, went around to the other side of the bed and turned on the lamp. When he sat down beside her again, he was carrying a plastic bag from Arnotts. 'This isn't the ideal way to celebrate your birthday, I know. You deserve better. But I got you this,' he said, handing over the bag.

Inside was something she'd wanted, something everyone wanted: a Walkman. Now she'd be able to listen to music wherever she went. She'd be like the girls on the Tube, headphones over their ears, nodding to a mystery beat.

Despite everything, she felt a smile spread across her face. 'That's a brilliant present. Thanks.' Then, she saw a problem. 'How will I explain it to the others?'

'Ah. I thought of that. I'll hold on to it until tomorrow and hand it over properly. I'll get a card and everything. I might even buy some wrapping paper.' He winked. 'I'll have to get something similar for the other three. When they celebrate their birthdays, I mean. We can't risk Birdy becoming suspicious.'

Loretta tried to swallow her disappointment. She didn't like the idea of the other girls receiving an equally thoughtful, and expensive, gift.

He dropped the Walkman back into the plastic bag and placed it on the bed. 'So, are we still together?'

Loretta didn't reply. She was worn out, her brain sluggish. She needed space for her head to clear.

Kieran moved closer and ran one finger down her cheek. 'I'll make it up to you. You have my word. And for fear I didn't say it, you look amazing. The red dress is perfect for you.'

'I'm sure I look anything but amazing. My face is in bits.'

'You're too hard on yourself, that's your trouble.'

She closed her eyes and felt his arms wrap around her. The contact was unexpectedly reassuring. His breath was hot against her ear, his smell impossibly attractive. Still, she wasn't convinced that this was a good idea. *Not now,* she thought. *Not now.* She attempted to pull away, but he had encircled her and moving was difficult.

'I don't know,' she said, her voice muffled. 'What if we don't do this tonight? What if I just go home?'

'Shush now,' he whispered into her hair. 'Shush. Everything's going to be all right.'

She could keep on protesting but, honestly, she didn't have the energy. Giving in was easier. Kieran pressed against her, and they fell back onto the bed, his embrace so tight it felt as if they were sinking into each other. He kissed her throat, her cheeks, her mouth. His hand reached under her dress. Loretta responded, at first tentatively and then with more enthusiasm. Bruised as she was by the day's revelations, she couldn't let go.

Chapter 17

Now, Dublin

Stacey had a growing sense that someone was playing with her. The list of suspects started with Senan O'Reilly. He'd sent another email, this time suggesting she pay a visit to Steelstown. Apart from telling her that Birdy and Yvonne had grown up in James Connolly Park and that Gail was from the neighbouring All Saints estate, his email was short on practical information.

She had decided against questioning JBT, the YouTube poster with Birdy's initials. Instead, she'd responded to Gus McNamara, the viewer who'd posted about it being time for the real story to emerge. Her reply outlined who she was and what she was doing. 'If you know anything about The Diamonds, please email me,' she'd written. Every day, she waited for an answer. So far, none had arrived.

Next, she returned to Kieran Mitchell's Wikipedia page,

specifically the 'Personal Life' section. Like Vivienne had said, his story was far from straightforward.

Personal life

Relationships

- Mitchell's first marriage to his college sweetheart, Imogen Faulkner, was dissolved in 1986. He has said that while she was a wonderful person, he had been 'too young for commitment'.[27]
- In 1988, he married his long-time partner, Dairena Lennox.[28] They had two children, Ryan Joshua Mitchell, born 1982 and Rowena Atlanta Mitchell, born 1990. Ryan Mitchell has achieved some success as a visual artist. [citation needed]
- Lennox and Mitchell divorced in 1997.[29] The following year, he married New York model Faye Godfrey. The couple have two children. Georgia Ciara Mitchell, who was born in 2000, is also a model.[30] Sebastian Patrick Mitchell, born 2003, is a student at Princeton.[31]

Given that divorce had been illegal in Ireland until the mid-1990s, Stacey wondered how Mitchell had been free to remarry in 1988. Presumably money made everything possible. Searches for Imogen Faulkner yielded little. The same was true for Dairena Lennox. Mitchell's second wife had died in 2002. She'd been forty-four, which sounded young, but Stacey couldn't find a cause of death.

Although there were multiple hits for Faye Godfrey and

Georgia Mitchell, most were of no practical value. Even at the sharpest peak of her fame, Faye had never made the top tier of supermodels. She had, however, partied with the best of them. There were photos of her with Stephanie Seymour and Naomi Campbell, with Bono and Michael Stipe, Gwyneth Paltrow and Courtney Love. She was pictured on the runway in Paris, on the beach in St Barths and, most incongruously, in a bar in west Clare. In more recent shots, Faye was with her husband. If her skirts had become slightly longer and her hair slightly shorter, she remained taut and glossy. Their daughter, Georgia, had 976,000 followers on Instagram and 1.2 million on TikTok. She had recently shot a campaign for Gucci and been interviewed by *Vanity Fair*. She'd also featured in a *Vulture* article about nepo babies.

Jacqueline Troy Brown had messaged from Rotorua. She was flattered that anyone would believe she'd been in a rock band. She hadn't. The St Patrick's Day greeting was explained by her son's marriage to a Donegal woman. Now that New Zealand Jacqueline was no longer a contender, the online hunt for Birdy had reached a dead end.

For the next twenty minutes, Stacey scrolled through gossip sites. In particular, she was distracted by a Reddit forum on the music industry. Every kind of bad behaviour was catalogued, from mainstream sleaziness to allegations of violence and abuse. One poster had even gone to the trouble of compiling a spreadsheet. While some perpetrators were named, others were given pseudonyms like 'Mr Slime', 'Teen Lover' or 'Narco Boss'. Stacey had to remind herself that while Kieran Mitchell might not be the soundest guy on the planet, he'd done nothing illegal.

She checked the time, then closed her laptop. There was somewhere else she needed to be.

*

The line stretched down the street and around the corner. There were at least sixty of them. Mostly, they were polite, but the politeness had an edge, one that said, 'We can smile and chat, but if I had to put on running spikes and trample over your dead body, I would.'

Stacey was in the middle of the queue. Ahead of her, a young couple shifted from foot to foot. A step or two behind, a man with hair like a Lego figure huffed and puffed and said it was all pointless because, in the end, the landlord would rent the flat to a relative. A woman announced that she was there for her daughter who was at work. Another woman accused her of breaking the rules. Lego-man claimed there were no rules any more. 'They abolished them,' he said. 'Did you not hear?'

Number 22 Mayberry Hall had been listed on a property website that morning. The studio apartment, which was described as 'exquisitely presented with ample bespoke storage', was one of only three currently available in Briarstown. According to the listing, viewing was between five thirty and seven. The queue had started to form at lunchtime. With every minute, it grew. Towards the back, two men were arguing about who had arrived first.

'At this rate, they'll have to bring in crowd control,' said the woman who was there for her daughter.

While Stacey waited, she tapped at her phone. Before uploading the latest edition of 'Whatever Happened To . . . ?' she needed to do some fact checks. Her next visit to the celebrity graveyard featured a former businesswoman. Cheryl Burke had organised conferences and run marketing campaigns. She'd been strong on empowerment, fulfilment and the pursuit of cash. She'd also been a frequent guest at the sort of lunches where expensively dressed women gave awards to each other. Then, a little introspection had caused her to question the superficiality of her existence. That she was deeply in debt, and that her creditors were circling like raptors, might have played a part in this disenchantment. Cheryl had packed up her wardrobe of navy shift dresses, nude heels and caramel-coloured athleisure wear and headed west. She now lived in a caravan in north Mayo.

Stacey also replied to Ronan, who'd sent a message about his mother. Her health problems were more serious than he'd thought. Stacey told him she was sorry to hear this and hoped his mam was soon on the road to recovery. Clichéd as her response was, she couldn't think what else to say. The Covid lockdowns meant she'd met Ann Egan only once.

When she got to the top of the queue, she discovered that the landlord was actually a landlady. Fiona Tansey had a sharp black bob, gleaming coral nails and a bunch of keys so large it looked as if she could open every door in Briarstown. With her la-di-da accent and tendency to exaggerate – the décor was 'stunning', the view 'delightful' – she sounded like the presenter of a TV property programme.

Although the studio showed signs of wear and tear, it was clean. While Fiona showed Stacey around, she asked rapid-fire questions about her job and her plans. When they'd finished, she placed the keys on the kitchen counter and smoothed her fingers through her hair. 'I'm going to be honest,' she said. 'I don't think this property's for you. Your work situation sounds a touch precarious. And with the way the world is at the minute, I can't afford to take a risk.'

'I've never missed a rent payment,' said Stacey, 'and I don't intend to start now. Like I told you, I'll be boosting my podcast income with public-relations work. That's what I did before the pandemic, and that's what I'll be returning to. The pod's just a side-hustle.'

'So you say, but I'm not convinced you could meet the payments on your own.'

'I can, and I'd treat the place well. You could get students in here, and it'd be parties twenty-four seven. Where would you be then?'

'Believe you me, there will be no students in this property,' said Fiona. 'This is an apartment for a professional couple.' She held up her hands. 'I know, I know. That's not what you want to hear, but it's the truth.'

'It's your decision, but are you sure there's enough room for two adults?'

The landlady gave a quick bark of laughter. 'Enough room for two? Are you having me on? There are property owners who'd have three sets of bunk beds and a cot in here. As you'll discover, that's where the market's at.' She scooped up the keys and gave them a rattle. 'Anyway, like I said, it's a no from me.'

Before Stacey could respond, Fiona was making for the door.

'If you don't mind,' she said, 'there are quite a few potential tenants outside, and I think it's best if we don't waste any more of each other's time.'

Stacey was close to tears. At this rate, she would end up like Cheryl Burke, in a caravan at the end of a boreen with only sheep for company. *Oh, please God, don't let me cry*. 'Cow,' she whispered.

Fiona Tansey must have heard because she stopped, turned around and, to Stacey's surprise, appeared slightly embarrassed. 'Look,' she said, 'I know this isn't easy, and I'm sorry if I was too blunt with you. But I've been burnt before and I can't allow it to happen again.'

'It's okay.'

Of course it wasn't okay. It was a million miles from okay. But there was no point in arguing. The woman had made her decision.

Chapter 18

The next morning Stacey uploaded the latest podcast before going to Instagram, Twitter and Facebook to let followers know where they could listen to Cheryl's story. Then she walked over to the Pear Tree for a coffee. In the hope of shutting out the chatter in her head, she put in her earbuds and found her favourite playlist.

She'd decided that, rather than reading about the sounds of the late 1970s and early 1980s, what she needed to do was listen. It would be a lie to say that all the music from those years appealed to her, but there was more than enough to compile a substantial playlist. Every time she listened, the rhythms, riffs and lyrics brought her closer to The Diamonds.

Mayberry Hall had forced her to acknowledge the seriousness of her predicament. Continuing to live on her own wouldn't be possible. The one other place she'd viewed had been wallpapered with mould, and even then, the rent had been too high. While the thought of sharing a house with strangers made her feel unwell, she didn't have a choice. She did, though, draw the line at sharing a room. That would be a humiliation too far.

Ronan's offer kept jumping into her thoughts. Was it too late to say yes? Perhaps she could make it work. Perhaps they could behave in a civilised manner until she found a long-term solution. Then she would think again. They'd split up for a reason. She needed to move on, not slither back into temptation's way.

She was knocked from her reverie by the clunk of a cup being placed in front of her.

'All right if I join you, Missus?' said Rhiannon.

Stacey lifted her head and removed her earbuds. Her neighbour appeared preoccupied. That was how everyone in Whitethorn looked these days. Their nerves were scraped raw from unanswered emails, crowded viewings and unaffordable rents. 'No bother,' she said.

'What are you listening to? Anything good?'

'"The Message" by Grandmaster Flash and the Furious Five. And, yeah, it's amazing.'

'I'll take your word for it.'

Stacey lifted her cup. 'We don't usually see you here in the morning.'

'I should be working, but I can't find the energy. Carmel and Mia have gone to the seaside. We were due to go on holiday next week, except the housing carry-on means we've had to cancel. We can't flit off to Italy when we're about to become homeless.'

'What a bummer. I'm sorry to hear that.'

'Thanks. What about you? I gather you went to see the place in Mayberry.'

'The Whitethorn bush telegraph's been busy,' said Stacey.

'One of the lads down the corridor spotted you. He had a look too. He said it was grand but out of his price range.'

'I would have taken it, only the landlady made it clear she could do better. She probably did me a favour. The only way I could have afforded it was if I didn't eat.'

'We've still got two months,' said Rhiannon, her tone less confident than her words. 'Or so I keep telling myself. If I don't make an effort to be positive, I end up in a loop of doom. And that's not fair on Mia. We don't even know if she'll be going to the same school in the autumn. What if we have to move to the other side of the city?'

'God, that's an awful thought. Poor Mia.'

'I know. We're not sure how much she understands, but she definitely knows that something's up.' Rhiannon licked the froth from her spoon. 'So I'm looking for a distraction. What are you up to? Any good celebs gone bad?'

'I could lie and say I've been hard at work but I've actually been doing some mindless gawking at the rich and famous. Oh, and listening to forty-year-old music.'

'Tell me more about the mindless gawking.'

Stacey outlined her pursuit of The Diamonds, running through their short-lived success, Kieran Mitchell's multi-layered love life, and the latest email from Senan O'Reilly. She explained how she'd become fixated on their story – and on what had happened afterwards.

'That's a cracking tale,' said Rhiannon. 'Why don't you take this Senan guy's advice and go to Steelstown?'

'Because I'm not a detective. I can't knock on doors and say, "Hi there. Do you happen to know what became of someone who lived around this way in the early 1980s? Black clothes? Plenty of hair? Handy with a guitar?" '

'But isn't there a good chance that at least one of the four went home again – and stayed? And the story's got under your skin, I can tell.'

'It has. But what if I don't find anything in Steelstown? I'll have wasted a day . . . and spent a fortune on petrol.'

'Ah, come on. It sounds like an adventure.'

'We're talking about Steelstown, not Monte Carlo.'

'Give me Steelstown any day. Here, let's get another opinion.' Rhiannon turned towards the café owner, who was wiping the next table. 'Detta, we need some advice.'

Detta, who had shoulder-length blonde-ish hair, was wearing her warm-weather uniform: bright T-shirt, cropped trousers and clumpy sandals. 'Go on,' she said. 'What is it?'

Stacey began her story. She hadn't got far when Detta's face was split by a grin.

'You don't have to tell me about The Diamonds. I remember them well. I saw them two or three times. As we used to say back then, they were fab.' She sang a snatch of 'Too Much Not Enough', prompting bemused looks from two young guys at a nearby table. 'A classic, lads,' she said. 'A stone-cold classic.'

'You don't happen—' started Stacey.

'To know what became of them? I haven't a clue. I'd love to find out, mind.'

Rhiannon clapped. 'So Stacey should go to Steelstown and track them down. Amn't I right?'

'Absolutely,' said Detta.

When the café owner had gone, the conversation returned to their search for somewhere to live. Stacey hadn't known whether to tell Rhiannon about Ronan's spare room. She decided to sound her out. 'What do you think?' she asked. 'Would it be a mistake?'

Rhiannon was slow to reply. When, finally, she spoke, her voice was hesitant. 'I wasn't sure if I should tell you this. Carmel thought not, but I said there was every chance you already knew.'

'Knew what?'

'Carmel was in town a couple of nights ago with some of her gang from the salon. She met Ronan on South William Street.'

'And?'

'He was with a woman.'

Stacey felt a flash of pain over her left eye. 'He's a free agent. There's nothing to stop him moving on.' She rubbed her eye. 'Anyway, are you positive he was *with her* with her? There are several women in his office. He could have been out with one of them.'

'Does he hold hands with the women from work?'

'Not that I'm aware of. Well, apart from the one he slept with. They might have done a bit of handholding first.'

'To be honest, I don't think Carmel got any work vibes from them.'

'I see,' said Stacey, thoughts swinging back to the week before. She'd assumed Ronan's offer was a ruse, a way of re-entering her life. She'd been wrong. Again. She reminded herself that he was entitled to hook up with other women. It just seemed too . . . too hasty. Actually, it was ridiculously hasty.

'It doesn't bother you, does it?' said Rhiannon.

'No,' she lied.

'You could take it as good news. If he's seeing someone, there's no reason why you can't move into his house.'

'Ah, Rhiannon. Think about it. Imagine me lying there, listening to my ex and his new woman having sex. Imagine the queue for the shower in the morning. It would be Cringe City.'

'Sorry. I'm an awful fool. I hadn't thought of it like that.' Rhiannon ran a finger around her cup. 'You're not regretting your decision, are you?'

Stacey put on what she hoped was her positive face. 'No. No regrets. I couldn't trust him. It wouldn't have worked out, so there was no reason to waste any more time. I mean, we bonded over a shared dislike of weddings. Maybe that should have told me something.'

'If that's what you really feel.'

'What are you driving at?' said Stacey, who was beginning to get annoyed. It was all right for Rhiannon. She'd been with Carmel for twelve years. Her first serious relationship, and she'd hit the jackpot. Did she not realise that Stacey had spent hour after hour, day after day, dwelling on all of this? It hadn't been an easy decision but it was the right one.

Rhiannon must have sensed Stacey's irritation because she raised a hand. 'What I mean is, are you one hundred per cent certain about ending things with Ronan? I always thought you were such a great match, and so did Carmel.'

'Yeah, well, so did I, but now I see things differently. I would have been settling. And, considering that he's already seeing someone else, Ronan probably feels the same.'

'I suppose, only . . .'

'Only what?'

'Okay,' said Rhiannon. 'I know I'm at risk of sounding like an old-fashioned agony aunt here, but hear me out. It's like you think everything in a relationship has to be perfect, and if there are any flaws, the best thing to do is walk away. And that's fine, if it makes you happy. But you're obviously not happy.'

'You're forgetting that Ronan cheated on me,' said Stacey.

'Yes. At the very start when you hardly knew each other. I'm not saying that was right. Of course it wasn't. But he owned up and apologised.'

'It wasn't much of an apology.'

Rhiannon sighed. 'I'm not going to argue with you, Stace. I've said what I wanted to say.'

Stacey drank the remains of her coffee. It tasted sour. She couldn't forgive Ronan. It wasn't just that he'd cheated on her. It was that he'd been so blasé about it. The knowledge of what he'd done would always simmer in the background, ready at any moment to boil over. So, yes, she'd made the right decision. The problem was, she still felt as though life had chopped her off at the knees.

Chapter 19

May 1982, London

Kieran stood with his back to the wall, addressing the four as though they were the dimmest pupils in a particularly dim class.

'This isn't the biggest show you'll ever play,' he said, 'but, believe me, it's one of the most important.'

As he spoke, one hand sliced through the air. If recent events had done anything to puncture his sense of invincibility, he hid it well.

Birdy scanned the dressing room. Yvonne appeared to be focusing on what their manager was saying. Gail was rolling a joint. Loretta was fussing with the ends of her glittery chiffon scarf.

Tonight's gig was different from any they'd played before. Not only would the staff of Supreme Records be there, a sizeable number of journalists, DJs and TV producers had been invited. Thankfully, tickets had also been given to some of The Diamonds' most enthusiastic supporters. Without them, the show was in danger of being all suits and no soul.

They were less than a week away from the release of 'Too Much Not Enough'. 'Ordinary Girl' would be on the B side. Already the band had been interviewed by several music magazines. They'd spoken about their influences and ambitions before having their photos taken in a studio with smooth white walls and harsh lights.

'Are you watching, Vera Cheevers?' Gail had said, provoking snorts of laughter from the others and a confused look from the photographer. Over the months, Vera had become the symbol of all they wanted to leave behind.

The record company was honouring its commitment and had created a buzz around the band. The pluggers were working their magic, trying to ensure that the single was on every radio playlist. 'You won't be able to escape yourselves,' Kieran had said. While Birdy would have liked to think that records succeeded on merit alone, she suspected the business was shadier than that. No one ever spoke directly to them about how the system worked. She didn't know if this was because Supreme considered them too dizzy to understand or if the company believed that some secrets were best held close.

Her thoughts snapped back to the present. Kieran was in full flow.

'The people out there this evening? They're the star makers. The men who'll decide your future. In a year's time, you can be travelling the world. You can be in the charts and on TV shows. You can be rock stars. Or you can be back in Steelstown, slumped in front of the telly and claiming the dole.' He tilted forward, like a singer reaching out to the audience. 'So, what I'm saying is, you've got to go out there and make an impression. You need to give it every fucking thing you've got. Because if you don't, there's a hundred other bands who'll be happy to take your place.'

Yvonne's eyes widened. 'Jesus, Kieran, when did you become Colonel Tom Parker?'

'All I'm doing is telling you how it is.'

Loretta gave an uneasy smile. 'We get you.'

'And with that in mind,' he said, nodding at Gail who had lit her joint, 'you should probably keep a clear head.'

She blew a stream of smoke in his direction. 'Settle down, Kieran. It's only hash. I play better when I'm relaxed.'

'Any other night you can do whatever you like. Tonight, I want you to play it safe.'

'That's not very rock 'n' roll of you.'

The two continued to spar, Kieran adopting his 'I'm the reasonable one here' tone and Gail doing what she did best: winding him up.

Birdy allowed her mind to wander again. This, people kept telling her, was the best part. The Diamonds were in the golden zone, waiting for their adventure to unfold. Every conversation focused on what they could achieve and how far they could go. But instead of enjoying the moment, she was constantly on the lookout for mistakes and failings. It was almost as if she wanted Supreme to let them down.

In her heart, she knew the real flaws were within the band. On the surface, all was perfect. They were in a rarefied place. Opportunity was all around. The truth was more complicated. Rather than bringing them together – and bringing Loretta to her senses – the revelation about Kieran's baby was prising the band apart.

'I agree we've got to talk to her,' Yvonne had said, 'but only when everything has calmed down. After the record's been released and life isn't so frantic, that's the time.'

Although Birdy disagreed, Yvonne had always been their leader, and disagreeing with her wasn't easy. Gail swung one way and then the other. She had become fascinated by the war in the Falklands, poring over every detail, her chatter filled with references to Port Stanley and Goose Green.

The four bickered about things that had once made them laugh. Gail's gig-day tapes had become darker, with multiple downbeat tracks. Joy Division were a staple, as were The Fall.

Eventually, Loretta tackled her. 'We need to dance,' she said. 'That's not dancing music.'

Gail pulled a face. 'You take over, then. I've other stuff to be doing.'

The argument dragged on until Yvonne intervened. She made a tape of songs that begged them to dance: from Candi Staton to Blondie, from Gladys Knight to Plastic Bertrand. Then she gave them a talking-to. They were under pressure because of the weight of expectation, she said. They ought to take it handy. Snapping at each other wouldn't achieve anything. *No*, Birdy wanted to reply. *If we're under pressure, it's because of Loretta and Kieran. It's because no one tells the truth any more.* The band's behaviour reminded her of being thirteen or fourteen when life was all raw nerves and perceived slights. Every incident, no matter how trivial, was a triumph or a disaster.

She waited for Loretta to say something about Kieran or for him to mention the baby. Nothing came. Of the two, he was better at masking his emotions. She was moodier, more withdrawn. There were times when she looked squashed, as though the world was pressing down on her. She would sit in the flat, chain-smoking menthol cigarettes and drinking cheap vodka. She must know about Dairena Lennox. And yet Birdy was convinced that she was still sleeping with Kieran.

When he left the dressing room, Yvonne grimaced. 'That was quite a sermon.'

'He always gets worked up when important folks are about,' said Birdy.

Gail took a final pull on her joint. 'I don't think he's ever met a powerful person he didn't like.'

At first, no one replied. The support band had taken the stage and their strident sound poured into the room.

Finally, Loretta spoke. 'That's not fair, Gail. Kieran's got a lot riding on this.'

'What do you mean?'

'I think it's kind of petty to criticise him when all he wants is for us to succeed.'

'I'm entitled to my view. Once I go out there and play my part, I doubt he gives two hoots what I think.'

'And do you have to snipe at him when we're all under so much pressure? I know it gives you a laugh, but it doesn't make life any easier for the rest of us.'

'I hate to break it to you,' said Gail, her voice cool, 'but Kieran's an adult. He should be able to handle a few jokes. And I can't see why you're so het up on his behalf. Or maybe . . .'

She stopped, as though thinking better of what she'd been about to say.

'Or maybe what?'

Gail smoothed back a lock of hair. 'Oh, you know.'

Loretta paused, as though she, too, had spotted danger ahead. 'This is daft,' she said, almost to herself. 'I'm asking you to hold back a bit, that's all.' She picked up her makeup bag and began sorting through it, an action that said, *Conversation closed.*

Birdy tingled with anger. For a few seconds, she wavered. *Not here. Not like this.* But if she didn't confront Loretta tonight, when would she get another chance? Gail had provided an opening. She had to climb through.

'He's got you under his spell, hasn't he?' she said.

A long beat of silence followed.

'I'm sorry?' replied Loretta, with an ill-at-ease laugh.

'Let it go, Bird, would you?' said Yvonne.

But she couldn't. For months, she'd pretended not to be bothered by her bandmate's double life. She'd thrown a blanket over her disquiet, her concern, her anger.

'We know, Loretta. We know about you and Kieran. And about Dairena Lennox and the baby. We know the whole story. And we've known most of it since last Christmas. Honest to God, whatever you saw in him at the start, I can't understand why you're still with him. None of us can.'

'Birdy,' snapped Yvonne, 'I asked you to cool it. This isn't the time.'

The makeup bag fell from Loretta's grasp. Eye-liners and eye-shadows went skittering across the lino. A lipstick kept rolling until Birdy stopped it with her foot.

When Loretta spoke again, there was a tremor in her voice. 'Whatever you think you know, you're wrong.'

Music thundered through the walls. Birdy found it hard to look at Loretta so focused on a fire extinguisher slightly to her left. 'I'm worried about you. We all are. Especially since we found out about the baby. We're also upset that you've been seeing Kieran behind our backs. Why didn't you tell us?'

For five, ten seconds, Loretta stayed quiet. Outside, the other band's vocalist was howling something about police brutality. When, at last, Loretta spoke, she changed tack. 'I did want to tell you but I was worried about how you'd react. I had the feeling you'd get all judgemental on me.' She shrugged. 'I guess I was right. Besides, it's none of your business.'

'Did it not occur to you that we'd find out? Dublin's not a big place. People talk. You must have heard about the baby news being in one of the Sunday papers. It's a miracle you haven't ended up in the papers yourself. And, by the way, if it affects the band, it is my business.'

'That's the problem, isn't it? You don't care about me and Kieran. All you're interested in is that fucking album. There's more to life than The Diamonds. Every hour of every day doesn't have to be about music. We're all entitled to have other lives, and I'm making the most of mine.'

Birdy was surprised by the force of Loretta's response. She'd expected something meeker, more apologetic. She would have to reply in kind. 'I've plenty going on in my life. For starters, I've got Andy, who doesn't have to dash off home to his wife or other mistress. Tell me, does Kieran have any more women stashed away?'

'Of course not.'

'And what about his wife?'

'It's a really shit marriage.'

Birdy looked directly at Loretta. Her neck and cheeks were splotched with pink. She wanted to grab her wrist and say, *Stop it. You're so much better than this. He's using you.* Instead, she said, 'Obviously, if he's sleeping around, the marriage can't be up to much.'

'Why can't you listen to me? He's not sleeping around. He's not seeing Dairena Lennox any more. And his marriage was an open arrangement.'

Gail, who'd said nothing for several minutes, threw her eyes to the ceiling. 'He told you that, and you believed him? You've got to wise up, girl. They're in Dublin, not Hollywood. He might like to think he has some type of special arrangement, but I guarantee you, he hasn't.'

A thousand thoughts ran through Birdy. She kept waiting for Yvonne to get involved, but their words were zooming across the room at such speed that intervention was almost impossible. She met Loretta's eye. 'You said his marriage *was* an open arrangement. Does that mean it no longer is? Or that he's split up with Imogen?'

'Not that it's anything to do with you, but they're taking a break.'

'And the baby?'

'A boy called Ryan. He was born last week.'

'But Kieran was here last week.'

'He had to prioritise. He'll see the baby when things are quieter over this way.'

'That sounds like classic Kieran,' said Gail. 'He'll always put the good times first.'

'No,' said Loretta, 'he's putting us first. I don't see why you have to twist everything.'

'She's not twisting anything,' said Birdy, who was taken aback to hear about Kieran and Imogen living apart. That didn't tally with what Vivienne had said about them staying together no matter what. 'She's telling it like it is.'

'That's enough,' said Yvonne, with a brisk clap of her hands. She stared at each of them in turn. 'You might not have noticed because you've been so busy yelling at each other, but the support band has finished. We'll be on in a few minutes.'

Loretta bent down and scooped up a lip gloss. 'What if I decide I'm not able to go out there tonight?'

'That'd be stupid. Whatever has happened in here, you don't want to let the band down. Or even if you do . . . you don't want to let Kieran down.'

There was a sharp rap on the door. A gruff London voice called, 'You'll have to get a move on, ladies. They're waiting for you.'

'Give us a moment, would you?' replied Gail.

Loretta continued to gather her makeup. 'I can't walk out there like nothing has happened.'

'I know it's not ideal,' said Yvonne, sending another stern look in Birdy's direction, 'but we can't do the gig without you.'

'They're getting restless,' hollered the man on the other side of the door.

Loretta straightened up again. 'All right, all right,' she shouted. 'We'll be with you in a tick.'

'Thanks,' said Yvonne, taking this as confirmation that the vocalist would join them on stage.

There were questions Birdy hadn't asked. 'Do you love him?'

Two lines appeared at the top of Yvonne's nose. 'How many times do you have to be told? We can't go through this tonight.'

'You know what?' said Loretta. 'That genuinely is none of your business.'

'What's the holdup?' roared the man, giving the door three loud knocks.

'Do you intend to keep on seeing him?' said Birdy.

This time, Loretta was less cagey. 'Yes,' she replied, 'I do.'

Chapter 20

When Loretta suggested that she might not take the stage, she hadn't meant it. She'd been lashing out to annoy Birdy. But now, standing in front of the microphone and waiting for the opening drumbeat, she wondered if she should walk away.

The stage was bathed in purple light. In front of her, the crowd shimmered, their voices fusing into a roar.

She instructed herself to forget Birdy. More than ever before, she needed to focus. She needed to act as though her entire life had been leading to this night.

If only it was that easy. Focus? She could barely breathe.

Even without Birdy's interference, tonight would have been daunting. Say what you like about Kieran, he rarely spoke to them the way he had in the dressing room. They couldn't afford to screw up.

Loretta had never felt less like performing. It was as if her clothes had been torn from her body and every single person in the room knew her secret.

Months, Birdy had said. They'd known about her seeing Kieran for months. How many times had they gossiped behind her back or waited for her to slip up? Gail and Yvonne she could forgive. Okay, Gail had been irritating, but she hadn't been the main aggressor. Yvonne had brought the haranguing to an end. Birdy was different. Her attack had been premeditated. She'd waited for the right moment to launch an ambush. And then? Then she'd been as pious as a reverend mother.

The past few weeks had been among the most difficult Loretta had known. Every time Kieran flew home, she would feel abandoned. She would fret that he'd see his son and not return. Then he'd come back to London and reassure her of their future together. Pathetic as it might sound, his praise had become more important than ever.

Her desire to turn and run intensified. What were the others doing? She looked around. There was Gail, poised, ready to begin. There was Yvonne counting them in. And there was the ring of Birdy's guitar.

It was too late.

This is what you love, she told herself. *This is why you defied your mother.*

As the sound pressed against her, she pushed herself forward. She gulped in air and sang the opening lines of 'Ordinary Girl'.

Loretta had a sense of being at one remove from the stage. No matter how hard she tried to concentrate, the questions tumbled in. What would she say to Kieran? Would the others insist on talking to him? Her thoughts topsy-turvy, she missed her cue at the beginning of 'Friday Afternoons'. Then she flubbed the lyrics of

'Shadow And Smoke', singing the first verse twice and la-la-la-ing her way through the middle eight.

At least, the audience was all right. Loretta had worried, they all had, that the guest list meant trouble. They'd pictured ranks of jaded men with 'Go on, impress me' faces. Sure, she'd spotted a few. In the main, though, the crowd was up for it. They were singing and moving like normal people.

'Brighter Than The Sun' came towards the end of their set. In the six months they'd been playing it, they'd learnt it was a guaranteed crowd-pleaser.

Row after row of pebble-dashed houses,
Dreaming of places where they say we don't belong,
Girls with skipping ropes, short hair, high heels,
The girls I know are brighter than the sun . . .

In the main, they all contributed to The Diamonds' songs, but 'Brighter Than The Sun' belonged to Birdy alone. It was about the girls of Steelstown, how brilliant they were, and how special their friendships. Tonight the lyrics stuck in Loretta's throat.

As she had countless times before, Birdy moved closer to the mic. Usually the two sang the chorus in harmony, their voices blending. But how could Loretta sing with someone who had spoken to her the way Birdy had in the dressing room?

She opened her mouth. Nothing came, not even a croak. She tried again. Nothing. The two shared a look.

You want me to fail, thought Loretta. *You want to punish me, humiliate me.*

The chorus ended. She had to sing the second verse. She gazed at the crowd, at their expectant faces, and, with every single part of her, she let fly.

Keep your head down, keep your voice low,
Tell us everything we say and feel is wrong,
But you know when we're talking, singing, dancing,
Every single one of us is brighter than the sun . . .

This time, when they reached the chorus, Loretta was ready. She filled her lungs and sang with a voice she hadn't known she possessed. Beside her, Birdy joined in. Every note was perfect. It was like a battle for territory, each challenging the other to do better. Despite their differences, their voices had never sounded more in harmony. Behind them, Gail and Yvonne were ferocious. They were as tight, as intense, as they'd ever been. Loretta imagined the walls blistering with the heat of their performance.

'Sing it,' she roared, hoping the band's passion would spread across the floor. It did. The audience became a collage of open mouths and raised hands and swinging hair. The room belonged to The Diamonds, and they knew it.

They blazed through the rest of the set. Birdy returned to the mic for 'Away From Me' and 'Too Much Not Enough'. Their encore started with a cover of 'Love Is The Drug' and ended with a scorching version of 'Harder'.

The energy in the room was immense. There was Birdy, striding across the stage. There was Gail, posing like a queen. There was Yvonne, hammering the drums like she might not get another chance. Loretta felt a tear slide down one cheek. Part of her wanted to run. Part of her wanted to stay on stage for ever. Up here, she had no problems. Up here, she just *was*.

The Diamonds tore into a second encore. As they had on the

night they'd first met Kieran, they revisited 'Too Much Not Enough'. Their final song was one of the first they'd written, 'The Fire Inside'. They left with the sound of the crowd erupting around them. They'd done it. They'd achieved what Kieran had asked of them.

In the past, they would have hugged and laughed. Instead, Loretta had an urgent need for calm. Head down, half running, half walking, she returned to the dressing room and lit a cigarette. Presently, the others joined her. Gail and Birdy avoided eye contact.

'Holy smoke,' said Gail. 'That was something else.'

Yvonne turned to Loretta. 'You looked upset out there. Are you okay?'

As she prepared an answer, the door was pushed open.

'Well done,' said Kieran, his voice strangely stilted.

Loretta mumbled her thanks, as did Yvonne.

'Weren't we class?' said Gail. 'Go on, Kieran, admit it. They were *begging* for more. We could have played the theme from *Sesame Street*, and they'd have lapped it up.'

He ignored her. 'The thing is,' he said, 'you might be able to fool the crowd, but you don't fool me. What the hell was going on?'

Chapter 21

Now, Steelstown

As she parked her car, Stacey thought of the opening lines of 'Brighter Than The Sun': *Row after row of pebble-dashed houses, Dreaming of places where they say we don't belong.* Other countries were blessed with honey-coloured stone or brightly painted clapboard. Ireland had pebble-dash, acres and acres of it swaddled around buildings in every town and city. Connolly Park was a testament to its durability.

Reluctant as she had been to make the journey, the only alternative was to abandon her search. Kieran Mitchell was out of reach. The internet had thrown up more questions than answers. Dublin's possibilities had been exhausted. And even though The Diamonds had imploded in London, trying to get the truth there would be like trying to find a rusty needle in a farm of haystacks.

It was Steelstown or bust.

Connolly Park was her first stop because, according to Senan

O'Reilly, two of the band had lived there. If she didn't make progress, she'd move on to All Saints Park. She'd emailed the mysterious Senan asking if he knew whether any of the band had returned to the town. In a predictable development, he hadn't replied.

She'd spent the previous night in Limerick with her parents, Colm and Ellen. Their house, the house where Stacey had grown up, was in a similar estate to Connolly Park. She wondered if this helped to explain her fascination with the band.

Twenty years ago, the area had thrummed with the sound of children. Nowadays, its residents were more sedate. Even when older people left, few young families could afford to buy. Stacey's mother, who shared her low opinion of WhatsApp groups, said theirs was filled with passive-aggressive messages about the perils of untidy gardens and door-to-door salesmen.

Her parents had asked about Ronan, and about her efforts to find a new flat, but hadn't done too much probing. 'Remember, there's always a spare room here,' her dad had said. Their understated kindness had landed like a jab to the stomach – and deepened Stacey's concern that she'd let them down. There they were, in their early sixties, health strong, mortgage paid off. Her dad played medium-handicap golf. Her mam was in two book clubs and did yoga three times a week. In September, they were going on a walking holiday in Croatia. They didn't need a thirty-year-old daughter getting in the way.

Stacey had been blindsided by Rhiannon's news about Ronan. Yes, she'd been the one who'd instigated the split. Yes, she'd nixed any chance of a reunion. But, and it hurt to acknowledge this, loosening their bonds wasn't easy. He was the first man she'd lived with, and because of the lockdowns, the experience had been pretty intense. He was also the first man to whom she'd said, 'I love you,' and really, truly meant it. She had been properly in love, and leaving that behind was more difficult than she'd expected.

Ronan had been there for the start of the podcast, and when it had taken off, he'd encouraged her to quit work. To be fair, he'd always cheered for her. His ability to find joy in the achievements of others was one of the many things she'd liked about him. In a world of game-players and shape-throwers, he'd seemed so wonderfully straightforward. At the moment, she couldn't imagine hooking up with anyone else. Even the thought was exhausting. Yet there he was, carrying on as though the last two years hadn't happened.

Stacey's parents were intrigued by her attempts to find The Diamonds, asking if she was Jessica Fletcher or Nancy Drew. 'I'll go for Nancy,' she'd said, 'although I don't think I'm on the trail of a murderer. At least, I hope not.'

There were a hundred and fifty houses in Connolly Park. A hundred and fifty possibilities. If any members of either the Troy or Hayes families still lived locally, they shouldn't be hard to find. Stacey approached three teenage boys who were sitting on a low wall, laughing to themselves. No, they said, they hadn't heard of either Birdy or Yvonne, but the woman in number thirty-seven gave animal-welfare advice on local radio and a guy in the next estate had been in the papers for selling cocaine. According to the boys, they were the only famous people in the area.

Reasoning that older men and women were more likely to remember The Diamonds, Stacey targeted the over-forties. Again, she had no luck. Oh, most people were polite, talkative even, but the names meant nothing.

Twenty fruitless minutes later, she was about to give up when a young guy walked over to her. He had curly copper hair and wore a Clare GAA jersey and khaki shorts.

'I overheard you there,' he said. 'Are you Stacey Nash? I listen to your podcast every week. It's great stuff.'

'Aw, thanks a million. That's fantastic to hear.' Bumping into listeners always gave Stacey a lift. With any luck, this particular listener would also provide information. 'I suppose there's no chance you've come across either the Troys or the Hayeses?'

'Afraid not. I'm only living here for the past twelve months. But I heard the mention you gave The Diamonds a couple of weeks back and I asked a few people about them.'

'Did anyone know anything?'

'Nah, they were all blow-ins too.' He shifted his weight to the other foot. 'You know who I was thinking might be able to help? You see that woman over there?' He pointed towards a middle-aged woman in a nearby front garden. 'Joan Slattery's her name. She's been living here since these houses were built. She also likes a chat, if you get my drift. If anyone knows about the girls, it'll be her.'

Stacey thanked the man, whose name was Scott Gunning, and promised to find out what had happened to a former boxer who should have made it big. Then, she made her way to the garden where Joan Slattery was deadheading roses with vigour. She explained who she was and what she was doing.

Joan, who had freckled arms and wings of wiry blonde hair, looked her over, as though seeking to find fault. 'It's hot today, isn't it?'

Stacey agreed.

'Far too hot for the likes of me,' continued Joan. 'But, as I always say to my husband, these beds won't weed themselves. I might as well be talking to the wall, mind.'

'Uh, I'm sorry to hear that.'

'Do you have a garden yourself?'

'I don't.'

'You've no idea how lucky you are.'

Stacey feared that Scott had played a trick on her, and that she was dealing with Connolly Park's resident crank. She was about to leave when Joan turned around and began marching up the path towards the open front door.

'Mike,' she shouted, 'there's a girl out here enquiring after Birdy Troy. Can you have a word with her?'

Mike Slattery sat back in his powder-blue armchair. He was a spare-framed man with clear green eyes and a thatch of pale grey hair. They were in the front room, a place so immaculate that Stacey worried her presence was making it untidy. She pictured Joan following her around, removing stray specks of dust with a mini-Hoover. After she'd outlined how her attention had been drawn to The Diamonds' story, Mike told her that he and Joan had been at school with Birdy and Gail.

'And you've been getting emails from Senan O'Reilly?' he said. 'I reckon someone's been pulling your leg.'

'Why so?'

'There was a Senan O'Reilly in Steelstown. He lived up in Pearse Park, near the health centre.' Mike's tone made it sound as though Stacey should know where this was. 'He taught Birdy to play the guitar.'

'You say "lived"?'

'He died about ten years ago. Funnily enough, the last time I saw Birdy was at his funeral.'

Stacey felt her body spring to life. 'Really?'

'It was the year with all the snow. What year was that?'

'Um . . . 2010?'

'That's when it must have been, so. I remember the ice outside the church. A fellow went flying, and the rest of us were doing our best not to laugh.'

Stacey took a drink from the glass of water Mike had given her, then placed it carefully on a coaster. She could return to Senan but, first of all, she needed to ask about Birdy. 'How was she? Did you have any problem recognising her?'

Mike gave an unexpectedly impish smile. 'God, no. I'd have known that woman anywhere. I won't say she hadn't changed. But she hadn't changed that much. It's hard to describe. It's like she's one of those women who doesn't alter. As the politicians are fond of saying, the fundamentals are sound.'

'Have you any idea what she was doing for a living?'

'Between you, me and the wall, Joan wouldn't be mad about Birdy, so I wasn't talking to her for long. She was living above in Dublin, that I do remember. And she was married with two children. When I say children, they'd be grown-up by now. Like our own crew.' He dipped his head towards a series of framed photographs. Graduations, weddings, grandchildren: they were all there.

Birdy was in Dublin. Or she had been twelve years ago. Stacey took another moment to digest the information. 'Did you get the idea that she was involved with music in any way?'

'No. To the best of my knowledge, she left all that behind years ago.'

'That's a shame. Does she have a married name or does she use Troy?'

'I can't tell you. She was just Birdy to me. Always was, always will be.'

Stacey smiled. And then it hit her. Or, perhaps, she saw how dumb she'd been. 'It's her, isn't it?'

Confusion passed across Mike's face.

'Sorry. I should have explained what I meant. I think Birdy's been using the name "Senan O'Reilly".'

'I wouldn't put it past her to play games. But why?'

'Because she wants the band to be remembered? Or because she wants to draw attention to the reasons they split up?'

'Why not use her own name? Why wouldn't she contact you and say, "I was in this band, and it didn't work out for us. I think we've got an interesting tale to tell"? She could be fairly direct, the same girl.'

At the start, Mike had given the impression that Birdy had just been a classmate. Now Stacy sensed there was more to the story.

'You knew her pretty well?'

He closed his eyes. 'I should have been more upfront with you. I went out with her.'

'Ah, I see.'

When Mike opened his eyes again, he told her that Birdy had been his first proper girlfriend. They'd begun seeing each other at school and had only broken up when The Diamonds got a manager and moved to Dublin.

'We were very young,' he said. 'Of course, I thought we were grown-up. When I look back, I can see what an eejit I was. It's mad to think she'll be sixty next month. Her birthday's the fifth of August.'

He stopped, and Stacey searched for a response. Before she'd found one, he was talking again.

'In a way, I was jealous of how much music meant to her. If I'd had any cop on, I'd have listened to what she was saying. To my shame, when the band disappeared, I was . . . not happy but . . .' Once more, he faltered. 'It felt like vindication. Like I'd been right all along. I regret that now. I'm only sorry I've never had the chance to talk to her properly. Like, Joan is the best in the world but . . .'

'. . . she wouldn't understand.'

'Yes.'

There was something almost childlike about Mike's directness, and Stacey found it touching. She also had a feeling he wasn't usually so candid.

'Hopefully,' she said, 'Birdy's still in Dublin. If – when – I track her down, maybe you'll get an opportunity to talk about those days.'

'Maybe.'

'Has she got family around here?'

'No. Neither of her parents made old bones. Oliver died in the early nineties. He can't have been much more than fifty, the poor fellow. Mary, God rest her, died about ten years later. Birdy's got one brother, Declan. He's in Chicago, as far as I know. Actually, now that I think of it, you can find him on Facebook. I've seen him on the oldies' page.'

'The oldies' page?' asked Stacey.

'Here, I'll show you.'

Mike took his phone from the coffee table, searched, then handed it to her. He'd brought up a page called 'Steelstown Memories'. The group was dedicated to photos and newspaper clippings from the seventies, eighties and nineties. Someone would post a picture of, say, a drama group or a school disco. Others would respond by tagging people they thought were in the photo or by telling brief anecdotes about those involved.

Some of the comments were funny. Under a photo of a group of teachers, a woman had written, Back row, third from left, Mr Crotty. Smoked ten Major in class every day. Best teacher ever. Others were poignant. Under a school sports-day photo, a message said, That's our Barry winning the one hundred metres. RIP bro. Gone too soon. More were sentimental. A newspaper article about a victorious football team prompted the post, Those were the days. When you could grow up on the streets without anyone thinking you were neglected. Would give anything to have them back.

Every post was soaked in nostalgia.

After a minute or two of scrolling, Stacey struck gold. A bleached Polaroid depicted two teenage girls on a tinsel-decorated stage. One gangly, the other short, they appeared to be singing. The caption read, Jackie 'Birdy' Troy and Gail McGeehan, Christmas 1976. The first comment said, Anyone familiar here, Declan Troy? He replied, The state of them!! Looks like the school Christmas Concert. I'll have to let her know.

'Wow,' said Stacey, holding the phone out so that Mike could see what had attracted her interest. 'Are there any more like this?'

'Not that I can remember, but Declan has commented on several other pictures. I'm nearly sure you can access the page yourself. You have to be a member to post anything, though.'

Stacey resisted the temptation to continue scrolling. At any moment, Joan might finish her gardening and disrupt the conversation. She suspected that Mike would be less talkative in his wife's presence. She asked if he'd seen the *Top of the Pops* video on YouTube. He hadn't, so she showed it to him. The comments might mean something. His response was as unexpected as it was fascinating.

'I'll tell you one thing,' he said, with a throaty laugh. 'Whoever's been impersonating Senan O'Reilly has also been busy on here.'

'Because they used JBT, Birdy's initials?'

'There is that, right enough. But I'm thinking about one of the other lads, the one claiming to be Gus McNamara. Gus was a neighbour of Birdy's.'

Stacey's heart quickened. 'So he should know what he's talking about?'

'If he was still with us, he would. God be good to him, Gus passed away twenty years ago. The thing is . . . he was a ferocious gossip. The man could talk for Ireland.'

'You're saying?'

Mike's laugh returned. 'I'm saying that whoever used his name knew what they were doing. Gus was a mighty man for the stories, not all of them true.'

'Right,' said Stacey, trying to gather her thoughts. 'If Birdy is pretending to be Senan O'Reilly, isn't there a chance she's also responsible for the YouTube comments? Or for some of them, at any rate?'

'There is. Only the more I think about it, if someone is playing games with you, Birdy isn't the most likely candidate.'

'No?'

'When we were at school, Gail was famous for her pranks. This is like something she'd do.'

'People have told me she was great fun.'

'She was that, all right. And, as we've discovered, she's not short of brains either.'

'What do you mean?' said Stacey.

Mike's brow crinkled. 'Do you not know about Gail? I would have mentioned her at the start, only I assumed you'd have heard.'

'Heard what?'

'Ah, here,' said Mike, 'wait until I tell you about Gail.'

Chapter 22

Listening to Mike talk about Gail, there were two things Stacey could say for sure: one, if she learnt nothing else in Steelstown, the trip had been worthwhile, and, two, she would never make a detective.

'What you've got to remember,' he said, eyes glittering with amusement, 'is that when we were at school, Gail was pure wild. Honest to God, there wasn't a trick she didn't have. And that was when she turned up. Half the time she was behind the handball alley, smoking cigarettes, or in someone's house listening to music. She was *obsessed* with music. All the girls were.'

'Did she ever show any enthusiasm for books or studying?'

'If you'd asked me, I'd have said no. Other people have different memories. They say she was always interested in the news and in what was happening around her. I don't want to give the impression that I thought she was thick, but folks tended to judge her by her family. I doubt the other McGeehans have a

Leaving Cert between them, so we all took it for granted that school wasn't for Gail. Her turning out to be an intellectual caused quite a stir.'

Mike said 'intellectual' in the way that others might say 'Martian' or 'cyborg'.

Stacey drank the last of her water. 'When did you hear about her going to college?'

'I didn't see her after The Diamonds broke up. It was ages before I came across any of them, Birdy included. I remember bumping into Gail's sister, Donna, one night. Joan and I weren't long married, so we're probably talking about 1984 or '85. I enquired after Gail, and Donna laughed. "Did you hear she's going to university," she said. "In London, no less. The Brits are after giving her a scholarship. Isn't that priceless?"'

'What happened next, do you know?'

'As I understand it, Gail did her doctorate in London too. That was where she met an American fellow. Leon Davis, his name is. At some point in the nineties, they moved to the States. If you pick up your phone there and look for "Gail Davis, University of Massachusetts", you won't be long in finding her.'

Stacey followed his advice. As she did, she noticed a message from Ronan. Perhaps he wanted to tell her about his new girlfriend. He would have to wait.

Within seconds, she was staring at one of the women she'd been searching for:

UMass, Boston.
Gail M. Davis, Professor of Political Science, College of Liberal Arts
Areas of Expertise: Contemporary Political Theory, Political Behaviour, Welfare Policy

The accompanying photo showed a woman with spirals of dark hair and a broad smile. She was wearing a red jacket and hoop earrings. If you squinted, she was just about recognisable as the teenager who'd been in a rock band and had lived for partying and pranks.

While Stacey read about Gail's achievements, she contemplated telling Mike the truth. Dare she confess that she'd seen The Diamonds' bass player on Twitter but had moved on? That she'd decided an outspoken girl from Steelstown couldn't have morphed into an American academic? The thought that she could have contacted Gail weeks ago made her dizzy. *Damn damn damn.* What an idiot she'd been. More than that, she'd been a snob.

Feeling ashamed, she kept her blunder to herself.

Beside her, Mike looked like a man who'd pulled an entire warren of rabbits from his hat. 'And that,' he said, 'is what happened to Gail McGeehan. Isn't it gas?'

'It surely is. Have you met her lately?'

'No. It must be fifteen years or more since I last saw her. I'll say this for her, she was the same old Gail. She was enquiring after half of our year at school. She hadn't lost her accent either. I said something polite about how successful she'd been, and she said it was okay to be surprised because she was too. I love how well she's done. It goes to show you never know what people are capable of.'

Mike veered off on a tangent about unlikely success stories. Stacey suppressed the urge to hurry him along. The podcast had taught her that you had to give people time to tell their own story in their own way.

Eventually, she found an opening to ask about Yvonne.

'I liked her,' he said, 'but I can't say that I kept in touch with what she was doing. She was two years ahead of us at school. In those days, the place was coming down with youngsters. So unless someone was in your year or lived in the same row of houses, you mightn't see much of them. She has a brother knocking around somewhere, but I think both of her parents are dead.'

'Which brings us,' said Stacey, 'to Loretta Saunders.'

'Ah, the lovely Loretta.' He paused, allowing his wife's voice to sail in from outside. Thankfully, Joan had found someone to talk to. Because of Loretta's relationship with Kieran Mitchell, Stacey was especially keen to hear more about The Diamonds' vocalist. She couldn't shake the suspicion that Loretta was central to the band's split.

Mike picked a thread from the hem of his navy shorts. 'The first thing I should say is that Loretta was always a bit of a mystery to me. She went to another school, for a start.'

'Did that matter?'

'It did. The girls who went to the convent were seen as a step above the girls in the community school. And, listen, I know that was wrong but it was how things were. Then again, even if people didn't know Loretta personally, everyone knew who she was.'

'Because of how she looked?'

'Mmm. Growing up in a town like this, three groups stood out: the troublemakers, the people who were obviously crazy, and the beautiful ones. Everyone knew their names. Everyone looked out for them. The rest of us were making up the numbers.' Mike smiled a wistful sort of smile. 'Anyway, even after she was in the band with Birdy, I can't say that I ever became friendly with her. It was like she held herself apart. But here's the mad thing: I hadn't seen her in years . . . and then, three or four days ago, I spotted her.'

'Are you certain it was her?'

'A hundred per cent. She was walking near her mother's house. She's changed, but haven't we all?'

'When you say she's changed, in what way?'

'Well, you'd never guess she'd been a rock star in her youth. Mind you, I always say that most people have lived bigger lives than you think. You can meet a fellow and think he hasn't much to say. Then you ask the right question, and away he goes.'

'And how did Loretta seem?'

'I wasn't speaking to her. I nodded in her direction, and she nodded back. She looked weary, as though everything was an effort. I've an idea that life hasn't been too kind to her.'

'Are her parents still in Steelstown?' asked Stacey.

'Her father's dead these last ten years or more. But the mother? You couldn't kill her. She's a notorious snob. Local gossip has it that Loretta's husband wouldn't have been the mother's first choice. I get the feeling they don't see a lot of each other. To be honest with you, if Patrice was my mother, I'd give her a wide berth too.'

Stacey needed to get Patrice Saunders' address. Before she did, there was something else she wanted to ask.

'You said that after The Diamonds broke up, it was quite a while before you saw any of them again. Did they ever say anything about why they'd gone their separate ways?'

'Realistically, the only one I could have asked was Birdy. I did try, but I got the sense that whatever had gone on, she'd closed it off and moved on.'

For the first time, Stacey was disappointed. Given everything Mike knew, she'd been banking on him having some insight into the split. It was interesting to hear that Birdy hadn't been keen to discuss The Diamonds. She'd have thought that being in a band, and having a hit single, would have supplied a lifetime of tales.

'At the time,' continued Mike, 'I was surprised by her reluctance to talk. That wasn't Birdy's way. Don't get me wrong, she wasn't a "me, me, me" person, but she'd always been honest. Still, if someone doesn't want to speak about something, what can you do?'

'Nothing,' said Stacey.

That was another lesson the podcast had taught her. While the occasional person got a kick from playing hard to get, if someone said no, they usually meant it. All the wheedling in the world wouldn't change their mind.

She was also beginning to understand that, despite nearly forty years of marriage, Mike had never stopped caring about his first girlfriend. Was this, she wondered, another case of flawed nostalgia? Or was it how memory worked? Was there always a period in your life that lodged in your brain? A time you returned to because it seemed central to everything that happened afterwards?

'What do you think yourself?' he said. 'Has anyone said anything to you about what happened?'

She considered opening up about Loretta and Kieran Mitchell. But until she heard directly from Loretta, she didn't feel it was her tale to tell. Instead she gave a lame answer. 'They must have fallen out over something. I wish I knew what.'

'Ah, no. That wouldn't have been enough. Getting to where they were? For kids from around here, that was like travelling to the moon. If it was no more than an argument, they'd have sorted it out. They weren't stupid.'

'What do you think went on, then?'

For a few moments, Mike stayed quiet. The only sound came from the ticking of the carriage clock on the mantelpiece.

'I've always believed,' he said, 'that something really poisonous must have happened in London. Otherwise Birdy would never have allowed that band to fall apart.'

Chapter 23

May 1982, London

The bar would not have been Birdy's choice. It was bright and filled with self-consciously glamorous people when what she wanted was somewhere dark. Somewhere they could drink without having to put on a show or pretend to be something they weren't.

The music was wrong too: all plinkity-plonk pop when she yearned for driving guitars and raw vocals. Now that she thought of it, she'd like a night in Steelstown, three hours in Shaker's disco with the boys banging their heads to 'Highway To Hell', the girls waving their arms to 'Kids In America', and sweat running down the walls. In Shaker's, anyone in a biker jacket actually rode a bike and anyone in work boots did physical work.

The venue had been chosen by Kieran, who'd insisted they come here to mingle with people who mattered, many of whom had been at their gig.

Despite their successful show, he'd stood in front of them in the dressing room like a headmaster who'd discovered his star pupils sharing a bag of glue behind the science block.

'At one point, I thought you were all going to lose it,' he'd said. 'And then at the end, Loretta was crying like a kid. What's the story?'

To begin with, none of them had given a proper answer. In halting sentences, Yvonne had spoken about a 'bit of a row'. Gail had been unusually quiet, while Loretta had said nothing at all. It was as if telling the truth would mean crossing into a different territory, one they weren't yet ready for.

The adrenaline surge of performing made Birdy more reckless, and tonight the feeling was especially strong. Even though she always claimed that fame wasn't the point, there was something intoxicating about the approval of a crowd. She'd been compelled to cut through the nonsense.

'Listen,' she'd said, interrupting Kieran, 'you might as well know what we were talking about before we went on stage.'

If she'd anticipated a firecracker reaction, she'd been wrong. He'd listened without comment or expression. Then he'd looked at Loretta and asked if what Birdy had said was true.

'Yes,' she replied.

'You pick your moments,' he said to Birdy, voice still measured. 'The one night I ask you to make a special effort, and you do your best to sabotage the band.'

'I didn't want to sabotage anything. The way things were, I don't think it was fair on any of us.'

'And ambushing Loretta before an important gig was fair, I suppose?'

Yvonne butted in, pointing out that they had people to meet and couldn't hang around in the dressing room all night.

Fast forward half an hour, and here they were, drinking vodka tonics, chatting to journalists and record executives and pretending that all was right in their small world. A close observer would have spotted the cracks. They would have seen how Loretta turned her back to Birdy, how Yvonne appeared distracted, how Gail was trying too hard to entertain. But there was no close observation. Apart from The Diamonds, the group was exclusively male. They told filthy jokes, bragged about people they'd met and swapped insider gossip: who was secretly gay? Who was having sex with a fourteen-year-old? Who couldn't stay away from heroin? The men had all the answers.

Birdy knew there would be a reckoning for the way she'd confronted Loretta. Right now, she didn't care. She would handle Kieran later.

After two or three drinks, Gail signalled to her and they escaped to the toilets. While Gail smoked a joint, Birdy reapplied her makeup: black eye-liner, peach blusher and burgundy lipstick. Then she hoisted herself up beside the washbasins and let her legs dangle. Gail sat on a closed toilet seat. Apart from a thin silver belt, she was dressed entirely in black. They all were. These days, even without trying, they were managing to coordinate. Kieran should be proud of his work.

'Be-you-ti-ful,' said Gail, admiring Birdy's makeup. 'Like a real pop star.'

'That might be stretching it, but I'm presentable.'

'How are you doing?'

'To be honest with you, I'm all over the shop. I mean, I don't regret telling Loretta what we knew. And she can't have been shocked that we'd found out. But I'm wondering if I should have been gentler.'

As the minutes passed, Birdy's feelings swung back and forth. She hadn't wanted to make Loretta cry. Had she screwed up?

A woman wearing a zebra print dress and magenta ankle boots tottered in. She looked at them with questioning eyebrows. 'All right, girls?'

'Just putting the world to rights,' said Birdy.

'Take my advice, darling. If it's about a bloke, he's not worth it.'

'I like your boots,' said Gail.

When the woman had gone, leaving a trail of Opium in her wake, Gail and Birdy resumed their post-mortem.

'I wouldn't worry about Loretta,' said Gail. 'There was never going to be a good time to tackle her. If she thought this day wasn't going to come, she was kidding herself. I assume Kieran's pissed off because we know all about Dairena Lennox and baby Ryan.'

'I'll have to talk to her. Not to apologise or anything . . . but to let her know that when I said we were worried about her, I meant it. Oh, and no doubt I'll get an almighty earbashing from Kieran.'

Gail tipped her head to one side and launched into her well-practised Kieran impression. She always made him sound like Bob Geldof. 'You look at Loretta, right? You're looking at someone who could be on the cover of *Smash Hits*. No, fuck it, she could be on the cover of *Vogue*. But the rest of you? You'd be lucky to make the back page of the *Farmers Journal*.'

Birdy laughed. 'Will they be more open with us now, do you reckon?'

'I don't know. I'd figured that after you'd spoken to him in the dressing room, he might be more tactile with Loretta. Like, I didn't reckon he'd be slobbering all over her or anything, but I did think he'd be less uptight. Watching him out in the bar, though, it's like nothing has changed. You'd swear he barely knew her.'

'I noticed that. Perhaps it'll all take a while to get used to.'

Gail stood up. 'We'd better go back outside, or he'll come looking for us. No Andy tonight?'

'He's got to work. They're pulling a late one with some new band, so I'm all on my own.'

'Come on so. I don't know about you, but I'm planning on getting wasted.'

At the end of the night, Kieran peeled away from the crowd and approached Birdy.

'We need to talk.'

Here we go. 'Do you mean tonight?'

'Yeah, only the bar will be closing soon. We'll have to go elsewhere.'

A small part of her worried that she was too tired – and too drunk – for this conversation. But she'd have to face him some time. Best to get it over with. 'Will we go back to the flat?'

'The hotel's closer, and we can get another drink.'

'The hotel it is, then.'

She would have liked some support, but Yvonne had already left with her boyfriend, Sam, while Gail was wrapped around a music writer with a lopsided haircut and a fringed suede jacket. The last time Birdy had looked in her direction, Gail had responded with a thumbs-up and a grin. She wouldn't be home tonight.

Birdy had presumed that Loretta and Kieran would leave together. After all, the need for secrecy was gone. She'd been surprised when, half an hour earlier, Loretta had announced that she was getting a cab home.

Outside, the night was unexpectedly cold. Birdy pulled her jacket around her and took small, careful steps. It was important that she appear sober and responsible. How often had she pictured this scene? How many times had she rehearsed what she'd like to say to Kieran? Now that she had the opportunity, many of her lines had flown.

Around them, late-night London flickered and glowed. Drunken voices, all pointless aggression and dim-witted hysteria, crashed through the air. She heard the purr and squeal of a black cab, the singsong of a police siren, the thump of a door being closed. Kieran told a meandering anecdote about one of the men in the bar, something about how he'd had the opportunity to sign Dire Straits but had missed out.

Birdy had assumed the promised drink would be in the hotel bar. These places served all night, didn't they? When the two arrived, they found it had closed early.

'No problem,' said Kieran. 'We can go up to the room. Don't worry, it's tidy.'

She smiled. What else could she do? 'Grand so.'

His room was shabbier than she'd expected. The carpet had bare patches, and there was a smell of disinfectant. A standard lamp with a frayed lemon shade threw shadows across the magnolia walls. What the place lacked in luxury, it made up for in space. There were two beds, one double, one single, with polyester bedspreads in a green and yellow floral pattern.

After he'd poured two drinks from the minibar – a neat brandy for him, another vodka tonic for her – he sat in one of the two hard-backed chairs. Birdy, her tiredness growing, would have liked to stretch out on one of the beds. That wasn't an option, so she took the other chair.

When Kieran began speaking, he left his genial act behind and reverted to his 'more in sorrow than in anger' tone. His face changed too, becoming harder with a hint of tetchiness. Birdy was familiar with this look. Usually, it was reserved for promoters and journalists he reckoned had let him down. For the hundredth time, she wondered what Loretta saw in him.

'I don't intend to go on and on about this,' he said, swirling the brandy around his glass. 'And I don't intend to discuss my private life with you. But we've got to talk about tonight. Believe me, it's not easy to get the entire industry to turn out for a bunch of unknown girls from the arse end of nowhere. But I pulled it off. And what did you do? You decided to throw a grenade into the works. The whole thing could have been a catastrophe.'

'It's a shame you feel that way,' said Birdy, fighting to keep the irritation from her voice. 'If you ask me, we were the best we've ever been. We lit the place up. You must have seen that.'

'I congratulated you in the dressing room.' He stopped to take a drink. 'Do you have any idea how many demo tapes I get in an average week? A bin bag full, that's how many.'

Birdy didn't like the direction this was taking. 'Maybe you should try to see it from my perspective. It's been really frustrating to know that you and Loretta were in some sort of relationship but chose to keep it hidden from the rest of us.'

'We did what we felt was right.'

The argument continued, their language gradually ramping up, until Kieran's words were like machine-gun fire. Quick. Lethal. She had 'crossed a line'. She wasn't the band's 'moral guardian'. He didn't ask who she was screwing. When she'd told a journalist about one of The Diamonds leading a double life, she'd been playing a 'low game'.

Drunk as she was, it struck Birdy that he was too defensive. He knew he was in the wrong but was determined not to admit it. Throughout, his accusations had a not-so-subtle message: she was guilty of ingratitude.

'I'm not going down the "You'd be nothing without me" route,' he said, although that was precisely what he was doing. 'This is real life, not a Human League song. But it wouldn't do you any harm to reflect on what I've achieved for you.'

Birdy took another gulp of her vodka, her second drink in the hotel. Or was it her third? The alcohol had stopped being enjoyable. She was drinking as a reflex action and had moved from that place where she was pleasantly blurred to one where she was wary of standing up.

She tipped the glass back too far and the vodka dribbled down her chin. 'I'm aware of what you've done. And I must have thanked you a thousand times.'

Kieran started speaking again, his voice fading in and out, like a radio not quite on the station. Wilting with tiredness, Birdy couldn't take any more. Their conversation had degenerated into two separate speeches. She didn't want to get dragged into the quicksand of his personal life. What mattered was the band. What mattered was music. She hoped she'd made that clear.

She shut her eyes. The room was spinning, and she had to put a stop to it. When she opened them again, Kieran was studying her.

'What?' she said.

He smirked. 'The inscrutable Birdy Troy. You know, in your own way, you're an attractive woman. When the band takes off, you'll build up quite a following. Girls with electric guitars always appeal to men.'

'Uh, thanks,' she replied, her tongue feeling too large for her mouth. She wasn't altogether comfortable with his remark, but a compliment felt better than another lecture.

'Are you all right?' he said.

'Uh-huh.' The room was spinning again. 'The day has caught up with me. That's all.'

'From here on in, every day is going to be a long one. You understand that, don't you?'

'Could I get a glass of water?'

When Kieran went to the bathroom to fetch some water, Birdy angled her head to catch her reflection in the dressing-table mirror. There were two of her. Neither Birdy looked as rough as she'd feared. Her hair was a mess, but that was nothing new.

The water was tepid and tasted of chlorine. Up until this, she hadn't worried about being sick. Now she feared it was a possibility. What she needed was sleep. Half an hour would do. Then, when she was feeling better, she could call a taxi and go back to Shepherd's Bush.

Kieran was examining her again. He could probably tell she was in danger of throwing up in his hotel room.

He took her arm. 'Come on, you need some rest. You can stay here.'

Although her head was swimming, Birdy wasn't certain that this was wise. 'For a little while just. I'll take the small bed. And I'll be gone before you know it.'

'You should take off your boots. And your jeans.' She must have looked unconvinced because he quickly added, 'Now, Birdy, don't be unreasonable.'

''Kay,' she heard herself say. 'But only for a small while.'

Her words were muddy and indistinct, and she didn't know if she was making sense. What she did realise was that Kieran was also very drunk.

Sleep came quickly. At some point, she woke up and told herself to get out of bed and go home. Before she had time to think of the practicalities, sleep had claimed her again.

The next time she woke was different. It took her a few moments to work out why. Lying on her side, she surveyed part of the room.

Save for a square of golden light beside the door, everything was the same fuzzy black.

What had changed was that she was no longer alone in the bed.

She heard him first, the heavy, jagged sound of his breath. Then she felt him. He was rubbing against her back, one hand on her thigh. Finally, she smelt the stale mix of sweat and alcohol. She went to say something, to say stop, but her face was squashed against the pillow.

Did he know she was awake? She wasn't sure. His hand had moved and was trying to peel down her underwear.

At last, she managed to speak. 'No, Kieran, this isn't . . .'

Without warning, he flipped her over. His face was scraping against hers, his voice in her ear.

'Sssh,' he said, 'and we can both enjoy this.'

Birdy was frightened, agitated, but moving was impossible. Kieran was much heavier than her and he was in control. She tried to press her legs together. Her effort was feeble. With one hand, he prised them apart again.

'That's better,' he said, his voice no more than a rasp.

Once more, Birdy attempted to speak. The right sounds wouldn't come. It was as if she was paralysed, her mouth too numb to form the words. At the same time, every cell in her body was screaming that this was not what she wanted.

Chapter 24

Night was falling, light draining from the bedroom. Birdy lay on her back and listened to the others move around. She heard Gail's gurgling laugh, Yvonne clattering about in the kitchen, Loretta singing along to a record. Normal sounds on a normal evening in a normal flat.

She'd crept out of the hotel while Kieran slept. Or while he appeared to sleep. She had a sense that he'd watched her leave.

Yvonne had met her at their front door.

'You look like you've been dug up,' she'd said. 'What's the story?'

Birdy had mumbled her answer. 'It got late, so I crashed in Kieran's hotel.'

'How was the showdown?'

'Not great. I'll tell you about it later.' *Hold it together. Hold it together.* 'Is Loretta here?'

'You're in luck. She's gone over to Hammersmith to get her hair streaked. Important days ahead and all of that. I was talking to her earlier. She didn't mention Kieran. You'd swear no one had said anything last night, and that we were all one happy family. Mad, huh?'

'Yeah, mad.' *Hold it together.* 'And Gail?'

'Not back yet. She's a dirty stop-out, like you.'

Birdy felt her face slacken, and Yvonne added, 'Well, obviously not at all like you. I assume she's actually having a good time.'

'Ahm, okay. I'm going to bed for a while. I'll see you later.'

Ten hours on, that was where she remained, running the previous night's events around her head.

She had told herself that when she was in her own bed she could cry. Tears wouldn't come. Neither could she sleep. Every time she was about to drop off, something – fear, she supposed – shook her awake again. This, she knew, was ridiculous. She was safe here. No one, Kieran included, could force their way into her bed.

Had that really happened?

Yes. Yes, it had.

Even if Birdy couldn't remember every detail, the stinging between her legs and the ache in her thighs were reminders of what he'd done.

Hours passed before she was capable of asking herself the most basic question. The event. The incident. The assault. Had that been rape?

Birdy wasn't stupid. She knew that rape wasn't just carried out by hooded strangers who lunged at women in alleyways, held a knife to their throat and left them for dead. Not all rapists were the Yorkshire Ripper. Then again, if she hadn't got drunk, if she hadn't gone to his room, if she hadn't passed out, would she be in this position?

Growing up, they'd all been warned about their behaviour. There were men who couldn't help themselves, and no good would come of placing temptation in their way. Don't give them the wrong idea. Don't put yourself in a dangerous situation.

Was that what Birdy had done?

Tomorrow, the carousel of meetings, interviews and performances would start up again. What would she do then? What would she say to Kieran? To Loretta? How would she tell Yvonne and Gail? Could she tell them? Suppose she did, how would they react?

Birdy wished she had a visible injury. She longed for a split lip, a broken wrist, a gash to the head. Then she'd be allowed to take time off.

For two things, she was grateful. Even though it was barely wider than a corridor, she had a room of her own. She could hide in here. She was thankful, too, that this was England, not Ireland. When she'd started seeing Andy, she'd got a prescription for the pill. To find yourself pregnant after sex you hadn't wanted must be grim beyond words.

Jesus. Andy. He couldn't find out about last night. Of that much, Birdy was sure.

It was fully dark now, the only light coming from the lamps on the street. Birdy turned to face the wall. Absentmindedly, she picked at the woodchip wallpaper. She prised away one chip. Then another. And another.

There was a knock on the door, followed immediately by Gail's voice: 'Are you alive?'

'What is it?'

The door opened. Birdy twisted around. Gail was in silhouette against the hall's dirty yellow light.

'Andy's on the phone for you.'

Not now. 'Can you tell him I'll give him a shout in the morning?'

'I can . . . but are you all right? You haven't stirred all day. It's not like you.'

Hold it together. 'I'll be fine.'

'Will I tell him you had a bad pint?' asked Gail, voice coated with laughter.

Birdy attempted a smile. 'Yeah. Tell him that, will you?'

Graham Baxter always reminded Birdy of a priest. His hair was marbled with grey and he wore a black jacket with a light blue shirt. She could picture him producing a set of rosary beads and recommending a quick decade. He also had a degree in classics from Cambridge and a passion for steam-powered trains. It was difficult to imagine anyone less rock 'n' roll.

An outsider would never guess that he was the boss of Supreme Records. Neither would they know that he was familiar with every dive bar and dilapidated venue in Britain and Ireland, that his nickname, 'Whizzer', stemmed from his one-time fondness for amphetamines, and that as a former tour manager, he had witnessed wild and wanton behaviour on four continents.

Sometimes, he treated The Diamonds like a novelty act. He would claim not to understand their accents or expressions. 'An interpreter,' he'd say. 'That's what you lot need.' He was also massively supportive and, so far, he'd kept every promise. Birdy liked him a lot.

Along with their manager, The Diamonds were in Graham's office in Notting Hill to discuss plans for the release of 'Too Much Not Enough', now only five days away. It was the first time in twenty-four hours that Birdy had seen Kieran. She tried to push Tuesday night to the back of her mind. If she was careful, she didn't have to look at him, much less engage with him. But the office was small, and he kept directing questions at her. It was as if he was taunting her.

After a restless night, she'd got up early and run a scalding-hot bath. She'd thrown in several capfuls from a bottle of Dettol left behind by a previous tenant. Even if disinfecting herself didn't serve any practical purpose, she'd reckoned it would make her feel better. She'd watched as the amber liquid made contact with the water and turned white. Then, she'd sat in the bath until her skin had shrivelled, her nails had softened and Yvonne had threatened to kick the door down. On the Tube, Gail had asked why she smelt like a hospital.

What had happened between the band went unmentioned. Birdy had a hunch that Loretta wasn't speaking to her but, honestly, there was so much else on her mind that she couldn't find the space to care.

The office was decorated with gold discs, framed band photographs and album covers. Many included small notes of thanks: *To Whizzer, the only man who believed in us* or *Cheers, Whizzer, you old bollocks*. If the room had been designed to impress, it worked.

Cuttings from that week's music press were strewn across Graham's desk. The Diamonds were everywhere. He went through the reviews and interviews, his clipped voice sounding like he was bringing them an update from the Falklands.

'Too Much Not Enough' was Single of the Week in the *NME*. According to the reviewer, it was 'pure adrenaline' and would be sung by 'every girl who'd had enough of being messed around'.

Single of the Week. In the *New Musical Express*.

'Put that in your pipe and smoke it, Vera Cheevers,' said Gail, clapping with delight.

Taste this, Birdy said to herself. *Savour every single word.*

In *Sounds,* the record was described as 'three minutes and twenty-two seconds of teenage perfection', while *Smash Hits* called it 'confident, melodic, right on the button'. In Dublin, there was a rave write-up in *Hot Press*. 'It's impossible to imagine,' read Graham, 'that only a year ago, The Diamonds were unknown. Now they're poised for the big-time, and their blistering, provocative debut doesn't disappoint.'

Birdy should have been ecstatic. Instead she was having trouble feeling anything at all. She was overly conscious of Kieran's presence. No matter that he was on the other side of the room, it was as if he was breathing in her face.

Graham was first to notice. 'You're quiet today, Birdy,' he said, his voice suggesting he was irritated by her muted response. 'Is something wrong?'

'She's waiting for you to get to the *Clare Champion*,' said Gail.

'She wants to be in the Steelstown notes,' added Yvonne.

'Between a notice about the Tidy Towns committee and news of a priest home from the missions. Then she'll know we've made it.'

'Where's that interpreter when I need him?' said Graham.

Birdy realised that she was expected to say something. 'Everything's good. Cheers, Whizzer.'

On and on, the good news went. Their single had made it to the Radio 1 playlist. Mike Read, Peter Powell and all the rest would be playing The Diamonds. Back home, the record was already on every show on Radio 2. One DJ, the great Larry Gogan, had called it the best Irish debut in years. When Yvonne heard this, she punched the air.

Opportunities were rolling in. John Peel wanted The Diamonds to do a session. There had also been an approach from *The Old Grey Whistle Test*. And how did they feel about going back to Dublin for a day or two? They could be on *The Late Late Show* before it wrapped for the season. Then there was the international interest. Supreme were fielding queries from the Netherlands, Germany, the United States and Japan.

'Will we get to travel to any of these places?' asked Loretta.

'That's the plan,' said Kieran.

'Yes,' said Gail. 'Yes, to it all.'

Birdy examined her hands. Not looking at Kieran, not talking to him, wasn't working. She was lightheaded. Nauseous.

Finally, the pressure became too much. 'I'm sorry,' she said, rising from her chair so quickly that it toppled and fell backwards. 'I need some air.'

In the toilets, she splashed cold water on her face. She couldn't believe how normal she looked. It was as if nothing bad had happened. She expected Gail or Yvonne to come looking for her, but they didn't. She leant back against the wall and told herself that she could get through this.

When she left, Kieran was in the corridor, waiting for her. She flinched. If he noticed, he didn't say.

'Yes?' she said, praying he wouldn't hear the panic in her voice.

'The others are worried about you dashing from the room like that. It was . . . um . . . unsettling for them, especially when everyone's hyped up anyway.'

Birdy's eyes didn't leave the grey carpet tiles. *Hold it together*. 'I'm grand. I'm coming back now.'

A brittle silence hung around them. She could smell the Dettol on her skin and wondered if he could too.

'Okay.' Kieran cleared his throat. 'Oh, and as we're here. About the other night . . . You were drunk. I was drunk. Things got kind of messy. It's best if we don't dwell on it. Agreed?'

Birdy didn't want to have this conversation here, in the corridor, with other people scuttling about, and the band only metres away. 'What are you saying?'

'You know what I'm saying. We work together. Everything's flying. Let's not allow one drunken night to damage the band.

Because that's what will happen if you overreact. You saw how thrilled the other girls are. You don't want to ruin this for them, do you?'

He put a hand on her arm, causing her to jerk away as though his fingers were radioactive rods.

'Don't touch me.'

'You've got to calm down,' he said, his voice hitting her face like a fistful of nails. 'Or you'll give people the wrong idea.' She didn't reply, so he continued, 'You saw what the press are saying. You've got Single of the Week in the *NME*, for God's sake. This should be the best day of your life.'

'But—'

'And, like you always tell us, it's all about the music. Isn't that right?'

Birdy needed to escape. A trickle of sweat ran down her spine. If she argued, she would be trapped.

'Yes,' she heard herself say. 'Yes, that's right.'

Throughout the day, Birdy spun between wanting to talk about Tuesday night and wanting to hide. Although her body was exhausted, her mind was on fire, thoughts thrashing about. One thought won through: for months, she'd complained about a lack of honesty. That was the charge she'd thrown at Loretta. Keeping a secret from the others would be a mistake. She was also furious at the way Kieran had downplayed what he'd done. Did he really believe what he'd said in the corridor? Did he really think that everything could be blamed on alcohol?

In the early evening, she gathered her bandmates together. Outside, the sun was obscured by gauzy cloud. Warm air drifted through the sitting-room window.

She sat in one of their low-slung mustard-coloured armchairs and went through what had happened in Kieran's hotel room. Occasionally, she peered up to see Gail sucking on her cigarette or Yvonne playing with a rip in her jeans. Loretta was motionless. Tension filled the room to its corners.

Birdy had worried that she would ramble. Somehow, she managed to keep her story concise. If anything, it was too brief because when she stopped they began asking questions. Some of their queries suggested they hadn't understood what she'd told them.

'Just so as we're fully clear,' said Gail, 'you woke up to find Kieran in your bed . . . and he insisted that you have sex with him?'

'Yes.'

'And you told him it wasn't what you wanted?'

'I tried,' said Birdy, acid collecting in her mouth.

'But he kept going?'

'Yes.'

'Christ,' said Yvonne. 'No wonder you came home looking rough. Why didn't you tell us about this yesterday?'

'Because I didn't have the right words. I thought that if I slept I'd wake up feeling differently. I know that's mad, but my head was all over the place.'

The tears were beginning to flow, and Birdy placed her fingers under her eyes to prevent her mascara from running. Irrational as it might sound, she didn't want to look a mess.

Loretta, who had been hunched forward in another of the armchairs, sat up straight. 'Are you saying he raped you?'

The word cut through the room like a chainsaw.

'I'm telling you what happened. And what happened . . . well, it wasn't what I wanted.'

'It sounds like rape to me,' said Gail.

'That's a heavy accusation,' said Loretta. 'I know you're not his biggest fan but . . .' She didn't finish the sentence.

'Do we have to get hung up over a word?' asked Yvonne.

Birdy's belief that she was doing the right thing began to melt away. There were good reasons why these incidents stayed in the shadows. Why people used slippery-slidey language and relied on nods and winks. She dabbed at her face with the hem of her T-shirt.

'I promise you, Loretta, whatever you think of me, I'm telling the truth.'

'What I don't get is why you were in bed in his room.'

What could she say? Do you want to see the big purple bruise on my right thigh? Would you believe me then? Or what about giving me an internal investigation? Would that satisfy you?

'I told you. I was smashed. I passed out. And it wasn't like I got into the same bed. There was a spare. It never occurred to me that he'd do something like that.'

'Even so, wouldn't it have made more sense to get a cab?'

Gail sighed heavily. 'Ah, Loretta, would you listen to yourself? You're making excuses for him.'

'All I'm doing is trying to understand what went on.'

The atmosphere had grown even chillier.

Yvonne put up a hand. 'What are you going to do, Bird?'

'I'm not sure. I'm finding it hard to think straight.'

This was true. Her thoughts were ragged, incomplete. As soon as one idea arrived, it was chased away by another.

'That's okay,' said Yvonne. The others stayed quiet.

Birdy lifted her head and looked at her bandmates. With a terrible certainty, she saw that, whatever she did, Loretta wouldn't support her.

Chapter 25

Now, Steelstown

Before Stacey approached Loretta's mother, she needed to sift through what Mike Slattery had told her and put some structure on the information.

What could she say for sure? And what could be ruled out?

She sat in her car with the windows open and a notepad on her lap. On balance, she agreed with Mike. Whoever was using the name Senan O'Reilly was also likely to be behind some – or all – of the YouTube posts from JBT, Gus McNamara, AllSaint62 and Steelstown4Eva. Chances were they'd also added The Diamonds to Kieran Mitchell's Wikipedia page. The anonymous correspondent had either been a member of the band or was connected to them. How else would they know who'd taught Birdy to play the guitar? How would they be familiar with her story-telling neighbour?

It was easy to see why Mike was leaning towards Gail. She had a record of playing tricks. She'd also turned out to be far smarter than many had believed.

But, and this was a substantial but, why would a Boston university lecturer contact a podcast in Ireland? Proud as Stacey was of her work, she didn't fool herself about its international reach. The majority of her interviewees had enjoyed limited fame. Few had been household names outside Ireland. It was hard to see their stories resonating with someone like Gail, who hadn't lived in the country since the early 1980s.

Stacey returned to the one-time bass player's Twitter page. Was there a chance that she remained engaged with the country of her birth? If so, there was scant evidence of it online. Most of Gail's tweets were about the university. She promoted extracurricular events, welcomed visiting lecturers and congratulated high-achieving students. The few non-academic tweets were about missing pets and American political controversies. There was no hint that she'd once been a professional musician.

Could anyone else be responsible for the emails and comments? What about someone with connections to Kieran Mitchell? No, that was laughable. Mitchell, with his gilded life and roll-call of platinum-selling bands, had made plain that The Diamonds were of no consequence to him.

It dawned on Stacey that a family member of one of the band might be posing as Senan O'Reilly. But, if that was the case, why all the cloak-and-dagger stuff? Why manipulate her?

Questions, questions, questions.

More than a month after the first email, and Stacey felt as if she was tackling a ten-thousand-piece jigsaw of sea and sky. It was hard to tell what she had and what was missing. At least, she was starting to get answers. She had found one Diamond and would email her later. She also knew that Birdy had a brother called Declan, who should be easy to contact on Facebook.

Reflecting on her conversation with Mike, she was struck by his sincerity. Birdy, he insisted, wouldn't have allowed The Diamonds to fall apart. Vivienne Lane Power had said something similar. But, not only had the band split up, Birdy had left music behind her. Forty years later, someone had decided this still mattered. But who? And why?

Patrice Saunders lived in a white-fronted bungalow surrounded by a neatly clipped hedge. Although modest compared to the houses of the past two decades, Stacey reckoned that in the 1980s it would have been considered a substantial family home. The car in the driveway indicated that someone was in, presumably Mrs Saunders. Or . . . was it possible that the red Opel Corsa belonged to Loretta? After all, Mike had seen her a few days ago. The prospect of coming face to face with an actual Diamond caused one of Stacey's knees to give an abrupt wobble.

Before leaving her own car, she'd smoothed her hair and applied a fresh coat of lipstick in a respectable peachy pink. By the sounds of things, Mrs Saunders was a sucker for respectability. Stacey wished she was wearing a more sober outfit. The scarlet leopard-print dress could have waited for another day. On the short walk, she'd given herself a pep talk: tread carefully, be polite and, most importantly, don't allow Loretta's mother to wriggle away.

Mike had warned her that Patrice might be hostile, but the woman who answered the heavy wooden door had a startled expression. She also appeared wrung out. There were dark half-moons beneath her watery blue eyes, and her face was the pale grey of dental putty. Her beige cardigan had been made for a larger woman.

'Yes?' she said, the word embedded in a sigh.

'I'm sorry to bother you, Mrs Saunders. My name's Stacey Nash and—'

'I don't want to switch my electricity provider. I already donate to three charities. And I'm fully stocked with cleaning products. So, if you'll excuse me . . .' She stepped back and began to close the door.

'It's about Loretta,' said Stacey.

Patrice stopped and opened the door again. Stacey couldn't quite decipher the look she gave, but confusion was in there somewhere.

'You mean my daughter?'

How many Lorettas did this woman know? 'Yes.'

'What about her? Is something wrong?'

Stacey launched into her sales pitch, placing emphasis on the serious nature of her work and its popularity. As she did, she examined the woman in front of her. Apart from having a similarly thin nose, she bore little resemblance to the girl in the *Top of the Pops* video. Then again, Loretta had been a teenager. Her mother must be in her early eighties. Patrice also reminded Stacey of someone else, but she couldn't pinpoint who or why.

She hadn't got far with her speech when Mrs Saunders put up one hand. 'No, thank you,' she said. 'I'm not interested and I doubt my daughter would be either.'

'If you give me her contact details, I could ask her.'

'No.'

'Or how about I leave my number and email address with you, and Loretta can contact me if she wants?'

'I said no.'

'I promise I wouldn't put out anything that made her uncomfortable. I just think lots of people would be interested in The Diamonds' story.'

'Why do you think she'd be uncomfortable?'

Stacey was surprised by the question. 'No particular reason. Sometimes the past makes people feel awkward, that's all.'

When Patrice spoke again, her voice had a more militant edge. 'It's much too late to be dragging all this up now. No good can come of it. What happened happened. She was only a young girl.'

So pointed were her words that Stacey paused for a moment. 'I heard she was here the other day.'

'Who told you that?'

'Someone who saw her on the street and recognised her.'

'What she was doing is no concern of theirs.'

'They weren't being nosy,' said Stacey. 'They happened to spot her.'

'Look, you probably don't mean any harm, but you're not wanted here. What you're talking about is ancient history. I'm asking you to leave me alone . . . and to leave my daughter alone. Do you understand?'

Before Stacey had the chance to reply, the door had closed.

Chapter 26

May 1982, London

Loretta needed to escape. With the release of their single only two days away, she felt as if the walls were closing in. At the same time, she felt isolated. Did that make sense? Maybe not. But what did, these days?

She strapped on her sandals, clicked on her Walkman and left the apartment. With The Go-Go's in her ears, she walked past the Green and the Market. Then, keen to escape the snarl of traffic, she turned away from Uxbridge Road and onto a street of redbrick houses. Her hair was in a high ponytail, and the sun burnt the back of her neck.

The trees were in full leaf now, the gardens coming into bloom. Loretta wished she could keep on walking, one foot in front of the other, until she was far, far away.

Kieran had returned to Ireland. The timing wasn't ideal, he said, but Dairena had asked if he wanted to meet their son. Despite his claim to be prioritising The Diamonds, Loretta suspected that his schedule was being dictated by Dairena. She'd decided he could see Ryan and, as fast as you could say 'son and heir', Kieran was on the plane to Cork.

Loretta hadn't said anything to him about Birdy. What could she say? *Wasn't that a cracking review in* Sounds? *Ian thinks 'The Fire Inside' needs more work. Oh, and by the way, Birdy claims you raped her. Is that true?*

Because of Birdy's accusation, Loretta was relieved that Kieran was out of their lives until later in the week. She wanted to think it all through, and his presence would be a distraction. It was hard to make a decision about someone when they were breathing down the back of your neck.

She was beginning to doubt her future with him. That didn't mean she accepted Birdy's claims. Tough as it was, she replayed her bandmate's story. It didn't ring true. Kieran wasn't a sad old loser or an ill-at-ease teenager. He could sleep with Loretta. He could sleep with Dairena or Imogen. He could walk into any bar on any street and find a woman willing to go home with him. Why would he force himself on Birdy Troy? He didn't even like her. How often had he complained about her being too intense or hard to read?

Over the past three days, Loretta and Birdy had settled into a stand-off. If they weren't openly sniping at each other, they weren't friendly either. They used Gail and Yvonne as buffers. While Gail plainly found this tedious, Yvonne was more skilled at hiding her feelings. Gail was also firm in her belief that Birdy was telling the truth. She didn't have to say anything. When Kieran was in their company, she radiated hostility.

Loretta had been walking for fifteen minutes when she came across a pub and decided to go in. A drink. That was what she needed. A peaceful drink in an old man's bar with no danger of meeting anyone she knew and no chance of having someone else's taste in music foisted upon her. At home, she would be wary of going into a bar on her own. There were plenty of places where she wouldn't be served and plenty more where she'd be leered at and harassed. London had made her braver.

The pub was decorated with dark wood and sagging red velvet. It smelt of boiled dinners, Old Spice and unwashed hair. In other words, it smelt Irish. This impression was bolstered by the framed posters behind the bar. 'Only Our Rivers Run Free,' said one. 'Ireland Unfree Shall Never Be At Peace,' said the other. The handful of drinkers ran their eyes over her but said nothing. The barman, a middle-aged guy with blank eyes and vampire ears, asked if she was looking for someone.

'No,' she said. 'I'd like a double vodka and orange, please.'

No sooner had she sat down and taken the first welcome mouthful than a hand touched her shoulder. She jumped.

'My boyfriend will be here in a minute,' she said, hoping her voice sounded firm.

'Everything's cool. It's only me.' Yvonne walked around to face her.

Loretta put down her glass. 'Have you been following me?'

Yvonne winked. 'I'd make a good detective, don't you think?'

'I'm entitled to do my own thing. You don't need to spy on me.'

'If you don't mind me saying so, that's not much of a welcome.' She nodded towards the bar. 'I'm going up for a drink.'

Yvonne returned with a pint of Guinness. She took a box of Rothmans from the pocket of her denim jacket and offered one to Loretta.

'So,' she said, when they'd both lit up, 'how are you?'

'You've trailed me around west London to enquire after my health?'

'There's no need to be ratty with me. We've had a tough few days.'

'You've not come here to give me a talking-to, have you?'

'Nope. I can't imagine your life's a bundle of laughs at the minute. Birdy shouldn't have got stuck into you the other night. But I'm worried about her. Right now, when she should be flying, she's as miserable as Lent.'

Loretta blew out a curl of smoke. She couldn't believe Yvonne had followed her. Was this what they'd become? A band of mad women who bickered and sulked and stalked each other around the city? 'There's not a whole lot I can do about Birdy's state of mind.'

'Are you sure? Whatever happened between Bird and Kieran, it's had a bad effect on her. And, whatever you think of the way she spoke to you, her heart was in the right place. She genuinely thinks you can do better than him.'

'She's not my mother.'

'Thank heavens for small mercies.'

For what felt like the first time in days, Loretta smiled. 'I got a letter from Susannah during the week. She claims Mam has thawed towards the band.'

'Has she heard you on the radio?'

'Mam? I doubt it. She's not an RTÉ 2 listener. Anything more up to date than Roy Orbison and she claims it's just noise.'

'We'll all be like that one day,' said Yvonne.

Loretta wanted to argue. She would *never* be like her mother. She would never settle for bland music and suffocating respectability. She would never wear tan-coloured tights and pleated Crimplene skirts. But this wasn't the time. She took a pull on her cigarette, then stubbed it out. 'Going back for a moment . . . You said "whatever" happened between Birdy and Kieran. Does that mean you doubt her story?'

'Before I answer, what do you think went on? You know him an awful lot better than I do.'

'I think . . . I think there was a bit of fooling around. Perhaps it got out of hand and they ended up having sex. And I think that afterwards Birdy regretted it. The fact that she's given me so much stick for going out with him probably deepened that regret.'

'Could he have forced her to go further than she wanted?' said Yvonne.

'Listen, Kieran can be very persuasive. He can make you feel like you're the sexiest woman alive. And he can make you feel like you'd be mad not to jump into bed with him. But that doesn't make him a rapist.'

'You haven't said anything to him?'

Loretta had been waiting for this question. How could she answer without sounding evasive or cowardly? 'No. I haven't had the chance. I will, though. I will. I mean, if he did have sex with Birdy, he was out of order. I don't want anyone thinking I'm fine with it because I'm not.' She drank the last of her vodka. 'I'm going to get us another drink. Then I want to hear your view.'

When she returned, Yvonne lit a cigarette and blew smoke rings towards the yellow ceiling.

'Okay,' she said. 'I told you I'd give you my read of things. And the honest answer is . . . I don't know what to believe. Everyone was so drunk, there could have been . . . I don't know . . . a misunderstanding. Because of the row, and because of what had happened on stage, there was a funny kind of atmosphere. You must have noticed that.'

'I did. Kieran said I should go home because he wanted to talk to Birdy. I didn't think for a minute that she'd go back to his room. You've got to remember that I was upset. My read of the situation wasn't great.'

'What are you going to do?'

'You mean am I going to stop seeing him?'

'Uh-huh. But, before you say anything, I'm not telling you what to do. It's your decision.'

'That's good because I've had it up to here,' Loretta tapped the top of her head, 'with folks telling me what to do. "Think this, study that, wear this, sing that." And on and on it goes.'

'I hear you. At the same time . . .'

'At the same time what?'

Yvonne pulled on her cigarette. 'We're up to ninety with the band. We don't need this hassle. And we don't need Bird moping around like part of her is missing.'

'Your point being?'

'You could help to lighten the mood.'

'What is it you want me to do?'

'If you could be a bit friendlier towards her, it might help. You don't have to say you believe her, but maybe you could ease up on the questions. What do you think?'

There was, Loretta guessed, a certain logic to what Yvonne was saying. Every day, Birdy became more withdrawn. The way things were going, her unhappiness would drag them all down. 'All right. I'll give it a go.'

'Good woman.'

Loretta took a long drink. The alcohol was doing its work, spreading warmth inside her, making the world a little fuzzier.

'After all,' she said, 'we don't have to like each other, do we?'

Chapter 27

Birdy had been waiting for Loretta to leave. That Yvonne had followed seemed like an omen, a sign she should press on with the idea at the back of her head. Gail had also gone out. The journalist with the lopsided hair was bringing her to a gig in Brighton.

Birdy had spent another night without proper sleep, heart thumping, questions tugging at her. *What if I'd been sober? What if I'd fought harder?*

She could have fought. She could have kicked and bitten and roared. For some reason, she hadn't. She'd allowed Kieran to hurt her. She wasn't able to forget what he'd done. It was as if he was always with her, ready to pounce again. No matter how many times she told herself that this was stupid, the fear persisted.

She had hoped that talking to the others would make a difference. She'd pictured Yvonne and Gail confronting Kieran, questioning him. Her hopes had been misplaced. It was as if they were all paralysed by having their record on the radio and their faces in the magazines. They were transfixed by the sight and sound of themselves, and Birdy couldn't break the spell.

When she'd spoken, she'd also been seeking comfort and reassurance. Since the band's earliest days that was what they'd done. *Tell me your story, and I'll tell you mine.* She'd thought of The Diamonds as a gang. She'd been wrong.

If nothing else, she'd learnt a lesson: you should only tell people what they were willing to hear. There was no point in burdening them with information that made them uneasy.

Birdy paced the flat, the nylon carpet scratching against her bare feet. She stopped to put on New Order, the twelve-inch of 'Temptation', her current favourite. Then she lit the joint Gail had left for her. With any luck, it would bring some calm.

The hash didn't work. The music couldn't drown out her thoughts. Her anger grew until it had a physical presence. It bubbled in her veins and tingled on her skin. She wanted to throw crockery and smash windows. She wanted to turn the furniture upside down and kick holes in the walls.

Somehow, Loretta continued to go about life as if nothing had changed. She had sauntered out of the flat looking as fresh as a snowdrop, her ponytail bouncing, her Walkman, a gift from *him*, clamped to her ears. While she wasn't dumb enough to say it out loud, it was clear she didn't believe what Birdy had said. *Why were you in his hotel room? Why didn't you leave until the following morning?*

How could Loretta stay loyal to someone who had humiliated her and who treated other women with contempt? Kieran must have courted her, flattered her. With Birdy he'd felt entitled to force his way in. That was all she was worth.

Birdy was also angry with herself. Why wasn't she more resilient? Being a woman in music wasn't easy. She'd always known that. She'd heard how women were mistreated, belittled and abused. They smoothed makeup over their bruises. They picked their teeth off the floor. They persevered.

The idea that had come to her in the early hours pushed forward again. Loretta and Yvonne would be back soon. If she didn't take this opportunity, she was unlikely to get another.

There were a thousand things she should be doing. For a start, she needed to return Andy's calls. Although he'd probably given up on her, she ought to talk to him. 'I'm not able to be a girlfriend right now,' she would say. That was the truth. She didn't want anyone touching her. Not even kind, funny Andy. She should also be working on new music. Oh, and all four of them should be rehearsing. Tomorrow night, on the eve of their single's release, they were playing the Marquee on Wardour Street. Everyone had performed there: The Rolling Stones and Jimi Hendrix, The Clash and Thin Lizzy. Tomorrow, The Diamonds would get to add their names to the graffiti-coated dressing-room walls.

And yet Birdy couldn't get excited. When she wasn't angry or upset, she felt nothing. Her other senses had been dulled. Frequently, she wondered what it would be like to disappear. She imagined walking into a rush of oncoming traffic and falling beneath the wheels.

Earlier, her mother had rung. International calls were expensive, and it wasn't something her mam would have done lightly. They'd heard 'Too Much Not Enough' on the radio. 'We're very proud of you,' her mother had said. Birdy had swallowed her tears. She'd wanted to say, 'Mam, I'd like to come home, please.' But she couldn't tell her parents. They would be devastated and, even if her dad didn't say, 'I told you so,' it was what he would think.

She lifted the needle and dropped it at the start of the record. One more listen, and then she would call. She waited for the slight crackle and for the smell of warm vinyl. She remembered being fourteen and worrying that she'd never escape Steelstown. That smell had given her hope. It was the smell of excitement and opportunity.

Arms outstretched, Birdy danced around the room. Hot tears ran down her face. Her head felt as though it was filled with shards of metal, as though they were poking at her brain. She heard herself scream, 'Why won't you listen to me?' Sobs pulsing through her, she gasped for air. She stumbled, sank to her knees and curled into a ball. Then, she placed her arms over her head, as though trying to ward away harm.

When the song ended, she was tempted to stay on the floor.

If you don't do it now, she told herself, *there won't be another chance.*

She stood and went out to the hall. Hands trembling, she picked up the receiver. The number was familiar: 00 353 61 . . . She paused before dialling the remaining digits.

'Hello, Mrs Saunders. It's Birdy Troy here. I was hoping to have a quick word. I'm worried about Loretta.'

Chapter 28

Now, Steelstown

Just down the street from Patrice Saunders' house, there was a small shop. Stacey decided to call in for an ice cream. She checked her phone. There was a missed call from Ronan and another message: Need to talk. When you get the chance, can you give me a bell?

She would, but not right now. Today was devoted to the podcast. The boost she'd received from meeting Mike Slattery had been tempered by her encounter with Loretta's mother. When Mrs Saunders referred to 'ancient history', she might have been alluding to her daughter's affair with Kieran Mitchell. Somehow Stacey sensed she had more on her mind. But what? After the revelation about Gail, she told herself to be wary of easy assumptions.

Although Mike had promised to call if he heard anything helpful, her expectations were low. If he didn't have an address for Birdy, it was unlikely any of his friends or neighbours would either. Stacey's best hope was Declan Troy. Fingers crossed, he would cooperate.

There was nothing of significance in her email inbox. Her news feed, which had become clogged with articles about the 1980s, all-women bands and irrelevant chart statistics, showed a new image of Kieran Mitchell and Faye Godfrey Mitchell. They'd been snapped in New York at a 'gala fundraiser' for survivors of domestic violence. The couple had the look that only the hugely wealthy could perfect. They were stylish but not in a brash way, tanned but not vulgarly so. Faye, who was in her early fifties, appeared to have been laminated to ensure she would never look older than thirty-five. Kieran, who was sixty-eight, had cropped grey hair, tortoiseshell-framed glasses and a sheen of power.

When she'd finished her ice cream, Stacey would try to contact Gail and Declan. After that, she would concentrate on her other tasks. Leaving aside her increasingly urgent need to find and fund a new home, the podcast required care and attention. She had a mountain of administration waiting for her – and a shortage of interviewees.

The next episode would feature a man called Macdara Grant. Macdara was an author whose novels had moved from quiet to inaudible. He wore a pork-pie hat indoors and had a selection of moody publicity shots. Fifteen years earlier, he'd made the Booker long list. His last work, *The Fractured Desolation of All Things*, had sold three hundred copies. His ego remained buoyant. Never had one interview contained so many references to 'my art' and 'the artistic sensibility'. Although he could – and did – rhapsodise for five minutes about the correct use of semi-colons, it was hard to avoid the suspicion that he disliked reading and readers. Stacey had recorded the piece several weeks ago but had been reluctant to upload it. Macdara was so pretentious he might drive away even the most loyal listeners.

Last August, the podcast had taken a break. This year, stepping aside for a month would be difficult. Stacey needed to keep earning. Also, the podcast market was increasingly crowded. All the influencers and comedians were out there, talking about themselves and interviewing their friends. When they ran out of friends, they spoke to their personal trainer or makeup artist. They didn't have to be any good. They were already well-known and well-liked. If Stacey's pod disappeared, even for a week or two, it gave listeners an opportunity to hit 'unsubscribe'.

Save for the woman behind the counter and two small boys, the shop was empty. When the boys had finished the complicated task of getting maximum value for a fistful of coins, Stacey went to pay for her Cornetto.

The woman, who wore a turquoise tabard and earrings shaped like palm trees, smiled. 'You're not from around here. Visiting family, are you?'

Stacey was about to give a vague answer. Then it occurred to her that the woman, who she guessed was fiftyish, might know something about The Diamonds. She explained what she was doing.

'Sorry, love,' said the woman. 'I'm in Steelstown for twenty years, but I never knew Mrs Saunders had a daughter who was a bit of a rock star. I've met both of the daughters . . . one more often than the other. I saw more of them when the father was alive. He was a gentleman.'

'You don't have any idea where they live?'

'The one I'm more familiar with, she's called Susannah.' The woman made a spiral motion beside her head. 'She's away with the fairies, that one. I've a feeling she lives in Spain. Or Italy. Somewhere like that.'

'And the other daughter . . . Loretta?'

'You say Loretta, are you certain that's her name? I thought it was something else.'

Stacey was confused. 'No, she was definitely Loretta Saunders.'

The woman made a clucking sound. 'She may well have been. But I don't reckon that's the name she uses nowadays. I'd remember "Loretta". It's quite distinctive, isn't it? Like Loretta Lynn. I'm a country-music woman myself.'

'Does Mrs Saunders ever talk about her?'

Another cluck. 'She's not the friendliest woman around, as you probably discovered. But I've an idea that the daughter you're talking about . . . Loretta, or whatever she's called now . . . I've an idea she lives in Galway.'

'In the city?'

'That's right. And she has a son. Mrs S did talk about him. Well, she used to boast about him, really. Give me a moment, and the lad's name will come to me.'

'Why did she boast about him?' asked Stacey.

'He was quite a talented athlete. He ran cross-country and such. Between you and me, the way her ladyship went on, you'd swear the lad was destined for the Olympics and all sorts. That was a while ago, mind. I'm not sure what happened. Perhaps he got injured.'

'Do you remember his name?'

'Let me see . . . it was an Irish name. Cathal? No. Rory? No, that wasn't it.' She smacked her lips together.

The room buckled.

It was as if Stacey was doing an eye-test. Everything was a blur. Then the optician turned the lenses and, all of a sudden, the picture was clear.

'By any chance, was his name Ronan? Ronan Egan?'

The woman's smile returned. 'Yes! That's it. Ronan Egan. Mrs S mentioned him quite a few times. Do you know him?'

PART TWO

Chapter 29

Now, Galway

They sat in the early-evening light, Ronan in one armchair, Stacey in the other. The woman originally known as Loretta Saunders was in the middle of the bottle-green sofa. Since they'd last met, she'd lost a significant amount of weight, and the sofa appeared to swallow her. Her face was pinched, her brown hair lank. She also had the watchful look of someone who'd been ill. Stacey recognised it from a couple of her interviewees. It was as if they were on constant alert for bad news.

This was the second time she'd visited the Egans' semi-detached home in Salthill. On her previous visit, she could never have imagined the circumstances that would lead to her return. The room looked and smelt the same. A patterned rug covered most of the varnished floor. A smudgy abstract painting hung over the black fireplace. The air contained traces of a sandalwood-scented candle.

Everything else was different.

Ronan's mother said she preferred to use her second name, Ann. She'd made the change more than thirty years ago when she'd met her husband and moved to a new city. It was a simpler name, less distinctive, and she'd seen it as part of a fresh start. A clean break with a difficult past. Back then, it had also meant she was less likely to be recognised as the woman who'd once been in a band.

'It wasn't as though I'd ever liked the name Loretta,' she said. 'It had always sounded too frilly. Like it belonged to an old woman in pearls and fur.'

To Stacey, the name change was an extreme measure, but she stopped herself saying so. She was about to discover why The Diamonds had broken up. Everything else was secondary.

'I had this idea,' said Ann, 'that I could seal away the past. That I could say, "That was me then. This is me now." But I've learnt you can't do that. Eventually, you've got to accept that it's all still there, waiting for you.'

It struck Stacey that her speech was overly polished. Then again, she'd had plenty of time to prepare. Forty years of time.

At the start, Stacey had been sceptical of Ronan's claim not to have known about The Diamonds. His mother had been in a rock band. They'd had a Top Ten hit in Britain. They'd been number one in Ireland. These weren't minor achievements. How could she have concealed that part of her life? Why would she have done so?

For half an hour, Stacey had paced the streets of Steelstown, phone clamped to her ear, a hundred questions on her lips. Throughout, Ronan's account had remained the same. While she'd been sleuthing around the town, he'd been at home learning about his mother's short-lived music career. Exactly why Ann had wanted to keep it secret, and exactly why his father had colluded with her, was still a mystery.

'If I'd known about the band,' he said, 'why wouldn't I have told you?'

'Because your mother had asked you not to.'

'Seriously? Why would I have missed an opportunity to make myself more interesting? I'd have loved to say, "I might look like a nerdy civil servant but, hey, my mother was a rock star." '

That made her smile. It also led to another question. 'Why didn't you say your mam was from Steelstown?'

'Was it ever relevant to anything? It's not like we ever visited that much. Besides, with all due respect to Steelstown, it's hardly the most fascinating place on the planet.'

Right then, that was exactly how it felt to Stacey, but she let the remark pass. 'In the interview I did with Ultan Dowdall, he said The Diamonds were from Steelstown. Did you not think, *Oh, Mam grew up there. Perhaps she can help?*'

'Which episode was that?'

'The Albie Laffroy one.'

'Apologies, Stace. Hands up, I didn't get to the end. Ten minutes of that pain-in-the-arse comedian were enough for me.'

In the end, she accepted his story. He told her that while his mother was keen to speak, she was reluctant to do so over the phone. Stacey abandoned her plans and set out for Galway.

On the drive north, she berated herself. How could she have spent the last month searching for someone she'd already met? Earlier in the year, they'd had dinner. But, while Ronan's mother had said she was from Clare, she hadn't specified a town. Nor had she given Stacey reason to suspect that her life had been anything other than run-of-the-mill. She'd spoken about her job as an administrator in an electronics company and about returning to the cinema after Covid. She'd told a few amusing stories about Ronan. At no point had there been even the haziest of hints about her former life.

Stacey tried to reconcile the woman on the other side of the room with the girl in the *Top of the Pops* video. Mike Slattery's observations had been accurate. Loretta had epitomised youthful glamour. She'd possessed the sort of chiselled beauty that made people stare. These days, Ann looked weary beyond her years. And yet, hair colour aside, Stacey found it hard to pinpoint a single dramatic change. It was more a case of life leaving its mark in a thousand small increments.

She remembered something else Mike had said: *Most people have lived bigger lives than you think*. How right he'd been.

Next, she considered Ronan. As usual, he had the crumpled appearance of a man who'd slept in his car. He had little in common with either the past or present versions of his mother. What his face did contain was an echo of his grandmother. That was why Stacey's brain had clicked into action when she'd met Patrice. She'd seen something, however slight, that had reminded her of Ronan.

Although he now knew about The Diamonds' existence, there were substantial gaps in his knowledge. He spoke about Birdy, Gail and Yvonne as though they were characters in a drama rather than real people who'd played a pivotal role in his mother's life. Stacey told herself that this shouldn't be a surprise. She'd spent weeks learning about the band. To Ronan, everything was breaking news.

His father, Brendan, had always known about The Diamonds. A tall man with plentiful pewter curls, he'd said hello to Stacey and then gone out. 'There's a lot to explain,' he'd said, 'and I'm going to leave ye to it.'

So far, they had only heard fragments of what threatened to be a complex story.

Stacey was excited, nervous, relieved. She'd gone to Steelstown hoping to find some of the chain's missing links. She'd ended up finding a Diamond. But she was also annoyed. For weeks, Ann had given her the run-around. Although reluctant to press too hard, she needed to know why.

'What I don't understand,' she said, 'is the way you went about this. You've waited for so long. If you wanted to talk, why didn't you reach out to someone? Why use a pseudonym? I take it you are Senan O'Reilly?'

'Yes and no. I came up with the name, but a friend wrote the emails. There are a few reasons why I had my doubts about coming forward, so you'll have to bear with me. You've got to appreciate that until relatively recently I didn't like talking about those days. And as time passed, I didn't reckon anyone would be interested either. In the last while, a few things have made me think again. Your podcast cemented those thoughts.' Ann gave a tired smile. 'I listen every week.'

There was warmth in her voice, and Stacey thanked her.

Ann continued: 'I've heard people describe their experiences, and I've thought, *I wish I could talk like that. I wish I could describe what it's like when everything is taken away*. In a funny way, I began to feel like this was meant to be. Like you were my opportunity.'

'That's great to hear. But why didn't you just give me a call?'

'Because I was in two minds. Part of me wanted The Diamonds' story to be told. That's if it can be told.' She hesitated. 'And, you know, maybe it can't. Another part of me was wary of breaking cover.'

That's if it can be told. Stacey was intrigued by this – and concerned. Had all her work been for nothing?

Ann must have noticed something in her expression because she quickly jumped in. 'Don't worry. What I'm saying is, you'll have to make up your own mind when you hear what happened. You know far more about telling a story than I do.'

'I see,' said Stacey, who wasn't sure that she did.

'Also, I've been going through a bit of a tough time, and I wasn't convinced I'd be able to follow through. I had to weigh everything up.'

'Ronan told me you hadn't been well. I'm sorry to hear that.'

Ann raised a hand, as if to signal that this wasn't a subject she wished to discuss. 'So,' she said, 'I chatted with my friend, and she suggested I dip a toe in the water. Using the name Senan O'Reilly gave me some scope to think. It's only been in the last week or so that I've thought, *Yes, I can definitely do this.*'

'Earlier today, I found out about the real Senan. Now I see his significance.'

'Oh, my Lord. Who told you about him?'

Stacey outlined her discussion with Mike.

Ann picked up a cushion and hugged it to her chest. 'I think I saw Mike the other day.'

'You did. He mentioned that he'd said hello to you.'

'I should have stopped to talk but I wasn't having the best of days. My mother tends to have that effect on me.'

'I met her too.'

'You're joking me. Did she speak to you?'

Stacey sketched out what had happened. She was, she feared, doing too much of the talking. Ronan's gaze moved between her and his mother. He was following every word but saying little. She could only guess how confused he must be.

While Stacey spoke, the room's fourth occupant, the family's black cat, Grover, circled her legs. She bent to stroke him. Then she asked another question. 'Were you not worried that Ronan would find out before now? What if he'd come across a photo of you or seen the video on YouTube?'

'When I first decided to stay quiet, I could never have known that something like YouTube would come along. So, yes, in recent years, I did worry.'

'And when you put all of this in train, were you not concerned that I'd see the video and recognise you?'

'Well, yes . . . but you didn't, did you? I've learnt that if you view someone one way, it's hard to see them as anything else.'

Stacey's cheeks burnt. Wasn't that the truth? No matter how often she told herself that the 'Irish Mammy' stereotype was outdated and offensive, she'd viewed Ann as Ronan's mother, not as a person in her own right.

'You have a point,' she said. 'I assume you're also behind the comments on the video?'

'Not really. My friend took over. I'm not entirely comfortable with everything she's posted, but she's been very helpful, very supportive, so I don't like to complain.'

The way Ann spoke about her friend stoked Stacey's curiosity, but before she had the chance to say anything, Ronan intervened. 'What video and what comments?'

Stacey found the relevant YouTube link and handed over her phone. For the second time that day, she watched while someone viewed The Diamonds on *Top of the Pops*. But, unlike Mike, Ronan had never seen the band before. She remembered the day she'd first come across the video. She'd been taken aback by how talented they'd been. For Ronan, the experience must be far more difficult. When the clip finished, she could tell he was deeply affected.

'You were amazing,' he said. 'All of you were amazing.'

'Thanks, Ro,' said his mother. 'Believe it or not, that was our last day together.'

Stacey took back her phone. 'When you say a friend was behind the YouTube comments, do you mean Gail? I gather she was keen on playing games.'

'No, I haven't spoken to Gail in years. I'm talking about another friend, a co-conspirator you might say. She's not from Steelstown, so I suggested the usernames. Did Mike tell you about their significance?'

'He did. He was amused by Gus McNamara. After that, I was convinced the comments were put there by Birdy or by someone who knew her. He reckoned Gail was the most likely culprit.'

'I emailed Gail a couple of months back, but she hasn't replied. I'm disappointed but not surprised. Her life has moved on.'

'Are you in touch with Yvonne and Birdy?'

'No.'

Ann's answer was quick. Abrupt. After a few seconds, she elaborated. 'I've tried contacting Yvonne. I'm hoping she'll get the chance to reply.'

Stacey considered what Ann was saying. One thing was plain: she wanted the band to meet again. But if she'd hoped that involving an outsider would help, Stacey had been a failure. Despite a month's worth of digging, she hadn't spoken to Birdy, Yvonne or Gail. Less clear was whether Ann wanted a wider audience to hear The Diamonds' story. What exactly had she meant when she'd expressed doubt that the tale could be told? Increasingly, Stacey was sensing that she hadn't thought this through. She was acting like a woman with a motto ('You can't escape the past') but no obvious plan.

Stacy took a long breath before her next question. It was one she needed to ask but doing so wasn't easy. 'And what about Kieran Mitchell? Do you ever hear from him?'

This time, it took a while for Ann's answer to come. When it did, it was in the form of another question.

'You know? About us, I mean?'

'Yes. Vivienne Lane told me.'

'My gosh, there's another blast from the past. I can't believe how much work you've done.'

'Woah,' said Ronan. 'Kieran Mitchell? The famous manager guy? Where does he fit into this?'

'He managed The Diamonds,' said Stacey. She dipped her head towards Ann, a way of saying, 'The rest's up to you.'

Ronan's mother put the cushion aside and patted her knees. Grover jumped onto her lap. 'Like Stacey says, he was our manager too. But, again, I haven't spoken to him in a long, long time. I've seen him, of course, on the TV and in the papers. He's done well for himself.'

'Hasn't he just?' said Stacey. She allowed her voice to trail away, hoping Ann would take her cue.

'You're wondering when I'll get to the split?'

'Yes.'

Ann stroked the cat's head until his purrs filled the room. 'I'm going to tell you about the final weeks, but there are reasons I haven't spoken before. I've spent a large chunk of my life regretting what happened back then.' She paused. 'What I wasn't always able to do was put everything in perspective, if that makes sense. Now I can . . . and I can see that we were thrown into the most toxic of circumstances.'

'How so?' asked Stacey.

'What I mean is, we'd grown up in a world where young women were supposed to know their place. And anyone with a whiff of importance about them had to be treated with deference. The best thing you could say about a child was that they were placid or obedient. So even when we thought we were rebelling, it was within fairly narrow limits.'

'*Keep your head down, Keep your voice low,*' said Stacey, quoting from 'Brighter Than The Sun.'

Ann smiled. As she did, a tear ran down one cheek. 'She wrote well, did Birdy. I don't think I appreciated how talented she was. Or perhaps I did and I resented it. Don't get me wrong, she wasn't Bob Dylan or anything, but she was writing songs about being a young woman from a small Irish town when no one else was.' Another tear fell, and she pulled a tissue from the pocket of her khaki trousers. 'How do you know "Brighter Than The Sun"? It was never released.'

'I got my hands on a bootleg. A gig you played in McGonagles?'

'Christmas 1981. That was an incredible night.'

'I'll play it for you later, if you like. The sound's ropy, but the songs are fantastic.' Once again, Stacey was scared of sounding too robust, but she also needed Ann to finish what she'd started. 'Anyway, you were saying . . .'

'I was saying that we'd grown up in that world, and then we were gobbled up by the music industry, a place famous for exploiting young women. And we weren't equipped to deal with any of it. I can see all that now. If only I'd been able to see it then.'

'You were what age? Nineteen?'

'Yes.'

'You shouldn't be too tough on yourself.'

'I suppose. But Birdy was young too. And I've never stopped wishing that I'd behaved differently.'

As she spoke, Ann's voice cracked. Stacey wondered why she'd singled out Birdy.

'If this is too tough,' said Ronan, 'you don't have to talk this evening.'

Yes, she does, thought Stacey, who worried that Ann would change her mind.

His mother tickled the cat's head. Grover responded with a stream of contented snorts. 'I've promised Stacey the full story and

I'd like her to hear it. I should say . . . it's not the sort of tale that any woman wants her son to hear.'

'If you'd prefer I wasn't here, I can make myself scarce.' Ronan's tone suggested that, while he felt he should make the offer, this wasn't what he wanted.

'No,' she said. 'It mightn't make for easy listening, but it matters. I hope you understand that.'

Chapter 30

May/June 1982, London

Three days after its release, the single was flying. The Diamonds were living in bursts of camera light. No matter how hard they worked, more was expected. Gigs, interviews, record-shop visits: the pace was frenetic. They were corralled from taxis to offices to venues with barely a second to take it all in. The following month, they'd be travelling to Italy and Germany. After that, they were due to play a number of dates in America. Their schedule would include recording a video for their second single. The decision to give 'Brighter Than The Sun' a proper video was a sign of Supreme's growing confidence. The record company had already approached a well-known director.

The Diamonds had a sense of being separated from the herd of hopefuls. The industry had decided they would be successful.

Birdy had been nervous about their gig in the Marquee. She shouldn't have worried. While they hadn't burnt the house down, they'd done enough. On stage, her troubles had felt less urgent. She'd been more like her old self. Confident. Sparky. As soon as she'd returned to the dressing room, the clouds had rolled in again. She'd wanted everyone to leave her alone.

Every morning, she woke with a sense of dread. She was convinced that someone was standing over her, watching her. When she cried out, no sound came. Then – poof! – the figure disappeared. At other times, she imagined her legs chained to the bed or her wrists tied together.

Kieran's trip to Cork must have gone well because his swagger had been restored. If Loretta had said anything to him about Birdy's accusation, he didn't let it show.

In her phone call to Steelstown, Birdy had told Patrice Saunders about Kieran. 'Loretta's seeing our manager, and we don't know what to do,' she'd said. It had taken a minute for Mrs Saunders to absorb what she was hearing. She'd thanked Birdy and hung up. Every day since, Birdy had expected a response. She'd thought Patrice would call to reprimand her daughter. No call came.

Perhaps she hadn't believed Birdy. Perhaps she'd dismissed her as a troublemaker, as one of those feral girls from Connolly Park who'd led her daughter astray. Truth to tell, Birdy was questioning the wisdom of her actions. What had once seemed logical now felt provocative, and she didn't know if she could cope with more drama. Also, Loretta had become less abrasive. While it wouldn't be accurate to call her supportive, she'd stopped asking hostile questions.

Early on Friday morning, Birdy was layering on her makeup when she heard the wheeze and clunk of the front door. It was Loretta, returning from a night with Kieran. For a minute or two, nothing happened. Then she heard, 'Jesus Christ,' followed by heavy footsteps. The bedroom door swung open.

'Tell me you didn't do this,' said Loretta.

'I'm sorry?'

'Don't act dumb on me. You rang my mother and told her I was going out with a married man.' She waved a letter. 'My mother. The woman who's terrified of scandal. You must have known it would send her into orbit.'

'I didn't have a choice,' said Birdy, getting to her feet. 'I told her I was worried about you. And I am.'

'Of course you had a choice. You could have kept your mouth shut.'

Yvonne arrived, wrapped in a pink-and-green-striped bath towel, hair dripping onto the floor. 'What's the story?'

Loretta told her.

Yvonne turned to Birdy. 'Ah, pet, I know you're upset, but was bringing Loretta's mother into this a good idea? We all know what Mrs S is like.'

'If we can't make her see reason, I thought her mam might have more success.'

'No, you didn't,' said Loretta. 'You were being vindictive.'

'Have you asked Kieran about what he did to me?'

'I haven't had the chance. We've been too busy.'

'So you keep saying, but where were you last night?'

'It wasn't the right time.'

Birdy sensed the balance of power tilt towards her. 'There'll never be a "right time", will there? If you trusted him, you wouldn't worry. You'd say, "Here's what Birdy told us. What's your response?"'

'It's not that simple,' said Loretta.

'Yes, it is.'

'Please stop treating me like I'm stupid.'

'I never accused you of being stupid. In most ways, you're far smarter than me. But when it comes to Kieran, you refuse to see what's in front of you. I mean, are you not curious about what he'll say? Does it not bother you?'

'You said yourself that you were drunk,' replied Loretta.

'That doesn't make any difference. If anything, it makes everything worse. He's pure scum, and it's a shame you can't see that.'

Loretta twisted towards Yvonne. 'I was prepared to patch things up, but when she behaves like this, why should I?'

Yvonne wrapped the towel more tightly around her body. 'To be fair, it might do no harm to have a chat with Kieran.'

'Thank you,' said Birdy.

'There's no need to get sanctimonious,' said Loretta. 'It's not as if she believes you either.'

Yvonne made a sound like something had caught in her throat. 'Ah, now. That's not what I said.'

'Yes, it is.'

'No, it isn't. Don't put words in my mouth.'

Loretta ploughed on. 'You told me there was a funny atmosphere and everyone was drunk, and you didn't know what to believe.'

For a moment, Birdy couldn't speak. When she found her voice, all she could manage was 'Is that right?'

Yvonne gave a slow shake of her head. 'I said I wasn't there so I couldn't know exactly what went on. I also said you were upset, and Loretta should make more of an effort with you.'

'You could have said you believed me,' said Birdy, her voice no more than a squeak. 'That's all you needed to say.'

Yvonne's eyes flicked from one to the other. 'I've done my best. I've tried to calm things down. And I've tried to make sure everyone's here, doing what they're supposed to do. But I can't enjoy a minute of what's happening with the band. And

I can't concentrate on playing or writing or any of the things I love because I'm forever watching out for trouble. And you know what? I'm tired of being the United Nations. You need to sort yourselves out.'

She turned and walked back to the bathroom, leaving a trail of water in her wake.

After that, their days played out in silence. The four went everywhere together but barely spoke. Even Gail appeared to have succumbed to the disharmony. Oh, she could turn on the charm when outsiders were there. But when it was just the four of them, she read her book (*Flowers in the Attic*: 'So twisted I think I should go to confession') or put on her headphones.

'Wait until the madness dies down,' she said to Birdy, in a conspiratorial whisper. 'I promise I'll put him in his place. We'll get a new manager then, I swear.'

But when would the madness subside? After this single, there would be another. And then the album. And then a tour. And then another record.

And on and on and on.

The knowledge of what lay ahead didn't bring Birdy joy. It was as if her energy and creativity had been stolen. Why was she putting herself through this? She no longer knew.

She realised she'd been wrong about Yvonne. Birdy had always assumed that because Yvonne was the most grown-up, she was also the bravest. She'd nursed the hope that the band's drummer would stand up to Kieran. Now, she saw that Yvonne was actually the most conciliatory Diamond. Or maybe, she hadn't always been that way. Maybe she'd changed because she thought that being an adult meant avoiding confrontation and carrying on. Either way, Birdy couldn't rely on her support.

At some point, Loretta spoke to Kieran. The first Birdy knew of their conversation was when he sidled up to her at the end of a record-shop visit.

'A word,' he said, shepherding her into a back office.

The room was scarcely bigger than a cupboard. A fluorescent light flickered overhead. Birdy's heart speeded up, as it always did in Kieran's presence.

He began by expressing annoyance that she wasn't taking care of herself. She looked wiped out, he said. People would take one look at her, and guess she was doing hard drugs. She didn't want a reputation as a smackhead, did she?

His words were level, controlled. He was full-on Lord Snooty. He was Trinity College and trips to the theatre. He was tennis lessons and restaurant dinners. She was the silly young girl from Save-A-Lot who hadn't placed his frozen food in the correct bag.

'No,' she said. 'I don't want anyone getting the wrong idea.'

She kept her answers short. She couldn't bear being trapped for a second longer than necessary.

He gave a laboured sigh, as if worn out by her inability to do as she was told. 'You need to make more of an effort. It's like I've said before: in the ideal world, nobody would care what you looked like. But we're not in the ideal world. You're letting the band down.'

'I'm sorry.'

Birdy hated the truth in his words. She hated her chapped lips, bleary eyes and limp hair. She tried to leave, but he moved closer to the door.

'One other thing. I thought we had an agreement.'

'I'm not with you.'

'We agreed not to lose perspective about what happened a couple of weeks ago. You said it to me outside Whizzer's office. "What matters is the music," you said. Only now I hear you've been talking to the others. Why did you have to go telling tales?'

As Kieran spoke, Birdy could smell the coffee on his breath. She could see the thin pink lines in his eyes and the pores on the side of his nose. He revolted her.

'I told the truth.'

'No, you didn't. You claimed I forced you to have sex. You made it sound like I kidnapped you and barricaded the door. We both know that's untrue. You were there of your own free will. You could have left whenever you wanted.'

She studied him, trying to spot any sign of discomfort, any sign that he was bluffing. Surely he must have some self-doubt. There was nothing.

'It wasn't what I wanted,' she said, her voice weak. She put a hand against the wall to steady herself.

'That's not how I remember it, and I doubt you can remember much at all. And calling Loretta's mother: what was that about? You know as well as I do that the woman isn't rational. You're determined to make life difficult for Loretta, aren't you?' Before she could reply, he tapped his watch. 'We need to get moving.'

Birdy edged out of the office and shuffled through the shop to the others. As she passed the rows of LPs and cassettes, she felt the eyes of the shop's staff and customers sweep over her.

Don't look at me, she wanted to shout. But, of course, she didn't.

It was Kieran's arrogance that got to her; his insistence that whatever he said had to be right; his confidence that no words of hers could damage him.

Then something hit her. Even though he constantly stressed how much the band needed him, the opposite was equally true. He needed them. Not only did they earn money for him, they gave him credibility. If they were a success, he was a success.

Throughout the day, this thought kept returning. While she couldn't claim it brought her solace, it did present her with possibilities.

That evening, she arranged to meet Andy in a café near the studio. They'd eaten there a number of times, and the owner, Silvio, greeted them like long-lost family. He'd heard The Diamonds on the radio. The entire café had listened, and they'd all clapped when 'Too Much Not Enough' had finished.

'You're famous,' he said to Birdy, who bowed her head with embarrassment.

Andy was needed for an evening recording session so couldn't stay long. That was good. If Birdy spent too much time in his company, she'd become emotional. Then who knew what she'd say?

They hadn't seen each other in almost two weeks. Since before Kieran had raped her. Even if others were reluctant to use the word, no one could stop Birdy saying it in her head. Not even Kieran could police what happened there.

As they sat down at the red-topped table, Andy echoed Kieran's view about her looking tired. In his words, however, there was concern rather than contempt. She was okay, she said. Promoting a record was more stressful than she'd anticipated, but she'd get used to it.

They both ordered sausages, beans and chips. They shared a pot of strong tea. While they ate, a fine drizzle misted the windows and Joan Jett drifted from the crackly transistor.

At the start, they pretended everything was normal. Andy spoke about his dislike of the studio's current occupants, a New Romantic band from the north-east. They were dizzy with their own importance, he said, which might be all right if their material was any good. It was unbelievably weak.

Birdy told a story about a condescending DJ who'd been tied in knots by Gail. 'I don't think the poor lad was prepared for a lecture about colonialism. Or at least it wasn't what he'd expected from a girl wearing the longest earrings this side of Las Vegas.'

While they chatted, she found herself relaxing. She'd forgotten what it was like to be in the company of someone who could give as well as take. Someone who genuinely liked her. But she'd come here with a task and she had to follow through. The trouble was, every time she opened her mouth, the words flew away.

'It's about us,' she said at last. 'I wanted to talk about us.'

'Oh?'

'For the next while, I'm going to be here, there and everywhere and I don't think you need a girlfriend you never get to see.'

For a cheerful person, Andy had a solemn face. Even at his most upbeat, he could appear earnest. Right then, he looked more hurt than she'd expected.

He put down his cutlery. 'Did I do something wrong?'

'God, no. I wouldn't want you thinking that. Not at all.'

'Take my word for it then. I don't mind you not being here.' He gave a half-smile. 'Well, of course I mind. What I'm trying to say is, I understand how record promo works. I understand about the travel and the insane hours and all the rest of it.'

'Yeah, but it's not fair, is it? I can't ask you to hang around for weeks while I'm somewhere else.'

She told him how the initial shoots of interest had sprouted into something more demanding. In the past few days, there had been approaches from TV shows in Belgium, Denmark and Sweden. There had been interview requests from *The Face*, the *Daily Mail* and the *Sunday Mirror*. *Smash Hits* were talking about a cover shoot.

Andy listened before giving her an enquiring look. 'I thought we were having a good time. I love your company, you must know that. And, up until two weeks ago, I thought you were happy too. Then you disappeared, and I can't figure out why.'

'I'm sorry.'

'There's no need to be sorry. Like I say, I'm confused.' When Birdy didn't reply, he moved his hand along the table until their fingertips were touching. 'Who else is going to tell me stories about Vera Cheevers, huh?'

Birdy swallowed over the lump in her throat. 'I'll bet there are plenty of girls with more entertaining stories.'

'Not in my experience, there aren't. And I can't imagine any of them being as lovely as you . . . or as good on the guitar.'

Oh, Andy.

Birdy hadn't expected saying goodbye to be this hard. It didn't make sense. She'd only known Andy for a few months. Even then, there'd been many times when they were too busy to get together. By comparison, splitting up with Mike had been straightforward, and she'd known him since junior infants.

'I've had a brilliant time with you,' she said. 'The best ever. But it wouldn't work out.'

He looked at her. His blue eyes were so clear, she could see the black circle around the iris. His gaze made her uncomfortable. She didn't want anyone looking at her, not even Andy.

'I don't want to pry,' he said, 'but did something happen to you? Or did someone say something about me?'

The lump in her throat grew larger. 'No. Why would you think that?'

'Because something's not right. I thought you'd be thrilled about how everything is going for The Diamonds. But, and I hope you don't mind me saying this, you look miserable.'

'I'm not, I swear.'

'Birdy, I know you, and I can tell you're about to cry. What is it?' He dragged one hand through his sandy hair. 'Have you met someone else? Is that what's going on?'

Maybe she should confide in him. He would listen. And he was clever. He'd know what to do.

But no. Who was she fooling? There was every danger he wouldn't believe her. She'd tried talking to her bandmates, and look how that had gone. Loretta had dismissed her story, and Yvonne's response had been wishy-washy. It would always be Birdy's word against Kieran's, and faced with a choice, few would come down on her side. If she lived to be ninety, she could never prove what Mitchell had done.

That wasn't all. Even if Andy did accept everything she said, their relationship would be tainted. He would be conscious of what had happened to her. She was damaged, not the same.

Tell him.

Don't tell him.

Tell him. He might understand.

Don't tell him. He'll ask questions you can't answer.

'Honestly,' she said, willing herself not to cry, 'there's no one else. It's like I told you. I'm finding the attention difficult. I mean, people keep looking for my opinion on stuff, and I don't have the right answers. The other day, this guy asked about my influences. I said "Steelstown", and he laughed. I hadn't meant to be funny.' She shook her head. 'I'll get used to it. But I can't . . . I can't do this right now.'

'Are you sure?'

'I am.'

'Does it sound arrogant if I say I think you're making a mistake?'

'No,' she said. *Why was this so hard?* She had to get out of here. She reached into her pocket and took out a five-pound note. 'I'll get this.' Then she rose from the chair. 'I've got to go.'

Andy wouldn't take the money. She couldn't bear an argument, even a trivial one, so took it back.

He stood and they hugged. She hadn't planned on touching him. Since the night with Kieran, she'd shied away from all physical contact. But once they'd pressed together, she didn't want to let go. She rested her head on his shoulder and inhaled his clean smell. She was weak from anger and exhaustion and the stress of lying to someone she loved. Because she did love Andy. Again, she came close to telling him what Mitchell had done. Again, she decided against.

'I wish only good things for you,' she whispered. 'I want you to know that.'

They pulled apart, and she picked up her bag.

'Take care of yourself,' he said. 'I'll miss you.'

'And I'll miss you,' she replied, her voice thick with tears. Then she opened the door and stepped into the evening rain.

Chapter 31

'Too Much Not Enough' entered the British charts at number eighteen. In Ireland, it was number two. Only that year's Eurovision winner prevented it from hitting the top. In both countries, the single was the week's highest new entry. The second highest? The Rolling Stones.

If the achievement didn't bring a full thaw in relations, it lightened the atmosphere. Everyone wanted a piece of them. They were 'white hot', 'a breath of fresh air', 'what music had been waiting for'.

The idea that had taken root in Birdy's brain was gathering strength. She decided her best course of action was to play along with the others and pretend she was coping. She became a sanded-down version of herself, her voice stripped of emotion, her face a perfect blank. Several times a day, she would worry that one of her bandmates had guessed what she was planning. Then she would tell herself that this was paranoia. She said nothing about breaking up with Andy. They would find out soon enough.

On Tuesday, the call came from the BBC. Were The Diamonds free to appear on that week's *Top of the Pops*? Yes, said Kieran. Absolutely, said Supreme Records.

'Who else is on?' asked Yvonne.

'Will we meet any famous people?' asked Gail.

'You're the famous ones now,' replied Kieran. 'Before long everyone will know who you are.'

'That's a scary thought,' said Loretta.

Birdy said nothing.

They strode down what felt like a never-ending corridor until they arrived at their dressing room. That week's *TOTP* was going out live. Unfortunately, this made no difference to the rules. Rather than playing their single, the band would have to mime. None of them was thrilled about it.

'Wouldn't it be easier to perform properly?' Gail had asked. 'Like, how do you pretend to play the drums?'

In reply, Kieran had used his long-suffering tone. 'Why don't you let Yvonne worry about that?'

When Birdy looked at the running order on the back of the door she felt queasy. Nerves bubbled up inside her in a way she hadn't anticipated. Siouxsie and the Banshees were on the show, as were Fun Boy Three and Echo and the Bunnymen. The week's chart toppers, Madness, would be live on a satellite link from Japan. Yvonne was keen to meet Siouxsie. Gail announced that she was off to find Terry Hall.

'Poor Terry,' said Yvonne. 'I hope he's prepared for what's about to hit him.'

This was the first time they'd been on television. Birdy liked how the woman doing makeup had transformed her into an altogether more sophisticated person. And she liked the sensation of putting on new clothes: bandage-tight black jeans, a forest-green silk shirt and black boots with towering heels. Impractical as the boots were, they gave her a sense of power.

While they rehearsed, she tried to let some of the magic sink in. She watched as men with large headphones and women with clipboards scurried about. Moving at speed appeared to be how you let others know you were important. Whatever happened next, she needed to remember this day. This craziness. At the same time, she fought her desire to lash out at Kieran. She longed to say, 'How could you have ruined this for me?' But the time for confrontation had passed.

That night's presenter, Kid Jensen, stood on a gantry, flanked by audience members. The metal staircase reminded Birdy of Save-A-Lot. Her thoughts leapt back to the day of Gail's prank phone call. The day they'd met Kieran. She pushed the thought away. She couldn't dwell on that tonight.

They were third on the running order. When she heard Kid Jensen say, 'Straight from Ireland, it's The Diamonds,' and when she heard the song's intro kick in, her heart lurched. She wished now that they'd been allowed to play live. She was confident they could have wowed the place. Whatever else had drained away, whatever had been stolen, her belief in their power remained.

An unusual feeling gripped her. It was as if she was up on the gantry, looking down on the stage. There were the girls, glamorous in their white dresses and red ra-ra skirts. There were the boys, their Panama hats and sailor caps straight from a fancy dress party. And there was Loretta, miming to perfection, as 'Too Much Not Enough' played out across the studio.

You want to control me, you claim that it's love,
But if I'm too much, baby, then you're not enough . . .

Birdy thought of her parents and Declan. She thought of Mike and the gang from the supermarket and everyone else in Steelstown. She pictured them, noses in front of their TV screens, doing a running commentary on the band. Those lucky few with video machines ('a total waste of money', according to her dad) would be hitting record.

As their song rang out, and as Birdy mimed her part, every nerve in her body hummed. She asked herself if she had any doubts. The honest answer was, yes, she did. But her doubts were wispy, insubstantial. They weren't enough to change her mind.

Afterwards, they piled into the BBC bar. The to-ing and fro-ing gave Birdy the opportunity she'd been seeking. While the others were soaking up compliments, she slipped away. She kept expecting someone to notice. She thought she heard Yvonne calling her name. She imagined Kieran's hand grabbing her shoulder.

But she was free.

From Television Centre, she could have walked to the flat, except that would take time she didn't have. She found a black cab and, within a few minutes, she was back in her bedroom. She removed her high-heeled boots. Fond as she was of them, they wouldn't take her very far. And she planned on going far. She replaced them with flat brown sandals. Otherwise, she didn't change.

Birdy's duffel bag was packed and hidden under the bed. Her letter was already prepared. Before putting it into an envelope, she gave one final check. There was more she would have liked to say, but this wasn't the time. There would be another day.

Dear all,

This will come as a surprise, but by the time you read this letter, I'll be gone. I've thought about it from every angle and have decided that what I'm doing is for the best.

You'll probably think I should have discussed my plans with you. But, let's face it, we would only have argued, and I think we've all had enough of that. I'm aware that I'm giving up a lot, but my heart is no longer in the band. Every day is tough. Every day I sink a little bit further. I wake up hating myself and hating the world. If I stay, I'll end up making a mess of things. There's also a danger I'll make life a misery for the rest of you.

I would have liked to say a proper goodbye, but that would have been too upsetting.

Please don't call my parents. I plan on returning to Steelstown eventually but not right now. I'll ring Mam and Dad in a day or two and tell them I needed a break. Mam will worry and Dad will think I've taken leave of my senses, but they're good people, and I know they want me to be happy.

Don't worry that I'll say anything to them about recent weeks. They wouldn't understand, so it's best if they remain in the dark.

I'm leaving my guitars behind. You can sell them to pay my share of the bills. I'd be really grateful if you could send what's left to my mother.

For a long time, this band meant the world to me. You all know that. I have tons of brilliant memories. Being a Diamond has also taught me that I don't always have to do what others want or expect.

I wish you all good luck. Honestly, I mean that.

Love always, Birdy xxx

A quick check of her watch, and Birdy decided she had time for one last walk around the apartment. Her eyes were dry, her head clear. She dropped her bag in the hall and placed the letter in the middle of the kitchen table. They couldn't miss it there.

She would be travelling light. Not only was she leaving her beloved guitars behind, her records would also be staying in London. She touched three or four sleeves: *Heroes, Marquee Moon, Easter, Boy*. They were a catalogue of her life so far. Then she told herself not to get sentimental about possessions. Possessions would only weigh her down.

Her sudden departure would cause difficulties, but nothing that couldn't be overcome. There were countless guitarists who would have no trouble picking up The Diamonds' chords. To begin with, Kieran would be furious. The thought of this gave her some degree of . . . not pleasure. Pleasure was too positive a feeling. It gave her a tiny stirring of satisfaction. She liked the idea of him losing sleep.

The record company wouldn't be thrilled either, but they would adjust. After a short while, everybody would be relieved that she wasn't there. They didn't need a constant reminder of something they wanted to sweep aside. If they referred to her, it would be as 'our first guitarist'.

From her perspective, she hoped she'd remember the good nights, the sliver of time when it had seemed anything was possible. She was sorry to miss the release of their album. She'd poured herself into the recordings, obsessing over every line and chord. But the songs had been contaminated and they were less important now.

She would also miss writing. Making music had always made her feel smarter. Hopefully the day would come when she'd be able to try again.

If Birdy had second thoughts, they were mostly driven by Gail. Life wouldn't be the same without her friend and ally. Andy, too, remained on her conscience. No, that was wrong. It made him sound like an obligation. His reaction the other night, the tenderness of it, had caught her off-guard. In a few weeks, she would write and explain. He deserved to know the true story.

Her new passport was in her bag, as was the money she'd withdrawn from the bank when she'd closed her account earlier in the day. While not a fortune, it was enough to get her started. She would take a taxi to Hammersmith. From there she could get the Piccadilly Line directly to Heathrow. Where she would go then, she wasn't sure. Greece or Italy, perhaps. The further she went, the less likely she was to see or hear The Diamonds.

Never having been on a plane, she didn't know how to buy a ticket. No doubt, someone would help.

Birdy hoisted her bag over her shoulder. Then she shut the door behind her and took the first steps into the next part of her life.

Chapter 32

Now, Galway

It was dark. The curtains were closed, the lamps throwing gentle light across the room. Ann waited while Stacey and Ronan absorbed what she'd told them. Her own head was a jumble of memories.

She remembered how, still giddy from their triumphant evening, they'd returned to the flat. Truth be told, she hadn't missed Birdy. The guitarist's blank eyes, grey-tinged voice and world-weary attitude had been dragging them down. The evening had been more fun without her.

It had been Yvonne who'd found the letter. Within minutes, the glitter of their success had been scrubbed away and the arguing had begun.

Yvonne had suggested that when she'd had an opportunity to think Birdy would return.

Gail had rounded on her. 'Did you actually read what she said?

She was falling apart in front of us, and we did nothing to help her. We let her down.'

'We did what we could,' Yvonne had replied.

'Come on, you don't believe that. Think about it, will you? She tells us a man raped her, and we expect her to carry on as normal. He calls her into an office on her own, and we stand around like everything's cool, nothing creepy going on at all. As soon as she spoke to us, we should have shown him the door. It's no wonder she's run away.'

Then Gail had cried. Ann would have expected her to be a loud, messy crier, but her tears had been quiet. One small *glug* and a quick intake of breath, those were the only sounds she'd made.

Later that night, she'd announced that she, too, was leaving. 'We were supposed to be friends,' she'd said. 'That's not true any more, so what's the point of The Diamonds? It's all been ruined.'

Initially, Ann had assumed Gail would change her mind. There was no reason for her to go. Surely she understood that they couldn't just shrug their shoulders and shuffle away? Their single was in the charts. Their album was ready for release. They had been on a television show watched by millions and millions of people. Everything was happening for them. *Everything.*

If anything, Gail's attitude became more fixed. 'What's the point?' became her catchphrase. She kept blaming herself, saying she shouldn't have allowed Birdy to leave the bar with Kieran.

Eventually, Ann was forced to accept the truth. Without Birdy, there was no band.

Now, she looked at Ronan. She hoped her son's judgement wouldn't be too harsh. Normally, she could interpret his gestures, gauge the inflections in his voice. Tonight, his face was opaque, his voice quiet. He'd said little, leaving most of the questions to Stacey. His few interventions had been halting, reticent. Had she told her parents why The Diamonds had split up? Yes, she'd said, but not until many years later. Had she ever considered joining another band? No, it would have felt wrong.

When she'd started her story, Ann had struggled to keep the emotion from her voice. But as she'd continued, her composure had returned. Was there a danger that Ronan had misinterpreted this? That he'd thought she accepted no blame for the events of 1982?

She broke the silence. 'Of course I should have believed Birdy. Above everything else, I regret the way I questioned her. There wasn't a reason in the world for her to lie.'

Stacey sat forward in her armchair. 'Have you told her that?'

'Not in person, no.'

'So when did you next see her?'

'I didn't.'

'Sorry. Maybe I didn't phrase that very well. What I meant was, when was the next time you had any contact with her? Like, did you see her after a few months? Or was it a couple of years?'

'No. I didn't see her. Not then.' Ann paused. 'Not ever.'

Even as she voiced the words, she had difficulty believing them. How much harder must it be for Stacey, and for her son, to accept their truth?

In the days after Birdy's disappearance, Ann's resentment had deepened. Whatever she'd put in her letter, she must have suspected that Gail wouldn't carry on without her. And with Gail gone, it was inevitable that Yvonne would leave too. For them, the band had been tarnished and its shine couldn't be restored. In the Shepherd's Bush flat, Birdy had been a ghostly presence. A hundred times a day, one of them would say, *I wonder where she is* or *Do you think she's okay?*

None of them could even take a guess at where she'd gone. It was as if she'd turned to vapour. Kieran's initial disbelief ('That's some fucking stunt she's pulled') had quickly been replaced by efforts at damage limitation. He'd railed against Birdy and then against Gail. Ann remembered Gail facing him down.

'In a fair world,' she'd said, 'you'd be on your way to Wormwood Scrubs. And if I was a better person, I'd tell Whizzer and Ian and everyone else what you did to my friend. In fact, I'd take out an ad in the *NM*-fucking-*E*. That's what you deserve.'

The following week, she'd left. Along with her boyfriend, she'd got a flight to what was then called Yugoslavia. As soon as she'd found somewhere to store her drums, Yvonne had taken a ferry to France.

Even in those early days, Ann had known that Kieran's first and last thoughts were for himself. What would the band's sudden split mean for his reputation? His bank balance? His plans for world domination? Despite his insistence that he'd done nothing wrong, he must have worried that someone would reveal the real reason for Birdy's departure.

He'd claimed the band could carry on. 'What we need,' he'd said to her, 'are new musicians. You're the heart of the band. As long as you're here, we can keep on going.'

That wasn't true. Birdy had been the beating heart of The Diamonds. Only a fool or a liar would say otherwise.

The record company and their producer, Ian, had reacted with fury. Amid legal threats, the album was shelved. There were two or three cryptic stories in the music press, but nothing more.

With hindsight, Ann could see how Supreme must have snuffed out any questions. In return for their compliance, inquisitive journalists had probably been offered access to bigger bands or long-distance jaunts to glamorous gigs. She still wondered how Kieran had explained the break-up. She assumed he'd framed the band as flaky small-town girls who'd chosen to spurn the gifts they'd been given.

Walking away from the rubble hadn't been easy. Until the group was gone, she hadn't appreciated how precious it had been. That was the blessing, and curse, of being young. You could only imagine the here and now. She could never have pictured herself as a fifty-nine-year-old woman, sitting in a suburban house, her teenage wounds not yet healed.

Once, she'd instructed herself not to mourn what might have been. *It was only a short chapter in your life,* she'd said. *You've got to move forward.* As anger had turned to sorrow, and sorrow to self-loathing, she'd tried to erase The Diamonds from her life. She'd even changed her name. Had it been possible, she would have scoured her head clean. Now, there was hardly a day when her former friends didn't ripple through her thoughts. In Ann's head, Birdy was perpetually nineteen, thin as a guitar string, a new tune never far from her lips.

'I'm surprised you didn't come across her in Steelstown,' said Stacey.

'It was two years before I went home. I never lived there again, and I don't think any of the others did either. We'd become different people. We couldn't walk back into our old lives and pretend nothing had happened. Can you imagine the questions? The slagging? It would have been miserable.'

For a decade, Ann had been adamant that she wouldn't go back to Ireland. She'd told herself that she treasured London's anonymity and freedom. That she didn't want to be known as 'Patrice Saunders' daughter' or 'the girl who'd been in that band'. She'd wanted to reinvent herself. She would sing in another band, team up with a new set of musicians. But she'd never been able to find the energy. Her life had been a mess. A complete ten-car pileup.

Brendan, a Galwegian who'd only spent a couple of years in England, had helped to change her mind. 'There's no shame in turning towards home,' he'd said. In Galway, she'd gradually realised how much she liked being with men and women who reminded her of growing up in Steelstown. She understood them, and she liked to think they understood her.

What had happened in London had left her with few stories. She couldn't reminisce about her wild youth. Her experiences weren't engagingly grubby. They were pathetic and infused with guilt. The summer of 1982 had left her alienated, not just from her former bandmates but also from her hometown.

'Did you try to contact Birdy?' asked Stacey.

'I wrote to her.' Ann smoothed a hand over Grover's warm fur. 'It must be twenty-five years ago. I didn't have an address, but Yvonne said she'd pass on the letter. Birdy told her to say thanks. She accepted my apology but reckoned there was no reason for us to get back in touch. I tried again five years later and got a similar response.'

Stacey joined her hands together. 'That must have been tough.'

'It was. It added to my fears that I'd been partly responsible for her breakdown. Well, I'm not sure if breakdown's the right word. Perhaps Birdy would call it something else. But to run away like she did she must have been in incredible pain.'

Ann willed Ronan to say something. Again, the response came from Stacey.

'When you wrote to Birdy, was she in Dublin?'

'The first time, she was in London. I have a feeling that, by the time of the second letter, she was in Dublin. I know she got married, but I don't know anything about her husband.'

'Yvonne wouldn't tell you?'

'No. I guess she worried I'd try to find Birdy when that wasn't what she wanted.'

Ann was about to continue when Ronan looked up. 'Are we not avoiding the real issue here? There's only one person to blame for everything, and that's Kieran Mitchell. He raped a teenager, someone he should have been protecting, and he got away with it.

And from the small bit I know, the guy's done nothing but prosper ever since. For as long as I can remember, there've been fawning articles about him in the papers and sycophantic interviews on the TV. He's treated like some sort of cultural guru.'

Whatever Ann had expected to hear, it wasn't that. She'd underestimated her son.

'I can't argue with you,' she said. 'I could never have imagined how successful he'd become. How respected.'

'This probably sounds naïve,' said Stacey, 'but did Birdy ever mention going to the police?'

'To be honest, I doubt she even considered it. It would have been her word against his. And if I didn't believe her, why would she have got anywhere with the police?'

'I see. And, if you don't mind me asking . . .'

'You want to know what happened between me and Kieran Mitchell?'

'Yes.'

'By then, any fantasies I'd had about him were fading. I didn't want to keep on seeing him. Not that he put up much of a fight. From his perspective, I'd been part of a set-up that was going to bring money and success. When that dream ended, my appeal went too.'

'And he went back to Dairena Lennox?'

'That's if he ever fully left her. How did you know?'

'The wonders of Wikipedia,' said Stacey. 'Did you have any further dealings with him?'

Ann shook her head. 'In the early years, when I was in London, our paths crossed a few times, but I haven't seen him in . . . oh, it must be thirty-five years.'

This wasn't entirely true. About five years earlier, when she'd been in Dublin visiting Ronan, she'd seen his face floating towards her. They'd been at the top of Grafton Street, near St Stephen's

Green. She'd known him instantly. He'd been wearing a navy coat, a black scarf and a glaze of success. He'd strode past without recognising her. She'd been another middle-aged woman in the crowd. One of the grey-faced masses. Easy to ignore.

'He was a predator,' said Ronan. 'Not just with Birdy, but with you as well. There are no excuses for the guy.'

'Obviously the way he treated me wasn't on a par with what he did to Birdy. But I was looking for approval, and he exploited that. And, let's face it, if it hadn't been me, it would have been one of the others. He viewed getting to sleep with the band as his reward for being our manager.'

'I can understand why you chose to keep those years hidden. All the same, I wish you'd told me before. It's too much to carry around in your head.'

'Thanks, Ro. Crazy as it might sound, I wasn't ready to speak. Not until now.'

The cat jumped from her knee, and she got up to let him out, wincing as she did.

'Are you all right?' asked Stacey.

'I'm grand. Don't worry about me.'

Ann would have loved to be a bystander when Stacey, in her crimson dress and emerald sandals, had called to her mother's door. She was surprised her mam hadn't rung to warn her that a cheeky young one was on her trail. To Patrice, any woman under forty was a 'cheeky young one'. At forty, they graduated to the 'old enough to know better' category. Despite the passing years, her talent for homing in on the shortcomings of others was undimmed.

Even though Ann had wanted Stacey to take an interest in The Diamonds, she was taken aback by how invested she'd become. She hadn't expected her to go to so much trouble. For the thousandth time, she wondered why Stacey had broken up with Ronan. When she'd asked, he'd been irritatingly vague.

After she'd fed Grover and let him out for a run, she returned to the sitting room.

'What about Gail and Yvonne?' asked Ronan. 'What became of them?'

Ann turned to Stacey. 'Am I right in assuming you've heard about Gail?'

'Mmm. Mike Slattery filled me in.'

Stacey told Ronan about the bass player's reincarnation as an academic in the United States.

'Fair play to her,' he said. 'From the way you described her, that's not what I'd imagined.'

'I didn't do her justice,' said Ann. 'These days, it's likely her potential would be spotted at school. Back then, everyone's judgement was clouded by what they thought of her family. They were the notorious McGeehans.'

'And Yvonne? Where's she?'

'She's in Sheffield. She married a Yorkshireman and had four children in quick succession. We stayed in touch for quite a while.'

'But you're not in contact now?' asked Stacey.

'No. I didn't make a conscious decision to cut ties with her. It just happened. I suppose she reminded me of the worst times. I suspect she felt something similar. It was like our connection had run its course.'

'I take it you no longer feel that way?'

'No. A lot has changed since then. Or maybe it hasn't. Maybe I've changed.'

Ronan stretched out his legs. 'Is that what you hope for? That you'll see them again?'

'Yes. I know that after all these years they might say, "What's the point?" And I wouldn't blame Birdy if she wanted to keep her distance. But, yes, I'd like to meet up with them.'

Ann kept asking herself why seeing the band mattered so much. Was it because she was seeking forgiveness? Yes and no. As Ronan had pointed out, she wasn't the one who had attacked Birdy. Was it because she was sentimental? No. Every happy memory was paired with a bleak one. She couldn't recapture the innocence of the early days. It had been stolen from them by someone who would never understand the value of what he'd taken. She wanted, needed, to see The Diamonds because she'd never stopped missing them.

Stacey rose from her armchair, walked across the room and sat beside her. 'I promise I'll do everything I can to help.'

Ann clasped her hand. 'Thanks. You're always told not to look back, aren't you? But, in this case, I think that's a mistake.'

'The question,' said Ronan, 'is whether you want to do more than that.'

'You mean would I like our story to be told? Up until recently, I'd have said no. But, having thought about it, I've changed my mind.'

'I get you,' he said, 'only—'

'Only it's far from straightforward? Like I said earlier, I appreciate that.'

Ronan nodded. 'Legally, it's hard to know where to start. I assume Mitchell has top-class lawyers and all the rest of it.'

'No doubt he does.' Ann gave Stacey's hand a squeeze. 'It's not just that, though, is it? Without the cooperation of the others, I can't do anything.'

Chapter 33

Stacey and Ronan sat outside a café on Shop Street. All around them, the city was coming to life. Shopkeepers pulled up their shutters; tourists slouched under the weight of their rucksacks; two seagulls squabbled over the remains of a sandwich. Stacey had forgotten about Galway's seductive power. Every time she visited, she asked herself why she didn't live here.

She looked at Ronan, deep in thought as he drank his coffee. They could, she reckoned, stay until nightfall and still not get around to everything they needed to discuss. Twenty-four hours ago, he'd never heard of The Diamonds. She'd been in Steelstown, knocking on doors and foraging for scraps of information. Neither had known that their lives were about to intersect again.

Stacey had spent the night in the Egans' spare room. Not that she'd had much rest. The revelations of the day had made sleep almost impossible. Her heart ached for the band, and for Birdy in particular. When she'd left London, where had she gone? How had she recovered? Had she found something else to bring her joy? Or had her life been blighted by what had been done to her?

According to Mike Slattery's description, she was doing well. The fundamentals were sound, he'd said. But appearances weren't always reliable. Few people paraded their wounds or wished to be seen as victims. Stacey didn't have to look far for an example. For decades, Ann had successfully shown one side of herself to the world.

Stacey's brain had raced until the birds were tuning up and pale light was peeping through the curtains. Not all of her thoughts had been about Mitchell. Every so often, her mind would alight upon something else Ann had said about The Diamonds: an episode from their months in Dublin or a story about a gig they'd played. Remembering an anecdote about Gail's gig-day tapes, Stacey had returned to her early eighties playlist. With U2 and Simple Minds providing unlikely lullabies, she'd finally fallen asleep.

Five hours later, here she was, eyelids heavy, throat dry, mind grappling with all she'd learnt. Ronan looked as worn out as she felt. There were dark smudges under his eyes, and his hair was even more unruly than usual.

'I emailed Gail first thing this morning,' she said.

Ronan smiled. 'I thought this was first thing.'

'No. This is eleven o'clock. Practically lunch time.' She returned his smile. When they'd lived together, she'd joked about his capacity for sleep. 'I also sent a Facebook message to Birdy's brother and to Yvonne Hayes, or Yvonne Marsden as she is now.'

'You're determined to talk to them all, aren't you?'

'I am. I'm desperate for the band to meet again.'

'Except Gail and Yvonne have ignored Mam's approaches, and Birdy has said no in the past. If they don't want to cooperate, what then?'

'That's a good question. I'd no idea this would turn out to be so explosive. You know the sort of stuff I deal in. Most of my subjects slid out of favour because that's the nature of fame. Unless you're monstrously successful, it's "Bye-bye, honey, move along now." This is the first time I've come across actual criminality. And it has me rattled.'

'You and me both.' Ronan scratched his throat. 'I watched the video again. Not just to see Mam. I wanted to see them all. Obviously I'm biased, but they should have been massive.'

'That's what's kept me plugging away for the past few weeks. They were way too special to disappear. By this stage, I must have seen that video a hundred times. Now that I know what was happening behind the scenes, it's even more poignant.' Stacey took a mouthful of coffee. 'How do you feel about everything this morning?'

'Where do you want me to start? It's too glib to say, "I feel like I've never really known my mother." But to find this out now is kind of unsettling. She had this whole other life, and I knew nothing about it.'

Stacey noticed the way he emphasised the word 'now', as though the timing was significant. She tilted her face towards the sun. 'Are you annoyed she kept it to herself?'

'Ah, annoyed is too strong. She had her reasons. I just wish she'd been able to tell me something about those times, even if she edited out the darker bits. I'm kicking myself too. I always knew she was interested in music and that she had a great voice. I grew up hearing her singing along to the radio. But never once did I wonder if she could do something with her talent.'

'Should I contact Kieran Mitchell again, do you think?'

'What would you say? The last time, you got the brush-off from one of his minions. If you mention Birdy, you'll get the brush-off again, only this time it'll be accompanied by a solicitor's letter.'

'But I feel like I've got to do something. And hearing the full story puts his email in a new light. He gave the impression that he barely remembered The Diamonds. That can't be true.'

'I'd say he got quite a land when your query arrived. He must have thought you knew something about what he'd done.'

'And I hadn't a clue,' said Stacey. 'Hopefully, it gave him an almighty fright. Anyway, you heard your mam. She'd like the story to be told. And she's right. Given how Mitchell treated them, it's sickening that he's prospered.'

While yesterday had provided a breakthrough, it wasn't the end. If anything, what she'd learnt had been too dramatic. Like Ann had said, the tale couldn't be told without the input and approval of the others. Even then, the legal barriers were high. People had this notion that if something was true, there was no difficulty in reporting it. If only. That Stacey believed every word Ann had spoken was neither here nor there. She couldn't just accuse someone of rape, especially when the allegation was forty years old and the alleged perpetrator was as wealthy and influential as Kieran Mitchell.

Men with power, and expensive lawyers, could always manipulate the truth. Vivienne Lane Power, who'd moved in the same circles as Mitchell, had described him as ruthless. He was a music-industry deity, a formidable adversary. So, yes, there was every danger Stacey would never get to broadcast the complete story. But that wasn't sufficient reason to give up.

Ronan's voice sliced through her thoughts. 'Take my word for it, Stace, I'd love Mitchell to get what he deserves. During the night, I had a look at some of his press coverage. Talk about gold-medal levels of hypocrisy. In one interview, he rattled on about how there were still too few women in rock music. But there's no sense in wasting your time. You'll never get to him.'

'Even if your mother wants me to give it a go?'

'I heard what Mam said but, trust me, she doesn't get how legally fraught this is. Realistically, the best outcome is that she gets to see Birdy again. I think that should be our priority. She needs peace of mind.'

His attitude didn't sit well with Stacey. 'I spend my life on defamation watch. I've had legal threats over the most stupid things. But even if the allegations are never broadcast, I want Mitchell to know that someone's on his case. I want to throw a few fireworks into his perfect life. Surely you want that too.'

'Yes. And I want world peace, and Galway to win the All-Ireland every year. But I spent the night thinking about this – and it's not going to happen. People like Mitchell are untouchable.'

'You're being too defeatist.'

'And you're not being practical,' said Ronan. 'There isn't endless time to play about.'

'I'm not "playing" with anything. I'm not some innocent let loose. I'm under no illusion about how tricky it is. And in case you've forgotten, I'd have got to this point a lot sooner if your mam had been more direct.'

A muscle twitched in his cheek. 'The circumstances changed. And I didn't say you were an innocent let loose.'

'It's what you implied.'

Stacey must have raised her voice a notch too far because the man at the next table, a middle-aged fellow with an elaborate comb-over, turned and gave her a disapproving look. *Oh, mind your own business,* she wanted to say. Instead she gave him her widest, fakest smile.

'Please, Stace,' said Ronan. 'Let's not fall out.'

'Okay.' She sighed. 'Football or hurling?'

'Come again?'

'Which All-Ireland is it you want Galway to win?'

He laughed. 'If you can fix it, I'll go for both. By the way, Mam's friend, the one who put the comments up online, is calling around later.'

Stacey had planned on returning to Dublin. Not only was her work piling up, the Egans could do with some space. But she didn't want to be rude, especially after Ann had been so honest. Plus, she was keen to meet the woman behind the YouTube aliases.

'Grand,' she said. 'What's her name, do you know?'

'I don't. Mam didn't say, but I've a feeling she's not one of the usual crew.'

Stacey lifted her cup. She had hoped to raise Ronan's chance meeting with Carmel. Did he have a new girlfriend or had that night been a one-off? Looking at him now, she shoved her questions aside. They felt too trivial. Too self-involved.

Across from her, his face remained preoccupied. Sombre, even. Throughout their conversation, he'd had the air of a man who was telling a tale but drawing back before the punchline.

'There's something you haven't told me, isn't there?'

'Nah,' he said, 'it's nothing.'

'So it is something, but you don't know whether to tell me?'

'Jesus, I'd forgotten how persistent you can be.'

'It's hard to get anywhere without persistence. I know you, and I know you're holding back on me.'

'I'm not sure that . . .' Ronan's words tapered off. He looked around, as though scared of eavesdroppers. Thankfully, Comb-over Man had left. 'Yes,' he said, weariness in his voice. 'I wasn't going to say anything this morning . . . but there's something I think you should know.'

*

Stacey had never given much consideration to Kieran Mitchell's first wife. If forced to think about Imogen Faulkner, she would probably have pictured someone harried and dreary, face etched with a lifetime of disappointment. Either that or a central casting south Dubliner: features distorted by one tweakment too many, limbs deeply tanned from a month in Marbella, attitude on the frosty side of indifferent.

The woman who sat on the Egans' patio drinking white wine fitted neither of these stereotypes. Imogen was small with ash-blonde hair and fine features. She was wearing a loose cream top, an ice-blue skirt and low-heeled espadrilles. Oh, and she fizzed with enthusiasm.

It turned out that she'd also married again. Her second husband was a retired orthodontist. ('Forget rock bands. You know where you are with teeth.') They lived in Dublin, and she'd driven to Galway to meet Stacey and Ronan.

The garden was a mosaic of colour: sweet peas jostling for space with lupins and aquilegia and other flowers whose names Stacey couldn't remember. This time, Ronan's father had joined them, and the five basked in the afternoon's warm glow. The cat dozed in the shade of a crab-apple tree.

The story that emerged was this: two months previously, at the same time as she'd tried to contact Gail and Yvonne, Ann had written to Imogen. She wanted, she'd said, to apologise for her role in the collapse of Imogen's first marriage. She knew that after four decades her letter might seem inappropriate, but she'd been thinking about those times, and the affair remained on her conscience.

'To begin with,' said Imogen, 'I wasn't going to reply. Hand on heart, when it comes to my first husband, I'm past the point of caring. Or, at least, I thought I was. But it was a persuasive letter, and I was intrigued. It bothered me that Ann was still beating herself up over something that happened half a lifetime ago so I dropped her a line.'

Imogen's voice belied her delicate appearance. It was firm, determined. She would, Stacey reckoned, have made a good broadcaster.

Ann trailed one hand along the patio table. 'We had a chat on the phone, and I soon learnt that the picture Kieran had painted of Imogen was . . . well, misleading doesn't begin to cover it.'

'We arranged to meet,' said Imogen.

'That was when I told her about the final days of The Diamonds. Even though we barely knew each other, I felt I could confide in her.'

'Going back to 1982, I remember wondering why The Diamonds had disappeared. But I was fighting so many battles of my own that I didn't give them much thought. I'd only just found out about Dairena Lennox and the baby. Then Kieran announced he was going to live with her. He also let something slip about Ann, or Loretta as she was then. I was an absolute wreck, and my parents were devastated. In their world, it didn't matter how unhappy you were, you offered up your suffering and you stayed married.'

'I can't imagine how awful that must have been,' said Stacey. 'Kieran Mitchell left quite a trail of destruction.'

'Didn't he just?' Imogen wrinkled her nose. 'We were young when we met, still at college. I was flattered he knew who I was. He had a big reputation – and a big welcome for himself. Compared to other men I'd known, he seemed larger than life, better than real. And I fell for it all. I was so naïve.'

'When Ann told you about Birdy, were you shocked?'

'How do I put this? Shocked? Yes. Surprised? Not really. He was never good at taking no for an answer, and I can see how that might have tipped over into something worse. He wouldn't have stopped to consider what Birdy wanted. And I can see how afterwards he would have bullied and intimidated her.'

'When did you decide to involve Stacey?' asked Ronan.

'I'd told Imogen about the podcast,' said his mother, 'and, like me, she'd become a regular listener.'

Imogen nodded. 'As you know, Ann was trying to get back in touch with the other Diamonds. She was also increasingly annoyed that Kieran had never faced the consequences of his actions. We were mulling over everything, and I suggested she write to Stacey to see if she could set up a reunion.'

'Like I explained last night, I was still in two minds. That was how Senan O'Reilly was born. Or perhaps I should say reborn.'

'I also thought it'd do no harm to put a few comments on the YouTube page. I'm afraid I got carried away.' Imogen raised her hands. 'That's always been a failing of mine.'

Until now Ann's husband, Brendan, had been a mostly silent presence. Stacey wondered what he made of the turn their lives had taken. How was he coping?

'Do you ever see Mitchell?' he asked.

'No, but he comes back to Dublin fairly often. I'm friendly with the children from his marriage to Dairena Lennox, and they fill me in. Well, I say children . . . Ryan's forty and Rowena's in her early thirties. They have a cordial relationship with their father, but I can't say they're close. He didn't treat Dairena very well and that continues to hurt them.'

'What happened to Dairena?' asked Stacey.

'The poor woman was killed in a car crash. It was a desperate tragedy. Rowena was only a little girl at the time. And, of course, Kieran was in New York with his new wife and new family.' She gave a slight shake of the head, as if to say, *What else would you expect?*

Stacey felt sweat gathering at the nape of her neck and in the small of her back. The heat of the afternoon and the stress of the past two days had combined to give her a vicious headache. She was winded by it all, by all she'd learnt and all she had to do. She was also on constant alert for a reply from Gail, Yvonne or Declan. *Please don't ignore me*, she thought. Even if the replies were negative, they would be the start of a conversation. They'd give her something to work with.

With every hour that passed, she became more determined. The Diamonds would have to meet again. And, whatever Ronan said, there must be some way of getting to Kieran Mitchell.

On the other side of the table, Imogen picked up her wine glass. She appeared to be thinking about what she was going to say. She put the glass down again and looked directly at Stacey.

'I've thought a lot about this over the past two months. There are days when I've thought of little else. And new questions keep popping into my head.'

'I feel the same,' said Stacey.

'And there's one thing in particular that's been nagging at me. We've been assuming that The Diamonds were Kieran's only casualties and Birdy his only victim. I wonder if that's the case.'

Chapter 34

'I still can't believe it,' said Rhiannon, as she pushed Mia's swing. 'I was getting more and more depressed. And then the call came.' She gave another push. 'Is it our dream home? Probably not. But it's a lot better than the three of us having to share a room in a bed-and-breakfast.'

Mia turned and gave a smile as wide as the Liffey. 'And I'll still see my friends and I can go to the same school and everything.'

'That's right, chicken,' said her mother. 'If anything, we'll be closer to school and to work. So, yeah, it's good.'

Every couple of minutes, Rhiannon made an attempt to hide her delight at having found somewhere to live. She would mention one of their new apartment's failings ('The curtains in Mia's room are ten types of ugly') or say something reassuring about Stacey's situation (It's your turn next. I feel it in my bones'). Then her joy would break through, like beams of sunlight in a slate-grey sky. She even looked different. Her face was less strained, her walk more confident.

Through a client of Carmel's, they'd heard about a two-bedroom apartment in a nearby development. It was smaller and more expensive than their home in Whitethorn. But it was clean and well-maintained and moving wouldn't involve any significant upheaval.

Be happy for your friends, Stacey told herself. *Be happy for Mia who'll still be able to come to this playground with its swings and slides and lovely treehouse.*

Rhiannon's good news should have provided her with solace. It proved that, with enough work, a breakthrough was possible. Instead she was having one of those days when the world felt like a bleak, unfair place. Her mood hadn't been helped by the arrival of another letter from Silver Eagle. This one reminded her that she was due to vacate the apartment in less than eight weeks' time. The company also wanted to arrange a date for someone to view the property. In formal language, the letter informed her that, unless the inspection was carried out successfully, she would forfeit her deposit and be left without a reference.

Before uploading the latest episode of 'Whatever Happened To . . . ?' she'd made a sprinkling of edits and written a sharp introduction. Unfortunately, no matter how slick her sales job, she couldn't make Macdara Grant sound appealing. Actually, it was worse than that. His self-absorption caught in her throat. 'Oh, get over yourself, man,' she'd said to the screen.

Twenty-four hours after her return from Galway, what she'd learnt was like a drumbeat running through her head. However hard she tried to focus on the rest of her life, The Diamonds wouldn't go away. So far, she'd heard nothing from Gail, Yvonne or Declan. If they didn't reply by the end of the week, she would have to try again. She'd called Mike Slattery and told him about meeting Loretta. She'd outlined the Senan O'Reilly connection but hadn't revealed anything about Kieran Mitchell. As helpful as Mike had been, it wasn't information she could share. He'd asked people in Steelstown about Birdy. Apart from a general belief that she lived in Dublin and was married to an Englishman, no one had much to offer.

Stacey gave Rhiannon the gist of The Diamonds' story. Not surprisingly, her friend was agog.

'There's lots more,' Stacey said, 'but . . .'

'. . . it's not suitable for small ears?'

'Got it in one.'

They resolved to talk back in the apartment where Mia could be distracted by cartoons.

They were about to leave when Stacey heard her phone. Since Sunday, she'd tried to ration the number of times she checked her notifications. She didn't want to get distracted by every buzz or ping. Still, she couldn't resist one more look.

'Just a tick,' she said to Rhiannon. 'I need to check my . . . Oh.'

There it was. A reply from Gail. Stacey felt a jolt and a whoosh, as though she'd accelerated over a humpbacked bridge. She sat on the ground and read:

Dear Stacey,
Thank you for your email and for your kind words about my career and about The Diamonds.

I gather that you have also reached out to Yvonne and to Birdy's brother, Declan. I have spoken to Yvonne and Birdy so, although this response is in my words, please consider it as being from all three of us.

In one way, I'm amazed that this is happening now. In

another, I'm surprised it has taken so long for Loretta/Ann to try to bring us together again. I don't mean that as a criticism. We fell apart in miserable circumstances. It's tempting to think that a get-together could wipe away the bad memories.

Everyone knows that, as you get older, you gain more perspective. In many cases, events seem less significant. You find yourself asking why you wasted so much emotion on something of no lasting importance. But the opposite is also true. Some events are amplified by the passing decades. You realise that they can't be pushed aside or rationalised.

Please believe that I would like nothing more than to see Kieran Mitchell face justice for what he did to my friend. But it wasn't possible in 1982, and it isn't possible now.

Birdy was, she is, very talented. In taking away her desire to make music, Mitchell took away one of the most important parts of her life. If he spent the rest of his days in prison, it wouldn't be enough to make up for that. He also shattered her confidence and made it hard for her to trust people.

I accept that you're sincere in your desire to bring The Diamonds together again and to tell our story. I'm afraid, however, that too much time has passed. Even if it was legally possible to tell the truth, which I doubt, I'm not sure it would bring any particular comfort to Birdy.

Neither are we convinced that meeting would be a wise idea. What would we talk about? It would be nice to think we could just reminisce about the good times, but we don't get to pick our memories, and the conversation would inevitably turn to Mitchell. After four decades, what purpose would that serve?

I bear no malice towards Ann. She, too, was a victim of a manipulative man. I should have replied when she wrote some weeks back. I guess I found it too difficult.

For fear she imagines that the rest of us see each other regularly, we don't. We are, however, in contact, and like I said at the outset, what I have written here represents our shared view.

In conclusion, may I wish you good luck with your podcast. Unfortunately, this is one story that is best not told.

With all best wishes,

Gail McGeehan Davis

As she read, Stacey blinked back tears. It was hard to think of a more dispiriting response. Her heart filled with affection for Ann. There didn't have to be recriminations. They didn't have to rub vinegar in each other's sores.

One thing was clear: nothing would happen without Birdy's agreement.

A week passed. And then another. Stacey replied to Gail, saying that if any of them had second thoughts, she'd be happy to talk. She didn't hear anything further. Every day, her frustration grew. There would be no reunion.

As she'd predicted, the Macdara podcast went down like a day-old pint. On social media, listeners suggested various ways he could supplement his writing income. Among them were unblocking hotel drains, cleaning portable toilets, and working overnight shifts in a meat factory. He sent her a poorly punctuated email in which he complained that she'd belittled his art and couldn't be trusted.

Thankfully, she was able to rustle up some more entertaining guests for the next three episodes. One, a television presenter turned garden designer called Amber O'Leary, was genuinely funny about her years in the shark-infested waters of children's TV. She was also unusually candid. In Stacey's experience, few people in the media were honest about being let go. They were 'stepping away for a fresh challenge' or 'seeking projects that fed their curiosity'. Amber admitted that her contract hadn't been renewed. 'A former Miss Ireland with two hundred thousand Instagram followers wanted the job,' she said. 'Plus, she has a big-name agent. So what do you think happened?'

Looking for a new home took up most of Stacey's time. She'd viewed seven different house-shares. These included one where the bedrooms were divided in two by curtains made from refuse sacks and another where the vacant room was actually a garden shed. Even then, they weren't the worst of what was on offer. That honour went to a bomb site of a place near the South Circular Road. While the landlord had been showing her the bathroom, a well-fed rat had emerged from behind the skirting board. In every case, the rooms had been snapped up by other people.

The one streak of light on her horizon had been provided by an email inviting her to a job interview with a PR consultancy. Hayley O'Connor and Associates specialised in fashion and beauty, and Stacey reckoned it might be the company for her.

The following weekend she was going to a college friend's wedding. The week after that, she was invited to a hen weekend in Westport. She had the money for neither. On top of this, she'd just received an electricity bill, and her television licence was due for renewal. She'd already resolved to get rid of the TV and was wondering if she really needed a car.

No matter what else she did, The Diamonds were never far

from her thoughts. She stayed in contact with Ann and Ronan. He'd confirmed that he did have a new girlfriend. Her name was Jill McGrath, and they'd met through one of his housemates.

Stacey had feigned polite indifference before spending half an hour stalking Jill online. Her Instagram was a familiar mishmash of family celebrations, misty west-coast walks and colourful cocktails. She was thin, pretty and conventionally employed.

As far as Stacey could see, Jill's only flaw was her taste in music. My God, it was *awful*. If she wasn't fan-girling over geriatric boybands, she was swooning over saccharine ballads. The knowledge brought Stacey unexpected pleasure.

In the main, her conversations with Ronan were confined to the search for Birdy and to the more contentious issue of what to do about Kieran Mitchell. Sometimes, they fell into easy chat. On other occasions, they were as awkward as two strangers in a hotel lift. She continued to find friendship difficult, but they'd been thrown together again, and there was nothing she could do about it.

Stacey rang Ultan Dowdall and Vivienne Lane Power to tell them about her progress. She skirted around the reasons The Diamonds had split, hoping that one day she'd be able to reveal the full story. She asked them both to keep an ear open for anything relevant. Even as she made the requests, she was convinced they were futile.

She decided to check in with Mike Slattery. He sounded surprised to hear from her again and asked if he could call her back. When he did, the background noises suggested he was outside. Stacey could make out a dog's bark and the chimes of an ice-cream van. She suspected his wife wouldn't approve of more talk about Birdy Troy.

'I've got a small bit of news,' he said.

Stacey felt a prickle of excitement. 'Oh? That sounds good.'

'I wouldn't get ahead of yourself because it's not much. I was talking to a fellow at work whose sister met Birdy a few weeks back.'

'In Steelstown?'

'No, the sister was above in Dublin for the weekend. She was in a café, and the woman at the next table looked familiar. She said hello. And who did the woman turn out to be? Only Birdy. The sister, Trisha's her name, was two years behind us at school.'

'What did she say about Birdy?'

'Not a huge amount. They had a quick chat. Birdy told her that she works in a GP's surgery. It sounds as though she runs the office.'

'She didn't say where?'

'No.' Mike stalled, as if he was considering what to say next. 'Her husband was with her. Like I'd heard, he's English. He said something about how they'd known each other when Birdy had first moved to London, but a few years passed before they met again and got married.'

'That's interesting,' said Stacey, hand curling more tightly around her phone. 'There's no chance Trisha got a name for him?'

'Only a first name, and that's hardly of much use to you.'

'Honestly, Mike, at this stage I'd be grateful for any small scrap of information. I'm desperate.'

'Okay.'

She heard him breathe out. 'What is it?'

'Look,' he said, 'I know I agreed to help you. But are you doing the right thing here? If Gail has said Birdy isn't keen on meeting Loretta, or Ann, I should say, is pestering her a good idea? I'm not saying you should let it go, but maybe you could ease up a bit.'

Stacey dug her teeth into her bottom lip. 'I won't pester her. It's just . . . Gail doesn't know the whole story. And if I could talk to Birdy, I think she might see things differently.'

There was another moment's silence before he answered. 'Grand, but you're not to go upsetting her. I'd be very annoyed if you did. Honest to God, I would.'

'You have my word.'

'I'll give you the name so, only I'm not sure you can do much with it. Trisha said Birdy's husband introduced himself as Andy.'

'Thanks,' said Stacey. 'You never know. It might help.'

'There's something else, isn't there? Something you're not telling me.'

Stacey's first impulse was to sidestep the question. But that would be wrong. At the same time, she couldn't tell him the truth. 'It's kind of complicated. It's like, for now, I've said as much as I can. But I swear to you, when I can say more, you'll be the first person I call.'

'I'll have to trust you,' he said, his voice revealing that this trust was already frayed.

When she'd thanked Mike again and reassured him that she wouldn't harass Birdy, she thought about what she was doing. Was he right? Was there something problematic about pursuing a woman who'd made it clear that she didn't want to be disturbed? Perhaps there was, but Stacey had made a promise to Ann. That wasn't all. Her search for Birdy was what shook her awake at four in the morning. It made everything else seem inconsequential. She couldn't give up now.

She called Ronan's mother to ask if the name 'Andy' meant anything to her.

For one, two, three seconds, there was no reply. 'Well, it does,' Ann said eventually, 'but it's unlikely to be the same man.'

'What do you mean?'

'When we were recording the album, Birdy was seeing a guy who worked in the studios.'

'A producer?'

'No, he was a young lad who did the admin work and suchlike. He was quite keen on Birdy, but after she went away, I never heard of him again. His name was Andy.'

Stacey bounced on the balls of her feet. 'Do you remember his last name?'

'Gosh, now you're asking.'

Please, she thought. *Please remember*. 'If you like, I can give you another ring when you've had time to think.'

'No,' said Ann, 'bear with me. It was Andy . . . Andy . . . Andy Chisholm. That was it. Andy Chisholm. But I doubt we're talking about the same man. How would she have come across him again? They were in London, not Steelstown. You don't just bump into people.'

'Maybe they'd kept in touch. Mike's friend said they met up again after a few years. So it does make sense.'

When they'd hung up, Stacey did an internet search for Birdy Chisholm. Nothing appeared. Ann had been right. It was too much to hope for.

Without any particular confidence, she decided to look for Jacqueline Chisholm. If that didn't work, she would try to track down Andy. No sooner had she typed in the name than a number of matches appeared. She was offered Facebook pages and Instagram accounts. There was an American Jacqueline Chisholm who'd written a book about crystals, a Londoner who ran a grooming service for pets and a woman in Brighton who worked in local government.

And then . . . there she was. Tolka Medical was a large GP practice on Dublin's northside. According to its website, the office manager was called Jacqueline Chisholm. There was even a photo. Her hair was shorter, and she was wearing glasses. But it was definitely, undeniably, her. Mike had been right. She was one of those people who didn't change.

Stacey let out a breath.

She had found Birdy Troy.

Unsure what to do next, she paced the room. If she called the doctor's office, there was every danger Birdy would hang up. Alternatively, she could set everything out in a letter. Was there, she wondered, a magic formula of words that would convince Birdy to talk to her – and to Ann? If there was, it eluded her.

The more she paced, the more she knew there was only one solution. The best way to persuade Birdy to think again was to meet her face-to-face. Stacey picked up her phone and located the GP's surgery. The map told her it was off the Drumcondra Road, close to the Tolka River.

First thing in the morning, she would be there.

Chapter 35

If you asked Birdy, there was no pleasing some people. She was early for work, the first appointment was thirty minutes away, and already Francie McAuliffe was sitting on the wall, complaining.

'A fellow could catch his death out here,' he said, as he eased himself up.

'It's a beautiful morning,' she replied. 'Whatever kills you, it won't be the cold.'

'That's easy for you to say, a woman in the prime of your life. Take it from me, Mrs C, in ten years' time, you'll be singing a different tune.'

Francie always called her 'Mrs C'. On the board beside the reception desk, where the staff photos were displayed, she was referred to by the name on her passport, Mrs Jacqueline Chisholm. The practice founder, Dr Gerard Feherty, maintained it sounded more professional. Everyone else called her Birdy.

Once inside, she switched off the alarm and placed her handbag on a chair. 'Have you an appointment, Francie?'

'No. Isn't that why I'm here early? I was hoping Dr Killian could fit me in.'

She feigned exasperation, something at which she was well practised. Francie was close to being an anchor tenant of Tolka Medical. If they handed out loyalty cards, he'd be in the gold circle. There was no point in telling him that the days when a patient could saunter in and expect to see a doctor were long gone. In Francie's world, rules were for young people.

She hung up her jacket. 'Go into the waiting room, and I'll see what I can do for you. No promises, mind. Dr Killian's very busy.'

'The blessings of God on you,' he said.

Birdy wasn't lying about the doctors being busy. In the decade she'd been working here, this was the most hectic July she'd known. Pandemic restrictions had left a backlog of sickness. Minor aches had morphed into life-changing pain. Acute conditions had become chronic. Cancers had quietly moved up the stages. That explained why she felt the need to accommodate patients like Francie. It would be easy to say, 'Oh, go away and take a paracetamol.' But you never knew what was really going on, did you?

Ordinarily, she wouldn't have been expected to manage all of the patients on her own, but her colleague, Basia, had returned to Poland for a holiday. When she got back, it would be Birdy's turn to take a break. In the meantime, she tried to keep her complaints to a minimum. There were few people more tedious than the man or woman who wanted everyone to know how hard they worked.

Dr Feherty, as solid as a mahogany sideboard and about as animated, was first to arrive. Next came Dr Lucinda Woods, the most diligent doctor in the clinic. If Birdy was worried about her health, she'd seek out Lucinda. She was followed by Francie's mark,

Dr Killian McSweeney. A beefy man who'd once played club rugby, his eyes roamed the ceiling while Birdy talked through the situation. Eventually, he conceded that, yes, he could squeeze in one more patient.

'Mark my words,' he added, 'there won't be anything wrong with the man.'

'I know, I know,' she said, 'but short of barring him, there's nothing I can do.'

The phone was ringing now. Patients were trickling in. There was a rustle of laughter as the nurses, Althea and Niamh, arrived. A baby, waiting for his vaccinations, began to cry. Outside, a bin lorry rattled and whined. The morning promised to be noisy and chaotic. Just how Birdy liked it. When it was quiet, she had time to think. At the moment, thinking wasn't her friend.

Three years earlier, when Andy had reached his sixtieth birthday, he'd become weighed down by petty worries and slights. He'd insisted he didn't want a party, then been disappointed that his wife and daughters hadn't thrown one anyway. In two weeks, Birdy would be sixty. She was better at coping, or so she told herself.

Perhaps it was because her parents had died young, or perhaps it was because she spent every day surrounded by ill health, but Birdy felt fortunate to be nearing sixty. There was a reason doctors referred to people's fifties as 'Sniper's Alley'. In recent years, she'd lost several friends. They'd been claimed by bad luck and bad choices, hereditary quirks and random misfortune.

More and more, she was preoccupied by those who'd once been part of her life. She spent too much time holding up her memories to the light and turning them around. In particular, she thought about her parents. She pictured her father, sitting at the kitchen table, polishing shoes and giving out about something of no consequence. She saw her mother, leaning over the ironing board, listening to the radio news.

Over the past two weeks, she'd also been thinking about The Diamonds. First, Gail had contacted her. Then Declan. Then Yvonne. A podcaster was making enquiries. Apparently, she'd been talking to Loretta, or Ann as she was now known. As Birdy understood it, Ann had only recently told her son about The Diamonds. This struck her as odd. Admittedly, the band had taken up a tiny part of their lives. But wasn't it an important part?

The podcaster, whose name was Stacey, knew what had happened in 1982. Although Birdy was uneasy about this, she figured there was nothing she could do. After years without contact, she could hardly ring her former bandmate and ask her to be quiet. No doubt the podcast woman wanted Birdy to explain why she'd chosen to walk out on The Diamonds – and what she'd done next. She would probably talk about 'setting the record straight' and 'telling her truth'.

No offence, thought Birdy, *but the answer is no. It will always be no.* The less she said, the sooner the trouble would go away.

In her reply to the podcaster, Gail had said something about no one getting to pick their memories. How right she was. Birdy always smiled when she saw people on social media talk about #makingmemories. The innocence of them. As if anyone got to choose what remained and what faded away.

Those who mattered knew what she had done after leaving The Diamonds. She'd moved and kept on moving. She'd travelled across the continent, taking work wherever she found it. Then she'd gone to Asia. She'd waitressed and cleaned and taught English. She'd slept in hostels and caravans and squats. She'd visited city after city, as though she was on the world tour the band had never got to make. Looking back, she could see how she'd wanted to feel the world didn't start and end in her head. Her brain had needed constant distraction.

On the road, she'd made friends. While her relationships had been brief, some of the friendships had endured. Every Christmas brought a flurry of cards from around the globe.

Three months after leaving London, Birdy had written to Andy. At the time, she'd been picking grapes in the Rhône Valley. The letter had taken weeks to compose. She would say something, then scribble it out. Finally, she decided to tell the complete story. She hoped he would write back but warned herself not to expect anything.

Before leaving France for the Peloponnese, she received a reply. He believed her. Her disappearance had frightened him and he urged her to return to London. He also told her about the band breaking up, news she found genuinely shocking. Andy said that Ian, their producer, had gone into meltdown. That upset her. Working with Ian had been a privilege.

She didn't go back to England, but they did continue to write. Two or three months might pass between letters. When Andy married a solicitor called Minna Renshaw, the gap lasted for six months. In their wedding photo, Minna looked like the sort of regulation posh girl Birdy had always thought he'd marry.

Somewhere along the line, her pain dulled. That wasn't to say it ever fully disappeared. Neither, perverse as it might sound, did she want it to. What had happened, the way Kieran Mitchell had pinned her down and raped her, the way he had lied about it, the way he had intimidated her, had changed the course of her life. It was part of her, and she couldn't wish it away. Even now, there were times when the pain flared up again. In 1982, she hadn't known the word 'predator'. Like 'misogynist' and 'narcissist', it was a word favoured by her daughters' generation. But it had described him then and probably still did.

Despite his arrogance, Mitchell must have realised that he alone had been responsible for The Diamonds' split. They'd been a valuable commodity: young, talented, innocent. And he had destroyed them. Not that this had halted his forward march. He was like a cat. No matter how steep his fall, he landed on all four paws and walked away. Over the decades, she'd seen him in the papers, looking suave and self-satisfied. His wife was hyper-glamorous, her entire life devoted to enhancing and preserving her good looks. Andy urged Birdy not to read about them. 'You'll only upset yourself,' he would say. Sometimes, though, she needed her body to flood with anger. She needed to remember what this man had done.

Eighteen months passed before she went home to Steelstown. After a short visit, she hit the road again. Four and a half years later, she returned to London. She was almost twenty-six. At the time, that had seemed alarmingly old. Now she wondered if there was anything more absurd than a twenty-something worrying about her age. By then, she no longer played the guitar. While happier, she remained rootless, skittish. London felt even more overwhelming than it had at the start of the decade. To her eyes, it was wealthier but more divided. If the number of City boys drinking champagne had increased, so had the number of old men in sleeping bags and cardboard boxes.

Birdy found work in a supermarket. Fortunately, there was a spare bed in Gail's flat, and she was able to live there for a reasonable rent. Gail was doing a politics degree. Although she downplayed her academic ability, her classmates said she was nailed on for a first. She no longer played the bass.

The papers, with more than a touch of sarcasm, dubbed that summer 'the second summer of love'. For many of Birdy and Gail's friends, it slipped by in a haze of acid and dry ice. This, they told themselves, was different. This was about rejecting greed and embracing solidarity. Not everyone was swept up by the new mood. Always the most grown-up Diamond, Yvonne had married and moved to Sheffield. By the summer of 1988, she had two children, a two-year-old girl and a baby boy. Her life was measured out in feeds and nappy changes. She was obsessed with sleep.

One weekend she travelled to London. After a few beers, she began to cry. She asked Birdy to forgive her. 'I should have listened,' she said. 'I should have fought the temptation to smooth everything over and carry on.' Birdy reassured her that none of it had been her fault. Then she asked about Loretta. Yvonne said she was living with a guy in Camden Town. They did a lot of drugs and not much else. 'But it's her life,' she said. 'It's not my place to interfere.' Yvonne no longer played the drums.

Andy's marriage had ended after a year. He'd left the record industry and was working in insurance. They joked about this. They joked about lots of things. While Birdy had been away, music had moved on. She no longer knew who was on the way up and who was on the slide. Where once she'd been able to reel off lists of producers and engineers, now she found herself asking, 'Who's he?'

Musically, her fellow travellers had been trapped in the 1970s. Their soundtrack had been crammed with James Taylor and Gordon Lightfoot, 'American Pie' and 'A Horse With No Name'. Anything more recent than *Rumours* was dismissed as inauthentic or gimmicky.

Andy made her a mixtape of music she'd missed. They had frequent chats to debate his selections. From The Smiths to

Madonna, REM to Public Enemy, The Jesus and Mary Chain to Prince, everyone was dissected. Those were her favourite evenings.

They were astounded that U2 were being called the biggest band in the world. Birdy remembered how, along with Gail and Loretta, she'd seen them in the TV Club in Dublin. Andy had been at one of their early gigs in Bristol. Because of a bus strike, only fifty people had turned up.

It was a mad world, they agreed. A mad world.

Birdy tried not to recall how The Diamonds had been compared to U2. Suppose they had stuck together, what would have happened? If they'd progressed to bigger venues, how would they have sounded? Could they have made it in America? Might they have added a ballad or two to their repertoire or would their sound have stayed hard and uncluttered? When she thought about what might have been, it was difficult not to cry.

Andy encouraged her to join another band. 'You should be making music,' he said. 'That's where your heart is.'

But she couldn't go through all that again. What was more, she no longer felt she had anything to say. As Mitchell had once reminded her, she was a nobody from the arse end of nowhere. No one needed to hear her.

On her travels, Birdy had learnt self-preservation. That was why she couldn't get back with Andy. Not even for a one-night stand. It would be easy to fall in love with him. But if it went wrong, and it would go wrong, what then? She would have lost him for a second time, and she couldn't bear that. Apart from Gail, he was the best friend she had.

Her behaviour annoyed Gail. 'I know you want to hop on the lad,' she said. 'And I know that's exactly what he wants too. I see the pair of you there, practically dripping with desire. Would you not do the decent thing and go for it?'

It took a further six months of Gail's wheedling and cajoling for the two to admit the strength of their feelings. They married in 1990. Birdy suspected that a few years earlier her parents would have objected to their only daughter marrying a divorced Protestant. By the time she finally said, 'I do', any misgivings had dissolved. 'Please God, this means you'll stay put for a while,' her father said. 'Maybe you'll even come home.' Oliver Troy died in 1991. He never had the chance to meet his granddaughters, Molly and Sorcha.

To this day, Birdy was grateful for her marriage. Whatever their ups and downs, she felt fortunate that life had given her Andy.

In 2000, the Chisholm family packed up and moved to Dublin. Birdy's mam was already ill. Andy was surprisingly keen on the move. He needed a change, he said, and his work skills transferred easily. The girls took to their new home with enthusiasm. They spoke Irish in their London accents and played Gaelic football.

Birdy was the one who couldn't adapt. She'd thought that returning to Ireland would bring comfort. The opposite was true. She associated Dublin with those golden months when it had seemed as though The Diamonds' possibilities were infinite. When she had believed the music would last for ever. Somehow, the city exacerbated her sense of failure. One day, she would be fine. The next, she would feel as though she was surrounded by trapdoors, as though she was one misstep away from falling into the darkness.

She paced the city, looking for places that had once been hers. McGonagles? Gone. The TV Club? Gone. The Magnet? Gone. Some things hadn't changed. O'Connell Street, with its stained pavements and stench of fast food, was still shabby and unloved. The affluent youngsters in Trinity College still dressed like poor old people. Buskers continued to annihilate 'Grace' and 'Dirty Old Town'.

Even Birdy had to admit that some changes were for the better. She'd grown up in a country where hopelessness had clung to people like stale cigarette smoke. That had been replaced by an air of positivity and self-belief.

Finally, after a heartfelt request from Andy and an intervention by Gail, she looked for help. She found a counsellor and sought the therapy she should have received twenty years earlier. Did it wipe away her troubles? No. But it did aid her understanding of how she felt. It also provided her with coping skills.

She realised that for too long she'd been pinned down by all the things she couldn't say. That was why, as soon as they were old enough, she told her daughters about The Diamonds and about being assaulted by Kieran Mitchell. The girls, then in their mid-teens, were curious about the band. Fortunately, Andy had made a copy of what would have been their album. At some stage in the nineties, he'd burnt it onto a CD. For a long time, Birdy hadn't been able to listen. What should have been one of her proudest achievements was also the sound of her world falling apart. That night they played it over and over again. After a few days, Molly and Sorcha asked about Mitchell. 'You were right to leave,' they said, their words among the most important Birdy had ever heard.

Rewinding to 1982, she had no regrets about running away. The longer she'd stayed, the more damaged she would have become. In an ideal world, she would have left Mitchell's hotel bedroom and walked straight to a police station. But all the power had rested with him. It still did.

What she did regret was abandoning music. Although she made occasional attempts at keeping up to date, the pull of the late seventies and early eighties remained strong. Lately, she'd been re-listening to The Pretenders. When no one was watching, she danced around the front room to 'Middle Of The Road'. She pretended she was Chrissie Hynde, a Telecaster at her waist: angular, beautiful and for ever cool.

Music could still transport her to another place and ease her troubles. She was reminded of a Bruce Springsteen concert where the man beside her – sixtyish, navy raincoat, neat beard – had been still and quiet for most of the night. Towards the end of the show, the band had played 'Backstreets', and the man had sung every word as if it was his own composition; as if all the pain and desire were written on his soul. For almost ten minutes, from the first piano note to the final drumbeat, he'd been young and uninhibited again. When the song ended, he'd reverted to silence. That was what music could do.

If Birdy's father had liked to grumble about the bands of the 1980s being 'just noise', she had the opposite complaint. In her view, too many contemporary bands weren't noisy enough. She wanted more anger. More attitude. She assumed it was out there, just not easily accessible to her. What she truly couldn't stand was the fashion for anodyne cover versions. Why would you remove all the verve from 'Teenage Kicks'? Why would you take the sex from 'Because The Night'?

From time to time, she read about women who wrote their debut novel or recorded their first songs in their sixties. But that wasn't her. She no longer had the drive. Nor, she feared, would anyone care about her songs. Culturally, the world had little interest in ageing women. When it did, they had to be sad and withered. They were expected to be in mourning for the looks they'd lost or the man who hadn't loved them enough. Or they could be 'feisty'. The word made Birdy shudder. If feisty was the only alternative, she'd opt for sad and withered.

Gail had a saying (she had a great many sayings, but this one was especially apt): 'The problem with being a woman is that you're too young until you're too old.' And wasn't that the truth?

These days, Birdy had little contact with Steelstown. Every couple of weeks, she would check the deaths on the parish website. Once, the notices had been for the mothers and fathers of her contemporaries. Now, they were more likely to contain the names of classmates. She pictured funerals where the mourners reminisced about their carefree youth and the low-level lawbreaking of the deceased. She could almost hear them: *We were half cracked in those days*, they'd say. *And it didn't do us any harm. Sure, God love the poor youngsters nowadays. They've no freedom.*

Then Birdy would go to RIP.ie to offer her condolences. She'd even left a message for the family of Vera Cheevers. Vera had died two years previously at the age of seventy-five.

Andy, Molly and Sorcha were bemused by her fascination with the deaths of people she hadn't seen in decades. They didn't understand that, no matter what had happened afterwards, there was a part of Birdy that was for-ever Steelstown.

The phone rang. She put away her thoughts and answered it. A man who couldn't shake off a painful cough needed an appointment. A young mother was frightened because her baby wouldn't stop crying. A woman asked if the hospital had forwarded her test results. In every case, their fear vibrated down the line.

Birdy longed to offer reassurance. 'Listen,' she wanted to tell them, 'everything will be all right, and even if it's not, you'll cope.'

But those weren't her words to say.

Chapter 36

The woman sitting on the wall had shoulder-length dark hair and long legs. She appeared to be in her late twenties or early thirties. Almost immediately, Birdy was hit by a troubling suspicion. She found her phone and searched for Stacey Nash. Suspicion confirmed.

The skin on her neck tightened. How, she wondered, had the podcaster found her? A moment's reflection told her that it probably hadn't been hard. Young people were good at connecting dots and following trails.

Every few minutes, she tiptoed to the window and peeked outside. Stacey barely moved. Presumably she was waiting for Birdy to take a break. Then she would pounce.

This was not a situation Birdy had anticipated, and she wasn't sure what to do. Could she call the guards? *Hello, Officer, I know you're busy, but there's a harmless-looking young woman who wants to have a word with me. No, she's not trespassing. No, she hasn't actually approached me. All the same, would you mind moving her on?*

Birdy ran through the options. She considered leaving through the clinic's back door, but it was only there for fire-safety reasons, and people would question what she was doing. *Well, Dr Feherty, it's like this. Forty years ago, I played the guitar in a rock band . . .*

Besides, why should she skulk away? She'd done nothing wrong.

There was a chance Stacey would get bored of hanging around or that she would have somewhere else to go. But what if she loitered indefinitely? Maybe Birdy could ask one of her colleagues to have a word. Again, this wasn't realistic. She would have to do a lot of explaining, and that could get awkward.

Resignation sank into her bones. Daunting as it was, she needed to talk to Stacey. She reminded herself that she was fifty-nine years old. Every day, she dealt with complex situations. With people who were scared, upset and angry. With people who railed against the health service, God, and their own bad luck. The woman in the car park looked to be a similar age to Birdy's daughters. Handling her should be a cinch.

She waited until the nurses had a quiet moment, then asked if one of them would take over on Reception. 'I won't be long,' she said. 'If you need me, I'll be out the front.'

Niamh gave her a quizzical look but agreed.

As Birdy walked down the steps and across the small car park, her anger rose. 'Can I help you?' she said, doing her best to sound assertive. 'You've been sitting out here for quite a while, and if you don't move on, I'll have to give the guards a ring.'

'Birdy?' replied Stacey, getting to her feet.

'Yes. You know who I am . . . and I know who you are. But you've already been told I don't want to take part in what you're doing. Isn't that right?'

Rather than giving a direct reply, Stacey launched into a speech.

She didn't wish to be a nuisance, she said, and she wouldn't normally turn up at someone's workplace, but she had to press her case. The wobble in her voice gave away her nerves.

'Look,' said Birdy, 'I've no doubt your heart's in the right place, but I'm not comfortable with you poking around in my private life. I'm asking you to leave me alone. Please.'

Stacey's fingers pressed against the bridge of her nose. 'I'm sorry for coming here like this, only I didn't know what else to do. I wouldn't want to upset you. It's just . . . I've heard how good you were, how good the band was, and it annoys the hell out of me that you never got to be a big success. That was what you deserved.'

'Yeah, well, most of us don't get what we deserve. I know about your podcast, and I honestly doubt that anyone gives a hoot what happened to Birdy Troy. The simple answer is, I'm here and I'm fine. And all the stuff you want to drag up? It happened a lifetime ago. Like I say, no one cares.'

'I care, and if other people knew how Kieran Mitchell had treated you, they'd care too.'

'I've asked you to leave me be, and if you have any respect for me, that's what you'll do.'

'I have tonnes of respect for you. That's the reason I'd hoped we could talk about what happened.'

Birdy put up a hand, as if directing traffic. 'Okay, let's say I gave you an interview. What then? You couldn't put any of it on your podcast. Mitchell would sue you . . . and me as well.'

'Not if—'

'Let me tell you about Kieran Mitchell: things have always worked out for him and they probably always will. Some people are like that. It's something I've learnt to accept, and I'm afraid you'll have to do the same.'

Stacey took a few seconds to reply. 'I'd love you to do an

interview, but if you don't want to . . . well, that's your choice. If I could convince you to do one thing, it would be to have a chat with Ann. You've no idea how much that matters to her.'

There was, thought Birdy, something ridiculous about this. Here she was, standing in a car park, arguing with someone who hadn't been born in 1982. Someone who had grown up at a different time with a different perspective on life. Like Birdy's daughters, she'd been brought up to believe that the truth mattered and wrongdoing would be punished. Birdy's parents had been at the other end of the spectrum. They'd believed in stoicism and deference and the meek inheriting the earth. And Birdy's generation? They were caught in the middle. They were the ones who'd wanted to raise their voices but had usually been too scared to do so.

'Listen,' she said, 'I don't have any animosity towards Ann. We were teenagers. Mitchell preyed on her need for approval, and she was dazzled by his attention. Did I see that at the time? Sort of. But over the years it's become more obvious. She apologised, and I accepted her apology. What else does she need to hear?'

For a few seconds, Stacey was quiet. When she spoke again, she appeared to change tack. 'Vivienne Lane also said hello. She said you were brilliant, and she's never forgotten you.'

It took Birdy half a moment to place the woman Stacey was talking about. 'Vivienne the photographer?'

'Yes.'

'Does she still have the Jack B. Yeats?'

'You've lost me.'

'There was a painting in her parents' front room. You wouldn't believe it, an actual Yeats surrounded by people drinking beer and smoking cigarettes. It was—' Birdy slapped the top of her head. 'Oh, what does it matter? If you come across her again, tell her I said hello . . . and thanks. She was cool.'

'I'm sure she'd love to talk to you. And Mike – Mike Slattery . . . he was asking after you.'

Jesus, this was like being tracked by the CIA. 'You were in Steelstown?'

'A couple of weeks ago, yes.'

This was becoming more of a challenge than Birdy had expected. What Stacey didn't know was that she'd listened to several episodes of the podcast. To Birdy's surprise, she was quite a skilled interviewer: empathetic but not gullible, persistent but not rude. Still, that was beside the point. She needed to take no for an answer.

'This isn't like a shoebox of old Polaroids,' said Birdy. 'It's not "Wasn't our hair funny?" and "Weren't our clothes crazy?" and "Look how thin we were." There's no fluffy nostalgia here. No bland walk down Memory Lane. You get that, don't you?'

'I do.'

'What you're talking about, what Mitchell did to me, I couldn't even tell my mam and dad. They went to their graves without knowing the truth. It took me ten years to tell my brother. Can you imagine what that was like?'

'No, I can't.'

'So what are you doing, then? Why are you bothering me about something that happened when I was a kid? Are there not other programmes you could be making?'

Stacey opened her mouth, then paused and tucked her hair behind her ears.

'I've got to go,' said Birdy, conscious that two men were staring at them. Word would spread, and Dr Feherty would ask why she'd had a row with someone in front of the clinic. 'I meant what I said about calling the police.'

She didn't. Of course she didn't. The longer they stood there, the more this woman reminded her of Sorcha and Molly. She would hate anyone to be rude to them or belittle their work. But neither could she allow herself to be ground down.

'All right,' said Stacey, the wobble returning to her voice. 'You want to know why I'm doing this? I'll tell you.'

Chapter 37

Ann sat into the car, placed her bag on the passenger seat and leant back. Although the heat had lost much of its ferocity, the day was mild, and she brought down the window to get some air.

She had assured Brendan that she could manage the hospital appointment on her own. If she was honest, she needed to feel she was still capable of doing something for herself. She'd already dealt with weeks of bad news. Every meeting, chart and scan teemed with bad news. How could today's consultation be any worse?

That was something she needed to remember: worse was always possible.

Back in the spring, when she'd first felt unwell, she'd had a stock response: 'It's no big deal. I'm a woman in my fifties. I feel like roadkill all the time.'

Eventually, under pressure from Brendan, she'd gone to the doctor. He'd referred her to a consultant. That was when everything had speeded up, and she'd been plunged into the world of the seriously ill: a place of sympathetic looks, hushed voices and embarrassed smiles. She'd learnt to use its language of biopsies, stages and markers. She'd grown accustomed to the hospital's polished floors and stark light, to the hum of daytime TV, to the people who walked quickly and the ones who could hardly walk at all.

At the start, she'd thought what everyone thinks: I don't deserve this. I'm too young. Too busy. I've got too much left to do. But unless you were evil beyond belief, who did deserve to be diagnosed with stage-four cancer? She was no more or less deserving than the next patient. Besides, there was no novel way to think of death. No fresh take or clever response. There could be only one winner.

For a little while, she'd done her best to be optimistic. She'd read all the literature and agreed to all the treatments. She'd asked about drug trials. She'd learnt about special diets. There was, however, a point at which optimism turned into foolishness or, worse, delusion.

Fast forward to this morning, and the doctor's silky voice and unreadable face. The palliative chemotherapy wasn't working quite as well as he'd hoped. Did that mean less time? He couldn't be sure.

Ann tried to see the appointment from his perspective. What was it like to be the bad-news man? She couldn't imagine anyone being blasé, but did the task become less onerous? Did you arrive at a place where you shook off the misery as soon as you left the consulting room?

As she'd sat and listened, she'd fought an irrational desire to attack the doctor. Had she possessed the energy, she would have slapped his ruddy cheeks or kicked his hairy calves. Her real anger was with herself. Or, to be more specific, with her body. She'd taken its strength for granted. It had let her down.

She'd heard people with a terminal diagnosis say the joy had been stripped from everything. The world had turned flat and grey, they said. Her experience was different. It was as if her senses had been heightened. Even relatively mundane experiences – coffee with a friend, an hour in the garden, a favourite album – were freighted with more sweetness than she could bear. Small displays of decency had a similar effect. A considerate health-care worker, an elderly man picking up litter, a cheery bus driver: they all had the power to knock her sideways.

Others found this difficult to understand. As she was discovering, however, there was no uniformity to happiness. No precise prescription. Something might bring her pleasure one day and fill her with despair the next.

After she'd accepted the truth, one thought had come to the fore. Ann wanted to see The Diamonds again. Like she'd explained to Stacey, there were times when this felt like a straightforward task, and there were others when it felt like foolishness. She told herself that she should be concentrating on her family, not on the ghosts of a past life. But she could no more wish away the yearning than she could wish herself healthy again.

Stacey had sent her a link to The Diamonds' gig from Christmas '81. Ann had listened with mixed feelings. She kept spotting the mistakes, most of them hers. Maybe, she thought, they hadn't been anything special. Maybe they would never have made it big. But then . . . There was something about how unapologetically loud they were, how exuberant, how raw, that made her think again. They'd been magnificent.

She also listened to a playlist Stacey had made. All of the songs were from the late seventies and early eighties. She guessed that, to Stacey, they must sound as dated as Glenn Miller or Josef Locke had done to her. And yet to Ann's ears they were timeless. She hadn't foreseen how the music would affect her. How hard it would hit. When Brendan had found her moping, he urged her not to listen.

Every day she warned herself against surrendering to mawkishness and sentimentality. During one of her long conversations with Imogen, she'd mentioned this. Imogen said she could be whatever she wanted. She hadn't expected Imogen's friendship. Or Stacey's. It was easier to have an honest talk with someone you hadn't known for very long. They were less likely to get upset.

She was such a funny thing, Stacey. So driven. God, to have her energy. Last night she'd rung to say she'd found Birdy. To listen to the excitement in her voice, you'd swear a winning lottery ticket had floated through the window.

Ann was unsure about her plan to visit Birdy's workplace. Wasn't there a danger Birdy would feel she was being stalked? When she'd voiced her misgivings, Stacey had listened before arguing that there was no alternative.

Ann glanced at her phone. She'd expected to hear about the meeting by now. The only message was from Brendan: Any news? What could she say? Nope. Still dying.

She'd discovered an unexpected attraction to gallows humour. Unfortunately, it wasn't shared by her husband and son. They spoke as if an upbeat attitude could provide a miracle cure. She didn't blame them. They were casting about for the right thing to say. At the same time, they were preparing for life without her. She had the freedom to say whatever she liked. No one would chastise a dying woman.

She would have to call Brendan. Five minutes, and that was what she would do. She was suffocated by tiredness. It was the sort of exhaustion she'd never experienced before, one that couldn't be chased away by sleep.

She checked her phone again. Still no word from Stacey.

The events that occupied Ann's thoughts had taken place over a few short weeks. Back then, every day had felt endless. As she'd got older, time had speeded up. How could the 1990s have been thirty years ago? When had that new film turned into a classic? When had the ingénue become a matriarch? When had the heartthrob become a character actor? It was as if entire years had gone missing.

She knew she should be making the most of now. Who could say when meeting friends or enjoying the outdoors would no longer be possible? Instead, she kept getting drawn into the past. Every day she thought of the band. Sometimes her memories were fleeting. On other occasions, they were more insistent. The throb of Gail's bass. The chop and swoon of Birdy's guitar. The relentless beat of Yvonne's drums. The roar of the crowd. The sense that your best stories were yet to be told.

When those moments came, she wanted to sing. She longed to be nineteen-year-old Loretta Saunders, narrow hips swaying, long hair swinging. She dreamt of being on stage, giving it everything she'd got. Then, when the memories became unbearable, she would take a deep breath, wrap her arms around herself and try not to cry.

Chapter 38

Stacey had used every argument she could think of, and still she'd failed. She'd babbled on about Vivienne Lane Power and Steelstown and the Lord knew what else. And she'd failed. That wasn't all. Last night, Ann had ruled out mentioning her illness. 'I don't want Birdy to feel I'm blackmailing her,' she'd said. And what had Stacey done? She'd played the sickness card. She'd hoped someone who worked in a medical centre would understand that pancreatic cancer wasn't to be taken lightly.

Birdy had closed her eyes against the news before growing pale. She'd repeated her line about not having any animosity towards Ann. 'I wish her well,' she'd said. Then she'd turned and gone back into the surgery.

In truth, Stacey hadn't been at her best. She'd watched nineteen-year-old Birdy so many times that she'd been overwhelmed by the present-day version. It wasn't just that Birdy remained recognisable:

she remained compelling. Her round grey eyes had lost none of their intensity. Her voice had authority.

Stacey's thoughts flew back to the sun-splashed morning in Galway when Ronan had told her about his mother's diagnosis. 'That's the curse of this form of cancer,' he'd said. 'By the time you realise what's happening, there's a danger the damage has been done. In Mam's case, it's already spread to her liver.'

She had responded with platitudes about treatment being better than ever before. 'There are breakthroughs all the time,' she'd said.

He'd had the good sense to stay quiet.

The information had forced Stacey to re-evaluate Ann's actions. From her desire to meet Birdy to her correspondence with Imogen, everything made sense. She had set the entire process in train because her time was running out. The news also explained why Patrice Saunders had been so worn down and wary. No matter their strained relationship, she couldn't have foreseen losing her daughter.

Ronan was struggling with his mother's diagnosis. Some days, he was remarkably positive. At other times, his focus floated away, and he became hard to reach. Most of their friends had both parents. Quite a few had grandparents. These days, people didn't die in their fifties. Except they did. A quick trawl through the death notices confirmed how severe illness could strike at any age. Many forms of cancer were breathtakingly unfair. They attacked at random with neither cause nor warning. They multiplied and metastasised in silence.

When, finally, Stacey found the courage to call Ann, she told her everything about the conversation with Birdy. 'I'm sorry,' she said. 'I know I wasn't supposed to tell her you were sick but I panicked. She was slipping away from me, and I wanted to stop her.'

Ann said it didn't matter and that she would have done the same. 'It's best if you don't bother her again,' she added, her voice leaden with disappointment. 'I don't want to become a nuisance.'

Talking to Ronan was no easier. Stacey had hoped she'd be able to say, 'Ta-dah, it's all sorted.' But she'd blown her opportunity. He sounded as dejected as she'd feared.

She went to the supermarket and spent money she didn't have on groceries she didn't need. She piled her basket with crusty bread and olives, aubergines and tomatoes, basil and Parmesan. She bought peaches, almond biscuits and a bottle of sauvignon blanc. She would go home, make aubergine parmigiana and try to forget her troubles. Cooking a proper dinner felt like a way of saying, 'I'm not completely useless.'

Outside Whitethorn House, two men were placing large cardboard boxes in the back of a van. A saucepan handle poked out from one. A tangle of coat hangers peeked from another. Every day, another flat became vacant, and more life seeped from the building. Even Pat and Bróna had found somewhere new to live. Actually, it wasn't accurate to say *even* Pat and Bróna because, as it turned out, they were well-connected. According to Rhiannon, Pat had a wealthy uncle with a spare apartment. So much for their WhatsApp agitation. If you asked Stacey, they were like the people who claimed they hadn't studied for the exam but got top marks anyway. They'd convinced everyone their situation was hopeless until – hey presto! – their problems were magicked away.

This, she told herself, was how the world worked. Connections would always trump effort, and getting upset about it was futile. Her mother said that in the eighties the same rule had applied to finding a job.

The more things changed . . .

In a few days' time, Rhiannon, Carmel and Mia would also be

gone from Whitethorn House. Stacey pictured herself as the last woman in the building, Silver Eagle's bailiffs dragging her out by the heels. In the past week, the WhatsApp group had lost its fire. Apart from the occasional message from someone who'd found a new home or the odd gripe about lax security, all was quiet.

Her job interview with Hayley O'Connor and Associates was at twelve thirty the following afternoon, and she planned on devoting the rest of the evening to preparation. First, she decided to check online for any fresh references to Kieran Mitchell. The news sites yielded nothing of significance. The same was true of Facebook, Instagram and Twitter. Before closing her laptop, she took a look at the Reddit forum on rock 'n' roll sex abusers. Traffic there was relatively light, and it took her only a few seconds to spot a new message. It had been added three days previously. Her hands trembled as she read: I know this is kind of different to what's normally posted here cos it's not about a musician. But word has it that there's media interest in an early-rising manager (he's been lucky until now). Lots of skeletons in lots of closets. Never too late for justice.

There was one response: Luck of the Irish?

The original poster replied:

Briefly, Stacey felt a buzz of excitement. Was this cryptic message, with its apparent references to One Scarlet Morning ('an early rising manager') and The Latecomers ('never too late'), about Kieran Mitchell?

Then reality hit. She was looking at Imogen's work. After all, it had been Imogen who'd raised the possibility of her ex-husband abusing other women.

While she prepared dinner, Stacey considered the post. She had to assume it was fake. But, even so, wasn't there a chance that Mitchell had offended again?

She poured a glass of wine before calling Ultan Dowdall. She began by telling him that she'd found the elusive Birdy Troy. Then she asked a question. 'I was wondering if you'd ever come across any rumours about Kieran Mitchell?'

'What sort of rumours?'

'Um . . . sleazy stuff, I suppose.'

She heard Ultan suck in air through his teeth. 'I thought the affair with Loretta Saunders was consensual?'

'It was,' said Stacey before outlining the claim she'd seen on Reddit. She decided not to mention her suspicion that the post was a hoax.

'An internet message board,' said Ultan, his tone halfway between amusement and despair. 'That's a top source you've got there.'

'I know. It's pathetic. But that doesn't mean the post is untrue.'

'Fair enough. Mitchell's had a busy personal life and he's not to everyone's taste. But I've never heard anything out and out nasty about the guy. Then again . . .' His voice trailed off.

'Then again?' said Stacey.

'When he was in his heyday, the world was a different place. You've just got to think of all those rock stars who went out with fourteen-year-olds. Even in the regular world, men in their twenties dated schoolgirls. Back in the day, it wasn't viewed as any big deal.'

'So for something to have caused a stir, it would want to have been pretty hard-core?'

'That's about the size of it, yeah.' They fell into an uncomfortable silence. Finally, Ultan spoke again. 'If you like, I can give the tree a shake. See if anyone knows anything.'

'That'd be really helpful. Thanks.'

'Honestly, though, Stacey, you'll have to tell me what this is about. I get that what you're dealing with is sensitive and that people might have spoken to you in confidence. But you can't expect me to give you a dig out when I don't know what you're looking for.'

With her spare hand, she massaged the back of her neck. Ultan wasn't being unreasonable. He'd helped her without seeking anything in return. 'I promise I'll fill you in,' she replied. 'Just not today.'

Later, while her dinner bubbled in the oven, she received a call from Imogen. To begin with, she considered not answering. She was still feeling low about her encounter with Birdy. Besides, she should be focusing on tomorrow's job interview. Then, her conscience got the better of her.

'Ah, Imogen,' she said. 'I was about to ring you.'

She took a large gulp of wine before running through what had happened with Birdy. As she spoke, the sun dipped towards the horizon and the room became glazed with gold.

When she'd finished, Imogen made a tut-tutting sound. 'That's a shame. I've no doubt this is tough for Birdy but, all the same, I thought she'd be willing to have a chat with Ann. Even a few words would mean a lot.'

'I keep asking myself what I could have done differently,' said Stacey.

'Please don't blame yourself, pet. Perhaps when she's had time to think, she'll change her mind.'

'That's what I want to believe. I'm not holding out any great hope, though.'

'Please God you're wrong. Anyway, the reason I'm calling is . . . guess who's in town?'

'Are you serious?'

'A friend of mine was at a party last night, and he was there too. I rang Rowena, and she confirmed that her father will be in Dublin for the next two days.'

Stacey was aware that her judgement was clouded by defeat and frustration. She was no longer sure what to do for the best. It was unlikely she would make a podcast of The Diamonds' story. Nor would she succeed in getting the band back together. What she could do was chip away at Kieran Mitchell.

'Where would I be likely to find him, do you think?'

Imogen told her that while Mitchell's house was in Dalkey, he also had a city centre office. It was off Merrion Square, close to where Stacey was due to go for her interview.

'What do you think?' said Imogen.

'You mean do I plan on going to see him?'

'Yes.'

'I've a feeling others would advise against.'

'Only you reckon you should?'

'Uh-huh. I think he should know that what he did hasn't been forgotten.'

There was a delay before Imogen replied. 'I tend to agree, but what would you say to him?'

'There's a question. I'll have to think it through.'

'You don't need me to tell you that he can be intimidating.'

'Don't worry,' said Stacey. 'I'll bring someone with me.'

Chapter 39

'I think,' said Stacey, 'we should play it as bad cop and very bad cop. If we give this guy any reason to wriggle away, that's what he'll do.'

She was talking to Ronan – but also to herself. The meeting with Birdy continued to play on her conscience, and she didn't want to be hobbled by self-doubt. It was important that when they confronted Kieran Mitchell, they did so in a full-hearted way.

At half past nine on Wednesday morning, they were sitting in Ronan's car, which was parked down the street from the Dublin base of Mitchell Artist Management. All around them, coffee-toting men and women hurried to their redbrick offices.

Although she'd had doubts about involving Ronan, Stacey hadn't been able to think of anyone better suited to the task. He was a reluctant accomplice. When she'd called, he'd maintained that he couldn't take time off work. He had things to do, people to meet. *Haven't we all?* she'd thought.

Then he'd questioned the point of the exercise. What could

they achieve? She didn't know, she'd said, but if nothing else, they would knock Mitchell's day off course. Finally, he'd suggested they wait another day or two. She'd explained that if they did, they'd miss their chance. According to Imogen, Mitchell was due to travel to the south of France before the end of the week. 'I'd be delighted to stalk him around St Tropez,' Stacey had said, 'but I don't have the budget.'

It was only when she'd announced her intention to go to the office with or without him that Ronan had relented.

'Do you think Mitchell will turn up?' he said now. 'Maybe he's at home snorting lines in his Jacuzzi or whatever it is that music moguls do, these days.'

'Apparently, when he's in Dublin, he always visits the office. He likes to remind them that he's the boss. He's bound to appear at some stage.'

'Suppose he does arrive, how are we going to get a meeting? Or do we just accost him on the street?'

Ronan was more uptight than Stacey had expected. She removed her sunglasses. 'I was thinking we could pretend to be a new band looking for representation.'

'You're having me on.'

'Don't worry, I am.'

'Thank God for that. Although, to be fair, you look the part.'

'Thanks. Even when you're meeting out-and-out scumbags, it's good to make an effort.'

Stacey's outfit was midway between her usual style and the more subdued look expected at a job interview. She was wearing a teal green silk shirt, a cream knee-length skirt and tan block-heeled sandals. Fearing Ronan would use the interview as an excuse to postpone their pursuit of Kieran Mitchell, she hadn't said anything about it.

'Anyway,' he said, 'do you have a more serious suggestion for tackling this guy?'

'I think we should stick to the truth. We'll tell whatever gatekeeper he has in place that we want to talk to him about The Diamonds.'

'Assuming that gets us into his office, and that's quite a big assumption, what then?'

'We keep on telling it like it is. I'll go through what I know, and if you want, you can reveal your connection to the band.'

Stacey had lain awake until the early hours thinking about how best to approach The Diamonds' manager. In the end, she'd concluded that all she had on her side was the truth. In an email, she'd been easy to push aside. In the flesh, she was more of a challenge.

Ronan fiddled with the lapel of his jacket. 'And when Mitchell says, "Nope. Never happened," what then?'

'We tell him that's not true, and that lots of other people know the real story.'

Stacey sensed that Ronan was about to argue but before either of them had the chance to speak, a rangy figure carrying a copy of the *Financial Times* strode around the corner. He had cropped grey hair and wore navy chinos, a blue shirt and a black suit jacket. Although his clothes were nondescript, he exuded the 'look at me' confidence of the rich and successful.

'And there he is,' she said. 'Mr Low-Life Music Manager.'

They gave Mitchell a few minutes to enter the office.

'Let's go,' she said eventually. 'The sooner we're in, the sooner we get to talk.'

Ronan brushed her hand. 'Good luck to us.'

'Good luck to us,' echoed Stacey, slightly taken aback by the gesture.

Mitchell's offices were on the first floor. As they climbed the stairs, Stacey's breath came in short puffs. She was doing her best to appear calm when in reality she was riddled with nerves.

The reception area was decorated with gold discs and awards. Many, but not all, belonged to the band that had made Mitchell's name, One Scarlet Morning. A woman with a waterfall of amber hair and shiny maroon nails was behind the desk. She was wearing a dress that Stacey recognised as Reformation. The woman confirmed that, yes, Mr Mitchell was in his office today. Without pausing, she added that they couldn't see him. He was busy, and they didn't have an appointment. There was an upswing to her voice so that every statement sounded like a question.

'Will you tell him that we need to talk about The Diamonds?' said Stacey.

'Who are The Diamonds?'

'He'll know.'

'You'll have to do better than that, I'm afraid. Mr Mitchell's diary is chock-a-block.'

Stacey tilted forward and in her most sugary tone said, 'Believe me, he'll want to talk to us.'

'And, believe me, he doesn't meet anyone without an appointment, especially not randomers who have just walked in off the street.'

The woman managed to inject 'randomers' with a sturdy dose of derision. Just as Stacey feared an extended tussle, a head appeared from around an office door.

'Is there a problem, Carissa?' asked Mitchell.

'This man and woman wanted to talk to you, but I've explained that you have a hectic schedule.'

He stepped out of the office, sizing them up as he moved. Up close, Stacey could see that, for an Irishman of his generation, his teeth were unusually white and straight. She also suspected that his eyebrows had been professionally shaped.

'If you're journalists seeking an interview,' he said, 'you need to go through my publicist in New York. I thought that was outlined on the website. If it's about one of my clients, you ought to contact the media representatives at the relevant record company. To the best of my knowledge, none of the Scarlets is doing interviews right now. They've recently finished recording and they're shattered. Iona Daunt is on tour in Australia and New Zealand. The Latecomers are doing the festival circuit on the continent, and Tania Reader is recording in LA.'

His voice was deep, his accent stranded between Dalkey and Manhattan, so that 'shattered' became 'shaddered' and Tania was pronounced 'Tonia'.

For the second time in twenty-four hours, Stacey was hit by a strange sensation. Someone she'd only seen on a computer screen was standing in front of her. Thousands of pixels had come to life. She was also struck by the absurdity of his statement. He was two metres away, yet in order to talk to him, she was supposed to contact an office on the other side of the Atlantic. Mindful of how intimidated she'd been in the company of the real Birdy, she willed herself to sound firm.

'It's about one of your former bands,' she said. 'The Diamonds.'

'I told her I'd never heard of them,' said Carissa, 'but she wouldn't listen.'

Mitchell removed his glasses. He squinted, causing the network of lines around his eyes to deepen. His look gave the impression that he was hauling vague memories of The Diamonds from the deepest crevices of his brain. At last, he spoke. 'Is this about some podcast or other?'

'That's right. My name is Stacey Nash, and I emailed your assistant in New York. She claimed you'd nothing to say about the band, but I don't think she had the full picture.'

'You're mistaken there. First, I wouldn't let the formidable Maren hear you describe her as an assistant. She's a director of the company. And, second, when it comes to The Diamonds, there's not much to say.' He put his glasses back on. 'Who's your minder?'

'I'm Ronan Egan. I gather you knew my mother.' He paused, as if for effect. 'Loretta Saunders?'

'Briefly, yes,' said Mitchell, scarcely missing a beat. If the name caused him any discomfort, he hid it well.

Carissa appeared puzzled. 'So is this about a band or about someone's mother?'

'Both,' replied Ronan.

Mitchell made great play of looking at his watch, which to Stacey's uneducated eye was worth at least a year's rent. 'I can spare five minutes to put whatever's bothering you to rest. You'll have to wait, though. As Carissa has made clear, I'm exceptionally busy.'

Carissa gestured towards two moss-green armchairs at the far end of the room. 'You can wait over there.'

Because they were within the assistant's earshot, Stacey reckoned the best way to communicate was through texts. (And, yes, she was aware that in its own way, this was as bizarre as Mitchell's directive that she contact his New York office.) She wrote: What do you think?

Ronan replied: Think he's legged it out the fire escape.

For truth!?

No! But he'll probably keep us here a while. I don't know what Mam saw in him. He's weird.

Would you say that if you didn't know what he'd done? 🤔

Don't know. ☹

They continued to text, trading comments about Mitchell and his office. Carissa kept sending what she probably thought were furtive glances in their direction. Stacey monitored the time:

10.15, 10.34, 10.51. In a little over an hour, she would have to leave for her interview.

Somehow she doubted that Mitchell was busy. She had a vision of him sitting in his office, trawling through Instagram or TMZ or whatever it was that attracted the attention of sixty-eight-year-old multi-millionaires. Dodgy porn sites? Expensive cars? Elon Musk fan pages?

Every so often, another woman walked past. Stacey had read enough about Mitchell Artist Management to know that her name was Melanie Adams. She handled the day-to-day business for Tania Reader and Iona Daunt. Her crease-free face, wavy blonde bob and sculpted arms spoke of careful maintenance. Stacey's fashion radar told her that Melanie was wearing Isabel Marant.

She texted Ronan: We're with the Stepford Wives, boho edition.

He snorted with laughter, prompting a disapproving look from Carissa.

11.02, 11.14, 11.23.

Anxiety was creeping up on Stacey. They needed to get into Mitchell's office. She glanced towards Carissa, who shrugged as if to say, 'Don't blame me. I did warn you.'

Another text to Ronan: Beginning to think you're right about the fire exit 🙄

He replied: Am tempted to storm the office 😠

You're on

Would rather not do jail time for Kieran Mitchell

🤣🤣

She put down her phone and studied her former partner. Despite her fascination with The Diamonds, this was just a story to her. She would move on. She would have to. To him, it was personal. It was about his mother's life. However reluctant he'd been to accompany her, she could tell he was fully invested. He caught her gaze and smiled the slightly goofy smile she'd always found appealing.

'All right?' he said, the first words he'd spoken in at least half an hour.

'All right.'

This wasn't true. She was running out of time.

11.29, 11.41, 11.50.

If Stacey left, she would blow her chance of tackling Mitchell. She was unlikely to get another. If she stayed, there was every danger she would miss her interview. She wished she'd told Ronan about the job, but it was too late.

11.59, 12.12, 12.24.

This was her last chance. Leave now, and she would be only five minutes late. She looked at Ronan, his face rigid with concentration. She thought of his mother. She thought of Birdy. There wasn't really an option, was there? They would have to stay until Mitchell decided he had time for them.

Another ten minutes passed before that moment came. When he re-emerged, it was with maximum bustle, as though he didn't have a second to waste.

'Let's get this over with,' he said. They stood and picked up their phones. 'And you can leave those outside.'

'But—' started Stacey.

'My office, my rules. Carissa will tell you that it's standard procedure around here.' He looked at his assistant, who bowed her head in affirmation. 'I don't like technology interfering with my conversations.'

He was worried they would record him. Interesting.

Mitchell's office was not subtle. A shrine to his achievements, it appeared designed to overwhelm. Along with more gold, silver and platinum discs, the walls were decorated with tour programmes, magazine covers and photos. Most were of artists he managed. Here was One Scarlet Morning's Shaun Mannion, baring his teeth and tattoos on the cover of *Rolling Stone*. There was Iona Daunt, looking other-worldly on the front of American *Vogue*. Elsewhere, there were framed and signed photos of other musical gods. Stacey spotted Eric Clapton, the Eagles, the Red Hot Chili Peppers and Madonna.

As they sat down, a slice of sunlight glinted off a set of discs, making the room feel like a rock 'n' roll wonderland.

'So,' he said, from behind his large black desk, 'what is it you want to know about The Diamonds? I don't get many queries about bands that didn't make it. And, as Maren has already told you, I don't have much to say.' He gave a self-deprecating laugh then looked at Ronan. 'I've been kind of busy over the past four decades. But I'm guessing you know more about the band's current lives than I do.'

Stacey crossed her legs at the ankle. 'We were keen to hear what you had to say about why such a promising band split up.'

'Now there's a question. Why does any band split up? Because they fall out. Simple as that. If we're talking specifically about The Diamonds, they were young and they found the life tough. Unless you've worked in the industry, you can't appreciate how much hard graft is involved. Outsiders imagine that it's all parties and fans, but it's way, way more than that. Some people don't have the aptitude for endless work, and unfortunately The Diamonds fell into that category.'

'The break-up was nothing to do with you, then?'

Apart from the smallest of facial twitches, Mitchell gave no indication that the question bothered him. 'I have my critics, but The Diamonds' decision to go their separate ways was just that: their decision. I hate it when artists don't achieve their potential. Sometimes, though, despite the best advice, it happens.' He made a steeple shape with his fingers. 'Look, I'm going to be honest with you. I'm getting the sense that you've got an unrealistic idea of what was possible.'

'What do you mean?'

'We-ell, you've probably read some of the puff pieces from the time: "U2 for girls" and all that hype. The truth is, they were never ever going to be in U2's league. In those days, being from Dublin had a certain cachet, a certain gritty authenticity, if you will. The Diamonds didn't even have that. When it came down to it, they were an unremarkable bunch of girls from an unremarkable town. What they had going for them was naïve charm and novelty value. No more, no less.'

It was Ronan's turn to reply. 'That's not true. We've seen and heard them. They were very talented. No one's saying they could have been megastars, but there was plenty for them to achieve.'

'I think you might be more than a little biased. I'm not claiming The Diamonds couldn't have racked up a few hits. Sure they could. But compared to the people in this room,' Mitchell glanced at the walls and gave a proprietorial smile, 'they didn't possess the right stuff. When you've been around for as long as I have, you understand that.'

Ronan rubbed his hands together. 'You're saying The Diamonds weren't good enough for long-term success?'

'Well, plainly I'd hoped they'd be more than one-hit wonders. So did their record company. Supreme had invested a significant amount of money in recording an album and honing the band's image. They didn't take a kind view of the girls' behaviour.' Mitchell shook his head, as if to indicate the difficulties The Diamonds' split had caused him. 'But even if the band were still together, they'd be well down the bill on the heritage circuit, performing songs they'd written as teenagers. That was their level.' His smile returned, this time with an apologetic twist. 'Sorry. I know that must be hard to hear, but I've never been one for sugar-coating the truth.'

Stacey's body was taut. 'We all know that's not the real story.'

The smile faded. 'Do we?'

'Yes.'

'Enlighten me then. What is this "real story"?'

His voice was crisp, matter-of-fact. His expression grew cold. For the first time, she saw the menace in him. It was a side that mostly stayed hidden, a side that Carissa and Melanie probably didn't get to experience. Or if they did, they were paid to look the other way.

Stacey took a steadying breath. 'The Diamonds broke up after you raped Birdy Troy.'

'Jesus,' said Mitchell, his face falling as though he'd never heard the accusation before. 'That's a lunatic allegation. Lunatic and extremely dangerous. You can't go around telling forty-year-old lies. That's how lives get ruined.'

'It's not a lie.'

'Yes, it is.'

A lengthy pause followed, but there was something artificial about it. He wanted them to believe he was shocked by the allegation.

When he spoke again, his voice was lower, as though he was sharing a confidence. 'I admit we had sex. I was always upfront about that. Afterwards, she must have felt guilty. She'd betrayed her bandmate, her friend. We both had. But that's a hell of a long way from rape. I mean . . . Christ, you can't be serious.'

Stacey gripped the side of the chair. Otherwise, he might see her hands shaking. 'There's no reason for Birdy to lie.'

'What age is she? Sixty? Sixty-one?'

'Fifty-nine.'

'So, she's probably struggling with the fact that it's too late to achieve her ambitions. And maybe she's casting about for an excuse.' Stacey tried to interject, but Mitchell kept on speaking. 'The music business can be tough on women. I'm the first to admit that. With the odd exception, they don't get to start again. If it doesn't work out when they're young, it's "So long, sweetheart, nice knowing you. Show the next girl in." But that's no reason to blame me for her own bad choices.'

Stacey wanted to tell him that, far from looking for someone to blame, Birdy was wary of saying anything at all. Then she decided this might backfire. Right now, Mitchell was under the impression that the two people in front of him had his victim's backing. However confident his appearance, he was under pressure. The temperature in the room had nudged up, and there was a film of sweat over his upper lip.

'Birdy's not making anything up,' she said.

'Let's be kind to her, then. Let's say she chooses to remember things one way. I remember them differently.'

'It's not just what she remembers. It's what she said at the time. She told the rest of the band.'

Mitchell shook his head. 'Tell me, if Birdy Troy cares so much, why isn't she here?'

'Because, even after all this time, she wouldn't want to be in the same room as you.'

'No. I'll tell you why she isn't here. It's because she knows that what happened in 1982 – before either of you were born – is of no consequence.'

'That's not true,' said Ronan. 'I believe what she says.'

'So do I,' said Stacey. 'And so do the other Diamonds.'

'I can't influence what they choose to tell themselves. I can only reiterate that they're mistaken.' Mitchell leant in towards the desk. His eyes were steady on hers. 'Let me also be straight: if this lie is repeated in public – and have no doubt, it is a lie – I will sue. Presumably you understand the implications of any legal action?'

Stacey's mouth felt as though it was filled with dust. Before she had an opportunity to reply, Mitchell was speaking again.

'I don't usually waste time on amateurs, and I only agreed to this conversation because of Ronan's connection to the band. I have warm memories of his mother. Of the four, she was the only one whose talents might have transferred to another group. It's a shame that wasn't an avenue she chose to pursue. But, again, that was her choice.'

Stacey noticed that he hadn't enquired after any of The Diamonds, even Ann. In 1982, he'd discarded them like bruised fruit. He'd been indifferent to their feelings back then and remained so today. And yet, as she studied him, he didn't look like a monster. He didn't even look particularly hard. She could imagine him enjoying a meal with his family or celebrating with one of his acts. She was reminded of a college friend who'd worked with a man later convicted of child abuse. 'And you know,' Stacey's friend had said, 'I thought he was the least weird guy in the office.'

Mitchell stood up. 'Now, if you don't mind, I have other things to do.'

He walked around to their side of the desk. They stayed put.

'Don't make fools of yourselves,' he said. 'You asked your questions, and I answered them. Considering how you've insulted me, I've given you more than enough of my time.' When they didn't move, he spoke again. 'Oh, and, Stacey? A word to the wise. I looked up your podcast and was disappointed to see that it's a small-time affair. Ask yourself this: if I wasn't successful, would you even be here? I think we all know the answer.'

'I'm sorry?'

'Come on now. You know what I'm saying. I've encountered a

few grifters in my time. I can always spot an attempted shakedown.'

He stepped uncomfortably close to her, effectively forcing her to push back the chair and stand.

Ronan also got to his feet. He was first to reply. 'That's a disgusting allegation,' he said, voice serrated with anger. 'But no one would expect better from you.'

'We'll see,' said Mitchell, as he opened the office door. 'And, like I say, it's best not to let yourselves down in front of Carissa and Melanie.'

'Don't worry, we won't say anything to shame you,' said Stacey, picking up her phone. She sent a half-smile in Carissa's direction, but rage was washing through her.

By the time they reached the stairs, Mitchell was back in his corner of the rock 'n' roll hall of fame, his office door shutting with a firm *clunk*.

Vivienne, Imogen, Birdy: they'd all been right. He was impenetrable. Immovable. It was as if he was surrounded by a force field of self-righteousness. In his own head, he'd done nothing wrong. The Diamonds had been mediocre, ungrateful, ill-disciplined. Birdy was bitter. Stacey was looking for a pay-out. Anyone who disagreed would be crushed like a ladybird beneath a size-twelve boot.

Out on the street, she looked at her phone. It was half past one. She'd missed the interview. She'd also missed three calls from a number she assumed belonged to Hayley O'Connor and Associates. She shoved the phone into her bag. Later, she would ring to apologise. If necessary, she would grovel. But she had no reasonable explanation. Not only had she failed to pierce Kieran Mitchell's armour, she'd allowed another opportunity to pass her by.

Chapter 40

Once again, Ann was waiting for news. Ronan had called to say that he and Stacey were going to see Kieran Mitchell. He wasn't keen, but Stacey was impossible to dissuade. Despite the grim nature of their visit, the idea of Stacey stalking into the offices of Mitchell Artist Management made Ann smile. The girl had missed her calling as a detective.

Ann's head was thick with tiredness. Her eyes were scratchy, her back sore. She'd lain awake for much of the night, grappling with Birdy's rejection. Recent weeks had taught her how to accept bad news. It was a skill she needed now. And yet accepting that she wouldn't see her one-time friend again was hard.

While she waited to hear from Ronan, her mother rang to talk about the latest miracle cure. Hardly a day passed without a call from Patrice. Her miracles took various forms. Sometimes they centred on bona-fide scientific breakthroughs. 'Why don't you ask your doctor?' she would say. 'It can't do any harm. This might work for you.' At other times, her stories featured people who had been staring at death but hadn't given up. Their faith had been rewarded, their tumours zapped, their strength restored. Patrice never said, 'These people fought. They made an effort. Why can't you?' But the subtext was there.

Occasionally she rang with news of a treatment that could, at best, be described as unorthodox. On the internet's flakier fringes, there were charlatans galore. Some claimed their cancer had been spirited away by crystals, spinach juice or colon cleansing. Others credited emu oil, magnetic fields or the power of positive thinking. Lazarus himself would have been impressed. While Ann's mother stressed that she didn't truly believe in these so-called cures, she spent a considerable amount of time seeking them out.

Once, Ann had come close to saying, 'Even the way I'm dying annoys you, doesn't it?' But then she'd heard the fear in her mother's voice. She had tried to explain that, rather than raging against the inevitable, she wanted to make the most of the remaining light. She had to accept – that word again – that her mam saw things differently.

Today's call was about a genuine breakthrough, a drug that appeared to have cured every patient in a trial. None of the participants had endured any significant side effects. The snag? The trial had been conducted in America. Oh, and the patients had been suffering from a completely different form of cancer.

'But it goes to show,' said Patrice, 'that a development could be just around the corner. You can't give up.'

'You're right,' replied Ann, who thanked her mother before lying about someone being at the door.

She placed the phone back on the kitchen counter and put on the kettle. In less than a minute, it rang again, the harsh *brrring* cutting through her like metal. She would have to change the ringtone. With Grover winding around her legs, she checked the number and was surprised not to recognise it. The caller must be connected to the hospital.

'Hello,' she said.

There was a pause. The voice that followed gave her a start. Although belonging to another time and place, it was instantly familiar. Like the smell of her first school or the opening bars of 'Too Much Not Enough', the voice was scored on Ann's brain. She had never forgotten it.

Chapter 41

'It would be easier,' said Ronan, putting his pint on the table, 'if the guy wasn't so persuasive. Unfortunately, he is. If you didn't know the real story, you'd swear The Diamonds were four messy young girls who went their separate ways because they were too lazy to do anything else.'

'Too lazy *and* untalented,' said Stacey. 'Let's not forget the untalented part.'

'Not to mention the fact that they grew up in an "unremarkable" town. How could anyone recover from that? Poor old Steelstown, huh?'

The bar was cool, the light muted. Nearby, four young lads of various sizes, but with regulation young-lad haircuts and pointy brown shoes, were tearing their boss apart. Three tourists were pretending to like the taste of Guinness. Otherwise, the place was empty.

It had been Ronan who'd suggested they go for a drink. He

would come up with an excuse for work, he said. They needed to talk about Mitchell.

While he moved his car, Stacey called the PR company to apologise. Hayley O'Connor and Associates didn't accept the apology. In a chilly voice, the HR woman told her she'd messed up their interview schedule and wasted their time. There would be no second chance.

Then, with perfect timing, Ultan Dowdall rang. No one he'd asked had heard of any serious allegations against Mitchell. They'd described him as a womaniser, a trickster, a cheat. Even the luminous Faye Godfrey couldn't be assured of his fidelity. He was arrogant, single-minded, vain. 'But,' said Ultan, 'you could say the same about half the people in the music business.'

Stacey sighed. 'And there's nothing illegal about being a bit of a bollocks.'

Ultan laughed. 'Which is probably just as well. The jails would be overflowing.'

Before hanging up, she promised that in the coming days she'd give him The Diamonds' complete story. She didn't reveal that she'd spent the morning in Mitchell's office. The experience had been too dispiriting.

Drinking wine on a midweek afternoon should have felt like a forbidden pleasure. But with everything falling apart around her, she was finding it hard to relax.

In advance of their meeting with Mitchell, Stacey had been convinced that he would display some form of weakness. She'd been wrong. His threat of legal action showed they'd got under his skin. As did his blackmail allegations. Not once, however, had he deviated from the claim he'd first made in the summer of 1982: Birdy had agreed to sex and then regretted it. Faced with his denials, there was no more Stacey and Ronan could do. And he knew it.

'Have you spoken to your mam?' she asked.

'I rang, but she was on another call. I'll try again in a while.'

Stacey sipped her drink. 'I hope she's not feeling let down. The whole thing still bugs me. I can't believe that in the forty years since Mitchell raped Birdy, he hasn't reoffended.'

'Only maybe he hasn't. He got away with assaulting Birdy because, like everyone keeps telling us, things were different back then. What if he was smart enough to realise that he mightn't be so lucky the next time?'

'It's possible.'

'Also, back in '82, The Diamonds' split must have been a head-wrecker for him. Whatever he says now, his behaviour cost him what could have been a good money-spinner. Only a fool wouldn't have been aware of that.'

'And whatever else he is,' said Stacey, 'he's not a fool.' She drained her glass. 'One way or another, it's unlikely we'll ever find out.'

'True, I'm afraid.' Ronan stood. 'Another?'

'Why not? It's my shout.'

'Nah, you're grand. You've put a huge amount of work into this. The drinks are on me.'

'Cheers,' said Stacey, with more gratitude than he could know. Her budget didn't stretch to afternoon drinking.

There were questions she would have liked to ask, but this didn't feel like the right time. His mother was up and about, living a relatively normal life. But for how much longer? Stacey hoped to stay in contact with Ann. She wanted to visit her again. Would Ronan be all right with that? Or, even if she didn't admit it, would Jill frown on an ex-girlfriend's presence in the family home?

When he came back, they sat in silence, each trapped in their own thoughts. Until today, Stacey had been able to keep her problems at one remove. Even when she'd been looking for a flat or a job, her mind had been occupied by hunting down clues and unearthing the truth. There'd been a bigger story to tell. Now that story was over, its resolution untidy and unsatisfactory. She could no longer play at being Nancy Drew.

Ronan was staring at her. 'What's up?'

'Ah, nothing.'

He took a drink. 'Go on, what is it?'

She closed her eyes. 'It's everything, isn't it? Every bloody thing.'

'You'll need to give me more than that.'

Before Stacey could stop herself, she was talking and talking and talking. She told him about the missed job interview, her failure to find a flat, her lack of income from the podcast and her fear that she'd have to move back home. She spoke about the wedding and hen weekends she couldn't afford, the bills she couldn't meet, the car she'd have to sell. Her words came quickly. As they did, her eyes grew watery, and tears ran down her face. She dabbed at them with the cuffs of her shirt. The brown-shoe lads looked on, sending knowing glances to each other. Oh, let them stare. She no longer cared.

Ronan nodded a lot but said little. If he was embarrassed, he didn't let it show.

And then it hit her: how self-indulgent must she sound? How spoilt? Compared to what they'd been discussing this morning, and compared to what Ronan's family was going through, her troubles were minor. Fearing he would point this out, she got in first.

'Before you say it, because I'm sure it's what you're thinking, I do know it could be worse. I think about your mam and dad, and I think about Birdy and all the rest of it, and I know I should be counting my blessings.' She sniffed. 'I can move in with my folks and go back to doing the podcast interviews over Zoom. Or I can get a proper job. Or I can do both.'

'I promise you, Stace, I wasn't going to say anything about

counting your blessings. It's an awful phrase, the sort of thing my grandmother comes out with.'

'Well, in this case, I wouldn't have blamed you. I've wasted so much time. I've let your mother down. I've annoyed Birdy. And what have I achieved? The square root of nothing. Mitchell is probably sitting in his office, telling his cronies about my "small-time" podcast. I can see them having a right old laugh.'

'Straight up,' said Ronan, 'I can't imagine him saying anything to anyone – except, perhaps, his lawyer. I'd say he's praying he's seen the last of you and that he can go back to pretending The Diamonds never existed.'

'I suppose,' she said, giving another sniff. 'If anything, he's probably packing his swimming togs and factor fifty for the family holiday in the south of France.'

'With any luck, it'll rain every single day.'

Stacey smiled. 'A drop of rain isn't nearly enough. He deserves a monsoon and a plague of locusts. No, he deserves a nuclear fucking explosion.'

'At least,' said Ronan before returning to the bar.

Despite their break-up, Stacey had wanted him to consider her dogged and capable. She'd wanted to impress him. Instead, here she was, snivelling like a child.

The more she thought, the more she saw how she'd fallen into a familiar trap. She'd waited until she'd found an excuse to end their relationship, and when it came, she'd seized it like a prize. Not that Ronan deserved to be absolved of blame. His attitude still hurt. But she should have been willing to engage – and to try again. The upsets of the past few days had forced her to accept the truth: she was pining for her old life. It wasn't just that she missed being with someone, she missed being with Ronan. She wanted to throw her arms around him and say, 'Come back to me.'

Initially, she'd questioned her motives. Was this a genuine change of heart or did she want to couple up again because doing so would help to solve her accommodation problems? Then she'd thought some more. Even with a partner, finding a new flat would be tough. She wanted to get back with Ronan because she wanted to get back with Ronan.

He returned with two drinks, a wad of paper napkins and two packets of cheese and onion crisps. Then he sat down beside her and passed over a bag of crisps with the napkins. 'Crying's hungry work.'

'I'm sorry,' said Stacey, blotting her face. 'I . . . ahm . . . I needed to vent a little. The past few weeks have been kind of intense.'

They began eating, their methodical crunching making further talk difficult.

'You know,' he said, eventually, 'listening to you there, I found myself thinking, *Isn't this where we came in?*'

'Did I really spend our first date weeping about my screw-up of a life? No wonder we didn't last.'

He laughed. 'No, I meant the wedding tyranny. Or the marital industrial complex, as one of the guys in the office calls it. The poor lad's going to a wedding next month: three days, three different venues.'

'That's outrageous. There should be a law against it.'

'Anyway, what I was going to say was, you don't have to go to any of that carry-on. Not if you don't want to. This evening, ring the bride and say you can't make it. And if it doesn't suit you, do the same with the hen weekend.'

'You're right,' said Stacey, 'except it feels like an admission of failure.'

Ronan finished his crisps then passed a salty hand across hers. 'No lie, as far as The Diamonds and my mother are concerned, the self-laceration is mad. You've been fantastic. No one else would have persevered the way you did. Even when you knew there was no chance of getting a podcast, you motored on.'

'But it didn't work out.'

'You can't let that keep on getting to you.'

'Thanks,' she said. 'And thanks for coming with me. I know you didn't want to. It meant a lot.'

'What else could I have done? And you were right. Even though Mitchell will probably shrug this off, it was worth getting a look at him.'

They became quiet again, but it was an agreeable quiet. Stacey was sinking into the afternoon, the alcohol making her pleasantly woozy. Minute by minute, her thoughts crystallised. Did the way Ronan touched her hand mean that he, too, was interested in sorting things out? Or had it been no more than a friendly gesture?

She took another swig of wine and thought about what she should say. As she did, his phone rang. He lifted the hand that had been resting near hers. 'It's Mam,' he said. 'I'd better answer it.'

'Of course.'

'Hiya. I rang earlier only you must have been on the phone. We went to Mitchell's office and—'

His sentence came to a sudden halt. Although Stacey could hear Ann at the other end of the line, she couldn't decipher the words.

'No!' said Ronan, turning towards Stacey and widening his eyes. 'You're not serious.'

Chapter 42

A minute into her call with Ann, Birdy worried that she'd made a mistake. Despite rehearsing what she would say, she was jumpy. If anything, Ann was worse. She sounded dazed.

'I was sorry to hear you're unwell,' said Birdy, as though the woman on the other end of the line was suffering from a bout of bronchitis or an ear infection.

'Thank you,' said Ann. 'I didn't expect to . . . I didn't expect to hear from you. Stacey said you hadn't changed your mind, and I thought, *Well, that's that so.*'

God, this was awkward.

'I thought it all through last night,' said Birdy, 'and I reckoned that not calling would be poor form.'

Poor form? What was she like? Had she forgotten how to speak?

Birdy's mind jumped back twenty-four hours. Even as she'd walked up the clinic's steps, she'd regretted sending Stacey away.

Put on the spot, she'd panicked and reacted too quickly. Thankfully, Stacey had run after her with a sheet of paper containing Ann's number. 'In case you change your mind,' she'd said.

For the rest of the day, and half of the night, Birdy had argued with herself. On the one hand, on the other, on the third hand, on the fourth: she became a study in indecision. It wasn't as though she'd been especially friendly with Loretta/Ann. Not in the way she'd been friends with Gail or Yvonne. Being in the band had given them a bond of sorts, but that had been broken a long time ago. Did she really need to contact her? Suppose she sent a card? Would that be an acceptable compromise?

But if Birdy had never been friendly with Ann, why was she being hit by flashback after unwanted flashback? She remembered sixteen-year-old Loretta Saunders auditioning for The Diamonds, how Gail had delighted in winding her up and how good-natured the singer had been in response. She remembered their early gigs and how they'd all been wonderstruck by Ann's talent. And she remembered how, when they'd sung and danced to Gail's tapes, Ann had been the most enthusiastic of the four. She'd always acted as though hamming it up in the kitchen was as important as belting it out on stage.

Birdy wondered if Ann's images of The Diamonds' later days were as dark as hers. Probably not. She'd noticed that when an obviously dangerous person like a heroin dealer died, their online condolences page still brimmed with sympathetic messages. The deceased was 'a gent' who should 'sleep tight among the angels'. His family was 'much loved' and would receive 'all our support'. She guessed that unless you'd suffered the full force of someone's badness, your feelings would always be watered down.

She spoke to Andy, who told her the decision was hers to make. But, he added, she couldn't afford to dither.

'You think I should call, don't you?' she said.

'I know you've always been determined not to revisit The Diamonds with her. And I was with you, one hundred per cent. But neither of us had imagined a situation like this. I'm not going to claim it could be cathartic for you because . . .'

'. . . because that would be a lie.'

Andy gave a sympathetic smile. 'If you do phone, it'll be hard. But if you ignore her, I don't think you'll rest.'

She rang Gail, who was enjoying her summer break.

'Fuckity-fuck,' said her old friend, in an accent that was equal parts Boston and Steelstown. 'Why didn't the podcast girl tell us this from the start? Why didn't Ann mention it when she emailed me?'

'I get the idea that she didn't want us to know for fear it came across as some sort of moral blackmail.'

'That's very noble of her. But, Jeez, this puts a whole different spin on things.'

'What should I do?' asked Birdy.

'Oh, honey, I can't tell you that.'

'What would you do?'

At least ten seconds passed before Gail replied. 'I'd call.'

The flashbacks continued, one so powerful that Birdy felt as if she'd been lifted from the ground. On the night she'd left London, she'd told herself that there would be another day. Another day to talk. Another day to settle their differences. She saw herself, alone in the Shepherd's Bush flat, pacing the hall, touching her records like they were saintly relics.

Later, she'd viewed things in another way. Distance was best, she'd decided. But what if that was no longer the case?

At three in the morning, she made up her mind. It was only a phone call. A phone call to someone she'd known a long time ago. It didn't have to be a big deal.

So here she was, sitting in the clinic's storeroom, surgical masks on one side, boxes of syringes on the other. To prevent interruptions, she'd jammed a chair against the door. Gradually, word by word, answer by answer, her conversation with Ann began to flow. Okay, flow was an exaggeration. But by dodging the difficult topics – cancer, Kieran Mitchell, four decades of silence – they managed to ease the tension.

Ann talked about Brendan. He was an engineer, she said, and they'd met in London. 'He was completely different from the crowd I was running around with at the time: solid, self-deprecating, sceptical of too much arty pretension. I knew straight away that he was for me.'

'It sounds like he could be from Steelstown,' said Birdy.

'Oh, God, yeah. When we first met, he'd say something, and I'd think, *That's exactly what a guy from home would say*. It must have been part of the attraction.'

Ann went on to speak about Ronan, who she said took after his father. 'Bless him, he hasn't a musical cell in his body but he's always been sporty. He's good fun too. And big-hearted. I think you already know that until recently I hadn't told him about the band. That always felt like the wisest move, and Brendan supported me. But now . . .'

'You wish you'd spoken sooner?'

'Yes.'

Their talk turned to the previous day. Ann said she'd been uneasy about Stacey's visit to Tolka Medical.

'I'll admit,' said Birdy, 'for the first few minutes, I was annoyed. But the more we spoke, the more I thought of my daughters. She's very persuasive.'

'Tell me about your girls.'

'Gosh, where do I start? Molly's thirty, and she got married last year. She's a nurse in the Mater. I've always thought of her as the steadier of the two, if that doesn't sound like an insult. Sorcha's twenty-eight, and she inherited my wanderlust. At the minute, she's working on an environmental project in Kenya. I don't know if she'll ever stay in one place long enough to put down roots. But that's cool . . . or so I try to tell myself. As you can probably guess, I'm very proud of them. Not only are they kind and clever, they're far more self-assured than I ever was. Then again, all the young women are.'

'It's funny you should say that. When I look at Stacey, I feel the same. She's so together, so certain of what she's about.'

'How did you come across her?'

Ann explained that the podcaster had gone out with her son. 'I don't know what happened but I get the strong impression the break-up was Ronan's fault. He's seeing someone else now, and I have to respect that. But . . .'

'You wish he'd get back with Stacey?'

'Is it that obvious?'

'Well, since you asked . . .'

'Every time I think that, I also find myself thinking, *Don't get involved. Don't turn into your mother.* Still, I guess it's too late to worry about that now.'

Then it hit Birdy. Ann was crying. Not sobbing, but the sort of quiet weeping that was hard to detect on the phone. Should she pretend not to know? That would be the easiest option, but it wasn't a day for easy options. 'Are you all right?'

Ann sniffed. 'I'm fine. Please don't pay any heed to me getting teary. You've been in my thoughts for a long time, not just since the diagnosis, though that did make everything feel more urgent. I've wanted to say sorry. I've wanted you to hear the words and understand that I mean them. That's all.'

This sudden candour affected Birdy in a way she hadn't anticipated. She saw that it wasn't possible to have a perfunctory conversation. She would have to go all-in. With her free hand, she made a fist, the nails digging into the fleshy part of her palm.

'It shouldn't have taken . . . this . . . for me to contact you. I know you've tried to reach me over the years. And I suppose I wanted to keep on punishing you for what I lost. For what we all lost. But it wasn't your fault.'

'Thanks.' Ann stopped for a moment. 'And, Birdy?'

'Yes?'

'You can say it. Dying. Death. Whatever. I'm okay with those words. I can't lie and say I've completely accepted what's happening, the inevitability of it. But I'm quite a distance down the road.'

'Ann, I'm so sorry. Because I work with doctors and because my daughter's a nurse, I feel I should know the right things to say, but I don't.'

'That makes two of us. At the start, I tried to behave in certain ways. To be endlessly stoic. Not to let myself down. Isn't that what people used to say when we were growing up? "Don't let yourself down." A few months in, I've started to wonder if there's a way to die that doesn't involve sentimentality. Wouldn't that imply that there'd been nothing good in your life? Nothing to get sentimental about?' She hesitated. 'Don't mind me. You don't need to hear my rambling thoughts.'

'Don't apologise,' said Birdy. 'Say whatever you like. Do you feel sentimental about the band?'

'About the early days, yes. But about everything afterwards, no. Obviously, no.'

'It's strange listening to you. You sound exactly the same.'

'So do you. We're pure Steelstown.'

'Only you're the slightly posher version,' said Birdy.

Ann laughed. Her laugh hadn't changed either. 'What about Yvonne and Gail?' she asked. 'How are they?'

'Yvonne's just had a new granddaughter. She's called Edie. That's six grandchildren now.'

'Dear God.'

'I know! How can we be so old? She works in a community centre. It suits her. Did you ever meet her husband, Bob? Bob Marsden?'

'Once or twice, but that was a long time ago.'

'He's retired. And Gail is . . . well, Gail's Gail. Despite everything, she's pretty much the same.'

'I envied that,' said Ann. 'Her Gailness, I mean. Even when we were kids, she knew who she was.'

'True. I've always felt the same. She has a son, by the way. His name's Caleb. He's twenty-four. Like his parents, he's super-smart.'

'Tell Gail and Yvonne I said hello, would you?'

'Of course.'

The conversation stalled. Birdy guessed this might be where they left things. Perhaps Ann had said all she'd wanted to say.

Then she spoke again. 'Do you ever play music?'

'No. What about you?'

'Same. Do you miss it?'

'Yes. Andy tells me it's not too late, but I think it is. Sorcha plays the guitar. She was in a band as a teenager. Thankfully, they were never that serious.'

'Andy's right. You were so good. I wish—' Ann's voice broke.

'I don't have the same fire,' said Birdy, her own eyes filling with tears. 'And I think to write and play well you need a rawness about you. You need to be obsessed. It's, like, I want to be as passionate as my daughters, but life has a way of knocking that out of you, doesn't it? Not that long ago, Molly gave me a speech about all that was wrong with the world. And I said, "Smash the patriarchy? I'd settle for a comfortable pair of shoes that don't make me look like a pensioner." Afterwards, I felt bad. I didn't mean to be flippant. But I have to choose my battles. I don't have the brainpower to get worked up about everything. Does that make sense?'

'Yes.' Ann was crying properly now, her sobs rattling down the line. 'I'm sorry,' she said again. 'I should be better at this. I have to get used to talking to people without coming undone.'

'No, you're fine,' said Birdy, digging her nails into her palms once more. 'You hadn't expected me to call. You weren't prepared. Did you have a medical appointment today or how does that work?'

'I've been having chemotherapy, not as a cure but to try and get a little more time. The trouble is, it's not making the difference the doctors had hoped for. I've discussed it with Brendan and we've decided that, maybe, it's not worth it. I haven't yet told Ronan and I probably won't tell my mother. She thinks I'm not trying hard enough.'

'Ah, Jesus, Lor—Sorry, Ann.'

'You're grand. You'll always be Birdy Troy to me. I'll probably always be Loretta Saunders to you. And about my mother? She doesn't mean any harm. This is difficult for her too. Susannah lives in Spain, and she doesn't see that much of her.'

'Would you . . .' Birdy hesitated. She could hardly believe what she was about to say. 'Would you like to meet up? I don't know how you're fixed or anything. If it's not what you want, that's okay.'

'Are you serious?' said Ann. 'I'd love that. I could come to Dublin, if that's what suits you.'

'No,' said Birdy, brain working all the while. 'As chance would have it, I'll be in the west at the end of next week. A short break in the Burren. Galway's not a million miles away, so I could meet you there. Would that be all right for you?'

'That would be brilliant.' Ann paused. 'It's only just hit me. It's your birthday soon, isn't it?'

'I can't believe you remember. It's next week.'

'And you'll be sixty?' Ann didn't add, *An age I'm unlikely to see.* She didn't have to.

'Yes, a big roundy birthday, as they say.' Birdy wiped her sleeve across her face. 'I'll give you another call in a day or two, and we'll arrange something.'

For a couple of minutes, they spoke about Steelstown, about Birdy's brother and Ann's sister. But Birdy's mind was already moving on. She had calls to make.

Chapter 43

'We're going to miss you,' said Rhiannon, as she locked the apartment in Whitethorn House for the last time. 'Will you miss us?'

Before Stacey could reply, the ever-practical Carmel intervened: 'We're moving down the road, Rhi, not going to Australia.'

'Aunty Stacey can come and visit us,' chipped in Mia. 'Isn't that right?'

'It is, chicken,' said Rhiannon, who looked surprisingly glum. 'It won't be the same, though. We had some fun times here.'

'We did,' agreed Stacey. 'And of course I'll miss you. Oh, and I'd be delighted to come visiting, Mia. I hear your new place is great.'

'It's good,' said Mia, in her considered six-year-old voice. 'Not as good as here but . . .'

By rights, Stacey should have been in Cavan, adrift in a sea of peach satin and fake tan, but she'd taken Ronan's advice and skipped the wedding. 'Covid,' she'd said to the bride, her old college friend Laura. 'A terrible dose.' While the excuse wasn't original, it remained effective. No one wanted their big day derailed by a plague-carrier.

She crouched to look Mia in the eye. 'Your new apartment will be fantastic, and I bet you'll make lots of new friends.'

Downstairs, she watched as her neighbours fitted the last of their belongings into the car. Before driving away, Rhiannon leant out the window. 'I'll be expecting regular updates on The Diamonds – and on the other business.'

'The other business' was a reference to Ronan. Three days earlier, having made a show of herself by crying, Stacey had felt she had nothing to lose. She would tell him that she'd made a mistake. 'Can we give it another go?' she'd say. Then, his mother had called with the news about Birdy, and the dynamic of the afternoon had shifted.

Even down the phone line, Ann's excitement had been plain. She'd kept on thanking Stacey, insisting that without her nothing would have happened. Stacey wasn't sure she deserved so much credit. In that moment, however, she'd been happy to accept it. She'd also been genuinely thrilled by the news.

When they'd finished dissecting Birdy's plans to visit Galway, Ronan had announced that he needed to go. He had arranged to meet Jill. One minute, Stacey had been in a happy blur, the next she'd been sitting alone among the detritus of their afternoon. After all the drama, she'd felt as though an entire warehouse of rugs had been pulled from under her.

Back home, her head cloudy from afternoon drinking, she'd confided in Rhiannon. 'I got it wrong,' she'd said, 'and now everything's screwed up.'

Rhiannon had managed to avoid saying, 'I told you so.' She'd also maintained the relationship could be salvaged.

Stacey was less certain. The way Ronan had bounced out of the bar to meet Jill suggested that she'd misread the situation. The encouraging words? The smiles and physical cues? They'd been no more than supportive gestures, a way of conveying his gratitude for the part she'd played in bringing two of the band back together.

As she'd talked to Rhiannon, Stacey had become conscious of how much she relied on her neighbours. Their departure felt like a turning point.

In the days since the meeting with Kieran Mitchell, she had called Mike and Vivienne and gone for a coffee with Ultan. Each conversation had provided its own challenges, but even if the wider world would never learn about the real Kieran Mitchell, the people who'd helped her deserved the truth. She glided over as much detail as possible. In particular, she obscured the falling-out between Birdy and Ann.

Vivienne was the least surprised. She promised to tell no one about The Diamonds' final days, not even her husband. She did, however, pledge to do anything she could to harm Mitchell. 'I've never been a great believer in karma,' she said. 'Let's be honest, the worst people are rarely punished, especially if they've got money. But in his case, I'm praying it exists.'

Ultan also promised to stay silent. 'With hindsight,' he said, 'it makes perfect sense. Those poor women. The fucker should be strung up.'

Stacey left Mike until last. For two reasons, she'd expected it to be the most testing conversation. First of all, he was a talker, and if he told anyone in Steelstown, it would be a serious invasion of Birdy's privacy. Second, she had a feeling that his reaction would be the most severe. On that much, she was correct. What she hadn't anticipated was the extent to which he would blame himself.

'I should have been kinder to her when she left,' he said. 'You know what my last words were? "I hope you don't get hurt." Honest to God, how miserable was that?'

Stacey attempted to console him. 'Take my word for it,' she said, 'Birdy's unlikely to remember.'

'It doesn't matter. I've never forgotten. What a mean-minded thing to say to a young girl who was excited about getting a break. "More power to you," I should have said, and left it there.'

Their call continued for some time, with Stacey telling him that he couldn't have known what would happen. The only person with questions to answer was Kieran Mitchell, she said, and he would never be called to account. All the same, when she'd put down the phone, she wondered if saying nothing would have been the wiser option.

On Saturday evening, in her empty flat in a half-empty building, Stacey found herself thinking about Ronan. He was at home this weekend. Was Jill with him? If so, did they share a bed or was she confined to the spare room? *You are better than this*, she told herself. But, actually, she wasn't.

As a distraction, she started to edit the next episode of the podcast. It featured a farmer who had made the headlines because of his campaign against a pharmaceutical plant. Her heart wasn't in it. Needing to do something, she decided to tackle the pod's administration work. She'd only been working for ten minutes when an email arrived. The address, containing as many numbers as letters, screamed 'fake'. The title, however, attracted her interest. It read, 'Info re KM'.

Her fingers flew to open it:

Dear Stacey,
We met the other day when you were in the MAM offices. Since then, I've been considering whether to contact you. I overheard some of your conversation with KM. There are things about him you should probably know, but I would rather not say anything here. If you would like to talk, please contact me at this address.
Carissa Dunbar

Goosebumps rose on Stacey's arms. Was this a trick? Even if Mitchell hadn't been spooked by her questions, he had been irritated. Was there a chance he'd asked his assistant to check on her plans? Then again, involving Carissa would mean telling her about Birdy's accusation, a risk he was unlikely to take.

Dear Carissa,
Thanks for the email. This sounds interesting. Is your information about The Diamonds? Would be happy to meet.
Best wishes,
Stacey

Within minutes, a response arrived: No, not about The Diamonds. I honestly hadn't heard of them until the other day. Don't want to say anything else here. Also, would rather not meet in the city centre. Too many eyes.

Stacey didn't know what to make of this. Either Carissa was suffering from advanced paranoia or she had something explosive to offer. *Don't get carried away,* she warned herself. Then, she sent a reply: Would Briarstown suit? I could meet you in the Pear Tree

Café tomorrow at 10.30 a.m. Everyone on hols so likely to be v quiet.

This time, the response took longer to arrive. Finally, Stacey heard a ping: Okay. See you then.

In black exercise gear, with her Disney-princess hair tied back, Carissa was barely recognisable. Without makeup, she looked younger too. Only her nails, glossy as fresh paint, were the same.

'I'm sorry,' said Carissa, who was fifteen minutes late. 'I'm going to be honest with you. I nearly backed out. I got a serious attack of the heebie-jeebies. This isn't the type of thing I do, you know?'

'Don't worry,' said Stacey, who was scared that Carissa might yet bolt for the door. 'I'm super-grateful you got in touch.'

As she'd predicted, the café was less than half full. On the Sunday morning of a holiday weekend, most people had somewhere else to be. They were in Courtown or Kilkee, Málaga or Magaluf, hoping that when they returned to the office, work would be a little more bearable. Carissa kept glancing over her shoulder, as though Kieran Mitchell might stun them all by abseiling down the front of the building. Outside, the sky was heavy with the threat of rain.

It was only now that Stacey realised how much she'd staked on this meeting. More than anything, she wanted Carissa to pass on some nugget of information that would prevent Mitchell from walking away. She smiled what she hoped was a reassuring smile. 'I was intrigued by your email.'

'Um, I couldn't think how to phrase anything so I kept it brief. Like I said, I overheard some of your conversation with Kieran. I was shocked . . . and not shocked . . . but I'll come to that in a minute. I should admit that as soon as I heard your voice, I knew who you were. I listen to "Whatever Happened To . . . ?" all the time.'

'Thanks a million,' said Stacey. 'It's always cool to meet a listener.'

Carissa passed a sachet of sugar from one hand to the other. 'The first thing I want to make clear is that none of what I'm about to say relates to me. Do I like Kieran Mitchell? Not especially. But I've never had a bad experience with him. Even though he comes back to Dublin quite often, the visits tend to be quick. He sweeps through the office, makes his presence felt and disappears again. In the main, I work with Melanie Adams, the woman you saw the other day.'

'I take it Mitchell spends most of his time in New York?' said Stacey.

'Pretty much, yeah. I started working for the company in 2019, and before the pandemic he also did a good bit of travelling. The Latecomers tour a lot. So does Iona Daunt. And he'd often go to where they were playing, especially if it was somewhere glamorous or interesting. Since the tours resumed, he hasn't been on the road quite so much.'

'Perhaps the years are catching up with him.'

'He wouldn't like to hear you say that,' said Carissa, smiling for the first time. 'Anyway, the other thing I need to stress is this: whatever you do with what I tell you, you're not to mention my name. It's vital that nothing is traced back to me.'

The steel in her words was at odds with her jumpy appearance. She was worried about the consequences of crossing Mitchell.

'Of course,' said Stacey. 'You have my word.'

Carissa stopped and drank her coffee. 'Okay,' she said, at last. 'Here goes. As you can probably gather, my role is relatively junior. Some of what I do isn't very exciting. I spend hours booking flights and making dinner reservations. At the same time, I get to meet amazing people, and I also get to hear a lot of sensitive information. I'm talking about stories that would send the tabloids and gossip sites into overdrive. But in our office, folks are all "Yeah, that's no big deal. What else is new?"'

'I can imagine,' said Stacey. 'I used to work in a newsroom and what wasn't reported was way more interesting than what made it to air.'

Carissa nodded. 'Then, about a month ago, there was a complete vibe shift. All of a sudden, the laidback attitude vanished. I was told that unless something was mega-urgent, I wasn't to bother Kieran. I was also told that if anyone contacted the office looking to speak to him, I was to take their details and pass them on to Maren in the New York office ASAP. At the start, I assumed that if there was an issue it related to one of the acts.'

'Do they usually cause trouble?'

'Not all of them, no. But The Latecomers are kind of problematic. Jonny has a reputation for being handsy with fans, and Hugo has a heavy-duty coke problem.'

Stacey thought of The Latecomers' wholesome image. On social media, fans spoke of being 'proud' of them, as though they were well-behaved toddlers. She was about to smile when it occurred to her that 'handsy' might be a euphemism for sexual assault.

'What happened next?'

'Kieran came to Dublin, and Maren was with him. I'd only met her three or four times before. She's sort of scary. Like, she's a serious New York blonde: Céline suit, whiff of old money, body just the right side of emaciated. You get the picture?'

'I do,' said Stacey, who was warming to Carissa. In the office, she'd considered her haughty. Today she saw that the brusque attitude had probably been masking her anxiety.

Carissa continued: 'I still didn't know what was up, so I did my best to tune in. It turned out there was a good reason for the secrecy. They were trying to deal with a journalist who was making enquiries about one of Kieran's old acts. A singer called Phoebe D'Amato.'

'I saw her name on his Wikipedia,' said Stacey, heart rate rising. 'She released a couple of albums in the nineties but never made a major breakthrough.'

'That's right.' Again, Carissa looked around the room. 'She's made an allegation against Kieran. Sexual stuff, you know? And a reporter, a guy from the *New York Times*, is on his trail.'

The information landed like a cluster bomb, its implications flying in every direction.

'Are you serious?' said Stacey, voice foghorning across the café. 'The actual *New York Times*?'

Carissa's face tightened. 'Please,' she said, in a furious whisper, 'don't draw attention to us. The last thing I need is someone listening in.'

'I'm sorry.'

'It's all right. You're cool. It's just I'm a bit rattled.' She leant in. 'That's not the end of it. From what I can tell, at least four or five other women have also made allegations against him. I'm pretty sure there's a second musician but I don't know her name. Another of the women worked for him back in the noughties. Her first name's Estelle. That's as much as I've got. Obviously, Kieran's lawyers are trying to shut everything down.'

'Wow.' Stacey's brain was spinning. Assuming all this was true, Imogen had been right, and Birdy wasn't Mitchell's only victim. 'Where do things stand at the minute, do you know?'

'Every few days there's a burst of activity. Like, at the start of the week, I heard Melanie on the phone to Maren. They were freaking out over a post on Reddit.'

'Oh, shoot. I think I know what they were talking about, only I've a feeling that post was a hoax. Bear with me a moment, while I find out.'

Carissa gave a questioning look, so Stacey tried to explain her suspicion.

'Jesus,' said Carissa. 'His first wife? Just when I thought things couldn't get any wilder.'

Stacey sent a message to Imogen, asking if she'd been responsible for the Reddit post about Kieran Mitchell.

The reply didn't take long: What's Reddit?

Stacey responded: The forums where people go for chat – and gossip.

Imogen: I'm afraid that one hasn't reached my demographic. What's the story?

Stacey: It's complicated. Will call you later.

'Well, it looks like I was wrong. Imogen hasn't a clue what I'm talking about.'

'Which means,' said Carissa, 'that Maren was right to get worked up about the post. It's legit. Someone else knows what's going on.'

Or, thought Stacey, *one of the reporter's sources is getting restless.* She needed to learn more about the *New York Times,* but she also found herself wondering how Mitchell had reacted to her enquiries about The Diamonds. 'If you don't mind me asking, did anything happen after our visit?'

'You bet it did. Kieran spent the rest of the day on the phone. He was supposed to be leaving early to go on holidays, but everything kept getting pushed back. I know he was speaking to his lawyer in New York.' Carissa picked up her cup. 'That was one of the reasons I sent the email. I thought you should know they were talking about you.'

'Thanks. Did you hear much of what we said the other day?'

'Very little. Just enough to know that one of The Diamonds was making allegations against him.'

'I ought to fill you in,' said Stacey, before giving Carissa an abbreviated version of what had happened in London.

When she'd finished, Carissa put down her cup. It clanked against the table. 'Oh, hell,' she said. 'That's shocking. What are you going to do?'

'I reckon I should talk to the journalist from the *NYT*. There's a chance he already knows about The Diamonds. But if he doesn't, he's bound to be interested. The snag is, he'd have to speak to Birdy, and I'm not convinced she'd be up for it.'

'But you can ask.'

'I can. Do you have the journalist's name?'

'Do I what! Despite everyone's best efforts to keep me in the dark, I must have heard it a hundred times. It's Mark Spiers. If you look him up, you'll see that he's done some big stories. He's the real deal.'

'You've no idea how grateful I am,' said Stacey.

Carissa's mouth twisted. 'I'm going to be straight here. There's one part of me thinking, *What am I doing? I can't risk my job.* But another part is wondering if I should keep on working for KM. You've got to understand: the job was absolute career goals for me. I love music and I've always been fascinated by the industry. But at the same time, I don't want to be involved in covering up abuse. And that's what this is beginning to feel like.'

'Will you find it hard to keep going in?'

'Yes and no. Even though I've probably painted the place as a museum of horrors, it's much more than that. I've got to know some cool people. The insane thing is, the biggest stars of all, One Scarlet Morning? They're absolute sweethearts. It's, like, they know they're legends, so they don't have to be snippy or sleazy with anyone.'

Stacey considered the situation. 'If I were you, I'd stay put. We don't know how this is going to play out. There's plenty of time to make up your mind.'

'Thanks. Will you keep in touch? For now, the email address is probably best.'

'Absolutely. And email's fine. I'll let you know how I get on.'

When Carissa had left, Stacey bought another coffee and combed through the *NYT* archives. Mark Spiers had a substantial list of stories, and achievements, to his name. He'd covered political corruption, mass shootings and civil unrest. He'd reported from Israel, Russia and Afghanistan. If he was working on something, it was being taken seriously.

For the first time, it hit her: if Mitchell was a down-on-his-luck manager with a stable of unprofitable acts, no one would care what he did. Readers had no interest in the wrongdoing of nonentities. The very things that had made him untouchable – his international success, his high profile, his wealth – now made him vulnerable.

The story wasn't over.

Chapter 44

Gail's cooperation was a surprise. Less than a month earlier, she'd written to Ann explaining why a reunion wouldn't be wise. She'd been adamant that no good would come of dipping into their memories. Now she was prepared to join Birdy in Galway.

The visit wouldn't involve any extra travel. Four years had passed since Birdy had last seen Gail and Yvonne, and they'd already arranged to come home for her sixtieth. Along with their husbands, they were due to meet Birdy and Andy in north Clare. Towards the end of her phone call with Ann, when emotion had got the better of her, Birdy had decided that all four Diamonds should get together. She hadn't given voice to the idea because she'd worried the other two would veto it. Reasoning that if Gail agreed, Yvonne would probably row in behind her, Birdy had called Boston first.

Her pitch was prepared. The get-together didn't have to last long. It didn't have to be about good times or bad. It could be about life as it was. They would stray into the past, of course. But it was worth remembering that there might not be another chance.

She didn't get far before Gail cut in: 'You don't need to justify your decision to me. She's all I can think about.'

'That makes two of us,' said Birdy.

'It's like . . . we live in a world where everything feels phoney, where phoneyness is prized like never before. But this is real. You can't filter it or spin it or dress it up.'

For a few minutes, Gail continued in this vein.

'Just to be clear,' Birdy said eventually, 'you are willing to come with me?'

A sigh fluttered across the Atlantic. 'It's not my place to tell someone how to die. If seeing us matters to her, yeah, I can do that. And, don't worry, I'll play nice.'

'You're the best.'

'We were all the best,' said Gail, 'only we didn't realise it.'

Ten minutes later, Birdy called Yvonne. After more than thirty-five years in Sheffield, the one-time drummer had a hybrid accent. People in Yorkshire asked where in Ireland she was from, and people in Ireland told her she sounded completely English. Birdy could have listened to her all day.

Yvonne's response was immediate. 'That's a relief.'

'What do you mean?'

'After you told me that Ann was ill, I was thinking I should go to see her. But I didn't know how to raise it with you. And there you were, several steps ahead of me. What did Gail say?'

'She got philosophical about death,' said Birdy.

'That's what too much education does to you.' Yvonne paused. 'And you? Are you okay with seeing her again?'

'Sort of. Listening to her was odd. She sounds the same, but so much is different. Even after I'd made the offer, I was saying to myself, "You can back out." Don't worry, by the way, I won't. Sometimes you have to dig deep.'

'I understand. You're doing the right thing.'

'Thanks. You know me, I've never believed in "closure". It's such a meaningless word, invented by journalists and self-help authors. Let's face it, bad memories always resurface. But this does feel like the end of the line. After next week, I never want to hear the name "Kieran Mitchell" again.'

'Amen to that,' replied Yvonne.

When they'd hung up, Birdy tapped out Ann's number. 'I have some news for you,' she said.

Chapter 45

Mark Spiers didn't know much about The Diamonds. He'd heard of them and had contemplated finding out more, he said. But their star had shone so briefly, and so long ago, that they'd tumbled to the bottom of his list.

It took Stacey two days to secure a call with the *New York Times* reporter. Throughout, Carissa's words echoed in her head. The picture she'd painted was of an office on tenterhooks, waiting for further allegations to emerge.

Spiers was suspicious of Stacey's interest in his investigation, a situation not helped by her inability to reveal how she'd discovered him. If he was wary, she was overawed. Talking to someone from the *NYT* made her feel as though she was in an outtake from *Spotlight*. (And, yes, she did know that was the *Boston Globe*.) She saw him sitting in a bustling newsroom in a building of glass and steel. She was perched on the edge of the bed, a mound of washing at her feet.

Before getting to the detail, she told him about confronting Mitchell.

'You just barged into his office?' said Spiers, incredulity in his voice. 'How did you even know he was in Dublin?'

'His ex-wife told me.'

'Isn't she dead?'

'No, his first ex-wife, Imogen. The woman he was married to in the early eighties.'

'What led you to her?'

'The Diamonds' singer, Ann, had written to her to apologise.'

There was a pause while Spiers thought through what Stacey was saying. 'What was she apologising for?'

'It's a long story. I'd better go back to the start.'

And that was what she did. In the main, she tried to leave the personal aspect of the tale to one side. She did, however, reveal her connection to Ann. She also spoke about the former vocalist having stage-four cancer. Gradually, Spiers accepted her bona-fides. She could tell he was looking her up online, something that prompted mixed feelings. As proud as she was of her podcast, she was embarrassed that it was so small-scale. Mitchell's disdain had got to her. When Spiers asked questions, his voice was rich, like the assistant district attorney in a court-room drama.

By the time she'd finished, he was forced to accept that The Diamonds' story had a singular importance. Even if it was only one thread in a larger tapestry, it also provided the template for much of what had happened afterwards. She sensed he was keen to find out more. But so was she. How many women had spoken to him? And why hadn't the story been published?

After some coaxing, he told her about his reporting. To begin with, his explanation was irritatingly abstract. She didn't want a history of sexism in the music industry. Nor did she want his theories about the industry's preference for vulnerable women. *Yes,* she felt like saying, *I know that record labels encourage women to bleed in public, then discard them when the blood flow becomes too messy. I've spent two months thinking about all of this.* Stacey held her tongue. She couldn't afford to alienate Spiers.

'So how did you come across this particular story?' she asked.

'It wasn't something I'd pictured myself working on, but out of the blue, a woman reached out to a colleague. She was keen to talk about a friend who'd worked for Mitchell. Her friend had been abused, she said. My colleague, who's a music reviewer, explained that it wasn't his beat. He put her in touch with me, and that's how it all started.'

'When you say "it all", how far have you got?'

Spiers hesitated before replying. 'When I began digging, I didn't expect to find much. It's not as though Kieran Mitchell is widely seen as brash or obnoxious. On the surface, he's an urbane guy. Sophisticated. He's influential too – and not just in the record business. Politicians have benefited from his largesse, as have people in other branches of the arts. He's in demand as a speaker. Even when I heard he was a well-known womaniser, I thought, *Yeah, him and every other guy in the music business. Tell me something new.* Then, when I dug a little deeper, I heard darker stories. Pretty soon I learnt that in some circles he was seen as someone who couldn't be trusted.'

Stacey thought of Mitchell's awards and honorary doctorates. She thought, too, of the obsequious television interviews and adulatory newspaper profiles. Of the fundraising galas he attended and the galleries he supported. He didn't just have a veneer of respectability, he had a thick coating.

'Have other women made allegations against him?' she said.

'Yes.'

'And are there many of them?'

'Including the friend of my original source, seven women have come forward.'

'What have they said?'

Again, he took a moment before answering. 'The complaints range from harassment to sexual assault and rape.'

Stacey paused to think. 'Were the women his clients or his employees?'

'A mixture.'

Spiers' caginess was annoying her. She was quivering with curiosity, and he was answering questions like a criminal suspect who'd been given a thorough briefing by his lawyer. He was only a couple of steps away from staring at a mark on the wall and saying, 'No comment.'

'I'm going to be blunt here,' she said. 'I know you have a duty to your sources, but I've provided you with a fair bit of information and I think we can meet halfway on this.'

'I can't give you any names.'

'That's fine. I wouldn't expect you to. But you can tell me more about the women . . . and about the pattern of allegations.'

'All right,' he said. 'That's not unreasonable. Of the seven women, two worked for Mitchell. Two met him through other people in the industry. One was a prospective client, a woman he strung along by saying he might agree to represent her. As you can imagine, that's a lot of leverage. Two were actual clients.'

'Was Phoebe D'Amato one of them?'

When he answered, Spiers' tone suggested he was surprised by how much Stacey knew. 'I can't tell you that.'

'A source gave me her name.'

'Okay, let's just say your source is a good one.'

'Gotcha,' she said. 'Had any of them made a complaint before or gone to the police?'

'None had gone to law enforcement. Two had received pay-offs and signed non-disclosure agreements, which is a bit of a tricky area.'

'I see.'

'You've got to remember how powerful Mitchell is. He has a stunning track record. If he agrees to manage your career, the potential rewards are phenomenal. And even for someone just working in his office, well, that's premium work. A different world opens up to you, a place of five-star hotels and first-class flights and cocktails with the stars. One of his victims said she was so seduced by this that she put up with his creepiness until it became unbearable.'

Stacey had a sudden sense of worlds colliding. Mitchell's platinum-plated New York life was far removed from The Diamonds' origins in Steelstown, from travelling to gigs in the back of a rusty Transit van and living in a ramshackle apartment. But while the settings might have altered, his predatory behaviour hadn't. Across the decades, he'd abused women who came into his orbit. He'd taken their talent and ambition and exploited it for his own ends.

'So you know that two of the women tried to speak out,' she said, 'and they received pay-outs. What about the others?'

'Two were advised to stay quiet. No one wants a reputation as a troublemaker. Or maybe I should say no woman wants a reputation as a troublemaker. In another case, the victim wasn't silent. She spoke to other people in Mitchell Artist Management. She also wrote to Faye Godfrey. But everyone found reasons to look the other way. She thought she'd go crazy, so in the end she left with nothing.'

Stacey was reminded of what had happened to Birdy. Ann hadn't wanted to listen, and Yvonne hadn't wanted trouble.

'*Keep your head down, Keep your voice low. Tell us everything we say and feel is wrong*,' she said.

'I'm sorry?'

'It's from one of The Diamonds' songs, one that should have been a big hit. It's about how they grew up. The more I hear about Mitchell, the more relevant it feels. Anyway . . . what I was wondering was, how close are you to publication?'

'We're close-ish. We've got to be certain that every single detail is rock solid, so there's a hell of a lot of fact-checking and due diligence. I've been chasing Mitchell for a response but he's a slippery guy – and his lawyers are extremely tough. Right now, the paper's dealing with a barrage of legal threats. We have to be careful, not just of Mitchell, but also of people the women have described as enablers.'

'Is it okay if I tell The Diamonds about your investigation?' asked Stacey. 'It's not as though they'll talk to anyone. They've hardly said a word since 1982.' She could tell that Spiers' mind was moving up the gears and she could guess what he was about to ask. 'They're meeting the day after tomorrow,' she added. 'It's the first time in forty years they'll all have been together.'

'You're kidding me, right?'

'No, that's how much damage Mitchell did. It wasn't just that he raped Birdy, he manipulated and intimidated her. When I said she ran away from it all, I meant it. She spent years avoiding people.'

'Have you given up on the idea of interviewing her for your podcast?'

'I have. It was never really a runner. I'm a one-woman operation. Kieran Mitchell would take me for everything I've got – which, believe me, isn't much. And Birdy doesn't need the hassle. She's reluctant to revisit 1982.'

'Do you think she'd talk to me?'

Stacey's hunch was that this would be a request too far. She still had difficulty believing that the four Diamonds were about to meet. But that was personal. What Spiers was asking was different. 'I don't know. She's been pretty successful at putting it all behind her, so I wouldn't think the chances are great.'

'I appreciate that. At the same time, it sounds as though she has a hell of a story to tell. Will you ask her?'

'I will.'

Later, Stacey met Imogen. She'd promised to fill her in on the other allegations against Kieran Mitchell. The afternoon was mild, with hazy sunshine, so they bought takeaway coffees and sat on a bench in Briarstown Park.

'It's hard to know where to start,' said Stacey. 'I'd just about given up, and then I got an email.' She talked through her meeting with Carissa and her conversation with Mark Spiers.

'I tend to agree with you,' said Imogen, when Stacey told her about the journalist's request. 'If Birdy spoke, she'd be turning a spotlight on herself, and from what Ann has said, I don't reckon she'd be comfortable with that. She's built a good life, and I can't see her doing anything to disturb it.'

Imogen appeared uptight, her voice low, her movements jittery. Once upon a time she had loved Mitchell. She'd trusted him. Listening to a roll-call of his crimes couldn't have been easy.

'I'm going to Galway on Thursday,' said Stacey. 'The plan had been to say a quick hello, but I can also tell them about the journalist. Mind you, even asking Birdy to talk to him feels intrusive.'

'I think you've got to ask. Whatever happens afterwards is up to her. One way or another, it's going to be difficult. Everything that

Kieran has done will be out there for the public to feed on. There's also the fact that not everyone will believe what the women are saying.'

Although Stacey suspected this was true, it wasn't something she had considered. 'Even when there are several women telling similar stories?' she said.

Imogen tutted. 'There could be fifty of them, and you'd still get fellows who insisted on accepting Kieran's version of events. Actually, that's wrong. I shouldn't say fellows because you can be certain some women will insist the victims are lying.' She stopped while a man walking three dogs passed by. When she spoke again, there was a tinge of sadness to her voice. 'This might sound odd, but I'm relieved that both my parents are a long time dead. They'd come to accept that Kieran was a bully and a cheat, but having the full truth out there for all the world to hear would be absolute hell for them.'

'And you? Will having this in the news be hard for you?'

'Yes and no. I suppose I feel fortunate that he grew tired of me so quickly. If he'd stayed, he'd have messed my life up too. Instead, I got to meet someone who genuinely loves me.'

Stacey felt as though her pursuit of The Diamonds had brought her through a series of rooms. Every day had introduced her to new people, places and situations. And yet, two months in, she still made mistakes. She came to decisions without giving sufficient thought to their consequences. She'd been oblivious to the fact that airing the truth about Mitchell would be hard for some of those he'd hurt. No matter how sensitively Mark Spiers worked, he'd be taking a knife to the survivors' scar tissue.

And then there were the others in Mitchell's life. What about his current wife? His sons and daughters? How would they be affected? Stacey had taken a jaundiced view of his younger children.

She'd seen them solely as the beneficiaries of nepotism. Rich kids with famous parents and a deluge of unearned opportunities. But was that fair? She thought, too, of Faye Godfrey. According to Spiers, Faye had ignored an approach from one of her husband's victims. Still, that didn't mean she was prepared for the incoming tide of allegations.

Stacey wondered if she'd been too caught up in her own concerns to consider the picture from every angle. She turned towards Imogen. 'I guess I only cared about getting to the truth.'

'And you were right.'

'I'm beginning to have my doubts.'

'Give it time,' said Imogen. 'Give it time.'

Chapter 46

It had been too long.

That was the only explanation Birdy could offer for her desire to visit Steelstown. They could drop by on their way to the Burren, she told Andy. No, she didn't have plans to meet anyone. Apart from her parents' graves, there was nothing in particular she wanted to see. She fancied a walk, a quick tour of her old haunts. That was all.

'Consider it a birthday treat,' she said.

'Your birthday isn't until Friday.'

'By then, I might be too old to enjoy the delights of Steelstown.'

Andy rolled his eyes, but the gesture was a humorous one. They would take the detour. Later they would meet up with Gail, Leon, Yvonne and Bob in the house they were renting near Ballyvaughan. Tomorrow the three women would make the short journey to Galway.

Birdy couldn't claim to be looking forward to The Diamonds'

reunion. But it was necessary. That she worried about meeting Ann was a given. What she hadn't expected was to find herself fretting about Gail. Ann's diagnosis, and the efforts she'd made to re-establish contact, had knocked something loose in Birdy's old friend. Usually so sure of herself, she kept questioning her actions.

'All these years,' she'd said, 'I've been telling myself that Ann was left unscathed. *Okay,* I thought, *hooking up with Mitchell was dumb, but she was able to get on with her life.* Only, if that was the case, why would she reinvent herself? Why would she keep her past hidden from her son?'

'I can think of several reasons why someone might change their name,' replied Birdy, trying to lighten the conversation.

'Don't get flippant on me, Bird. You were seven years old. That was totally different.'

'All right, then. The truth is, she was a long way from unscathed. She spent years beating herself up over what happened.'

'I was wrong, wasn't I?'

'Yes, only you can't blame yourself. You weren't the one who did the damage.'

'But I was wrong,' repeated Gail.

Andy was driving, and Birdy guided him past All Saints and into Connolly Park. Although he'd been there many times before, the web of estates and cul-de-sacs always defeated him.

'How can that house be number ninety-five,' he asked, 'when the one right beside it is number forty-two?'

Birdy laughed and said the town had developed a special numbering system, designed to repel outsiders.

On the journey, she'd delved more deeply into her reasons for visiting Steelstown. The best she could come up with was this: she wasn't just fifty-nine years and 363 days old, she was also all the other ages she'd been. She was the thirty-eight-year-old who'd moved back to Ireland; the thirty-two-year-old who'd doubted she would ever cope with motherhood; the eighteen-year-old who'd set out for Dublin with dreams of a life in music; the nineteen-year-old who'd been raped by a man who should have been protecting her. But, most of all, she was the girl who'd grown up here. She was Birdy Troy with the snaggle-tooth and wayward hair, the girl who'd played hopscotch to Olympic levels and covered her homework journals with pages torn from *Smash Hits*.

They passed the spot where the Connolly Park playground had been. Aged seven, a fall from the monkey-bars had left her with a gash to the side of the face. It was no surprise that the bars, swings and seesaws had been removed. A crunching fall to the tarmac was no longer viewed as a childhood rite of passage.

Andy parked beside the community hall. The fine weather had returned, and there was a hot, thick sun overhead. Before leaving the car, Birdy dabbed sunscreen on her nose and adjusted her sunglasses.

'Are you coming with me?'

'Why not? Let's see what's changed – and how much the change annoys you.'

He was right. Not only did she expect a time capsule, she wanted everything to match her childhood memories, even when those memories weren't reliable. Wherever you were from, she supposed the story was the same: the roads were shorter than you remembered, the houses smaller, the hills less steep. In her head, the community hall would always be home to the Friday-night disco. There would be a queue of teenagers, some in flares and platform boots, others in tight jeans and shoes so pointy they could have been worn by Rumpelstiltskin. The hall would smell of sweat and Clearasil and sickly 1970s perfume.

The two low walls where she'd broken up with Mike Slattery were still there. Three teenage girls with spider eyelashes, minuscule shorts and Day-Glo orange legs were sitting on one of them, chatting and laughing.

When Birdy spotted an abandoned shopping trolley, she laughed. 'I'll have to get on to Declan and let him know his skills are needed.'

'I doubt he'd be willing to work for fifty pence an hour,' replied Andy.

After he'd left school, Birdy's brother had moved to New York. It was what all the young people had been doing back then. To everyone's surprise, especially his own, he had discovered an aptitude for hard work. He was now the Chicago area manager for a chain of mid-priced hotels.

Birdy and Andy walked through a neat loop of lemon-coloured houses towards her old primary school. All the while, she hummed under her breath. The pale brown building had been renovated and remodelled. In her time, it had been possible for boys and girls to ramble away – and for outsiders to ramble in. Now, the building was surrounded by a high metal fence.

No matter the changes, there was something mercilessly evocative about the place. She remembered how overcrowded the school had been, with children spilling out of the cramped classrooms into prefabs and the sports hall. She remembered the thump of Miss Lynch's piano and the rhythms of morning roll-call. She remembered the smell of hot lunchboxes and damp duffel coats, vomit and disinfectant.

The memories continued to flow, as relentless as lava. What Birdy felt wasn't homesickness – she was content with her life in

Dublin – but a flutter of something else. Fondness? Admiration? Gratitude? Steelstown had given her grit and common sense. It had given her empathy with the underdog and a dislike of gaudy ambition.

Birdy and Andy turned and made towards her first home. She didn't know who lived there now. A young family, she assumed.

Some of Connolly Park's houses had aged badly. Their walls had grown mottled and stained, their fascia boards faded and warped. Other houses had never looked better. The doors and gardens were brighter, the pebbledash rejuvenated.

'I used to walk to work up that way,' she said, pointing towards a clump of trees.

Andy smiled. 'Save-A-Lot RIP.'

Twenty years earlier, her one-time workplace had been bought by a British supermarket group. To the best of her knowledge, Normoyle's Butchers had become a nail bar while the Hunter's Inn was a takeaway.

It was as they rounded the corner that Birdy spotted him. How many years had it been since they'd last spoken? At least ten, possibly more. They'd both been at the funeral of Senan O'Reilly, the man who'd taught her to play the guitar.

'Mike!' she shouted. 'Mike Slattery!'

He twisted towards her, an expression of pure disbelief on his face. 'As I live and breathe,' he said, 'it's Birdy Troy.'

When she'd completed the introductions and asked about Joan, she said, 'I hear you were enquiring after me.'

Mike mumbled something about talking to a woman who'd travelled down from Dublin. His embarrassment was painful to watch, and Birdy wondered how much Stacey had told him.

'Believe it or not,' she said, 'the four of us are meeting up tomorrow.'

'That's fantastic news. Fantastic entirely.' The warmth in his voice was unmistakable. He was genuinely pleased. 'From what Stacey, the podcast girl, said, I gather Loretta – or Ann, I should say – I gather her health's not the best.'

'No. She's in quite good form, though.'

'Will you give her my regards?'

'I will.'

'I'm sorry,' Mike said to Andy. 'Do you find the Steelstown talk hard going?'

'I've had forty years of it. By now, it's my specialist subject.'

'Your starter for ten,' said Birdy, adopting a formal, quizmaster voice. 'Prior to throwing in her good job, where in the industrial estate did Yvonne Hayes work?'

'Flexatron.' Andy winked. 'See what I mean?'

As they prepared to go their separate ways, Mike ran a hand over his light grey hair. 'Before you head on, I just wanted to say, I wish all the best for you, Birdy. I always did.'

'I know that, Mike,' she replied.

'Oh, and one other thing.'

'Yes?'

'Happy birthday.'

Afterwards, they crossed the strip of concrete at the back of the Troys' old house. A girl they recognised as one of the three from the wall was opening the gate.

'Hi there,' said Birdy. 'Do you live here?'

'Um, yeah,' replied the girl, voice wary.

'I did too.'

'For real? I didn't know the houses were that old.' As soon as the words had left the girl's mouth, she laughed. 'Sorry, I'm only messing with you.'

She had a lovely giddy tinkle of a laugh. Her soft brown eyes crinkled at the corners, and her hair was a dark cloud, like a twenty-first-century Gail.

'No offence taken. I left a long time ago. Birdy's my name.' She tipped her head towards her husband. 'And this is Andy.'

'My name's Ruby. By any chance, are you . . . ?' She frowned. 'Nah, forget about it.'

'Go on. What were you going to ask?'

'Are you the woman who was in the band?'

Birdy was floored. Apart from Stacey, it had been many years since anyone had asked about The Diamonds. 'Yes,' she said. 'That was me. How did you hear about us?'

'Because I'm in a band, and there's this woman down the street – her name's Mrs Clancy. I don't know her first name. Everyone just calls her Mrs Clancy because she's so old. Anyway, she said that years and years ago, there was a girl who lived in our place and that she was in a band too. She said you'd been on the TV and everything.'

Birdy wondered if Imelda Clancy knew she was considered too old to warrant a first name. As Imelda Quilligan, she'd been two years ahead of Birdy at school. Back then, she'd been famous for wearing leopard-print trousers and dumping Christy Clancy for his younger brother, Matty. 'She's nothing but a strap, that young one,' Birdy's father had said. 'She'll come to no good.'

Birdy forced back a smile. 'That's right. We were on television once. But, like Mrs Clancy said, it was a lifetime ago. Tell me about your band. What sort of music do you play?'

'We're a proper rock band. Like good hard stuff.'

'I'm taking a wild guess here, but do you play the bass?'

Ruby rounded her eyes. 'Wow, that's freaky. How did you know?'

'You remind me of someone, and that was what she played. What's your band called?'

'Tinseltown.'

'That's a good name,' said Birdy. 'Like the song? "Tinseltown In The Rain"?'

'I don't know that one.'

'Oh, you should,' said Andy. 'It's by The Blue Nile. It's from the eighties, but I think you'd like it.'

'Cheers,' said Ruby. 'I'll have to look it up.'

Birdy remembered that 'Tinseltown In The Rain' had been on the first tape Andy had given to her when she'd returned to London. She didn't know if Ruby would bother seeking it out. That was okay. To a teenager, the 1980s were as relevant as rural electrification or holy days of obligation. They were long ago and far away. There was only so much prehistoric music that any young person could care about. Let them have their own music and their own stories. Let them create their own memories and make their own mistakes.

She removed her sunglasses. 'We'll have to keep an ear out for you. It's time Steelstown produced a few rock stars.'

'Thanks. What was your band called?'

'We were The Diamonds. And we were a proper rock band too.'

When Ruby had gone inside, Birdy and Andy ambled back towards the community hall.

His voice broke through her thoughts. 'Have you seen enough?'

'I have, thanks. We can drive over to the graveyard if you like.'

'That's fine by me.'

'I don't know how to explain it,' she said, 'but it's like . . . before I do tomorrow, I needed to do this.'

'I understand,' he said.

And she knew that he did.

Chapter 47

Ann looked around the table, from face to face to face. For years, she'd thought about this moment, yet now that it was here, she was tempted to run back into the house and hide.

What do I say? How should I sit? What if the small-talk runs dry? How do I tell them about the newspaper?

They'd arrived together in a burst of greetings and exclamations. Gail had announced that she'd always wanted to live in Galway. Yvonne had admired the house. Birdy had hugged her and said, 'I'm glad we're doing this.'

There was a choreography about their comments that suggested they'd practised who would say what. Ann couldn't blame them. As soon as Birdy had told her about Gail and Yvonne, she'd understood the rules. With Birdy, it had been different. There had been things they'd needed to say. But this wasn't a day for dark honesty. This was about saying a cordial goodbye. With that in mind, Ann had compiled a list – an actual list! – of safe topics.

Then Stacey had called, and the list had become redundant.

A journalist from the *New York Times*, she'd said. Seven different women. Harassment, sexual assault, rape. While Ann was absorbing the news, Stacey had asked if there was a chance Birdy would talk to the reporter. Ann had given an honest answer: 'I don't think so. Knowing that others are telling the truth about Kieran Mitchell will be enough for her.'

Today she feared that even reading the stories of other women might be too much. There was a danger, wasn't there, that knowing how others had suffered would retraumatise her? Ann's own feelings were complex. As keen as she was for Mitchell to face some sort of justice, the thought of other victims made her feel guilty. What could she have done to stop him preying on women? She could have believed Birdy, that's what.

They'd all agreed that on such a lovely day it would be best to sit outside, and that was where they were. In her heart, Ann knew this was probably her last summer, an acknowledgement that tore at her. She'd come to view wet, blustery days as a personal insult. Could bad weather not wait until after she was gone? She wanted sunshine, long evenings, camaraderie. Brendan had booked a week away and, barring a catastrophic deterioration in her health, they would go to Kerry before the end of the month. She hoped that Ronan would join them for a couple of days.

Grover the cat had examined Ann's visitors before deciding they didn't have anything to offer. He was in his favourite place, snoozing under the crab-apple tree, dreaming of slow birds and easily caught mice. The fresh green of early summer was long gone, and the garden was looking more singed than Ann would have liked. This didn't stop Birdy, Gail and Yvonne from being extravagant in their praise.

They hoped she hadn't gone to too much trouble, but of course she had. After all, what was too much trouble for a day like this? There were thick slices of brown bread topped with smoked salmon. There were little cheese tarts and bowls of strawberries and a moist lemon cake. There was tea, coffee and lemonade. Oh, and there was wine for anyone who wanted it. Gail did.

One moment, Ann was on edge. The next, a glittery kind of happiness would wash over her. When she spoke, her voice was stiff with nerves. She'd told them that Stacey and Ronan would be dropping by but hadn't revealed the full purpose of their visit.

She wasn't helped by the tiredness that tugged at every part of her. Last night, she'd slept in twenty-minute blocks. Every time she woke, some new concern would emerge, like weeds poking up through concrete. At four o'clock, the hour of the damned, she'd decided to cancel the gathering. By then, her thoughts had been at screaming pitch. She could ring Birdy. 'I'm too sick,' she would say. 'Too tired. Too overwhelmed.' Thankfully, by the time the sun had come up, she was more composed.

Listening to her former bandmates, Ann was struck by how they knew each other's stories off by heart. They'd had four decades of swapping routine gossip and life-changing experiences. Of big days and mundane ones. They'd watched lines develop and hair fade. There was a casual intimacy to their conversation that she could never match. She'd been the outsider in 1982, and she was the outsider now. She saw how Birdy was trying to include her and was filled with gratitude. At the same time, it seemed wrong that the one who'd suffered most was making the greatest effort.

Stop it, she thought. *This isn't a day for being bleak or self-indulgent.*

In the week since Birdy's first call, they'd spoken several times. While these chats had been brief, they'd been long enough for Ann to know that she liked Birdy. They could have been proper friends.

If she had expected there to be a touch of the scatty professor about Gail, she'd been wrong. The Diamonds' bass player had acquired an air of accomplishment. It was there in her confident gestures, in the glow of her skin and in her casual, well-cut clothes. Physically, she was recognisable. But apart from a scattering of pronunciations – 'g'wan' for 'go on', 'fabalas' for 'fabulous' – just about every trace of All Saints Park had been eliminated.

Birdy wore glasses now. 'Play the guitar?' she joked. 'I wouldn't be able to see the strings.' Like all of them, her jawline was less firm, her eyes more tired. She had, however, retained her bony frame. If Ann had spotted her in the street, she would have known her.

The same was true of Yvonne. She had held on to her youthful face, her piercings remained in place, and her bobbed hair was still red.

Ann was intrigued by this. 'How can your hair be the same colour as when we were teenagers?'

Clearly pleased by the question, Yvonne pulled forward a strand and examined it. 'Well, to be fair, it's a bit more washed out, and there are a few highlights in there. But red hair? It's practically indestructible.'

'Oh, to be indestructible,' said Gail, refilling her wine glass.

While the comment prompted a pointed look from Yvonne, she didn't say anything.

Inevitably, the talk drifted to the fascinations of the late-middle-aged: the merits of experience, the folly of youth, the joy of not caring about the judgement of men. They traded quips about being more Billy Idol than Billie Eilish, more Neil Young than Yungblud. They lamented how social media had distorted the world and encouraged young women to turn themselves into cartoon characters.

'I'm sorry,' said Gail. 'I'm not buying it.'

'Not buying what?' said Birdy.

'The "age before beauty" schtick.'

'So you'd trade places with your younger self?' asked Yvonne, picking up a strawberry.

'Are you mad? Of course I would. In a heartbeat.'

'But what about wisdom? What about self-confidence?'

'What about them?' Gail dragged both hands through her hair, causing it to jump up like mattress springs. 'You know what I want? I want to be young and skinny and capable of obsession. I want to wake up in the morning knowing that no one depends on me and that I can fill the day with whatever self-destructive nonsense I like. And I want to sleep with men just because I can. Just because it amuses me. I'd bring you all back with me, by the way. We deserve a second shot at being young.'

Birdy gave a hesitant smile. 'Gail, I love you, but sometimes you talk an awful lot of rot.'

'No, I'm telling the truth. The benefits that supposedly come with age? All those sayings about adversity building character and experience bringing confidence? Those are just the lies we tell ourselves to make life bearable.' She breathed out heavily. 'Obviously, I'd never say any of this to my students. Or to my husband. They'd think I'd had a lobotomy.'

Ann tried to read Birdy and Yvonne's body language. Yvonne appeared surprised by Gail's outburst, Birdy less so. Both attempted to lift the tension but were quickly rebuffed. Ann wondered if more than twenty years in America had reinforced Gail's natural outspokenness. In Ireland, people remained reluctant to voice unpopular opinions. For all that had changed, it was still a country of nods and winks and 'Don't make a show of yourself.'

The talk moved back to safer ground: to children and grandchildren, to holiday plans and work anecdotes. That they were able to do this was surreal. There was no direct mention of Kieran Mitchell and only the occasional reference to The Diamonds. It was like being at a wake where everyone ignored the coffin in the centre of the room.

Ann needed to tell them about the journalist. If she didn't, it would look like she was deliberately withholding information. Gail's intervention might have been awkward, but talking about Kieran Mitchell would pitch them into a far more difficult place. Yes, they'd be interested in the allegations. But they would also realise that the news came with expectations. And they would have questions she couldn't answer. If Birdy spoke – and that was an enormous if – would she be able to hold on to her anonymity? What if Mitchell continued to deny her allegations? What if he denied all the allegations? Anxiety wrapped itself around her. *You have to do this,* she said to herself. *If you don't do it now, Stacey will be here, and Birdy will feel she's being ambushed – or manipulated.*

She wished she'd called Birdy last night and told her, but it hadn't been possible. She'd been with Gail, Yvonne and their husbands. Prior to that, she'd been in Steelstown. Her sentimental journey, as the others kept calling it.

The words were taking shape in Ann's mouth when she noticed Gail was looking at her. No, it was more than that. She was examining her, scrutinising her.

'How are you?' she was saying.

'I'm good.'

'No. How are you really?'

'Oh, well. You know.' Ann gave an uncomfortable laugh.

'That's the thing, I don't. I haven't a clue how you are. I'm not just talking about the cancer. I'm talking about everything.' She paused to take a slug of wine. 'I told myself I'd come here today and be polite and detached and dignified. But in my whole life, I've never been any of those things, and this doesn't feel like the day to start.'

'I'm good. You've got to take my word for it. Everything's all right.'

'No, it isn't.'

'Ah, Gail,' said Yvonne, face stern. 'This isn't the time.'

Gail ignored her and looked again at Ann. 'The way it is . . . I'm scared to talk about how sick you are and I'm scared to talk about the fact that for all these years we've excluded you. It's only three weeks since I wrote an email to the podcast woman, justifying that decision. And, I swear to God, I meant what I said. But now? Now I read it and I'm embarrassed by how cold I was. I want to press rewind, and it's too fucking late.'

'We're here today,' said Yvonne. 'Isn't that what matters?'

'We're only here because Birdy asked us. To be fair, you'd probably have contacted Ann anyway. But me? I'd have been trapped in my bubble of self-righteousness.'

'Is there any point in rehashing everything right now?' asked Birdy.

'I'm sorry, Bird,' said Gail. 'I know we agreed not to dwell on the past. And if that's what you think is best, that's cool. I won't mention any of this again. But I needed to apologise.'

Ann shook her head. 'That you're here now is enough.'

'It's not. I should have been a better friend. I shouldn't have abandoned you. We could have sat down and thrashed out our differences. The fact that we didn't . . . well, it makes me feel like I let that man win.'

'You didn't,' snapped Yvonne. 'You can't think like that.'

'Yes, I can. The one thing I'll say in my defence is that I was only a kid. We thought we were adults, and the world treated us like adults. But what did we know? What did we know?'

After Gail had stopped speaking, she appeared spent. It was strange to see her stumbling. When Ann had wondered if America had made her even more outspoken, she'd been wrong. Gail wasn't being aimlessly provocative. Of the four, she was the one who was struggling with the reunion.

Birdy stared into the distance. 'Perhaps you're right. Not about letting Mitchell win but about the rest of it. Ann and I have discussed everything, but I didn't think that was why we came here today.'

'It wasn't,' said Yvonne. 'We can't go back. We can't undo the damage. We've got to accept that.'

Listening to Yvonne, calm, rational Yvonne, Ann realised that, while they'd changed, most of the changes were superficial. Sure, they were a little wiser, a little more sensible. They had longer, and more painful, back stories. But they weren't harder or softer. They weren't more calculating or less honest. They were the women they'd always been, just older. Somehow she found that comforting.

Yvonne turned to her. 'You've gone very quiet. What do you think?'

Once again, Ann looked at the arc of faces in front of her. She could skirt around this – or she could jump on in.

'Okay,' she said, 'I hate to mention the man's name and, like you, I'd hoped I wouldn't have to. But there's something I need to tell you about Kieran Mitchell.'

Chapter 48

Stacey and Ronan were on their way. Without thinking, she had accepted his offer of a lift to Galway. Then she'd begun to fret. She remained embarrassed by her meltdown in the pub. So far, it had gone unmentioned.

Early that morning, she'd revisited Jill McGrath's Instagram. If anything, Ronan's new girlfriend had become slinkier and more appealing. This was not a woman who allowed her washing to pile up or the milk to turn sour. Letting Ronan go had been a mistake, but it was too late for Stacey to do anything about it now. Another lesson learnt.

As they passed the turnoff for Maynooth and the traffic started to thin, Ronan asked if she'd heard anything further from the *New York Times* journalist.

'Mark Spiers? I talked to him yesterday, and he sent an email last night asking again if he could speak directly to Birdy. I said that was up to her. He's fairly pushy, but I suppose you have to be. I promised to let him know how we got on today.'

Despite his guarded approach, Stacey could tell that Spiers was excited by Birdy's story. She was also certain that, no matter how many obstacles Mitchell placed in the American reporter's way, the fruits of his work would make it to print.

'Has he told you anything else about the other women?' said Ronan.

'Bits and pieces. Apparently, the other former client is a woman named Joelle Anderson. She played keyboards in a band called The Five Janes. They released an album back in the mid-nineties. I looked them up. They were really good.'

He gave a low whistle. 'Don't tell me they were an all-woman rock band.'

'How did you guess? Actually, they were a bit poppier than The Diamonds. They had a Californian surfer-girl look. But there are quite a few similarities.'

'I still can't get my head around the fact that Mitchell got away with this for so long.'

'You and me both,' said Stacey. 'According to Mark, Joelle Anderson's life went downhill, and she wound up with a serious drug problem. She's willing to go public, as are four of the other women including Phoebe D'Amato. The final two are using pseudonyms, which is something Birdy could do.'

'Except all the article would have to say is that she's Irish, and her name would be online within half an hour.'

'Yeah. Unfortunately, that's probably true. That's the trouble with a small country. There's not much scope for anonymity.'

Mark Spiers had also revealed that the most recent allegations came from a woman who'd worked for Mitchell just five years earlier. Despite all the talk about how much progress women had made, she, too, had suffered in silence.

The more things changed . . .

'Does it bother you that someone else might get to tell The Diamonds' story?' asked Ronan. 'I mean, you've done all the work.'

'I . . .' Stacey stopped and collected her thoughts. 'If I'm being one hundred per cent honest, yes. But, like Birdy said when I first approached her, we don't all get what we deserve.'

While this was true, it wasn't the full picture. Every day, she was thankful she'd heard about The Diamonds. Had she not become obsessed with them, she would probably have abandoned her podcast. 'Whatever Happened To . . . ?' wouldn't last for ever, and Stacey still needed to find other work, but she wanted to make the remaining episodes as strong as possible.

For the next while, they motored on in silence. Stacey prepared what she would say to the four women waiting for them in Galway. She also kept an ear on her phone. Last night, she'd been to view a house-share in Drumcondra and she was feeling optimistic about getting the room. Then again, she'd had similar hopes before and they'd come to nothing.

At least, the news about the pod was positive. In a bizarre quirk of taste, the Macdara Grant episode had gained traction and was lodged in the podcast charts. For some hard-to-pin-down reason, there were people out there who relished a good cringe. Give them a self-involved interviewee, a delusional world view and pompous pronouncements, and they were in listener-heaven. Then they could open Twitter and vent. Others would join in, and a small community of spite would form.

For a time, she'd had sympathy for Grant. Okay, he was an almighty pain, but he hadn't done any actual harm to anyone. He didn't deserve others tossing around his failings with such glee. When he sent another vitriolic email, threatening to destroy her 'nasty little enterprise', her attitude hardened again.

But she couldn't think about that right now. 'How's your mam doing?' she asked. 'I've been talking to her but it's not the same as seeing her.'

'Up and down. Thrilled about the reunion. Scared about it too. And scared about everything else as well.'

'I was about to say, "I understand," only . . .'

'It's impossible to understand unless you're the one affected? She enjoys talking to you. I get the feeling she says more to you than to me.'

'Some things, maybe. Not much, though. Mostly we talk about the band.'

'I worry that she doesn't say enough, but I suppose how she handles everything is up to her. Sometimes she can be quite funny about it all. At others, it's clear she'd rather talk about anything else. I know she's been meeting people to say goodbye, only she doesn't put it like that. Oh, and she talks to my dad about what she'd like at the end. She hopes to stay at home, except that mightn't be possible.'

Ronan's voice cracked. Stacey suspected that if you didn't know him, you might not notice. But she knew him well. 'And you?' she said. 'How are you?'

'Oh, God, Stace, I don't know. I try not to think too much. Mostly I feel useless. Mam will say something, and I won't have a notion how to respond. There are days when I forget about it all for an hour or two, and then it comes crawling back in.'

'At least you're seeing her all the time. You were home at the weekend and you'll be there again today.'

'It never seems like enough.'

They were nearing the services outside Loughrea and, concerned that Ronan was too upset to drive, Stacey suggested they stop for a few minutes.

They sat in the car, people to-ing and fro-ing around them, and spoke about Ann. Ronan said he was filled with regret. He recalled how often his mother had driven him to training or athletics meetings.

'I don't think I ever asked what she'd been passionate about as a teenager,' he said. 'It never occurred to me that she'd had ambitions beyond getting married and being a mother and having a regular job. Now I know about the band, it's too late. We could have gone to gigs together. She could have educated me.'

'Any of us could say that about our parents,' replied Stacey. 'Well, not the gigs part, obviously. I dread to imagine what sort of band my mother would bring me to. But if she was ill or if my dad was ill, I'd be the same. I'd be thinking, *I should have asked this* or *We should have done that*.'

'The worst part is, now that I know about her talent and what she did, I find I admire her more. That's wrong, isn't it?'

'I . . .'

'It's okay, Stace. You don't have to answer. It's not a fair question.'

'Please don't give yourself a hard time. You've done everything you can. And whether Birdy talks to the journalist or not, what matters is that all the band have got together again. Even a few weeks ago, that was impossible to imagine.'

'But I keep thinking . . .'

'. . . why couldn't it have happened before?'

'Yes,' said Ronan. 'All those years of silence. It's beyond crazy.'

'Your mam did try to contact Birdy.'

'True, and I can't imagine the strength it took to keep going when she was knocked back. Mind you, I marvel at Birdy, too, and the way she got her life together again.'

Ronan had always been a great believer in mental fortitude and perseverance. Stacey had assumed this came from endurance sport. Running kilometre after kilometre through sticky mud and squally rain must have left its mark. Now she saw that she'd got it the wrong way round. He was able to run for hours through punishing, windswept fields because of the resilience he'd inherited from both parents.

Something else she'd come to understand was that Birdy's forgiveness was authentic. She hadn't arranged to meet Ann because of a blind sense of duty towards the sick. She was better than that.

Stacey looked at her watch. 'If it's okay with you, we should probably get going. It might be awkward if we arrive too late.'

'Before we do, there's a couple of things I wanted to say.'

'Oh?'

When Ronan began to speak, he didn't look at Stacey. Rather, he seemed focused on what was happening in front of them: on the men and women coming and going with bottles of water, cups of coffee and paper bags of fast food.

'I've never been good at saying sorry. When I told you about the woman at work, I made light of it because it wasn't a particularly big deal to me. The way I saw it, we hardly knew each other at the time. And I reckoned that if I was blasé about that night, you would be too. But it was a big deal to you. I got that wrong. Really badly wrong. And I'm sorry. I'm sorry about everything.'

Stacey swallowed. 'Thanks. I appreciate that. To me, our relationship was important, and anything that undermined it mattered.' She turned her head towards him. 'After we split up, I didn't think we could be friends, but the past couple of weeks have shown me that we can. And I'd like to stay in touch with your mother. Would that be okay?'

Ronan's eyes remained on the windscreen. 'That's one of the things I wanted to ask. Before the end of the month, Mam and Dad are going to Kerry for a week. I'm planning on joining them for a day or two and I was wondering if you'd like to come along.' He hesitated. 'Like, just as a friend . . . or not. It's up to you.'

Just as a friend . . . or not. 'Wouldn't I be in the way?'

'Not at all. I know my folks would be happy to have you. And it's what I'd like too.'

'But . . .' Stacey searched for the right words. 'What about Jill? Surely she'd be put out if I turned up. If I was in her position, I'd be wondering what was going on.'

At last, Ronan looked towards her. A lock of hair had fallen over his left eye, and he pushed it away. His gaze was sincere. Disarmingly so. 'The thing with Jill? That's over. I just . . . I don't know . . . I just stumbled into something. It wasn't very serious, and the more time I spent with you, the more I realised that going out with Jill was a mistake. It was dishonest to be with her when I still had feelings for you.'

'Weren't you with her the other day? When we were in the pub after seeing Mitchell? You left so you could see her.'

'I was meeting up with her to break it off. She wasn't surprised.'

'I see.'

Stacey was annoyed with herself. For someone who talked to people for a living, she was ridiculously inarticulate. And when her skills were most needed, she was at her most hopeless. Right now, her mouth felt semi-paralysed, as though she'd just left the dentist's chair. To be fair, Ronan wasn't much better. When he said 'as a friend . . . or not', what did he mean? She asked him.

'What I'd hoped . . .' he said. 'Well, what I'd hoped is that you'd think again. About us splitting up, I mean.'

She looked into his face. 'The trip to Kerry?' she heard herself say. 'When is it?'

'I was thinking of heading down on the nineteenth, if that suited you.'

She smiled. 'I could do that.'

'And we would be together?'

'Oh, yes,' she said. 'Definitely together.'

Chapter 49

When Ann began talking about the other women, Birdy was so surprised that she almost toppled over. Yvonne, sitting beside her, must have noticed because she touched her arm, as if to steady her.

In one way, this was wonderful news. When the paper printed its story, Kieran Mitchell would finally be held to account. In another way . . . God, it was too much to take in.

That wasn't all. No sooner had Ann started speaking than Birdy understood: this wasn't just about the experience of other women. The journalist, Mark Spiers, would want to know more about The Diamonds. Specifically, he would want to know about her.

She watched and listened while Ann detailed what she knew. The others did the same. Gail had become more subdued, leaving most of the questions to Yvonne.

As she spoke, Ann's ill health was painfully obvious. Her teeth had come forward, the way they do with serious sickness or advanced old age. Her shoulders sloped, as though they'd become accustomed to a heavy burden. She reminded Birdy of the clinic's regular visitors, the people who smiled and insisted everything was fine, when you knew that it wasn't.

A few minutes into Ann's explanation, the cat meandered up the garden and jumped onto her knee. This appeared to comfort her.

All the while, a briny taste grew in Birdy's mouth. Thankful that Yvonne was driving, she poured a glass of wine. Not only was she grateful for the slight sense of detachment the alcohol provided, she was glad to have something to do with her hands.

Before Ann had finished, Stacey and Ronan arrived. Stacey, who was wearing a primrose-coloured dress, long silver earrings and flat gold sandals, kept saying how brilliant it was to see them all. It was hard not to be distracted by her enthusiasm. Ronan was quieter, less effusive. He went into the house and fetched two more chairs, and they bunched up around the table. The looks swapped by the new arrivals belied what Ann had said about them splitting up. Birdy reckoned that if they hadn't already got back together, they soon would.

Stacey said she wished she had more detail. Mark Spiers had chosen his words carefully, however, and was cautious about revealing too much information. 'I had an email from him last night,' she said. 'Two of the women have asked not to be named or for a pseudonym to be used. The rest are content to go public.'

Birdy had heard of Phoebe D'Amato and The Five Janes. She'd known that both were connected to Mitchell. Had it occurred to her that they, too, might have been his victims? In truth, it hadn't. She'd assumed they were part of the legions whose dreams had stalled. The nearly-but-not-quites. No doubt, most observers had assumed the same about The Diamonds.

'Am I right in guessing,' said Gail, 'that Spiers wants to talk to Birdy?'

Colour rose in Stacey's cheeks. 'Um, yes. I had to tell him about The Diamonds, and he's keen on your story.'

Yvonne cradled her teacup. 'Does he need Birdy? Surely seven women is enough for readers to know that this is serious and that Mitchell doesn't deserve his position.'

'Except,' said Gail, 'you can see why The Diamonds' story would stand out. It shows how long he's been abusing women – and getting away with it.'

'And there's the fact,' said Stacey, 'that you were all so young.'

Birdy's mind wandered. She thought about these new women. How old had they been? Had there been one incident? Or had they endured years of harassment? Had they confided in someone right from the start? Or had it taken decades for them to talk? The questions circled her like a thunderstorm.

Meanwhile the others were throwing comments back and forth. Although they all stressed that the decision was hers to make, their positions became clearer. Gail argued that, if she was up to it, Birdy should do an interview. Yvonne maintained that, after all this time, there was little to be gained by talking. Ann reckoned that before committing to anything, Birdy should have an informal chat with Spiers.

'That way,' she said, 'you'd have a better idea of whether you can trust him.'

The conversation moved on to the difficulties in publishing the story. Again, Birdy stayed quiet. She was overwhelmed by thoughts of the lives affected. She pictured them all as part of a chart, with Mitchell at its centre. They'd entered his web because they'd loved making music or because they'd dreamt of working with musicians. He'd exploited that passion.

While she sipped her wine, a memory rose of the night Yvonne had told her about their record deal. She saw the two of them sitting in the dark, whooping and shrieking. She remembered how they'd trekked through the snow to the pub where they'd toasted each other with hot whiskeys, like a pair of old men. It was a memory of pure happiness.

She thought of what Mitchell had taken from them. He'd stolen their creativity, their opportunities, their friendship, their voices, and trampled them into the dirt. Then he'd sauntered away and found far greater success elsewhere. He'd also been free to abuse other women.

Yvonne had been right when she'd said they couldn't go back. That wasn't the point. Birdy had accepted that a long time ago. The point was to make it harder for other Mitchells to flourish. She thought of Sorcha's teenage flirtation with music and how relieved she'd been that her daughter's band hadn't been much good. A feeling came sliding in. Not certainty. She would never have certainty. But clarity.

She would consult Andy, Sorcha and Molly. They might have different views. If so, she would need to take them on board. First, however, she had to explain her reasoning to the other Diamonds.

She took another drink, placed her glass on the table and waited for a lull in the conversation. Eventually, it came.

'Yesterday,' she said, 'when I was in Steelstown, I met a young girl called Ruby. I'd say she's sixteen. Seventeen, at the most.'

Gail and Yvonne looked at her, as if to say, 'Where's this going?'

She continued. 'She lives in our old house in Connolly Park, and guess what? She plays in a band. They're called Tinseltown, and when she spoke about them, she came alive. Ruby loves music the way we did.'

Birdy paused, took in her friends' faces and saw that she didn't need to explain any further. They understood.

Chapter 50

Four months later

Ann was buried on a raw Thursday in early December, a day after the article about Kieran Mitchell appeared. In the months before her death, she'd told a sizeable number of people about how she'd once been a singer in a rock band. Still, some mourners were puzzled when an original copy of 'Too Much Not Enough' was among the gifts brought to the altar. The 45 was owned by Andy, who'd kept it even after Birdy had disappeared.

Sitting at the back of the church, Birdy imagined the whispers. *Did you not hear? Apparently, Ann was in* that *band. The one managed by the fellow who was on the news last night. Ah, you must have seen it. He sounds like a right piece of work.*

The final weeks of Ann's life had been difficult. Birdy had been to see her a few days before she died. Propped up on a bank of pillows, face yellow and wizened as a windfall apple, Ann had drifted in and out of sleep. Both had known it was likely to be the last time they met. Both had been afraid to say so. Ann had held Birdy's hand and whispered, 'Stay strong.' From anyone else this would have sounded corny, but you couldn't argue with the sincerity of a dying woman.

Only Brendan and Ronan were there at the end. Later, Stacey had called. 'Ann spoke about you yesterday,' she'd said. 'She was grateful that you'd all had the chance to meet up again.'

In August, following The Diamonds' reunion, Birdy had made contact with Mark Spiers. Three weeks later, he had travelled to Dublin. Over two days, he'd spoken to her about the tumultuous summer of 1982. He'd also talked to Gail about the impact of Mitchell's actions. Although they'd given Mark the full story, he'd agreed to gloss over some of the details. The wider world didn't need to know what had happened afterwards.

As they'd grown to trust each other, the journalist had revealed more about the other women. Among them were Estelle Hill, a junior assistant who'd been the victim of months of harassment, Samantha Douglas who'd been raped by Mitchell when they'd met backstage at a concert, and Camila Martinez whom he'd sexually assaulted when she'd asked for career advice. All had blamed themselves. All had worried that speaking out would do more harm than good.

In addition to Birdy and the original seven women, two others had come forward. Both had signed intricately worded non-disclosure agreements, proving again that Mitchell's lawyers were no newcomers to his behaviour.

Birdy's experience was central to the finished piece. Hers, after all, was the origin story. In advance of publication, she'd had to tell several people that they didn't know her as well as they'd thought. These included her colleagues at Tolka Medical. Dr Gerard Feherty had turned the colour of watery rice pudding before remarking that she was 'a very interesting woman indeed'. He'd quickly added that she had his full support.

When the allegations were put to Mitchell, he had lied and obfuscated. His lawyers had strung out the response and put up a series of roadblocks. Finally, on the eve of publication, he'd issued a disingenuous statement, talking about 'different times' and 'different recollections'. He'd answered questions that hadn't been asked and avoided those that had. 'Memories may vary,' he'd said, before resolving to 'do better'.

Although Birdy had known every line of the article, its publication had been tough. She'd scrolled through the words, as if seeing them for the first time. When she'd started to shake, she'd had to remind herself that talking had been her decision.

Mark had warned her to expect negativity. There would, he'd said, be people who questioned why the women were coming forward now. Had they wanted hush money? Were they embittered? Were they fantasists or attention-seekers? Mitchell was married to a supermodel. His life was a conspicuous success. Why would he waste his time on any of these also-rans?

Birdy had resolved to avoid social media and the shadier parts of the internet. This morning, she'd also turned down the notifications on her phone. Since the article appeared, the clinic had received calls from reporters and radio producers seeking to speak to her. It was only a matter of time before one of them found her number. She didn't want to deal with them. Not today. Besides, she'd already decided that her only other interview would be with Stacey. Along with Gail and Yvonne, she would record an episode of the podcast, and it would be uploaded the following week.

What Birdy had said to her former bandmates about looking out for young musicians was true. But, let's be honest, she'd also seen an opportunity to wrest power from Mitchell. Now she couldn't escape the fear that, once again, he was getting away with it. Oh, sure, the weeks ahead would be challenging. He'd have to disappear for a while. Some gold-rimmed invitations would be withdrawn. Some phone calls might not be returned. But the music industry was notoriously tolerant of abusers. How many musicians had been forgiven with lines like 'Trust the art, not the artist'? If you made enough money, there was always a second chance. And a third. And a fourth. And on and on.

After the burial, they gathered in small groups, shuffling from foot to foot, rubbing their hands to try to ward off the cold. Birdy was with Andy and Yvonne. They had offered their sympathies to Brendan and Ronan but hadn't yet had the chance to talk. Birdy recognised a handful of faces, most of them from Steelstown. She also spotted Imogen, whom she'd come to know over the past couple of months.

They were about to leave for the funeral lunch, where people would alternate between tears and laughter while reminiscing about Ann's life, when Stacey sidled up to them. Alone among the family grouping, she was dressed in bright clothes: a shocking pink scarf and an emerald coat.

As if guessing their thoughts, she shrugged and said, 'Ann made me promise not to tone down my clothes for the funeral. She reckoned it'd be sombre enough without me wearing black. I've a feeling Patrice is wondering what sort of madwoman her grandson is keeping company with.'

The jaunty words and vibrant colours were at odds with Stacey's face, which was lined with grief. During Ann's final weeks, the podcaster had spent a considerable amount of time in Galway. She had also reunited with Ronan, and while they'd had difficulty getting somewhere to live, they'd eventually found a new apartment in Briarstown, not far from their original home.

Ann had confided to Birdy that, while reuniting Stacey and Ronan had never been her primary motivation, it had been in the mix. 'Senan O'Reilly's work is done,' she'd said.

For a few moments, the group spoke about the funeral, about the large attendance and about the beauty of Brendan's tribute to his wife. Then Stacey reached into her handbag and took out her phone.

'I take it you've seen this,' she said, tapping at the screen.

'I haven't seen anything over the past few hours,' replied Birdy. 'We've had an unwritten code this morning. No Mitchell talk.'

Stacey's face lifted. 'For truth? You'd better take a look.' She handed over the phone.

Birdy took out her reading glasses. Again, the article appeared to be lengthy. As she read the opening paragraphs, her heart thumped in her ears.

> Following allegations of sexual harassment and assault, one of the music industry's most successful figures has resigned from the management company that bears his name. Kieran Mitchell's departure from Mitchell Artist Management came as several of the company's best-known clients sought to distance themselves from him.
>
> Speaking through a representative, the Grammy-winning band One Scarlet Morning said that without his resignation it would have ended its relationship with the agency.
>
> In a statement posted on Instagram, the chart-topping

singer Iona Daunt said the revelations had 'broken her heart'.

The allegations stretch back over four decades and come from musicians as well as former employees. In his initial response, Mr Mitchell had said that, while his behaviour may not have met contemporary standards, he was not guilty of illegality.

Twenty-four hours later, a spokesman for Mitchell Artist Management said that following a meeting of its board, the veteran manager would be severing all links with the company, and its name would be changed. Further details are expected in the coming days. The precise financial arrangements remain unclear.

Separately, the police in New York have started looking into some of the allegations.

Birdy sketched out the developments to Andy and Yvonne. Her instinct was not to believe what she'd been reading. Was it possible for Mitchell to be ousted from his own company? According to the article, it was. She thought of the artists, now so vehement that he needed to go. Where had they been before? Had they really not known? And what about colleagues who'd helped him to dodge and deflect? Would they, too, have to move on?

'What will he do?' she asked.

'Who knows?' said Stacey. 'He's unlikely to starve.'

Andy took Birdy's hand. 'It's all about money, isn't it? When others felt their livelihoods might be affected, Mitchell had to be removed.'

An icy rain had begun to fall. Birdy looked around. The mourners were dispersing.

For years, she had viewed Mitchell as poison spreading through water. He had contaminated everything he touched. His fall wouldn't turn back time or return what he had taken.

But it was enough.

The lunch had entered the companionable phase in which old stories were being rolled out, not all of them relevant or appropriate. Because many of those in attendance had only just heard about The Diamonds, Birdy found that she and Yvonne were objects of curiosity.

Most people were too polite to ask directly about Kieran Mitchell. They didn't want anyone accusing them of nosiness or insensitivity. This didn't prevent them from sending meaningful looks in Birdy's direction. That they meant well was beyond question. All the same, the attention made her uncomfortable, and the room felt as though it didn't contain enough air.

She was relieved when Gail called and she could abandon the function room for the hotel's blue-carpeted reception. Yvonne and Stacey came with her. Although Gail hadn't been able to travel home for the funeral, she wanted to feel she was taking part. She was also keen to discuss the latest news about Mitchell.

Birdy rested the phone against a thin vase of flowers so the others could see and hear Gail. Mitchell was everywhere, she said. Not just the *Hollywood Reporter*, *Variety* and *Billboard* but also the mainstream news sites and channels. The *NYT* was continuing to explore different angles, while *Fox* was gloating over his liberal credentials. It was as if, for the first twenty-four hours, people had been holding their breath. They'd been waiting to see in which direction the story travelled. Mitchell's departure from the management company had given them freedom to unearth long-buried stories and settle old scores.

The four women agreed that it was a strange, strange day.

Birdy took a sip of the brandy that someone had bought her. It burnt her throat, and tears gathered at the backs of her eyes. She still couldn't grasp that what had happened forty years ago in a down-at-heel hotel room was now being recounted in places she had never seen. Her name was in the mouths of people she would never meet. What had once been intensely personal was in newspapers and magazines, on phones and on the airwaves.

She needed something to hold on to, something to ground her.

'I was thinking about the day we were all together in Ann's house,' she said.

On the screen, Gail gave a smile of recognition.

Chapter 51

Four months earlier

On the day of their reunion, after Birdy had explained why she'd decided to talk to Mark Spiers, they'd sat in silence, the afternoon's warmth folding around them.

She'd also told them that she didn't wish to remain anonymous. There was no reason to hide away. This, she knew, would have implications for her former bandmates. Grainy photos would be unearthed. The bones of The Diamonds' brief history would be picked over.

Were the others okay with that?

They were.

The silence was broken by Gail. 'Listen, if you don't think this is the right time, that's cool. But when I was thinking about coming here today, I couldn't help myself. I put a few songs together. Like I used to do, you know?' She nodded towards Stacey and Ronan. 'On the day of a gig, I used to do this thing where—'

'We know all about the tapes,' said Ronan, his mouth curving into a smile.

'They're famous,' added Stacey.

'I'm feeling a certain amount of pressure here,' said Gail. 'I'm also conscious that some of us aren't as young as we used to be, so if all the moves aren't possible, that's fine.' She winked at Ann. 'Oh, and there's a special dispensation for the lady with the cat on her knee.'

'Much appreciated,' said Ann, 'but I intend to fulfil my duty.' She picked up Grover and put him on the ground. 'The next few minutes mightn't be for you, buddy.'

While Gail found the playlist on her phone, the others, including Stacey and Ronan, pushed back their chairs and kicked off their sandals. The grass tickled their bare feet.

Gail pressed play, and they were met by a familiar beat. In the eighties, many of her tapes had started with 'Once In A Lifetime'. This one was no different.

To begin with, they were stiff and self-conscious. Was this just silly? wondered Birdy. A foolish attempt to reclaim a time that was long gone? A time that had ended before she was twenty years old.

And then the music took over. They strutted and sang and twirled. Ronan spun them around. They spun each other around. They waved their arms and clapped their hands. Squeals of laughter rang out across the garden.

Fleetingly, nothing else mattered.

They were carefree. They were fans. They were rock stars.

Acknowledgements

Thanks to my agent, Nicola Barr. I'm very grateful.

Thanks to everyone at Hachette Ireland, especially my editor, Ciara Considine, and her colleagues Joanna Smyth, Ruth Shern, Elaine Egan and Stephen Riordan. Thanks to copy editor Hazel Orme, and to proofreader Aonghus Meaney. Thanks to all the booksellers, librarians and readers for your support.

Thanks to everyone for their patience while I became obsessed with researching the early 1980s. I spent far too many hours reading old editions of the *NME* and *Smash Hits* and watching *Top of the Pops* on YouTube. In case you're also a bit of a nerd for these things, the line-up for *TOTP* on the 3 June 1982 is accurate. In real life, The Diamonds' spot in the charts, number eighteen, was occupied by The Scottish World Cup Squad. 'House of Fun' by Madness was number one. In Ireland, 'A Little Peace' by Nicole was number one, and The Wolfe Tones' 'Admiral William Brown' was the highest Irish entry.

I've put together a playlist of songs mentioned in the book. I've also included some songs that I imagined would be on Gail's gig day tapes and a few Irish tracks from that time. I would have liked to include more Irish bands, but unfortunately their work hasn't made it to the streaming era. If you search for Birdy Troy on Spotify, you should be able to find the playlist.

Above all, thanks to my friends and family, especially my parents, Tony and Ruth, and my husband, Eamon Quinn.